Arctic adventure and cou........

C aptain Edward Devlin knew the treacherous waters of the Bering Sea better than any man alive in the 1890s. The only representative of U.S. law in the region, he dedicated his life to championing the cause of the Alaskan and Aleutian Eskimos. He was relentless in his crusade to find and prosecute the unscrupulous men who were cheating the Eskimos out of the seal pelts they hunted by selling them cheap whiskey. Death and devastation was what these men peddled in the name of profit.

Stanton Knowles first met Devlin when the captain transported him to the Arctic, where he made his rounds as superintendent of the Eskimo schools. Since Devlin's cutter Walrus was the only transportation to these remote areas, Knowles spent weeks and months aboard ship and saw firsthand the captain's heroism and hardness. Knowles disagreed with Devlin's methods, which sometimes seemed harsh, even brutal, but he showed up to support Devlin at the trial that could break him and put an end to his work on behalf of the arctic natives.

Thurston Godfrey, president of the Arctic Circle Corporation, believed things were changing in the Alaskan frontier. Being a màn of wealth and political influence at the highest levels, he was going to cash in on it. But there was a major impediment to his plans, named Edward Devlin. Godfrey was not the kind of man to let anything—or anyone—stand in his way.

Many Colors of White is the story of life in the 1890s, from the perils of the bone-chilling arctic wastes to the stunning revelations in a San Francisco maritime courtroom. It is best read by a roaring fire or under warm covers, because arctic winds blow cold whenever the book is opened.

MANY COLORS OF WHITE

MANY COLORS of WHITE

THE SECRETS OF CAPTAIN DEVLIN

A NOVEL

WILLIAM E. DUKE

DG EMMS Publishing
Los Angeles, CA

This book is dedicated to
Claire Carmichael, my writing professor,
for her inspiration, instruction, and patience
throughout the writing of this book.

FOREWORD

Following Alaska's purchase from Russia in 1867 until the late 1890s, the only consistent, visible manifestation of United States authority in the Bering Sea and along the possession's Arctic coast was provided by the small ships and the men of the U.S. Revenue Cutter Service, a predecessor of the U.S. Coast Guard.

September 2008

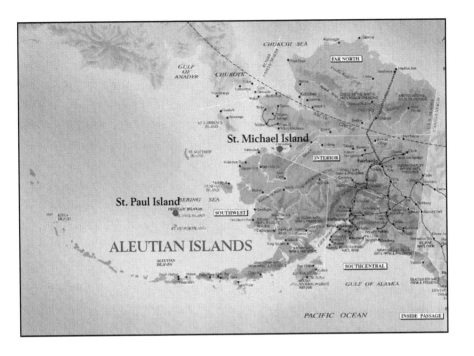

Locations & Main Characters

Aleutian Islands, Alaska

The longest archipelago of small islands in the world, it extends over 1,200 miles and forms the Aleutian Arc in the North Pacific. Comprising a series of 14 large volcanic islands, 55 smaller ones and numerous islets, rocks and reefs between the Kamchatka Peninsula in Siberia and the Alaskan Peninsula in North America, they divide the Bering Sea from the Pacific Ocean. The Aleutian Islands are divided into groupings known as Fox Islands, Islands of Four Mountains, Andreanof Islands, Delerof Islands, Rat Islands and Near Islands. Sparsely populated by Aleut natives, these rugged points of land are some of the most forbidding yet fascinating places in the world.

St. Michael Island

A small island on the southeast side of Norton Sound. It was named after the archangel Michael by traders of the Russian-American Company in 1833 when they built a trading post at the site of the current village of St. Michael.

St. Paul Island

The largest of the five islands comprising the Pribilof Islands in the Aleutian chain, is 40 square miles and today has one K-12 school, one post office, one store, one bar and one Russian Orthodox church listed on the U.S. National Register of Historic Places.

Captain Edward M. Devlin

"Roarin" Ed is an obsessed, hard-drinking captain of the Walrus, one of the U.S. Revenue Cutter Service's Bering Sea Patrol ships. As the highest federal authority in Alaskan waters, he fights illegal fur-seal poachers and violent liquor sellers, quells a riot of Chinese cannery workers and frees a native girl from a "floating brothel." Respected by natives and whalers for his navigation skills and fairness and feared by fur-seal hunters, his "take-no-prisoners" attitude leads to a politically motivated court martial and the revelation of his devastating secrets.

Doctor Stanton Knowles

A failed clergyman and newly appointed Alaskan education commissioner who accompanies Devlin on many of his Bering Sea patrols and develops both an admiration and revulsion for the Captain's reckless, violent and uncouth ways. He is instrumental in helping to introduce Siberian reindeer as a new food source to forestall starvation of the Eskimos in northern Alaska.

Sarah Cartwright

The pretty, strong-willed granddaughter of a Methodist missionary and the wife of Stanton Knowles. She teaches native children on the Aleutian Island of St. Paul. After being paralyzed by an epidemic that ravages Dutch Harbor, she is confined to a wheelchair and becomes head of an orphanage. Throughout her marriage, she emboldens Knowles to stand up to Devlin and Godfrey.

Thurston N. Godfrey

A former governor of Georgia during Reconstruction and head of the Arctic Circle Corporation, backed by Washington politicians and Wall Street investors to develop Alaska's lucrative fishing, fur-seal and mining resources. A white supremacist who persecuted Negroes and who has no sympathy for the fate of Alaska natives, he is intent on destroying Devlin's career.

Lieutenant Addison Heath

Godfrey's nephew by marriage and an onboard spy on Devlin's ship. He instigates charges against Devlin for cruel and unusual punishment, dereliction of duty and drunkenness, which leads to Devlin's court martial. In a twist of irony following the court martial, Heath, captain of a stranded ship, is saved by Devlin.

Jake Sykes

A cynical reporter covering the Devlin court martial for Joseph Pulitzer's *New York World* newspaper, narrates the politically contrived legal proceedings. The reporter interviews leaders of the women's Temperance movement and the seaman's union, learning that they have been bankrolled by Godfrey to get Devlin out of Alaska.

Crew members of the Walrus

Anderson ....Chief Engineer
Donaldson..Medical Doctor
Dowie ....Second Lieutenant
Jameson .... Boatswain
Mueller .... Third Lieutenant
Norris... First Lieutenant

PART ONE

The Awakening of Stanton Knowles

Chapter One

San Francisco, 1896

Shock and dismay overwhelmed me when I turned the corner and confronted a riot-in-the-making in front of the sooty limestone Customs House where the trial would be held. I realized at once Devlin's stubborn cantankerousness had stirred up more passion than ever, certainly more trouble than I had bargained for when I agreed to leave my students and come north to support him.

The Board of Inquiry wouldn't begin for another hour, but already more than five hundred shouting partisans were waving placards and hawking handbills printed in large, screaming typefaces. Despite the cold January drizzle that coated the cobblestones of Portsmouth Square and the smelly droppings of streetcar horses, I feared that the tinder that could ignite physical violence was present in that milling crowd.

From what I could determine, there were at least five contending factions, each with its own insistent, contrary opinion of the Captain. It made me nostalgic for the clear-cut certainty of confrontations we had had with poachers and liquor traders when I had sailed with him in the icy waters of the Alaskan frontier.

Here, clenched-fisted sailors with tar-stained jackets taunted well-dressed women in long skirts and fancy, feathered hats, their docile businessmen husbands in tow. Officers in the uniforms of the U.S. Revenue Cutter Service tried to ignore hostile enlisted men in bellbottoms. A score of men, whose ill-

1

fitting gear told me they were ship captains, argued loudly with a covey of nervous clergymen, a few of them wearing Roman collars. And, of course, there was a selection of local Barbary Coast bullyboys, the kind attracted by any opportunity for a scrap, with some pickpocketing prospects to boot.

The waving placards, mounted on potentially lethal poles, were as varied and insistent as the discordant chants of the people wielding them. Some signs were obviously produced by commercial printers, and had cost somebody a lot of money: *Devlin, Monster of the Arctic, Stop the Torture,* or *Whiskey: The Plague of Our Nation.* Others were homemade affairs with scrawled admonitions: *Protect the Whalers; Sailors Have Rights, Too; Save Devlin, Save Ships;* or *Stop Cruelty to Seamen.*

As I began to ease my way through the crowd, a sailor punched a handbill into my chest. In bold letters it stated "Devlin Saved One Hundred Whalers at Icy Cape."

Not to be outdone, a tiny gray-haired woman dressed all in black followed him and politely handed me another. It contained a reproduction of a local newspaper article under the headline "Captain Devlin Reintroduces Tortures of the Inquisition." While I was scanning it, a tall, thin, young man in a tweed suit pushed his way toward me, and tipped his derby.

"Doctor Stanton Knowles?" he asked. When I nodded, he said, "I'm Jake Sykes from the *New York World.* Can I speak with you for a few minutes?"

I was about to push him aside until he told me he had just arrived from the east, and wanted to make sure his report on "such an important case" was as accurate as possible.

"Know something about this Captain Devlin of the Cutter Service's Bering Sea Patrol from newspaper cuttings," he said with a sly wink, "but I'd really appreciate interviewing him for the real story. Some of the locals say you can help me."

Sykes, his breath smelling of alcohol, was pushed into me by the jostling crowd, and I almost slipped on the moist horse manure. I told him I had just arrived from Southern California myself, hadn't spoken with Devlin personally for years, and couldn't be of assistance.

"The problem, Doctor, is that all the articles about the great man praise his life-savin' and such. Nothing about the controversies and disputes that seem to follow the man."

He handed me a copy of something called "Frontier Stories," a penny magazine printed on cheap paper. The cover featured a faded photograph of Devlin standing beside a painfully thin man with an unkempt beard. Large cursive type declared "Heroic Captain Saves Stranded Mariner." It was a reproduction of a postcard circulated years ago, and reminded me of the sad incident I had shared with Devlin on the Siberian coast.

Sykes began to press his case further as I returned the tattered magazine, when we were accosted—that's the most accurate word I can think of—by Lieutenant Heath, in full dress uniform, his usually placid face contorted into a fierce expression.

"Is it true, Doctor, you've agreed to support Devlin despite his outrageous conduct?" he asked heatedly, without waiting for a reply. "I warn you that if you don't convince him to resign before the hearings get under way, certain information will come out. It will not be to that man's benefit or yours!"

"I'm glad you witnessed that, Mr. Sykes," I said as Heath pushed off into the crowd, knocking several protesters out of his way. "Now, perhaps, you understand how complicated—how ugly—this situation has become."

"Who in hell was that?" Sykes asked in amazement.

"Lieutenant Addison Heath," I responded. "He was one of Devlin's officers for many years, and I've been told he's now the instigator of many of the charges against him."

Sykes thanked me, but insisted he still didn't understand why, "A silly set-to among the brass buttons would cause such furor among civilians."

"Don't these San Franciscans know strikers are getting their heads bashed in all across the country, that there's a bloody revolution in Cuba?" he asked, waving his arm to indicate the crowd. "Those are the kinds of things to get riled up about. Not this blather."

As we spoke, portions of the crowd, those with admittance passes, began to move toward the building entrance. The movement broke up clusters of protesters, defusing, I hoped, the prospect for immediate mayhem.

"You may not think these proceedings are important, Mr. Sykes, "but I do, and I really must get inside before the hearing convenes. Besides, my hair and beard are getting soaked by the drizzle."

I looked directly into his bloodshot eyes, and said: "If you really want to know what's at stake here, meet me in the Occidental Hotel restaurant following today's hearings."

Sykes agreed, and I watched as he went off to join his fellows at the journalists' side-door entrance. I wondered if the newspapermen who had been so eager to extol Devlin as a hero of the north would now take delight in bringing him down.

Chapter Two

The second-floor chamber of the Customs House proved to be as somber as the San Francisco weather. Now arranged into some functionary's idea of a courtroom, the cavernous place was illuminated dimly by foggy light from soot-streaked high windows and kerosene lamps along paneled walls. The only splashes of color, in addition to some highly polished brass cuspidors, were the Stars & Stripes and the red-and-white stripes of the Cutter Service's ensign, which flanked a judge's table set on a low platform.

Those lucky enough to be admitted, mostly garbed in dark navy and gray, were gathered in small, discrete groups engaged in whispered conversation. Wet and uncomfortable, I felt somewhat out of place in my rumpled lightweight brown traveling suit. Then I spotted Heath leaning over in quiet conversation with three solemn, fancy-dressed men sitting near the aisle in the far corner of the room. I recognized immediately the diminutive, clean-shaven man with the pince-nez glasses in the middle. Thurston Godfrey, president of the Arctic Circle Corporation and Heath's uncle by marriage, was so tiny that his hands, cupped over the knob of his cane, partially hid his resplendent, violet silk cravat. I wondered what he, his investors and his Washington friends had to do with this inquiry into Devlin's actions.

I recognized a few of the whaling captains, most of the Revenue Cutter officers, and Mrs. Lucy Pitcher and her ladies from the Temperance crusade, but all seemed subdued. It was if we were all gathered in some kind of decrepit, chilly chapel waiting for a funeral to begin. Quite a contrast, I thought, to the raucous shouting on the Square, echoes of which could be faintly heard.

But when Captain Edward M. Devlin entered in full dress uniform, his wife Amy on his arm, the mood changed like a bolt of lightning shattering a humid summer day. After seconds of stunned silence, words such as "torturer," and praises of "atta boy" hissed from various corners of the room.

Amy smiled and patted my arm when he sat her next to me near the rear of the room. Then he strode down the aisle like a man about to take command of a frigate, not someone facing the destruction of a remarkable career. Frankly, I continued to be awed by the man's reckless effrontery in haughtily commanding attention as he was about to be put on trial.

Devlin nodded genially to his supporters among the whaling skippers, some enlisted men and warrant officers and to the press box. He ignored the disdainful tut-tuts and gasps of the gray-skirted ladies of the Women's Temperance Crusade, and hisses from members of the newly formed Seamen's Union. He looked around the chamber with his usual smugness, I thought, and finally shook hands with a white-maned civilian at the defendant's table, the attorney his supporters had urged him to retain.

Even in his uniform, complete with sword and old-fashioned tricorn hat trimmed in gold, I thought he didn't cut what you would call an imposing figure. He was not a tall man. Perhaps five foot four or five, but solidly built. It was his piercing stare and his bearing that marked him as a man who would not be ignored. His complexion was dark for an Irishman, weathered by years of salt spray and icy gales, and his curly black hair sprouted strands of gray around the temples. But, as I remembered, the solid ebony mustache required regular reliance on a dye jar even five years ago, when he was in his early fifties.

Devlin was just attempting to get comfortable on the hard chair and keep the useless ceremonial sword from rattling on the badly splintered floor when two court reporters with their oversized pads entered. They were followed by a young, clean-shaven officer I didn't know and a civilian loaded with law books. They took places behind the prosecutor's table.

Then a burly Master at Arms, who was stoking the pot-bellied stove, stopped and bellowed: "Attention in the court. All stand for the Board of Inquiry of the United States Revenue Cutter Service, by order of the Assistant Secretary of Treasury, signed October 1895."

The five who would render judgment entered smartly from a side door and found their places on a raised platform. One was a heavyset civilian with a luxuriant beard and an aura of self-importance. He apparently represented the Treasury Department which had ulti-mate authority over the Revenue Cutter Service. The second was a tall, sallow medical officer in the uniform of the U.S. Maritime Health Department. Then came two bearded Revenue Cutter captains in full regalia. Bringing up the rear was the President of the Board, Senior Captain Walter H. Johanson. I had been told he was a respected, no-nonsense skipper of the Cutter Service on the east coast, dispatched by Washington to get this embarrassing busi-ness over with as quickly and quietly as possible.

Johanson looked like some middle-aged, stern schoolmaster. He brushed his walrus mustache lightly, gave permission for all of us to sit, and loudly cleared his throat.

"As President of this Board of Inquiry," he declared, making sure we all were apprised of who was in charge, "I take the liberty of making opening statements. First, I want the record to show that the members of the Board are aware of the accused's record of saving lives and protecting natives. We are in possession of copies of the honors Congress and the Service have awarded him over the years for his service in the Bering Sea and the Arctic."

Then, flourishing the previous day's edition of the *San Francisco Chronicle*, he added:

"We also recognize the public outcry, lately very much in evidence in the newspapers, which these proceedings have generated." He waited for the spectators to quiet down, probably debating if he dared go further with the newspapermen absorbing every word.

"Captain Devlin, I would like to address you and your counsel directly at this point," Johanson said, as the accused came to full attention while still seated.

Johanson continued: "The charges in this case involving your actions in 1893 and last year are extremely serious. We are here to deal with those charges specifically, not your prior record when these were frontier waters."

He paused, pointed toward the defendant's table and continued. "Address if you can these accusations completely and honestly. Do not rely on the adulation you receive in some segments of the press to impress this Board. Do you understand my meaning, Captain?"

"I certainly do, sir." Devlin stood and replied with a declarative voice heard over a rising rustle of hushed comments from the audience. "I welcome this opportunity to clear my name and the reputation of my crew. I have been besmirched by forces that refuse to understand or appreciate the dangers we encounter facing lawlessness in the far north. They're not qualified to judge me."

Johanson, his cheeks turning crimson, pounded the gavel repeatedly, each stroke echoing in the dim chamber.

"This is the kind of thing I just warned you about, sir. Foreswear the speeches," Johanson said as he leaned over the judge's table looking fiercely at Devlin.

"As to your gratuitous statement, this Board *is* qualified to judge your actions, and we will do so soon enough, I assure you. Now sit down, sir, and let's get about it. Prosecutor, read the charges."

The young lieutenant, whose name was Jeffrey Wilson, marched forward as if he were on a parade ground. But the sour expression on his tanned face displayed what he thought of his assignment. He wasn't a lawyer, much less a prosecutor, but an active-duty small-cutter commander somewhere in Florida. He had been drafted into the prosecutor's role, Devlin had written me, because he once clerked for a judge in New Jersey for all of one summer. I was certain this was a role that could do nothing but harm his career. If he got convictions, the Administration's appointees at Treasury, the Temperance women, and some junior officers would toast him, while some important newspapers, certain western politicians and whaling captains would eat him alive. If he lost, the reverse would be true.

"Captain Edward M. Devlin stands accused on three charges, Mr. President," he said in a voice hardly audible in the packed chamber.

"Charge One: Employed cruel and unusual punishment on at least three seamen of the whaling bark *Hannah* at anchorage off Point Clarence, Alaska, on July tenth, 1893. Specification One: Used violent means to arrest an employee of the Arctic Circle Cannery in Bristol Bay, Alaska in July, 1888."

"Now, there's a lot of crap," cried the deep voice of a whaler captain. Less audible choruses of "monster" could be heard from other pockets of the room. This gave the President an opportunity to wield the gavel with vigor, while Devlin turned to smile and nod at his supporter.

"We'll have none of that!" Johanson thundered. "Any more outbursts and the Master at Arms will clear the room."

Wilson's voice was gaining strength now.

"Charge Two: Dereliction of duty and endangering his vessel and crew in dense fog and darkness near the Shumagin Islands, south of Alaska Peninsula, on September second, 1895."

Murmurs of assent from some in the audience caused Johanson to rap the gavel repeatedly and to issue his stern warning once more.

When he had silence, Wilson continued.

"Charge Three: Conduct unbecoming an officer and gentleman. Specification One: Drunkenness aboard a British naval vessel at anchor in Dutch Harbor, Unalaska Island, on September ninth and tenth, 1895, to the scandal of the Revenue Cutter Service. Specification Two: Using abusive language to junior officers of the Revenue Cutter Service during and after the Bering Sea patrol in 1895."

Johanson wasted no time. "How do you plead?"

William McGowan, the defense attorney, had pulled his considerable bulk to its feet. He answered for his client in what I presumed he felt was a proper stentorian baritone.

"Not guilty on all charges and specifications, Mr. President."

Devlin showed no signs of nervousness, starring attentively at the judges' table.

"Very well," Johanson replied, and stated that the Board would consider and render judgment on each of the charges separately. He then busied himself searching through a pile of papers with wax seals and ribbons. "I now will place into the record petitions filed by parties in the case who are at sea or otherwise unable to attend these proceedings."

As he droned on, naming petitioners and their interest for and against Devlin, I shivered with the realization that the charges had been bundled for maximum effect. Someone or -ones are really determined to get Devlin out of the picture for good, I thought. I'll bet he understands what's going on and that's why he wanted to fight it out in public.

I turned to look at Amy, the frail supportive woman who did all she could to smooth over my disagreements with Devlin. As a practicing Roman Catholic, she never hesitated to take this defrocked Methodist minister into her confidence, urging me to be friend and critic for a man who didn't make friends or accept criticism very well. I wondered what this calm, bird-like woman with her hands clasped tightly in the lap of her black dress was thinking when she heard these charges read so blatantly, so clearly.

Like all those present, she'd had to push her way into the courtroom through a mob of demonstrators carrying signs calling Devlin a torturer and a drunkard. That would've been a difficult encounter for anybody, but now she had to listen as the government he served for more than thirty years turned against him. He could be cashiered out of the Service without income; he could lose his highly touted reputation.

As the short first-day session came to an end, Devlin, still looking cocky, worked his way through the chattering crowd to collect her. He told us Johanson thought it best if they left through a back door to avoid the demonstrators.

Amy squeezed my hand and thanked me for "helping her through the day," and queried the Captain. "Things will get better when our witnesses begin to testify, won't they, Edward?"

"I don't think you should come to the court again, m'dear," Devlin said. "I hope Knowles will agree with me for once that all this blather is too much for any creature—man, woman or goat—to hear."

"Edward Devlin," she retorted, "I've sailed with you when you needed me. And you need me now, whether you know it or not. I'll be here every day I'm able, and that's all there is to say about it."

"All right, Amy, don't get sore," he responded with a tiny deprecating laugh. "If you want to sit through all this nonsense as ill as you are, I respect your wishes. Now, please, let's get out of here and back to the hotel."

As he turned to leave, Sykes introduced me and asked if either Devlin or his wife could spare him a little time.

"Not now," Devlin said with a frown. "Neither of us is to talk to the papers during the proceedings. Attorney's orders."

When he took Amy by the arm and walked to the front of the room, Sykes joined me and we followed the crowd to the main door. I received hostile stares from a few Temperance ladies who couldn't understand how a former minister could support a man they considered a drunkard. Several of the whaling captains, including Captain Collins, one of the Icy Cape survivors, gave me pats on the back and words of thanks for sticking with Devlin.

Sykes and I carefully made our way together down the slippery marble steps of the Customs House and into the milling humanity, now somewhat chastened by steady rain. I told the newspaperman I would meet him at the restaurant in an hour, explaining that I had to see how my wife was faring after our long trip from Los Angeles. He agreed.

I hoped I was not being too gullible; that I was doing the right thing. Splashing through the rain with my coat collar up, I wondered if this seemingly cynical Easterner would be objective, or would he twist whatever I tell him into sensational fodder for Devlin's enemies?

WESTERN UNION. JAN. 20 12:30 PM—TO EDITOR NY WORLD. ARCTIC HERO CAPTAIN ACCUSED OF TORTURE, DRUNKENNESS ON DUTY STOP NEAR RIOT IN SAN FRANCISCO STOP SAVE SPACE FOR SUNDAY PIECE COMING TOMORROW STOP SYKES.

Chapter Three

The darkened dining room of the Occidental Hotel was quiet this early on Friday afternoon. There were no customers, only two Chinese busboys who had almost finished setting tables for the dinner trade. Sykes had commandeered a corner table already set with plates and silverware, found a waiter and ordered ale. I opted for a pot of coffee.

Sykes and I exchanged a few pleasantries awaiting arrival of the drinks. He was a lanky fellow about six feet tall, probably in his late twenties, and with a full head of slicked-back, light-brown hair. He had a nervous tic which caused his left eye to twitch repeatedly, marring the aspect of his otherwise pleasant face.

As we waited, neither of us could ignore the ruckus emanating from the adjacent barroom, the same establishment where Devlin held court with elaborations of his adventures in the north. I hoped "Roaring Ed," as Devlin was called by his cronies, was being on his best behavior these days, and wouldn't be performing this evening. But his raucous friends certainly were enjoying themselves.

When the drinks finally arrived, Sykes flipped open his pad, took out a pencil, and said he needed my help to get to the bottom of stories he had heard about Devlin's "recklessness and his treatment of seamen."

"For example," he said, "some believe Devlin has continually taken outrageous, dangerous chances, pushing his crew unmercifully in pursuit of personal fame and glory, so to speak."

I resented his know-it-all attitude, and had started to protest when he cut me off.

"And what about this business of threatening to sink a British sealer and blow up a cannery?" With a flourish, he emptied a large manila envelope, containing a score or more of yellowing newspaper cuttings, onto the center of the table. "Seems to me," he said, "this fellow has been acting like a buccaneer who thinks he's on the wild frontier."

"Alaska still *is* the frontier," I retorted, trying to keep my dislike under control. "The fact is, sir, there was no law—and certainly no order—in the Bering Sea these many years except for Devlin and a handful of other cutter captains."

I'm afraid I rattled the dinner plates and cups as I leaned across the table to pick up some cuttings. "How could an experienced journalist such as yourself depend on the rumors and hyperbole in scraps like these? How can you ignore starvation in many native villages and what Devlin tried to do to help?"

I was sure he was baiting me, but resentment at his assumptions got the best of me.

"As a matter of principle," I went on, "how can you not realize American traders sell rotten whiskey, plunging natives into such a state they can't survive? Or that many are getting rich on illegal fur-seal slaughter?"

He said he had heard such things, but didn't understand what they had to do with Devlin's trial.

"They have everything to do with it, Mr. Sykes," I said, finally relaxing a little. "I readily admit I opposed some of Devlin's methods, was disgusted by his rough manners and his violence. But you must understand he's one of the very few white men willing to fight hard to improve matters."

"All right, Doctor," he said with a sneer, "that's your point of view as a former clergyman and a schoolmaster, but I don't believe that's how ordinary Americans will view the charges against your Captain."

I threw my spectacles on the table, ready to do battle, when the door to the barroom swung open, filling the echoing, oak-paneled restaurant with loud laughter and snippets of off-key singing. Framed in it momentarily was a short, wiry fellow in an ill-fitting civilian jacket and well-worn trousers. He brought a smile to my lips as he walked unsteadily toward us like a seaman not yet used to the solidity of land, or of sobriety either.

"Beggin' your pardon, Dr. Knowles," he said as he approached our table. "I was tole you were in here talkin' to some newspaper feller. Me and a few of the lads wanted to know how it looks for our Captain, what with this goddamned trial and all."

It was Boatswain's Mate Jameson, my genial companion on voyages on the Cutter *Walrus*. I introduced him to Sykes, saying he was a trusted member of Devlin's crew for many years standing.

Sykes offered his hand, but Jameson ignored it, apparently dubious about the stranger's intentions.

Jameson paused to collect his thoughts. "I'm sure glad you're back, Doctor, but what are you doing to help the Old Man?" he demanded. "Will you testify for him, despite the way you two argued all the time? Nobody seems to give a hoot and a holler about what the lot of us enlisteds what's served with him thinks."

Sykes broke in to tell him he was trying to capture an accurate picture of the Captain and his work for his newspaper in New York.

Jameson turned toward him, and shot back. "That's a damned good thing, Mister. There's a lot of cheap crap being tossed around against the Captain these days."

I assured Jameson I planned to testify to Devlin's good works, but couldn't address specific charges since I wasn't aboard when most of them occurred, adding quickly that I was certain enlisted men would be permitted to speak their piece.

"But you were at the cannery riot, weren't ya?" he asked me.

"Yes, but that's the only incident I witnessed personally, and I hope they wouldn't call on me to testify about that sorry episode."

"Anyway, this all smells like week-old walrus carcass to me," Jameson said with a slight slur. "Ya know that, don't ya, Doctor? You've been up there with us some of the time. You know what's it's like in the ice and all. Set this feller straight, will ya?"

Then leaning his hands on the back of an empty chair, Jameson focused on Sykes, whose arms were folded across his chest. "If ya want to know the truth, Mister, this bloody business was brought on by some what thinks the Bering Sea is like Boston Harbor, where everybody goes ashore for a tea party every night."

I tried to calm the old seaman, saying that all sides would have a chance to testify, but Jameson remained agitated.

"Me and the lads know what's what," he said pulling himself erect as if he were called to attention. "The Old Man came up the hawse pipe, made it from deckhand to the pilothouse. He's tough, you're goddamned right. But he's fair, and the best officer I ever served with."

Jameson clenched his fists as he continued to speak directly to Sykes. "Devlin's one of us salts who's done good in the godforsaken places the government sent him. Even captured seal-pelt robbers in the storms of winter, for chrissake!"

Jameson blanched, and rocked back on his heels. He realized he'd just revealed more than he should.

"Anyway, the Old Man made a name for his self, he did. And that embarrasses the brass hats in Washington and that prissy Temperance crowd all to hell."

"Now, Jameson," I said, "there's more to these charges than that, and you know it."

"There's just something fishy about all this altogether," he said, looking to me for support. "There's some big shots, I'll wager, that wants to get the Old Man out of their way up there."

"Jameson, the Captain himself decided to contest these charges," I said, "and to trust the Board to act responsibly, no matter what. Now please get yourself some coffee and sleep, man, before you get into trouble."

"Trouble, is it?" he shouted. "Them that bring down 'Roaring Ed' will have plenty of it from pissed-off sailors if they try to sail north without him. Mark my words."

Sykes put on an ingratiating smile and inquired about the seal-pelt robbers.

Jameson's eyes narrowed, and he stood at attention again.

"Can't," he said. "Orders from the Bering Patrol Senior Captain, his self."

Jameson then turned abruptly, and walked unsteadily through the swinging door into the noisy and brightly lit barroom, leaving the smell of stale whiskey and an unanswered question in his wake.

"Did I just hear a threat to disrupt the Bering Patrol if Devlin gets convicted?" Sykes asked. I had little experience with news-papermen, but suspected he was baiting me again, trying to tease out some inflammatory information for his dispatches.

"No, Mr. Sykes, you didn't," I said, shaking my head. "What you heard was an outpouring of affection from a man who has served Devlin in dangerous situations of many kinds."

I told him that Jameson was one of the men whom Devlin counted on for any risky task at sea, a man always willing to help with a smile, a quip, and an endless line of blarney to bolster his men.

"But here he was," I added, "very much in his cups, looking sour and angry, trying in his own way to help 'the Old Man' when he needed help the most."

"There's a lot more at stake here than meets the eye, Doctor," Sykes said. "In just one day, I've heard an outburst from an officer threatening his captain and another from a drunken salt spouting mutinous talk to support him."

"There's high emotion on both sides," I said, "but—"

In a loud voice, Sykes spoke over my response. "What did that fellow Heath mean this morning that 'certain information will come out' if the trial continues?" He rose from his chair, stretched his arms, and came to my side of the table.

I told him I really didn't know, but added that Heath had political connections; that his wife's uncle had been a Southern governor during Reconstruction. "Perhaps his mysterious information comes from that quarter. I saw Governor Godfrey in the courtroom this morning."

"Was that the dandy with a cane I saw chatting with Heath?"

"It was," I responded. "You should be aware that Godfrey is president of the Arctic Circle Corporation, a big investor in Alaska, and the unsuccessful bidder on the government's lucrative fur-seal-harvesting contract."

Trying to determine how far to go in describing Godfrey, I fiddled with the silverware. "Devlin and Godfrey have very different ideas about Alaska, Mr. Sykes. About how Eskimos and Aleuts should be treated; how the fur-seal herd can continue to survive."

Sykes began to pace the still-empty room. "Dr. Knowles, I expected this to be an easy assignment. Now, I have a potful of questions about Devlin and the people who despise him: questions you can answer."

"Don't know if I can help you very much. I've been away for five years."

Sykes strode back to the table and looked down at me. "Didn't you say Devlin actually insisted on contesting these charges? Create a public spectacle? Doesn't that mean the powers-that-be will be even more determined to get him?"

Weary of sitting on hard chairs all day, and getting annoyed with his prosecutorial approach, I stood and glared at him.

"As a matter of fact, Mr. Sykes, there are others who want to create 'a public spectacle,' as you call it, for their own purposes. You heard some of them on the Square this morning."

He took a step back, and started to interject when I jabbed my forefinger into his chest.

"Let me finish, will you? I believe some in authority are already taking it out on the Captain. I can guess, but I'm not really sure why." I took a breath to calm myself, and continued. "Those 'cruel and unusual punishment' charges, for example. Why weren't they lodged years ago when the incidents happened?"

I told him that as far as I could determine the other charges could have been handled without a formal trial.

"These are some of the questions *you* should be pondering, Mr. Sykes. I don't have the answers for you."

He agreed they were important queries but, with hands on his hips, continued to press me.

"I still want your opinion on accusations Devlin had often risked his ship to save whalers trapped in the ice, and even tracked down liquor traders all the way into Russian territory."

"And more pertinent than all that, Doctor, do you think Devlin is a drunkard, is guilty as charged?"

"That's enough, Mr. Sykes!" I shouted, my voice echoing off the restaurant's walls. "Let me ask *you* a question. Have you ever been to the Arctic or any place in Alaska?"

"Not me," he answered, "I've never been north of Chicago and I like it that way. I'm a man what likes his comforts."

"Well, then," I said, my face flushed with the anger deep inside me, "if you really want to educate yourself, I'll tell you what it was like for me to witness Devlin's relentless drive to control what happens up there. In the telling, maybe we can both understand better the character of that stubborn, difficult man: whether these charges are warranted."

Sykes backed up as I walked toward him. I was determined to force him to listen.

"Until I sailed with Devlin, I was as ignorant as you—as most Americans—of the vicious seas, the smothering fogs, the mud and the ice; of predators calling themselves Christians, who rob and debase people who have lived in those conditions for thousands of years."

I had to take a long breath before continuing. "When you learn what Devlin had to face in those years, you can judge for yourself if he let whiskey or anything else interfere with his concept of duty; whether he succeeded in shaping events, or if the brutal reality of Arctic life didn't shape him."

My uncalled-for fury spent, I sat down, continuing to look him squarely in the eye. "Then, Mr. Sykes, you might just be able to tell your readers the real reason this Board of Inquiry is important, not only for Devlin but for the future of Alaska."

"All right, calm down," he said, with a chuckle. "I don't have to send my article until tomorrow, and I'm sure your stories will be worth the price of a steak, so I'll buy you dinner, and be as attentive as a schoolboy."

He took his seat, adding, "I have one condition. You have to call me 'Jake.' I'm getting tired of that 'Mr. Sykes' palaver. That's what that old buzzard Pulitzer calls me when I miss a particularly salacious story."

Chapter Four

Bering Sea 1886-1888

My first exposure to Devlin and the Bering Sea, Jake, began at Dutch Harbor on the Aleutian island of Unalaska a decade ago, in 1886.

I had just arrived by steamer from San Francisco, full of unfettered zeal to begin my mission to educate native children throughout a vast region, as foreign to me as any place on earth. My spirits rose as we entered the wide harbor protected by imposing hills, vividly green with late July foliage and punctuated by patches of snow. From a distance, their flanks appeared to be awash with gentle ocean swells, as winds sculpted tall grasses into undulating patterns. Several snow-covered mountains were visible in the distance despite low-hanging clouds that shrouded their highest summits. The feeling of freedom, of clean-air freshness, exhilarated me.

I remember being heartened that this tiny Unalaska village with no more than twenty weather-beaten, wooden buildings strung along a gravel beach—a village hundreds of miles from any other settlement—had been able to sustain an imposing, onion-domed Russian Orthodox church on its waterfront. In my naïveté, I savored it as a good omen for a new career, a chance to start fresh in frontier Alaska.

Wonderment and optimism evaporated quickly when I finally met Captain Edward M. Devlin on the deck of the Revenue Cutter *Walrus*. With a jovial smile, I presented him with a letter from the Treasury Department requesting that he show "Stanton Knowles, D.D., the new General Agent of Government Schools, every courtesy and assistance in visiting facilities in the north."

He frowned as he read it. Folding it and placing it in his uniform pocket, his face became as expressionless as a bronze statue. He had noticed my degree was "Doctor of Divinity," and asked curtly, "What are we supposed to call you, 'doctor' or 'reverend?'" He pronounced "reverend" in three syllables so it rhymed with "never end." I told him "Doctor" or "Knowles" was sufficient since I was a government employee now, no longer a clergyman.

"Well, then, Doctor Knowles, we'll get you where you have to go." He paused for several seconds. "In good time."

After stowing my gear and assuring that school supplies were loaded onboard, I watched as he gave orders to get the *Walrus* ready for sea. His vile language in yelling at one hapless sailor who failed to secure a line properly made me flinch. But the vessel itself, from its white-painted hull to the tautly furled sails on its three masts, was a vision of orderliness. It was almost as long as the steamship I had just left and its smokestack and pilothouse were in similar positions amidships.

We left the calm of Dutch Harbor within the hour. Devlin set an eastward course around the island and then southeast toward the Alaskan Panhandle, not due north toward my first destination. I reminded him of my need to get to St. Paul in the Seal Islands as quickly as possible, for there were problems at the school there.

"Stand by, Rev-er-end", he said, ignoring my preference for mode of address. "We have work to do." He cupped his hands, lit a small, black cigar and stared, making me feel like excess baggage. I was taken aback when he added, "Just stay outta the way, and we'll give you a little something to write in your journal before we get there."

Once out of sight of the harbor, Devlin sent men ashore on a pint-sized island to collect some unidentifiable pathetic bushes that any decent farmer at home would trash as weeds. Underway and in open water, he once again changed direction; this time to the west, and now under sail, found his way to an anchorage behind a desolate island of tall outcrops of black, volcanic rock. He ordered the men to be as quiet as possible in lowering the topmost masts and climbing aloft to trim lower masts and spars with the greenery. To me, the rigging looked like a forlorn Christmas tree.

In this inhospitable spot we stayed for nearly three days, swinging at anchor and wallowing from side to side as well as forward and aft in the surf and eddies. The fog became so water-laden and low I couldn't keep my spectacles clear or light the soggy tobacco in my pipe. Every boulder on the nearby shore became familiar to me as I clenched the stern rail for hours, retching and heaving, eventually disgorging everything but my pride. All else of any use to man or fish had left my body in the first hours of convulsive motion, while the brackish stench of iodine, probably caused by rotting kelp beaten against rocks, clung to my tongue, adding to my misery.

On the evening of the second day, I gathered what little dignity I had left and went to complain again about the delay in sailing north. Devlin and three officers were playing poker in the ward-room filled with stale and newly exhaled cigar smoke.

Devlin looked up from his cards briefly, squinted through the haze, and offered an amused expression. He inquired dryly about my health. With my ashen face and unsteady legs, my condition was clearly obvious to him and all the old salts around the table, now covered with green felt.

"Can't be helped," he snapped, studying his cards. "We've gone and set a trap for the bastards—excuse my language, Doctor.

They can't see us here." After asking the dealer for two cards, he explained men were determined to shoot fur seals in open sea and they thought the *Walrus* was heading south. "That's what I told everybody in Dutch Harbor."

He suddenly sat erect, and gave me his full attention. "Poachers are waiting in Captain's Bay and when the fog lifts they'll come out and go about their killing. Then we'll do a little hunting of our own, by God."

Desperate for clean air, even the sickening salty iodine variety, I tried to steady myself to leave when Lieutenant Norris, the tall, thin first officer, took my arm and helped me up to the deck.

"If you ask me," Norris said, stroking his graying mustache, "it's criminal to kill them seals foraging at sea. They're mostly females, you know," he added shaking his head.

"I'm ignorant of such matters, Mr. Norris," I managed to say.

"For every one shot it's like killing three," he added, "the animal itself, the baby in its womb and the pup left on shore that no other female will feed."

The thought of such brutality and waste made me even more nauseous. I thanked him for his help, and was about to go to my stuffy, six-by-nine-foot, low-ceilinged cabin, when the ship's surgeon approached with a sympathetic smile. Dr. Donaldson was a short fellow with a protruding belly and a round, pleasant face. Instead of the regulation officer's jacket, he wore a woolen sweater that covered his neck up to his chin.

"Looks like you're having trouble getting used to all this lurching about," he said. "Brought you a concoction of my own that seems to do the trick."

He handed me a brown half-pint liquor bottle.

"Don't worry," he said with a laugh, "it's not hooch. I just use bottles confiscated from the men."

My face must have turned green at that moment, because Donaldson took me by the arm and led me to the rail.

"You *are* in a bad way," he murmured. "Now, don't sip this stuff. Take it all in one gulp and you'll feel better in a while."

His brew tasted like cod-liver oil laced with kerosene. I nearly gagged before I got it all down. Afraid to speak in my condition, I nodded my thanks, and seized any handhold available to go below. Tying myself to the bed frame to keep from rolling out, I tried to sleep amid half dreams of helpless seals being drowned in pungent cigar smoke. I had never felt so alone and useless and ridiculous in my thirty-four years.

About ten a.m. the following day, I felt vibrations as the engine strained to turn over the propeller shaft. Then I heard running feet on the deck above and loud metallic noises coming from the bow. Slowly making my way topside, I saw that the anchor was being raised from the rocky bottom with difficulty, the men swearing as they strained to get the windlass to bring in the chain. Devlin watched with a scowl.

To my blessed relief, the dyspeptic wallowing ceased as we moved forward. We were underway at last, slowly heading west among the rocks and treacherous shoals south of the Aleutians. The topmast was righted. Greenery was being thrown down to the deck and overboard by laughing and joking men. The spirits of all seemed to improve with the better stability of a ship doing what it was designed to do—sail into the swells.

By two p.m. the fog had disappeared, and Devlin had threaded the *Walrus* north through a narrow, twisting channel between two substantial volcanic islands with barren, snow-covered mountains. One was emitting smoke, its plume trailing in the wind, etching a long white gash against the robin's-egg blue sky. As we entered the mounting swells of the Bering Sea, I wondered how Devlin could have managed the channel so effortlessly with no buoys or other navigation aids to guide him.

Feeling much better, I was happy to stay on deck in the refreshing air, moderate temperature and unobstructed sunlight, observing Devlin at work. My superiors had described him as the best navigator in these waters.

Within an hour the lookout spotted a sail on the western horizon in what I was told were international waters. Devlin ordered a change in course to intercept the vessel, which was moving north at a slow pace using one sail. Small whaleboats, which I presumed were used by hunters shooting seals, were bobbing and curtsying around it. Under steam, the *Walrus* was closing quickly when Lieutenant Norris, who had a telescope on the vessel, said, "She's flying the Union Jack, Captain. Probably a sealer out of Vancouver. Could give us political problems. Do you want to proceed?"

"Let's see what the son of a bitch has to say for himself, Norris," Devlin said, pacing the width of the pilothouse. "If they're shooting seals I don't care what flag she carries or where she does her killing. This is our ocean, goddammit, and those seals are our bread and butter."

Devlin ordered assembly of an unarmed boarding party and, on further thought, told Heath, a boyish-looking second lieutenant at that time, to get the gun crew to uncover and run out the two-pound muzzle-loading cannon.

"Just to demonstrate our determination, don't you know," Devlin said, his dour countenance gone. Our captain was clearly having fun.

Norris was told to bring the *Walrus'* port side as close as safety would allow to the British ship's starboard and maintain the same speed as the other vessel. Its name, now visible in fading paint on her stern, was *Amelia*. But as we neared, the sealer captain decided to show some independence. As if to shoo away a pesky fly, he swung his vessel to the west, making it difficult for the *Walrus* to approach safely.

Norris made course corrections to compensate for the *Amelia's* action, and Devlin strode forward with a megaphone and called on her captain to "Stop playing games. Heave to, prepare for boarding, and call in your hunter boats."

It was difficult to hear, but it was obvious the gray-bearded sealer skipper was having none of it. This is what I recall of his response.

"...British registry in international waters," he shouted, gesturing as if presenting his old and ill-kept ship to an audience. "...Won't be boarded by anybody, let alone a bunch of Yankee revenue hunters."

"This is the Bering Sea, captain," Devlin bellowed, "I'm authorized to protect those seals your hunters have been shoot'n." Devlin paused for only a second. "I ask you again to heave to so my men can conduct a search."

The *Amelia* then turned sharply farther west and south, its mainsail and lines flapping loudly as they jibed through the wind; they were then lashed on the opposite side to pick up speed.

Devlin was all action, pointing to members of his crew in turn.

"Helmsman, hard to port and follow that piece of shit, but keep her a couple of boat lengths to starboard."

"Norris, post Jameson at the wheel when we near 'em. 'Boats' and I have done this before. And ring the engine room for a little more speed."

"Master at Arms, give loaded weapons to that boarding party and prepare to lower the launch."

"Heath, load the mother-lovin' cannon and stand by."

It was thrilling to watch, and I admit I was caught up as one might be while being behind stage while actors were performing a play.

When the vessels were about two boat lengths apart, the *Walrus* slightly ahead with the *Amelia* to our starboard, Devlin shouted: "Heath, don't miss, whatever you do. Send a round in front of that son of a bitch. I want graybeard to get soaked with the splash."

The blast was louder than I expected. The noise and the smell of cordite made me realize this was reality, not some entertainment: that people could get hurt. That *I* could get hurt. The noise also seemed to stun everyone I could see on the other ship. An American cutter firing on a British-flagged vessel was not an everyday occurrence, and the sealers stopped what they were doing to gawk at the still-smoking weapon.

The firing seemed to accomplish its mission, even though the shell landed wide and a half boat length ahead of the *Amelia*. The sealer captain ordered his mainsail lowered, even as Devlin stomped toward Lieutenant Heath, upbraiding him for the wide shot so everyone on deck could hear. From where I stood, it appeared as if Devlin was chewing the nose off the lieutenant.

When the two vessels were abreast, each wildly dancing to its own rhythm in steep swells, Devlin ordered the boarding party into the launch and resumed his shouting match with the sealer captain.

"If you try another trick like that, man, I guarantee you and your lads a long swim to Siberia. Do you understand?"

I learned later that *Amelia*'s captain was a Canadian named Macintosh. From my location at the *Walrus'* pilothouse, I couldn't hear his reply or fathom his actions. Heath, who was now beside me, said it appeared he had ordered his crew to refuse to assist our launch, making it impossible for Norris and his team to board. Out of habit I said a silent prayer as the boarding party's boat rose and fell precariously near the *Amelia's* unpainted wooden sides.

Somebody is going to get killed or badly hurt before this is over I thought. Devlin can't do anything but fire on that ship to get them to obey.

But Devlin, appearing as calm as could be, ordered Heath to bring the *Walrus* about in a long circle around the *Amelia's* stern so as to approach the other ship from the side opposite to where our boarding party's launch was positioned.

"Now give the wheel to Jameson," Devlin ordered. "'Boats,' you know what to do, don't you, lad? Watch for my signals to stop engines and turn away, but put me right into the grinning face of that bastard."

Devlin signaled to cut engines as the *Walrus* headed by momentum alone toward collision with the wallowing *Amelia's* stern.

Devlin then scrambled to the bow, an unlit cigar clamped in his teeth. He pulled himself over the rail and stood on the lines and cables used to hoist the forward sails, just as if he were preparing to harpoon a whale. Heath and the deck crew were aghast. I was transfixed. My heart beat rapidly when Devlin's foot slipped off the cable. He pulled himself back, regained balance and continued to move forward.

As the ships neared each other, our crouching captain gauged the motions of each vessel, and signaled Jameson with his free arm. The *Walrus* was rising in a swell, the *Amelia* settling. With amazing precision, he leapt onto the rear deck of the sealer, as the vessels were level in a tossing sea.

I braced for collision. Our bowsprit swept over the sealer's aft rail. It missed the *Amelia's* rear mast shrouds by what looked to be inches. "Good Lord!" Heath gasped, "He's acting like a pirate in a melodrama. It's crazy. Any small miscalculation and he would have been crushed. We would have suffered damage."

Neither of us could hear what was being said as we slipped along the dipping rail of the other ship, but Devlin, hands on his hips, had his dark face inches away from the taller man's beard. Whatever argument was made, Macintosh had his men throw lines to assist the search party onboard.

"Please understand, Dr. Knowles," Heath said in a low voice, "this is not the sort of thing we're taught in the Cutter Service. Captain Devlin left his ship at sea, for God's sake. A terrible infraction." The young man shook his head, and mumbled, "He took a high risk. Put the cutter in danger of collision. I'll say no more."

I confess the events of that hour frightened me as well. What kind of man was this Devlin, who was entrusted to deliver me safely to my far-flung schools? I realized I had to allow for conduct of government business, but such confrontations as this foul-mouthed man seemed to relish were not to my liking. I also didn't want to be brought into the confidences of one of his disapproving officers. I just wanted to get to St. Paul Island alive and well.

We were told later that Norris and his party discovered 210 fur-seal pelts and about 200 other recently harvested skins. Devlin had ordered its captain to sail to Dutch Harbor and turn the bounty over to the government warehouse, and pay a fine of $750 for evading the boarding party. Macintosh refused, saying the search and boarding were illegal under international law. Further, he would not require his men to work on the trip to deliver the pelts, and his company would refuse to pay the fine.

Devlin told Norris and four armed sailors to take charge of the *Amelia* and sail her to Dutch Harbor. Macintosh was to be confined to his cabin, he said, and any member of the ship's ragtag crew refusing to work would be put ashore. Norris was instructed to examine the *Amelia*'s papers, with particular attention to the names of any of Macintosh's financial backers residing in the U.S.

The orders given, the two ships sailed off in opposite directions after Devlin returned to the *Walrus* on the launch. He was animated and smiling as he virtually vaulted over the rail, taking the little cigar out of his mouth only long enough to shout, "We showed 'em the Union Jack doesn't mean crap in these waters, didn't we, boys?"

In the half-light of the late arctic evening, we were finally on course for St. Paul. My stomach problems had abated for the first time in three days, so I attended the evening meal in the officer's wardroom. Amid muted expressions of congratulations from Chief Engineer Anderson and Dr. Donaldson, Heath and two other junior officers raised concerns about the personal and political risks he had taken.

Devlin was dismissive. "Don't worry, gentlemen. I've sailed these waters in all kinds of vessels and in all kinds of circumstances. The men will tell you I can do anything they can, and maybe a little better."

He was in his element with a captive audience of subordinates and one rumpled, free-riding school agent who should have known to keep quiet.

"But Captain," I said impulsively. "You could have been crushed. Killed or crippled. And won't that captain make a fuss in London? And Washington, too?"

"Ah, Dr. Knowles, I thank you for your concern, and I'm glad to see you've gotten 'sea legs' and your color back," he said, grinning. "Since you're new to this godforsaken region, there's no reason you should understand what's at stake here: what we have to do to keep predators in line."

Pushing around the fish and boiled potatoes on his plate, Devlin proceeded to lecture us on his philosophy of cutter life in the Bering Sea.

"Washington is thousands of miles away," he said, waving his fork directly at me. "They've ignored Alaska ever since old Seward bought it in '67."

"But, surely, won't you'll get a scolding letter or something for today's action?" I asked.

"Nonsense!" Devlin replied. "Those teacup boys will love this. We proved we control these waters, and they can deny any direct responsibility. They'll have it both ways, the way politicians like it."

He said that although he only confiscated four hundred pelts that day, the news that he forced a foreign vessel to allow boarding by threat of gunfire would spread rapidly among sealers and whalers, and "the scoundrels trading whiskey to the natives."

"There's no law up here yet, Knowles," he said while keeping his plate from sliding away as the ship listed. "No judges. No marshals or jails for that matter. And no top hat diplomats either, right, gentlemen?"

The chief engineer said, "Amen to that."

"What I did today," he continued, looking at each of us in turn, "will instill a healthy fear of the Almighty—or at least of the Revenue Cutter Service—and prevent all kinds of skullduggery the rest of this season."

There were less-than-enthusiastic murmurs and nods of approval from the officers, but I'm sure they noted, as I did, his egotistical use of the first person singular instead of the "we" that would have encompassed praise for all hands.

Devlin then continued to lecture, telling us how he had handled Macintosh.

"That ignoramus made the mistake of saying I had no authority over him or his crew. He wouldn't sail his ship to Dutch Harbor. Can you believe that?" he asked. "I told him if he didn't, I'd tow his stinking bark to the end of some island and put the whole mob of them ashore. That got through his stubborn Scot's skull, I'll tell you."

His fish was getting cold, I supposed, so Devlin returned to eating, and with his mouth full asked the engineer about the remaining store of coal in the bunker. The lecture was over.

I didn't realize it at the time, but Devlin's decision to commandeer a foreign-flag vessel and confine its master to quarters would create a tidal wave of indignation in maritime nations. The diplomats called the incident the start of the Bering Sea Controversy, which, even now, continues to be a source of friction between our government and the British. To Devlin, it was all in a day's enjoyable work.

I couldn't decide whether to fear this man's recklessness or admire his bravado. So I took another helping of potatoes to stabilize my stomach, ignored the fish and left the wardroom.

The following morning, in heavy fog, I heard rather than saw the approach of St. Paul in the isolated Seal Islands, the small, rocky places the Russians called the Pribilofs.

The barks of tens of thousands of fur seals and assorted other pinnipeds, and the squeals and shrill cries of sea birds magnified and misdirected by fog, overwhelmed my senses. The cacophony was eerie and unsettling and visceral for someone experiencing it for the first time. It was as if the ship were heading blindly into a new kind of Hades, where discordant, grating noise replaced fire and brimstone.

When the rocky shoreline gradually appeared, I noticed weather-worn wooden structures on some higher ground. One or two of them, I was certain, constituted the only school on the island. It was run by a Methodist missionary, and I was charged with making sure it met government standards, such as they were.

A coxswain and several men rowed Devlin, Donaldson and me through the surf, which was quite high, toward a short, dilapidated pier protruding from a gravel beach.

As we approached, I saw Rev. Cartwright, whom I had met once before, and a tallish woman dressed in dark colors with boots visible beneath her calf-length dress. A second man, whom I suspected was Parker, the agent of the sealing company under government contract, stood beside them.

They waved at the Captain, who sat erect and returned the gesture. He poses like a sea lord acknowledging his landed subjects, I thought.

Holding onto the side of the boat with one hand and keeping my spectacles in place with the other, I was filled with uncertainty as I began my new role in this desolate place.

Nevertheless, I was anxious to leave the domain of this particular "sea lord" for a few days.

Chapter Five

"What kind of vessel was it?" Devlin demanded, shouting over blasts of wind rattling the windows of Pastor Cartwright's drafty cabin on St. Paul Island.

Soon after landing, Devlin, Donaldson and I had been ushered into what served as the old minister's kitchen-dining room area.

"Did you get the name or homeport of this son-of-a—er, renegade?"

"We couldn't see her plainly," the downcast pastor said apologetically. "She was anchored out beyond where your ship is now and the fog was heavy."

"Well, can you at least tell me how many masts she carried?" Devlin continued as he put his empty coffee mug on the table with a thud. "Was she a steamer, a sailing vessel or a combination?"

Cartwright coughed deeply and said, "I'm sorry, but I really can't say for sure, Captain."

"By God, we have to stop these hooch sellers." Devlin stood and began to pace. "But I have to know what I'm looking for before I can track 'em down, don't I? And to think we only missed them by two days."

I noticed immediately that Cartwright was much frailer than when I last saw him two years earlier. Now he was having difficulty breathing and seemed disoriented.

Cartwright's granddaughter Sarah gave the description as she poured more coffee. "It had two masts, I'm sure of that, and a smokestack as well." She put down the pot and continued. "I went to that little rise over the beach to get a better look, which, I guess, was silly of me with men from an unknown ship coming ashore."

"Please, Miss Cartwright, tell me everything that happened as best you can recollect." Devlin stopped pacing and gave her his full attention.

I focused on the young woman as well. I marveled at the poise of this energetic, lithesome girl who appeared to be in her twenties. Her dark-brown hair was swept back into the kind of long, intricate braid that many Indian women preferred.

Sarah said she had been concentrating on two beached whaleboats and the villagers flocking to them to trade when she heard crunching on the gravel path behind her. She then saw two men walking fast toward her. One was tall and bear-like, with a dark beard punctuated by a leer as if his upper lip had been cut away, she said. The other was a smallish fellow who surprisingly sported a battered derby. She heard the large one say, "Now here's a tasty morsel in an unexpected place."

"They kept coming up the hill, so I decided to hurry to the school," she said calmly. "I went to the work shed, grabbed the axe, and demanded to know what they wanted. The derby fellow was out of breath, but the other one was laughing at me."

"Good lord!" I said in amazement, joining the conversation for the first time. "That was awfully brave of you to stay and confront them. They could have overpowered you."

"I didn't know what else to do, Dr. Knowles," she said with no sign of embarrassment. "Especially when the big bear fellow said something like 'Now, darlin', that's no way to treat lonely sailors that only wants a little kiss'."

"Were they armed?" Devlin interjected quickly. "Did they keep approaching you? By any chance did you hear them call each other by name?"

"I didn't notice any arms or hear any names," Sarah said, shaking her head. "They stopped coming toward me when grandfather came out of the cabin and fired a shot over their heads from our old bird gun."

"You must have been frightened out of your wits," I blurted out. Devlin, who had ignored me until then, gave me a withering look of disapproval.

She said one of the two men then said something about getting back to business and they scrambled down toward the beach. The big bear shouted he might "pay me a little visit later." She blushed, and strode to return the pot to the kitchen coal stove. I turned to watch her, intrigued with a glimpse of white calf between her boots and the hem of her dress.

Cartwright said he was ashamed that he had heard nothing until Sarah arrived at the school; that he had not been there to confront the men earlier. Parker, the manager of the sealing station, said he hadn't heard or seen anything at all.

"That wasn't the worst of it," Cartwright continued. "Sarah and I had to stay near the cabin all day."

"A wise decision," Devlin remarked.

"But that evening about a half-dozen drunken natives came pounding on the door looking for more liquor," the old pastor said. "I recognized most of them, but had never seen them in that condition."

He said he'd tried to assure them no liquor was allowed at the mission, but they were too besotted to believe him. "Someone in the village must have seen the men talking to Sarah earlier and thought they sold us that terrible stuff, too," he added, and went on to describe how they trampled Sarah's tiny vegetable garden, tore doors off the sheds and completely shattered their only privy.

"Sarah tried to keep them away from the vegetable plot, but they wouldn't listen as they usually did when she spoke. It was really frightening," Cartwright said with a shudder. "They were out of control: utterly irrational from that poison."

The old man ran his fingers through his thinning hair, and I could almost feel his anguish, his shame in being powerless to stop them.

"I was down on my knees praying, but they took no notice in their rage," he said. "Thank the Good Lord they finally got discouraged and left on their own."

"We'll have to find those law-break'n bastards," Devlin said, pacing the small room again. "Make 'em pay for frightening you and your granddaughter and selling hooch to the natives."

"That's right, Captain," Cartwright said, slapping the table. "You really can't blame the Aleuts. They've lived in these seas for thousands of years without ever tasting grain alcohol. Their bodies can't figure out how to handle it."

Devlin nodded, and said it was troubling "these pirates," as he called the whiskey traders, would come to St. Paul, a sealing station that should have had at least a few armed men for protection.

"Their kind usually prey on isolated Aleut or Eskimo villages," he said with a frown. "Why did they come here and only stay for a few hours? They could have traded more of their swill easier on the mainland."

"I think they heard you were coming, Captain," Cartwright replied. "I told my little flock last Sunday Captain Devlin was due any day."

"Probably so," Devlin snarled as he ceased pacing and looked directly at the sealing station chief.

Parker's unruly black hair was bunched over his ears, sticking out from under a dirty slouch hat like a pair of wings. Combined with his equally unruly beard, long, pockmarked face and thick glasses, he had the most mournful countenance I had ever seen. He never smiled or changed expression during the conversation.

"It's odd as hell they would land here in any event," Devlin said. "We'll find out what's what when we catch 'em."

Sarah had busied herself at the pastor's desk, and now presented Devlin with a pencil sketch of the vessel she had seen. "I hope this helps you find them," she said.

He thanked her, saying the drawing was first-rate and would be very useful in the hunt.

In the meantime, he continued, a detachment of Cuttermen would be sent to scour the village and destroy any remaining alcohol, and the *Walrus'* carpenter and some men would repair the sheds and the privy.

"You can't survive in this climate without a privy, can you, Mr. Cartwright?" he added with a tight smile.

Without waiting for a response, as if one were needed, he told Parker, Dr. Donaldson and me to accompany him to the beach. Just like Devlin, I thought. He never asked, he ordered.

Once we were away from the cabin and somewhat sheltered from cold wind by the schoolhouse, Devlin braced the station chief as if he were a malingering Cutter seaman, not a civilian.

"Parker, where the hell were you when all this was going on? That old man and the girl could have been killed—or worse."

"The station is at the other end of the island, Captain," Parker tried to explain. "What with the goddamned seals bellowing and the wind blowing, I didn't know what was going on until some of my men didn't turn up for work yesterday."

Devlin's exasperated expression as he moved within two feet of Parker showed what he thought of that explanation.

"Anyway," Parker continued as he backed away, "there's only three white men at the station. Two replacements went south when they took one look at this place in May. The company hasn't replaced them."

"You have to be more alert in the future, assistants or no assistants," Devlin retorted, his face inches from Parker's. "Every honest skipper knows only authorized ships are allowed on sealing islands."

"I know," the station chief started to say, only to be interrupted by Devlin forcing him to step back until he was against the schoolhouse wall.

"I find this visit as suspicious as hell," the Captain said.

Parker, his face now flushed in anger, stood his ground, but agreed that the incident was disturbing.

"Protect those furs, Parker," the Captain said. "Disreputable people are trying to get your company's sealing contract. It's worth lots of money." He backed away a few feet. "They'll try anything to make you look like an incompetent, or a thief."

Then it was my turn to get the Devlin treatment.

"Knowles, I can't tell you your business, but you have to make a decision about this school," he said, grabbing the arm of my coat. "That preacher and his pretty granddaughter are your responsibility now." He looked over at the tiny schoolhouse, shook his head and continued. "They're vulnerable to all kinds of viciousness on this island and we can't protect them. You see that, don't you?"

I told him I was considering transfer of the school to another location, but would need more information. I added quickly that after first impressions, I planned to urge Cartwright to request retirement from his mission duties. "I'm praying for guidance," I added.

"A bit of advice, Knowles," Devlin said sternly. "Up here, act first and pray later."

He then informed us that the *Walrus* would scout the nearby seal foraging area for a few days to look for the liquor-seller. Donaldson would stay on shore to offer medical assistance to the Aleuts, and a couple of armed men would be stationed at the mission school until he returned.

"I'm short of officers, as you men know," he said, "but I'll leave Boatswain Jameson in charge. In a crisis, 'Boats' is worth ten times some of them new Academy officers anyway."

As he turned to leave, three Aleut men appeared near the top of the little rise, heading toward us.

"Mr. Ivanoff," Devlin shouted, walking briskly toward the man in the lead, a stern-faced fellow wearing a seaman's cap, woolen shirt, sealskin pants and muddy boots. The contour of his eyes spoke to his Aleutian ancestry, but his skin was lighter than his companions'.

Ivanoff pulled off his cap as Devlin shook his hand. "We come to say sorry to the pastor fellow," he said.

"That's a first-rate idea, Dimitri," the Captain responded, still gripping his hand.

"The council will punish those drunks," Ivanoff said. "You won't have to."

Devlin stared up at the man who was at least a head taller, and said, "We trust each other, Dimitri, so I defer to your council's judgment." He released the man's hand, adding, "But I still want my men to destroy any liquor that still might be around."

The big man nodded agreement, and was about to leave when Devlin took him by the arm and led him around the school-house. Over the sound of the wind, all I could hear was the Captain saying something like, "Now let's talk about keeping those bandits off the island."

Donaldson was grinning as Devlin walked away from us with Ivanoff. "My new friend," he said, "you've just witnessed how

'His Highness' lords over his domains along the Bering Sea." He slapped me on the back, stuck his pipe in his mouth, and went toward the village.

On returning to the cabin, I saw that Cartwright had not moved from the dining table. His head was bowed and encased in his splayed fingers, his wispy white beard touching the oilcloth. Sarah was rinsing coffee mugs in the kitchen, which consisted of an unenclosed area opposite the entrance.

The low-ceilinged room was spartan. On the north wall, over a well-stocked bookcase, hung the ubiquitous pastel-colored print of Jesus that I abhorred. Unlike the icons in Russian churches, this rendering depicted the Lord as weak and dreamy. To me it was not an ideal Christian image for a bleak, dangerous place like St. Paul.

Above a tiny desk in the south corner, several framed photographs of church groups and a diploma were visible. The area must have served as the pastor's office, since it was furnished with a worn carpet and two extra chairs. The coal stove was located next to a narrow staircase, presumably in the hope that some hint of heat would rise to the bedrooms above. A door to the schoolroom was centered on the south wall.

While drying her hands, Sarah said, "Dr. Knowles, would you like to see our school?"

I agreed immediately. Her invitation would allow me to leave the cabin with its lingering odor of coal smoke. It also gave me an opportunity to speak privately with this captivating young woman so utterly different in manner and appearance from the churchwomen I had known.

The classroom was dark and very cold when we entered. After opening a shutter for light, Sarah sat beside me on one of the long, rough-hewn benches. The shaft of light from the window illuminated her thin, angular face, pale even in mid-summer from long foggy months without dependable sunlight.

"Dr. Knowles," she whispered, "please help me convince grandfather to do something about his health. I don't believe he can last another winter on St. Paul without proper medical attention."

She said the old gentleman had suffered terribly with pneumonia during April and May, and had had several episodes of depression since she arrived after her grandmother's death a year ago.

"He blames himself," she said, looking directly into my eyes. "He believes she would still be alive if he hadn't insisted on staying at the mission instead of taking her home when she became frail."

I told her I also was concerned about Cartwright's condition and valued her candor.

"Given what you just told me, and based on my observation of your grandfather's condition," I said, "I'm going to ask him to request transfer to his mission headquarters in California as soon as possible. I hope he'll agree."

"I believe he'll be relieved to have your advice," Sarah said, smiling for the first time. "As long as you assure him it's for health reasons, not for any failure with management of the school."

I told her I would speak with Cartwright and would depend on her support.

"But first," I said, "I hope you will call me Stanton, and allow me to address you as Sarah. Conditions up here are far too difficult to require formality among colleagues."

"Thank you," she replied as she pulled her woolen shawl around her. "But I'm not really a colleague. I love being a teacher, but I'm here without appointment or salary from your department, only to support grandfather."

"That's of no consequence," I said, my breath visible in the cold. "Even though I've been ordained, I've elected to spend my life in college classrooms. Teaching is my first love, too." I explained I became bored with administrative duties and the rigidity of doctrine as a seminary dean and thought my new position would invigorate me. "But, please, tell me about your school here."

She said it was not as successful as she would have liked. Many of the Aleuts on St. Paul were men recruited in the Aleutians to kill and process fur seals in season and then return home to their families. There were some year-round families with children, she went on, but she was lucky if ten attended school on any given day.

"And what about church attendance? It's none of my concern these days, but it could indicate what we should do about the school."

Sarah said a "good Sunday" in summer would see no more than ten worshipers in chapel. Most Aleuts were very faithful to the Russian Orthodox Church, she explained, especially since several of them had been ordained as priests or appointed as lay readers.

Not wanting to end this intimate conversation, I gathered up my courage and offered to arrange for her to teach school in Oakland. She and her grandfather could return together on the fur-company's steamer when it came to collect the pelts, I added.

"That's really thoughtful of you," she said, relaxing for the first time since our conversation began. "But I want to stay with these children at least through this winter; until you can send a replacement next spring." She looked at me, and added in a plaintive voice, "I'm afraid if they stop school now, they may never return, and several show promise."

I argued against her position. I told her of Captain Devlin's warning of danger; that the school department couldn't provide support if the mission were closed. But she disarmed me with smiles that softened her steely determination. As I leaned closer to make my case, an unexpected desire to take her hand came over me. Unused as I was to this kind of emotion, I wanted to tell her immediately how much I admired her courage, how much I wanted to be with her in California over the winter. I overcame my desire with difficulty, but lost the argument as sounds of hammering and sawing echoed in the room, breaking the mood.

Outside in the persistent north wind, crewmen were repairing the damage to the sheds and privy with a smiling Boatswain Jameson urging them on with a line of patter.

"Good evening to you, Miss and you, too, Dr. Knowles," he said as if he were greeting us on a Market Street Sunday afternoon. "I'm 'Boats', Miss, and that feller over there with the rifle is Harry. We're to be your fearless sentinels for a few days."

Late that night, the long arctic twilight, visible through the window of our temporary quarters in the schoolroom, kept me awake. Donaldson was sleeping, but Jameson was even more talkative than usual, and I was happy to have the distraction. The emotional conversation after supper with Cartwright and Sarah had saddened me greatly. The good man finally agreed to retire, but made plain what he thought of my decision to allow Sarah to stay alone for another winter. Neither Cartwright nor I could shake Sarah's resolve, so I told them any supplies remaining under Cartwright's contract would be available to Sarah until next spring. It was not, I'm ashamed to say, a memorable performance for a new school agent.

Jameson broke through my musings. "Look here, Dr. Knowles. I did a little profitable trading myself today."

He proudly displayed ivory of varying sizes and shapes on one of the benches. "These two are almost perfect walrus tusks," he said, "but I'll get my boys to carve something grand on the smaller irregular pieces, too."

He held out his hands for me to see. His knuckles were the size of Brazil nuts, and two fingers were missing on one hand and one on the other.

"After too many years aloft, I can't do scrimshaw myself anymore, but my lads are mighty good at it." He handed one of the tusks to me. "At home we earn a few extra dollars selling the stuff and split the proceeds. Not bad business for ignorant sailors, eh?"

I asked if Devlin wouldn't disapprove, mentioning I thought he was a particularly stern and unforgiving commander.

"Not at all," Jameson said, lighting his stubby pipe. "The Captain was a seaman his self, ya know."

I said I suspected as much.

"And he knows enough to give us lads a little incentive to sign on for this rotten duty every year. A few extra dollars to enjoy 'Frisco's Barbary Coast' keeps us interested altogether."

"Why do you volunteer to serve with Devlin in the first place?" I asked. "Even in my short time on the *Walrus*, I can see how difficult your life must be. No fresh food, poor living conditions—"

"That's just it, Doctor," he interrupted. "Them what sails the Bering Patrol are the toughest damned sailors there is, and every other seaman respects us for it. We're probably crazy, but we're the best." He sat back and puffed his pipe for a minute. "Uncle Samuel lets loose a few extra dollars for the duty, but the best thing is nobody's ever bored on this Old Man's ship, believe me."

I certainly did believe him. I just worried about the price we all had to pay so Devlin could avoid boredom.

I only had four days on St. Paul before the *Walrus* returned. On the first two, I was able to observe Sarah and her tiny troop of pupils. It was delightful to see how the children gravitated to her, laughing and squabbling to hold her hand, quizzing her constantly about life "on the outside."

In the evenings around the pastor's kitchen table, her enthusiasm overwhelmed me. Without a hint of shyness she recommended practical ideas for making school more interesting for children who had only the faintest notion of the world beyond their villages.

"Mostly," she said, slowly shaking her head, "uneducated whalers and traders are the 'outside world' they know. Many have an inventive vocabulary of vile swear words, and love to try and shock me."

With passion she pressed me to provide every native school with easy-to-read books in English, posters illustrating the geography and the plants and animals of our country.

"I surrender," I said, laughing and throwing up my arms. I was completely captivated by her intelligence, her intensity. By her. "I'll draft a letter of petition to the School Administration this very night." Her lean, pale face was transformed into a thing of beauty by her wide smile. It warmed the chilly, bare cabin, and dazzled me.

One morning, Station Chief Parker joined us for toasted bread and coffee, saying he wanted to show me "Why we're all here, what all the fuss was about."

Despite everything I had read or heard before, my senses weren't prepared for introduction to the world of Callorhinus ursinus. Parker took me to a muddy bluff overlooking the world's largest northern fur-seal rookery. Thousands of barking, squealing, writhing fur seals of all sizes covered virtually every square foot of a sand and gravel beach as far as I could see. Pups the size of large dogs squirmed to locate their mothers. Some adults used strong fins to flip sand onto their backs, while others rolled and grunted while scratching their backs on the gravel. Each animal, it seemed to me, emitted proprietary throaty sounds, adding volume and disharmony to a chorus. The stench generated by so many animals overpowered the wind's best effort to disperse it.

The massive bulls, the size of steers, were the most fascinating. Their fearsome bellows were heard above the general roar as they pulled themselves erect with their fins and bared long, sharp teeth to protect their harems.

"See how fast those old bulls can move when they have to," Parker said, pointing at one nipping a rival's neck and chasing him into the surf. As the animal moved, several pups being weaned were crushed in the melee, squealing in a high pitch. One appeared to have been killed.

"They can be dangerous as hell," Parker explained over the din. He nodded toward a group of his Aleut hunters with their clubs warily trying to isolate a young bachelor for slaughter. "Under our contract," he said, "we're only allowed to kill a limited number of young males to keep the herd in balance."

As he spoke, I watched a cow and her pup closest to where we stood. "That one there, Parker," I said, pointing. "She seems to be talking to the pup, or am I just dreaming?"

"No, you're not," he answered. "Those sounds are the only way the youngster can identify its momma and get its food."

After walking above the beach for some time, watching flocks of sea birds on the lookout for seal afterbirth, I declined Parker's offer to observe the seal killing and skinning process. I was glad when we left the noise and the smell of the beach and went to the Sealing Plant, where skins were processed for shipment.

Parker was a man who took pride in his work, and he proceeded to educate me on what was involved. A dozen Aleut men were busy washing and soaking the skins while others, stripped to the waist, used two-handed curved ulu knives to laboriously scrape blubber off the inside surfaces. In another room, the skins were constantly agitated in a brine tank, then put through a large wringer device and placed on racks to dry for several weeks.

The adjacent warehouse was obviously Parker's centerpiece. It was here, he said, where pelts were packed tightly in salt by four of his most trusted workers, and placed in barrels for shipment.

"This is why we're all here," Parker said, waving his arm to encompass the large story-and-a-half room. "There's the makings of hundreds of fur coats and such for the fine ladies and gents in New York and Paris right here in my little barn."

He claimed that the royalty value of the pelts in that warehouse would pay for all the government's expenses in Alaska, including the costs of the Bering Sea Patrol and my schools.

"Aren't you afraid of theft?" I asked.

"Not really," the station chief said. "I keep good records on every seal killed, and the Cutters give us some protection." As he walked me to the entrance, he added, "But I'm damned sure the possibility of robbery is why your high and mighty Captain was so riled up by the liquor-seller that came sniffing around here last week."

The next day was the only sunny one I experienced on St. Paul. The temperature was close to seventy degrees with only a mild breeze. Sarah let the children go in the afternoon and led me huffing and puffing to keep up with her through fields of vividly colored wildflowers and berry bushes. She named them as she went: ruby-red fireweed, lemon-yellow arctic poppies and lavender lupines, commingled with wild moss berries and strawberry bushes.

I marveled as the flocks of sea birds swirling overhead in the clear, blue sky seemed to reflect the brilliance of the flowers. Horned puffins with orange and yellow beaks competed with less dense groups of crested auklets with their plumes, while the red-legged kittiwakes were everywhere.

"The flowers will be gone soon," Sarah said sadly, "and then we'll return to black and gray against the snow."

"Then why don't you allow me to help find you work in the States, or at least on the mainland or at Dutch Harbor?" I said as I took her hand in both of mine. "I don't want anything to happen to you, Sarah Cartwright, you're—you're too valuable—as a teacher, I mean."

She laughed heartily, but didn't pull away. "Why, Dr. Stanton Knowles," she said tilting her head coyly, "it wouldn't be that I'm the only white girl you've seen for a while, would it?"

I actually blushed and tried to stammer a reply, when she interrupted. "Well, I've grown fond of you, too, Stanton, and I'm a bold enough woman to say so. But I can't—I won't—leave these children before spring."

With that, she kissed my cheek and, her arms swinging, set a fast pace back toward the school. That sunny day on St. Paul, the flowers and birds, her chaste kiss and vibrant energy haunt my memory.

"Captain wants us aboard right now," Jameson said when we reached the schoolhouse. "Somethin' about a favorable westerly what'll help us go north by sail. Save the precious drop of coal we have left, and all."

And then with a wink, he leaned close to my ear and whispered, "The Old Man'll probably be as sour as a rotten lemon, ya know? Didn't even catch a sight of that liquor ship."

After praying with Cartwright and wishing him good luck, I gave him my letter to his Mission Board supporting his request for retirement. I asked Sarah to accompany me to the launch.

"Please reconsider," I said, as she took my arm when we

descended the hill. "There's still time. I'd feel better knowing you were safe in Oakland with your grandfather."

"I know you would, dear Stanton, but I wouldn't," she said softly. "I'd know I was abandoning these children. We'll see each other soon, and get to know each other much better, I promise."

To Jameson's great amusement, she kissed me again on the cheek and walked briskly up toward the school, the wind molding her skirts to her supple body. Reluctantly, I boarded the launch to take me back to the domain of Captain Devlin, wondering if I would ever see that intriguing girl again.

Chapter Six

I had no sooner boarded the Walrus than I was told that the Captain wanted to see me. He was on deck shouting orders as the crew prepared to get under way. A young third lieutenant stood stiffly beside him with a brass sextant tucked under his arm.

"You wanted to see me, Captain?" I asked.

"Knowles, are you crazy or just incompetent?" he asked, his back towards me while he gave full attention to the crew. "Jameson, get that goddamned mains'l up. Your lads are sleepwalking. Push 'em." He relit his cigar while still surveying work on the deck.

"I'm told you let that young woman stay on the island for the winter," he said.

He raised his voice. "And Jameson, tell the lazy bastard working that sheet to winch it down like a sailor, not a 'Frisco trollop! No, no, not that bastard! The red-haired one!"

Angry and determined to get his full attention, I spoke loudly over the wind. I explained that Sarah was adamant about staying. She was an independent woman, I said, and I had no authority over her actions.

He ignored me. He had turned his attention to the novice lieutenant, who looked no older than my nineteen-year-old nephew. "Carter, take another sighting and be accurate this time. We don't get a clear shot at the sun very often, and a tenth of a mile mistake can kill you up here."

"What were you saying about that pretty missionary, Knowles?" he said, finally turning toward me. I explained her status once again, bracing myself against the pilothouse as the sails filled, heeling the ship to starboard.

"Carter, for Jeezus sake, keep that instrument level. What did they teach you at that damned Academy, anyway?"

"That was a knuckle-headed decision you made, Knowles," he said in a lower voice. "If anything happens to her, it'd be your fault. I'll record your decision in my cruise report, noting it was contrary to my sternest advice."

Fuming, I followed him into the pilothouse. "Listen here, Captain, I—"

"Stand by, Knowles!" he ordered as he directed attention to the lieutenant. "Carter, plot a course to a spot ten miles off the entrance to Norton Sound, and another from that point to St. Michael, where the doctor here has to go."

He paused to survey action on deck as the *Walrus* began to gain speed, close-hauled to the wind.

"And Carter, try to keep us from running aground in all that open water, will ya." I was now certain sarcastic abuse was one of his favorite teaching tools.

Trying to contain my anger, I said "Captain, I appreciate I'm a passenger here, but I have my work to do as you do yours. I resent being treated like a schoolboy!"

"That's just too damned bad, Knowles," he said with a hard stare. "But if you act like a tenderfoot, I'll treat you like one. There's no room for stupidity north of the 53rd Parallel."

Barely able to keep hurtful rage to myself, I stomped out of the pilothouse and went below. For the first time since I wore short pants, I wanted to shout the ugly word, "bastard."

"Old Man got you down, Knowles?" Donaldson said as I strode furiously into the wardroom, muttering something about "unfeeling martinet."

"Don't take it personally." He handed me a mug of coffee. "He's rough on everybody. Except for me and Jameson, that is." He flopped into a chair, and smiled. "'Boats' is old-school, like the skipper. Me, I'm just the saw-bones who gives him a little quinine and whiskey when he's ailing."

"He has no concept of decency or manners or what effect he has on people's feelings."

"Oh, yes, he does. He just doesn't care about insignificant things like that." Donaldson put his feet up on an empty chair, and his hands behind his head. "You gotta understand something, my friend. He thinks he—and he alone—rules the Bering Sea. And he's out to prove it."

"That doesn't make me feel any better. I have important work to do, too, and it has little to gain by his ill-mannered blustering."

"He believes everything up here is his business. The man's on a mission, I tell you. Damned if I know what drives him so desperately."

"I have a mission of my own, and he should respect that," I said, taking a deep breath.

"He'll only countenance that when you have the same fervor for your job as he does for his, I 'spect."

In my cabin, a combination of disturbing emotions tormented me. I was full of hatred for Devlin. I had disparaged his crude manner and language since coming aboard, but this boiling anger seared my soul. It obliterated my rational defenses. It was savage, un-Christian. Sinful. But I couldn't bring myself to ask the Lord for forgiveness. Then something I can't fathom occurred. The intensity of these destructive urges became transferred somehow into a desperate longing to be with Sarah, a girl I barely knew. I wanted to hold her, to make her love me in body as well as soul. These unworthy, overpowering, comingled emotions were beyond reason. I tried to write, but couldn't concentrate. Reading was no help either, so later that night I pulled on my heavy jacket, lit my pipe and went on deck, hoping the reality of sea and cold wind would dispel them.

The sky was clear, the wind blustery and variable, shifting direction ever so slightly. The *Walrus* was obviously making good time under the watchful eyes of Lieutenant Heath. He greeted me warmly and asked how I came to volunteer for arctic duty.

"You were a college dean or something, weren't you?" he asked, inviting me into the pilothouse. "Why in heaven's name leave a comfortable job in the States for this?" he said, sweeping his arm broadly to indicate the rolling sea.

"Change," I said. "The humdrum of settling stupid squabbles among professors and correcting papers on the same subjects year after year had deadened my spirit." I pulled up my coat collar. "In truth, Mr. Heath, I actually believed I could do some good in frontier schools."

"But why here?" he persisted. "Surely you could have done good in a more congenial place."

Pointing to a barely discernible constellation in the northeast, I said I blamed my impulsive decision on the constellation Cygnus, the Northern Cross.

"Walking across the green after a contentious faculty meeting one night," I said with an embarrassed laugh, "I spotted Cygnus. The apex of the cross was pointing north. A few days before, I had received an Interior Department notice appealing for educators for Alaska. In my frustration, I took old Cygnus to be a sign for how to improve my life. So here I am."

With a hearty laugh, Heath said, "I've heard lots of reasons people give for coming up here, for the whales, ivory, or to get away from their wives. But following a star. That beats all. It really does."

"It is a bit overdramatic," I said, seeing the humor in my pompous explanation. "But, think of this, Heath, no matter what goes wrong, I can always blame my misfortune on a cluster of stars."

Still chuckling, he said to be careful in telling Devlin about my "revelation." "The Captain will think you're mocking him. He believes he's the only man aboard who can read destiny in the stars."

Even as we spoke the constellation became shrouded by a solid band of charcoal-colored clouds. Heath said it looked as if we were in for in a Bering Sea storm. He was right.

By morning, the old *Walrus* was performing its own dance to a concerto of contrapuntal sound. Wind sang and whistled as it vibrated through the rigging; the old ship rolled and lifted and plunged with a splash sounding like a bass drum as waves sluiced over the bow and along her deck.

I was the only one aboard who admitted being concerned with the violence nature threw at us. "No cause for alarm, my friend," Donaldson said. "It's just Old Man Bering letting us know who's boss." A steep plunge threw his chair into the bulkhead. "It's not unusual to encounter swells like that one," he said grimacing. "They exceed thirty feet sometimes, but we haven't reached that yet."

"I know I'm getting personal," he said with a warm smile, "but why in hell did you leave the solidity of college classrooms to be tossed around in the Bering Sea? You were a professor, weren't you?"

Trying to keep my growing seasickness under control, I told him I had grown weary of the strictures—the self-congratulatory certainties—of the subjects I taught.

"Reality, not sanctimonious theory, was what I wanted."

"I take it, then, you've never been married, professor, or you would've experienced giant doses of reality," he chuckled, bracing his feet against the bulkhead.

"Came close once years ago when the pastor I was working for pushed me to marry his daughter. She was pretty and willing, but I was never Calvinistic enough to suit her stern standards." I shook my head and smiled at my escape. "That's when I fled to the tranquility of the seminary classroom."

"As a married man with a nagging wife and three young ones," Donaldson said, "I applaud your decision, although, my friend, you'll not have to worry about being trapped in tranquility as long as you sail with Devlin."

It was difficult to get any rest sitting or lying down with the noise and the violent motion as the ship dove as if it would never rise again. I can't even imagine how the crew got any relief, swinging spasmodically in their hammocks in the forecastle, hearing the waves wash over the deck above them.

Since I couldn't stand the thought of being anywhere near Devlin, and violent seasickness had drained me, I was pleased that meal service in the wardroom was suspended while dishes, pots, pans and other utensils were stowed away by the stewards for safekeeping. Nobody seemed to have any appetite, anyway.

During such storms the wardroom became the gathering place for the off-duty officers, swapping tall tales of other tempests and adventures. Devlin stubbornly remained in the pilothouse on these occasions, so I went to the paneled sanctuary with its bolted-down table and heavy chairs to ride it out with the experienced Bering seamen.

Late the afternoon of the second day, Chief Engineer Anderson, Donaldson, and two others were trying to play cards on the gyrating table. Heath and young Carter, their feet braced against the table legs, were looking on.

"Dr. Knowles," Carter said, as he motioned me to a chair, "Lieutenant Heath told me how the Northern Cross brought you to Alaska. I think it's a wonderful story, I really do."

Donaldson couldn't resist. "Sounds to me like a bit of Methodist blarney," he said with a wide grin.

"Didn't know Methodists were even allowed to have blarney," Anderson retorted with a straight face. "Certainly aren't allowed to have much fun. That right, Knowles?"

The good-natured ribbing pleased me, but I just smiled and ignored it. I thanked Carter, and in the interest of filling time, asked how he came to be in the Cutter Service. He said he was the son of a Gloucesterman. "Dad thought I should be a Grand Banks fisherman like him," he said. "But, no, no, not me. I thought the Service would be a more pleasant way to make a living."

Suddenly, the ship rose and then dove radically in the swells. The pile of discarded playing cards scattered in every direction. Carter grasped the table ledge with one hand and with a wide grin shouted, "Then, I got assigned to this here Bering Patrol." He shrugged, threw up his free arm as if he were riding a bronco, and the others joined in his laughter.

Heath, on the other hand, remained serious. It seemed he couldn't wait to tell me his story. At even the prospect, Donaldson rolled his bloodshot eyes and groaned, "Not again, for God's sake."

Heath, his arms folded and his chin raised, explained he was the third son of an iron-foundry owner in Baltimore. His oldest brother was in the family business. The next oldest, he said with obvious pride, graduated from Annapolis and was a full lieutenant in the Navy.

"When I declined to go into the church as my father wanted," Heath said smoothing out his trim beard, "I was encouraged by an associate of his to enter the Revenue Cutter's School of Instruction. It was a consolation prize, I suppose."

"Not much consolation," Donaldson said as he laid down his cards and cried, "Gin! Your papa wanted a preacher and got a sea-going revenue agent instead."

There was general hilarity at the remark, even as other card players challenged Donaldson's victory call with everyone's cards in such disarray. Heath didn't join in the laughter or the challenge. "You can all laugh," he said, "but I fully expect to be a senior captain someday."

Ignoring the guffaws of the others, and looking directly at me, he said he would travel home in December to be married. "It will be a high-church wedding to the sweetest, most cultured, prettiest young woman in all of Maryland," he said. "Both families will be there, including her uncle. He's a former governor of Georgia, and now is a very prominent businessman."

As the others were retrieving cards and squabbling over who had won, Heath went on. "My bride's originally from Atlanta. Her family lost almost everything in the War, but to my great good luck, she was sent to live with relatives in Baltimore to attend finishing school."

"Her family doesn't object to her marriage to a Yankee who plans to move her all the way across the country?" I inquired to be companionable.

"Not at all, given their financial circumstances," he said haughtily as the *Walrus* took another dramatic plunge and recovery. "Besides," he continued, "they all know my family wasn't exactly strong supporters of Mr. Lincoln and the War. Not many prominent Baltimore families were, you know."

As he continued to entertain us with reminiscences of the Baltimore Heaths, their home overlooking the harbor, their Negro servants and the extravagant parties they hosted, Devlin, water dripping from his oilskins, made his presence known.

He said that freezing rain had coated the windward side of the *Walrus* with ice, making steering dangerously sluggish.

"Heath, call out your watch and get 'em to begin chipping

ice from rigging and rails with whatever tools they can find," he ordered. "We'll probably have to keep at it all night."

Heath was slow to respond, but not Carter. "I'd like to do it, Captain. I've pulled this kind of duty on my dad's boat many times."

"Very well," Devlin said, glowering at Heath. "But make sure the men rig life-lines and all hands are attached at all times. All times, ya hear me? It's damned dangerous on deck."

Turning to me, he declared I would need better foul-weather gear as we sailed farther north. "The steward will bring you a few parkas and boots to see if any fit. I don't want any frozen schoolmasters on my conscience."

That was all he said. Not even the slightest echo of our bitter exchange. Is this a peace offering of sorts? I wondered. Or is it just Devlin's way of controlling every detail, even down to the winter wear of his non-paying passenger?

At any rate, I proceeded to play the fool. I was determined to show that man I couldn't be dismissed so casually. So I put on oilskins hanging near the companionway bulkhead and followed Carter after he had roused the crew

"Please don't go on deck, Dr. Knowles," the young officer pleaded. "You're not used to this. Could be washed overboard or break some bones."

I lied. Told him I wanted to personally experience everything the Bering Sea could do to my schools along the coast. I had been a dedicated coward all my life, but now I was too stubborn and angry with Devlin to back down.

Carter waited behind the hatch cover until the ship rose on a swell, sending the water on deck sluicing beyond our location. He then pushed the hatch open, and we slid onto the icy, heaving deck and groped for handholds to reach relative safety behind the pilothouse.

In the eerie half-light of the arctic summer night, I was shocked and frightened to witness the mountain of angry water the *Walrus* was climbing. The vessel would pause, quivering for a second near its summit, and then plunge—it must have been at about a forty-degree angle—into the void, only to creak, roll and climb again. Looking aft, there was the same-sized mountain, having done its worst to us, rising thirty feet or more above our stern.

I clung to a support with all my strength when Carter left me. Crewmen soon began to make their way past on the wet and ice-encrusted deck, holding on to anything at hand when the furious sea swept aft. They were harnessed to lifelines and wielded belaying pins, hammers and other implements to pry ice from every surface, block and line within reach on the port side. There must have been more than three inches of ice covering the windward side of the pilothouse.

I gasped in horror as one man lost his grip and was swept violently against the stern rail. His body, held only by the lifeline, momentarily floated over the side. A shipmate risked his own life and pulled him back onto the deck. I was amazed when the rescued man coughed up the frigid salt water and went back to work.

That was the limit of my foolishness. I didn't stay to "experience" any more. I mimicked Carter's earlier actions, waited for the ship to climb and made it to the hatch before the next seawater surge came. I swore I would never again attempt to prove anything in a Bering Sea storm.

The tempest finally abated late that night. The old *Walrus*, with her stout oak-beam construction, had escaped relatively unscathed. One of her flying jibs became unfurled and was in tatters. A crewman suffered a broken arm and was in Donaldson's care. The rest of us were exhausted from lack of sleep and solid sustenance.

The following day was overcast, with relatively calm seas as we entered Norton Sound, and I saw floating sea ice for the first time. It was incredible that we had suffered through freezing rain less than twenty-four hours earlier, but now were visited by temperatures in the forties.

Two whalers, both the worse for wear, were anchored east of Nome. The mizzenmast of one was down and hanging precariously across her stern. The other's mainsail was shredded and its boom was lying across her deck.

Devlin visited both vessels, inquiring if they needed any help and delivering a few pieces of mail. He asked their captains if they had seen any unfamiliar ship in recent days or if they had visited the Seal Islands. Neither had any information about our mystery ship, but reported there was an unfamiliar freighter farther east into the Sound. They also declined our offer to help with repairs.

We found the freighter anchored off St. Michael. It was a sturdy-appearing vessel slightly longer than the *Walrus* with two masts and a smokestack. In his usual gruff manner, Devlin used his megaphone to ask its skipper to identify himself, his vessel and his business in the Sound. He also asked if he had visited the Seal Islands at any time.

The ship was the *Arctic Rose*. It had just supplied the Arctic Circle store and was now on route to supply coal mines further north. No, its captain said, he knew better than to stop at St. Paul and had not heard of any vessel that did so. The freighter's captain said his name was Shields and that he had served in the Navy until recruited to command this ship. "My company is buying other ships, Captain," he said, "and you'll be seeing more of us with the *Arctic* name pretty damn soon."

Devlin nodded, but couldn't resist telling the man any ship

found selling hooch or firearms to the natives would be fined and its captain could be imprisoned.

Shields said it wasn't necessary, but Devlin insisted on sending a boarding party, headed by Heath, to make a routine inspection. Devlin went below, but I watched Heath laughing and having a long, animated conversation with Shields on the deck of his ship. Probably regaling the poor man with stories of his Navy lieutenant brother, I thought. Heath was very excited when he came up to me on his return.

"I just learned, Dr. Knowles," he exclaimed, "the *Arctic Rose* is owned by the organization my bride's uncle organized, the Arctic Circle Corporation." He leaned on the rail and stared at it as if it were made of gold. "Captain Shields says they're building many more, that there'll be lots of opportunities in the future."

Later that day several crewmen rowed my crates of school supplies, the mail, and me to St. Michael while other crewmen were cleaning out and reorganizing the storerooms disrupted by the storm. The *Walrus* then sailed off to Nome so Devlin could perform marriages between whites and native women, and then go on to Port Clarence to take on coal.

Unlike the one on St. Paul Island, the school here was in fine order, run by a husband-and-wife team. The wooden school-house, sheltered from the northwest wind, boasted more than forty Eskimo pupils. The children were much better dressed— quite a few in western clothing—and in better general health than the Aleuts on the island, I thought. Over the four days of my visit, I sat in on school classes, and had opportunities to meet with villagers in their semi-subterranean dwellings, called "barabaras." One evening, I was invited, as a visiting dignitary, to participate in a meeting inside the "gargit," their place for rituals and feasts. The hanging harpoons, paddles, and buckets carved with representations of whales and other animals fascinated me, but I'm afraid my lack of recent speaking experience was obvious to all, even those with little understanding of English.

Other than the teachers' expected requests for additional funds and supplies, it was a refreshing visit that made me optimistic once more for the success of the Alaskan coastal schools.

When the *Walrus* returned, the Captain was in a fever to get me aboard and underway. It seems that a whaling captain had spotted an unfamiliar ship fitting the general description of the liquor trader heading west toward St. Lawrence Island, just south of the Bering Strait. Devlin was determined to investigate even though it was getting late in the season.

Chapter Seven

Three boatloads of Eskimos climbed aboard to trade when we reached a village on the flat, windswept tundra of St. Lawrence Island. They were the dirtiest, most grasping beggars I had yet encountered, and they clogged every inch of deck space on both sides of the pilothouse. The men had shaven heads, the women garish tattoos on their faces. Dressed in tattered, smelly skins and muddy, western castoffs, men, women and children alike had no hesitation in fingering our clothing and, unless pushed away, exploring the pockets of our jackets.

Devlin, however, was treated with great respect. The men waved arms and spoke loudly to him in pidgin, but kept their distance. No, they told him, they had not seen the "liquor ship," or anything like it for months. But the headman, a lanky individual taller than the others with many missing teeth and a long scar on his right cheek, offered something that captured the Captain's immediate attention.

It was a waterlogged scrap of planking about two feet long that villagers found washed up on shore the week before. Devlin, clearly excited, gave the headman some tobacco for the flotsam, ignored the rest of us, and disappeared into the pilothouse. Reappearing within minutes, he gave the visitors a bundle of clothing collected by the Women's Temperance Crusade, and ordered them off the ship. He circulated his prize among the officers without a word of explanation. I was puzzled by their glum expressions and groans until I examined the plank, and learned what it portended.

Crudely carved and difficult to read given the condition of the wood, were the words "Mary Beth," and longitude and latitude markings.

"*Mary Beth's* a whaler been missing for more than two years," Heath told me. "As far as I can tell, the position indicated is about three hundred miles west, somewhere in Siberia's Anadyr Bay."

"Is that a problem?" I asked.

"Expect so," he said shaking his head. "That message was probably carved two years ago by a seaman long dead." He pulled me away from the pilothouse. "But it'll be like a magnet, pulling the Captain to Siberia, and us with him."

A strong mid-September wind was blowing from the northwest, and blocks of ice of all sizes and shapes were floating around us. But nothing or nobody could discourage Devlin from searching for that vessel and possible survivors. I heard Heath tell him that all ships, other than whalers planning to stay the winter, were already heading south.

Devlin lashed out. "If you wanted to be coddled, Heath, you should have stayed home with your momma." The lieutenant recoiled, and muttering under his breath, pushed aside a seaman and stomped away.

A thick ice sheet hugged the shore and prevented the *Walrus* from reaching the location indicated on the plank. Within my hearing, Devlin refused suggestions from several other officers to use ice conditions as a reason to turn south. Instead he proceeded to search for pathways through the ice—the sailors call them "leads"—to reach a low outcrop of snow-covered rock farther northwest.

This was my first encounter with the ice pack. I was fascinated by the surreal, sullen immensity of it, by how quickly the ship was caught in its grip. The outcrop, barely thirty yards high, was one of the very few disruptions to the monotonous sameness of the white and faint gray-shrouded scene. Devlin ordered a search party with a sledge onto the ice at first light the next day. I kept my distance from him, but noticed that while they were away, he moved the *Walrus* a little forward and then astern to keep her from becoming trapped in the ice.

After about four hours, the shore party with Carter in charge returned with the news that an ice-crushed wreck they believed to be the *Mary Beth* was found north of the outcrop. What was left of her, Carter reported, was lying on the port side, the tops of masts missing and her cabin unreachable under the ice. What caused the most excitement was their discovery of the remnants of a long-abandoned camp of crude lean-tos in a gravel gully about a half-mile inland. There was evidence of fire pits, as well as seven low stone piles that Carter believed might be graves. He didn't disturb them since it was getting dark, and because one of the men found a small wooden plank fragment propped up on one of them.

"I wanted to get that plank to you as soon as I could, Captain," Carter said. In the dim light of the pilothouse, Devlin strained to read its message. Carved into it were only the English words: "village—south."

"Now the Captain will keep us here 'til spring, if he has to," Donaldson whispered to me.

At the urging of Donaldson and some others, and despite my distaste for having anything to do with Devlin, I tried to intervene before conditions got worse. The temperature gauge read five degrees, but snow and sleet blown by an angry north wind caused great concern. So, too, the constant screeching noises as the *Walrus'* hull chafed against the ice.

Devlin, in his otter-fur and sealskin clothing, was checking the buildup of ice near the rudderpost when I approached him.

"I hope you're aware the men are getting really concerned, and so am I, Captain," I said, overcoming my trepidation. "They're worried we'll be frozen in here for the winter."

"Concern noted," he said through his muffler. "There still might be survivors. I won't abandon them in this godforsaken place." He turned to resume his inspection. "We'll keep on searching, concern or no concern, understand?"

It took a full day and lots of cold, hard work by men aboard and on the ice before the *Walrus* was finally freed. Somehow, Devlin found leads through the floes as the vessel steamed at its slowest speed to a place twenty miles or so southeast. Carter told me that a thirty-year-old Russian chart indicated that a native village once existed inland from that location.

Chastened by the Captain's rebuke, I stayed below, seething with anger and immobilized by fear for our situation. We were using a chart made by some unknown Russians that "indicated" a village existed somewhere decades ago. My apprehension was heightened by the loud crashes and shrill scraping sounds reverberating through the hull as the *Walrus* inched and crushed its way forward, pushing large blocks of ice aside. I was not alone in blaming Devlin for putting us through this on the very slim chance any human had survived in this climate for two winters.

On deck the second day of our slow sail, I hardly recognized Jameson when he came toward me dressed in his fur parka and hood.

"It's colder than the other side of hell, ain't it, Dr. Knowles?" he said with a muffled laugh. I nodded as he continued. "And the hours of light are getting too short for my liking, altogether."

He took a few steps away, then turned and said, "Have you noticed the Captain never leaves the deck or the pilothouse? Even when the rest of us take turns below and it starts to blow like a banshee. Yesterday he climbed up to the topgallant yard in all that sleet to look for clear leads. It was grand, I tell ya!"

It was true. I went on deck intermittently when we could move during daylight. I saw Devlin constantly pace to the bow to determine a path and then back to the pilothouse to give the helmsman directions. He wouldn't allow anyone to speak with him, to break his concentration. Often I saw him climb up the rigging like an ordinary seaman to get a better look ahead. His mustache and muffler were coated with ice, but neither that nor the intermittent sleet blown sideways interfered with his task. To me, he seemed to have the same kind of closed-minded fanaticism that drove me from the ministry, and it frightened me.

When we neared the location marked on the Russian chart, as difficult to determine as it was in that featureless wilderness, a lookout spotted two natives on the shore. Devlin sent a new party, this time with Donaldson in command, to speak with them.

"Captain, I think I should go ashore with this party," I said in frustration over my lack of activity. "If there are any survivors, they may need consolation."

"Suit yourself, Knowles," he said, "but I guarantee, if survivors there be, they'll need the surgeon's help long before they want yours."

Through gestures and pidgin Russian, Donaldson said he learned there was a white man at a village several miles inland. In the wardroom, the news was greeted with disbelief at first, then with growing enthusiasm. Maybe some good may come out of this yet, I thought. Devlin acted as if he expected it all along. He instructed Heath to move the *Walrus* fore and aft to keep from being frozen solid, retrieved a sack of trade goods from his cabin and took command of the shore party himself. I went with him.

My borrowed parka, with its fur-lined hood, redolent of fish oil and tobacco, kept me warm enough with the exertion of the march. The sealskin trousers worked, too, but the boots—

mukluks, as they're called up there—were another matter. With my extra heavy socks, my feet barely fit into them, and I began to feel as if I were walking on stilts. Every step crushed my big toes until they ached.

It took us almost two hours, but guided by the two hunters, we reached a cluster of barabaras. They were low, sod-covered structures that appeared to be the upper portions of underground dwellings. Off to one side there was a small gathering of reindeer. Even in my exhaustion, I was amazed and exhilarated to see the animals. I had no idea that herding of those gentle beasts was a way of life this far north on the Siberian coast.

Our party was greeted by smiling villagers who emerged from the dwellings and from the reindeer herd. To me, they appeared to be healthy and vigorous, and looked similar to the Eskimos I met at St. Michael. By their excited chatter and arm-waving motions, it became obvious they were delighted by a visit from strange white men in late autumn.

A few children ran yelling into one of the structures, and before long a tall, thin figure in reindeer skins emerged blinking from the dark entrance. He walked awkwardly and silently into the circle of people. It reminded me of the Bible story of Lazarus rising from the dead. As it was, this smoke-stained skeleton of a man was James Howell, the only survivor of the *Mary Beth*. He had lived with these people, eating their food, sharing their quarters for two long years. He hadn't been raised from the dead, but his survival was miracle enough for me.

The short, stocky headman, with an almost perfectly round, flat face, invited Devlin and our party into the "kashim," their largest communal structure, to share a meal of reindeer. We hadn't had meat except for salt pork and salt beef for nearly two months at that point, so one and all devoured with great enthusiasm the somewhat stringy morsels in a stew-like concoction. Devlin traded some goods for more fresh meat to bring back to the ship, as Donaldson talked quietly with Howell. For some reason the survivor seemed detached from the companionable group, not someone whose salvation was at hand. He said nothing to any of the rest of us.

The Captain, who seemed especially well versed in using the pidgin understood here, lost no time in inviting the headman and some of his people to accompany us back to the ship. He told us to hurry as he hoped to get there before dark, which was arriving earlier every day now in the high latitudes.

His offer was accepted, and the headman insisted on providing two reindeer-driven, low-riding sledges to transport the meat and the survivor. I was deeply moved to see Howell walk slowly among the villagers helping to load the sleds, silently embracing the people who had saved his life.

Once onboard, and with Howell in Donaldson's care, Devlin initiated a ceremony to honor the villagers with the few trade goods still available that late in the season. Jameson said later they included two axes, four knives, some pots and pans and a tiny sack of tobacco.

"Do you have anything to offer, Knowles?" the Captain had asked on the trip back to the ship. I said I had a half dozen or so small, cheap metal "ABC" badges on bead chains, the kind presented to schoolchildren for success in learning the alphabet.

"We have to show these people our appreciation for saving that fella's life," he said. "Give them reason to help any other stranded sailor who comes along."

Devlin presented the gifts to the Siberians as if he were awarding Queen Victoria's Cross. In the wardroom, which was a thing of wonder to the natives, he placed my shabby little medallions around the necks of the visitors, including the headman's son. I almost laughed out loud as I had a vision of him attempting to kiss them on both cheeks. He didn't carry western rituals that far, thank God!

The chattering Siberians stayed aboard the *Walrus* through the dark hours; several camped on deck because the areas below were too warm for their taste.

The next day, Devlin sent Jameson and some of his men onto the ice to attempt to move some smaller blocks away from the rudder and propeller. The Captain stationed himself at the stern and signaled Heath to reverse engines for a few yards, stop, and then go forward at half speed. The good old *Walrus,* with its reinforced bow, broke through for several yards and then slid up onto more stubborn ice ahead. It rested there for several long minutes until the ice sheet broke. The men on the ice scrambled aboard, and this procedure was repeated for hours even after darkness enveloped us.

Temperatures moderated somewhat the following morning, the sleet ceased, and the wind changed direction. It now assaulted us from the Siberian shore. I had no idea what Devlin was going to do next or if he could do anything to free us. It certainly occurred to me again that if he couldn't, all aboard could suffer the same fate as the *Mary Beth* survivors.

"He's going on his instincts," Carter said as he joined me in the shelter of the pilothouse. "I'll bet he wants to get close to that rafted ice yonder." He pointed to a misshapen upcrop of dirty ice about fifteen feet taller than our rails. "Thinks it's being blown eastward toward open sea. Might help us outta here."

Devlin kept forcing the *Walrus* toward the upcrop, as I wondered how that would help us. He eventually positioned the bow as close as safety would allow, and attached us to it using a small anchor as a grappling hook. The engines were quieted for the night, and Devlin told Carter to keep the bilge pumps running continuously. Despite her solid construction and metal plating, the *Walrus* had begun to take on water with the pounding she endured, he said.

In the middle of the night, a terrifying crash reverberated throughout the ship like an earthquake. Fearful of disaster, I ran to the pilothouse only to discover that a large chunk of the upcrop had broken off, landing on our forward deck. No real damage was done, but the effect was jarring on the already frazzled nerves of all hands, which very much included me.

The next morning that wind-driven piece of rafted ice had forced its own lead through thinner ice, just as Devlin hoped it would. The *Walrus* was slowly freed and we began the first difficult mile of the thousands we faced heading to Dutch Harbor to collect Lt. Norris and the boarding party and then proceeding to San Francisco.

It had taken us five worrisome days to get free from the icepack in that Siberian bay. Now other dangers rattled me. Floating ice was everywhere. Some pieces were as large and ominous as small ships; others lay serenely in extensive sheets as flat as a prairie. Either could sink us if struck the wrong way in the October twilight that now entombed us most of each day.

Devlin never left the pilothouse for more than a few minutes as far as I could tell. He dozed in a corner chair, under orders to proceed at quarter speed and to wake him immediately if any danger arose. In darkness, we proceeded at "Slow Ahead," and extra lookouts were posted at the bow to search for heavy ice. It was fortunate for these poor fellows that temperatures had returned to the mid-teens and the wind had moderated. Just days earlier, we had twenty-five-mile-an-hour winds with temperatures well below zero.

Donaldson sent word to me several days later that Howell was feeling stronger and wanted to speak with a clergyman. In the sick bay, there was hardly enough room for the surgeon and me to squeeze in around the solitary bunk. Howell was sitting up with his back against the bulkhead dressed in borrowed seaman's clothes. His eyes held the same haunted look I noticed when we first found him.

I told him I was ordained, but no longer had a position in any church. He didn't care.

"Reverend, rotten stuff happened on that shore a year or so ago," he said, tears welling in his eyes. "I have to tell somebody, ya see."

He told us that about three months after his ship had been crushed, leading to the death of the captain and most of the crew, the eight who survived the first few days on shore had depleted what stores they had salvaged from the vessel. It was then that one of his shipmates—his best friend among the crew—died of injuries suffered in the wreck.

"We buried him under some gravel and rocks," Howell continued, "but within a week or so some of the lads started to argue we'd all die soon without something to eat. That we had to use anything we could get."

He choked and put his hands over his eyes. "Christ," he said, "they wanted to eat Charlie's leg." He started to weep and shake. I wanted to comfort him somehow, but was too shattered by revulsion to move.

"Oh God, Reverend," he said through his sobs, "two of them started to scrape the gravel off Charlie's grave and I didn't do nothing to stop 'em!"

His body shook convulsively for a time and he turned toward the bulkhead. "I watched, Reverend, and I wanted to eat so bad I ached." He turned to face us. "But as God is my judge, I didn't—I couldn't—do it."

"I'm sure you didn't join in," I said, not knowing anything else to say. "But it'll do you good to tell the entire story."

Howell said he left the others and walked aimlessly inland, believing he would die of the cold as old Eskimos were said to do when they could no longer hunt. The Siberians found him several days later, but he didn't remember anything for weeks as they nursed him back to some semblance of health.

"I didn't go back to the camp until I was thinking clear," he added. "It was too late to save 'em." He couldn't continue for several minutes, staring as if in a daze at the swinging oil lamp.

"They was frozen solid, Reverend. Two were sitting with their backs to some rocks. Old George, the black cook, had his eyes half open and, oh God, I couldn't find any part of Charlie's legs. Nothing!"

As we watched, this grown man—by all accounts a hardened sailor—cried like a child, burying his face in his pillow. "I'll never forget seeing them coated with ice like that; like ghosts, they were."

He then said he buried the corpses with the help of the Siberians who guided him and left the second message on a piece of driftwood.

"Howell," I said softly, "You did all you could, man. The Good Lord knows what's in your heart. Please join me in a prayer and try to get some rest."

Outside the sick bay, I leaned against the bulkhead and tried to calm my emotions; tried to erase the image of a frozen corpse staring at me; of desperate men forced to eat human flesh to stay alive.

"Good Lord, Donaldson," I said. "Do you think he actually did it? That his mind is shattered with guilt?"

"Don't know what to believe," he responded. "This isn't my kind of medicine."

He grabbed a handrail as the *Walrus* listed steeply to port. Until that moment, I hadn't realized the engines were silent, that we were under sail. After the horrors of Howell's story, this was a hopeful release, a good sign we were finally safe enough to sail in open water.

After some minutes, Donaldson convinced me we had to tell Devlin Howell's tale.

The Captain was resting on his bunk when we arrived, exhaustion showing around his half-closed eyes. He had a glass of what could have been whiskey in one hand, motioning us to sit by his desk with the other. Among the navigation tables and charts, I spotted a well-thumbed volume of poetry, open to a page with visible pencil annotations in the margins.

"Are you an admirer of poetry, Captain?" I asked, thinking to put him in a non-confrontational mood.

"It's Longfellow. The man has some interesting things to say, that's all," he responded as he rose, and quickly shut the book and placed it on a shelf crammed with similar volumes. Among them was a stout leather-bound book not usually found in a sea captain's cabin. It was a copy of the essays of Ralph Waldo Emerson.

After Donaldson and I told him Howell's story, he sat back in his swivel chair and thought for a long while. I thought the lion might have fallen asleep.

"I'll have to report this," he said wearily. "It could change everything; take attention away from the rescue."

"He's sick, Captain," I said. "The events of the last two years have affected his mind, I think."

When he didn't respond immediately, I risked outlining my thoughts. "Howell never actually saw men eating the leg, or even cutting into it. This could all be in his imagination after the trauma of the shipwreck and his survival while all the others perished."

"You have a point, Knowles," he said. "At any rate, whatever occurred happened on Russian territory, not any place where I'm justice of the peace." He sat up, and leaned his elbows on the desk.

"Gentlemen," he said, "the men who didn't make it have families—mothers, wives and kids, some of them anyway."

He paused, took a sip of his drink and said: "Nothing would be gained, but families would be hurt, by officially reporting the possibility of cannibalism. If you two will agree, and can get Howell to do likewise, I'll not mention this in my cruise report." We both agreed willingly.

"The report," Devlin said, "will say that Howell reached the village alone, and survived the scurvy and starvation that killed his shipmates by eating reindeer meat."

Maybe it was exhaustion or maybe the whiskey, but this was not what I expected. I had braced myself for hostility, but found agreement. I suggested that we organize a memorial service for the deceased seamen in San Francisco. Devlin nodded his agreement without hesitation, but added, "Make sure you keep Howell's sickening suspicions out of it, ya hear?"

While he was this accommodating, I asked him why the underfed people we met on St. Lawrence Island didn't herd reindeer like their Siberian cousins only a couple of hundred miles distant.

"Good question, Knowles," he said, once again returning to his commander's tone. "It's something I've puzzled over for some time." He fiddled with a pen, looking into a far corner of the cabin. "It would take important money to buy goods to trade for the animals," he said, "and I'd need permission to supply transport." He sat erect and looked directly at me. "But it's worth exploring, Knowles. Deer herds could keep whole villages from starvation, keep white exploiters at bay."

He drained his glass and headed toward his bunk. "Look into it, Knowles, and I will, too," he said. "We'll discuss it further when we know what's what."

A few days later in the last week in October, Jameson approached me on deck. "Ah, Dr. Knowles, how lucky we are to be going home, eh?"

I agreed, of course. "When we get back to 'Frisco," Jameson continued with a laugh, "this Howell thing will be treated as a bloody miracle altogether, and the Captain and us *Walrus* men hailed as heroes. Best of all, me and the lads will get free drinks for a month retelling the story."

Chapter Eight

The rescue of Howell caused a sensation in San Francisco throughout the winter of '86, just as Jameson predicted. If front-page newspaper articles were any indication, there seemed to be no limit to the curiosity people had about Howell, Devlin and the hazards of the far north in general.

The Captain's efforts to promote the rescue and the role he and his crew played in its success astonished and embarrassed me. Even while the *Walrus* was in the process of tying up at the wharf in late November, a reporter from the *Chronicle* asked permission to come aboard. Donaldson told me this was not unusual. The Captain was well known as an informed and willing source of exciting information and gossip about the coastal regions of northern Alaska.

Devlin related the essential facts of the episode, but didn't allow the young journalist to interview Howell, claiming that the survivor had to receive immediate attention at the hospital. He did oblige in detailing the problems the *Walrus* and its crew overcame in finding the survivor. He also recounted the discovery in the Siberian icepack of the crushed remains of the *Mary Beth* and the loss of every other man aboard.

I learned all this from an edition of the *Chronicle* the day after we docked. I was flabbergasted to see a long article covering the two right-hand columns under headlines reading

AMAZING RESCUE!
SHIPWRECKED WHALER FOUND ALIVE

TWO YEARS IN SIBERIAN ARCTIC
SHIP CRUSHED BY ICE IN '83
ALL OTHER CREWMEMBERS LOST
COURAGEOUS CUTTER CAPTAIN
REFUSED TO GIVE UP SEARCH

Within days it became apparent that the original story had been sent to newspapers in other major cities. Scores of telegrams of congratulation to the Captain arrived from across the country. One was a commendation from the highest authorities of the Cutter Service in Washington.

To my way of thinking, Devlin's masterstroke was how he manipulated the memorial service for Howell's lost shipmates. On the journey from Dutch Harbor, he asked me to "put on your minister's cap" and organize such a service as quickly as possible after we arrived home.

"Find yourself some decent clerical garb, Knowles, and get us a Catholic priest willing to say some prayers with you," he said. "I'll bet a good number of those lost lads were Irish, and their kin would appreciate a little blessing in Latin as well."

Two days after we arrived, Devlin stationed the scrubbed *Walrus* crew in clean uniforms behind a newly built platform on the *Walrus'* wharf. Five chairs were arranged on the riser between the Stars and Stripes and the ensign of the Revenue Cutter Service. The seats were assigned to Captain Benson, senior USRCS officer on the west coast, Howell, Devlin, Father O'Rourke from St. Catherine's and me.

A solemn crowd of sailors, longshoremen and off-duty Revenue Cutter officers and enlisted men gathered around the platform at the end of the wharf closest to the street. Even pungent odors from the newly creosoted pier and the sewage flowing into the bay couldn't keep a sprinkling of ladies with children from being intrigued. Among the throng, I counted five newspapermen with their stiff white collars and derby hats scribbling in their pads, and two photographers burdened with their bulky equipment. In all, there must have been at least two hundred in attendance.

Benson congratulated the Captain and crew with a very few words and then asked Devlin to introduce Howell. The Captain loudly praised the Siberians who had saved the seaman from certain death. He said Howell, himself, had displayed "uncommon grit" in surviving for more than two winters under the "most difficult of circumstances." Still looking pale and thin, the survivor spoke so softly his words were drowned out by boat whistles, gulls' cries and other sounds of a working harbor. Even standing nearby, I could barely hear him as he thanked the natives, Devlin and the crew, with special mentions for Donaldson and me. Then haltingly he expressed his grief at the loss of his shipmates. No mention was made of the tragedy that befell the seven who died at that awful shore camp, but I shuddered in the chill breeze off the bay when I thought about it.

The priest went on a little longer than necessary. Given my confusion about religious faith at the time, I declined to wear clerical regalia. I limited myself to recitation of the prayer for sailors lost at sea, and led the crowd in the Lord's Prayer.

I was in awe as Devlin strode to the front of the platform, removed his service cap and took command. The man has no sense of shame, I thought. How he did it so quickly, I don't know, but he had obtained a list of the lost ship's crew, all fourteen of them from either Massachusetts or Rhode Island. He asked us to say silent prayers as he slowly intoned each name, pausing to allow a *Walrus* crewman to strike the ship's bell once for each man. As it always has, tolling of bells evoked in me a feeling of loneliness and sadness. Howell wept. The crowd stood in respectful silence, many with heads bowed.

The ceremony prompted new articles in the newspapers. Most included interviews with Howell, conducted, I suspect, under the Captain's close supervision. There were no mentions of the possible cannibalism to mar the heroic rescue story.

As we discovered several weeks later, one enterprising photographer used his picture of Howell at the ceremony for a commemorative postcard available throughout the city. Devlin was pictured beside Howell and the caption read: "The *Mary Beth* survivor with the Revenue Cutter Service captain who rescued him in Siberia."

A week later as I was writing reports in my cluttered office at Fort Mason, a short, stout but fashionably dressed woman burst into the room. She identified herself as Mrs. Arthur Pitcher, president of the San Francisco Women's Temperance Crusade. Without any prelude or explanation, she announced that her husband was "a well-known banker downtown and we have many friends who are prominent in Washington."

"I know I can count on you as an educated man of the cloth," she said, her puffy face beaded with perspiration. "My ladies want you to introduce us directly to the right individuals of authority in the Cutter Service as soon as possible." She didn't give me a second to comment before explaining she had read of my role in the rescue.

"Of course you must realize," she said, "the unfortunate man was rescued only because the *Walrus* had been hunting criminals selling alcohol to the Indians."

I only had time to nod in agreement before she continued.

"We want to send letters to Washington that will get results, you understand," she said, her gloved hand presenting me with her embossed calling card. "We will praise that captain for his work, of course, but will demand more stringent measures to arrest evil whiskey traders."

Wagging her pudgy finger, she continued without taking a breath. "Depraved men are using liquor to lure Eskimo women into prostitution on whaling ships and in the shore stations, is what we hear. Disgusting for any Christian to even think about, don't you agree?"

I nodded, and she went on about "moral laxity" caused when the Cutter Service allowed its officers to drink alcohol aboard its ships. She shuddered. "That has to be stopped. Drunkenness, as you well know, is the prelude to sin and disaster."

Only then did she sit back in my sole visitor's chair, her unsmiling face flushed with satisfaction. I struggled to control my distaste. Her unquestioned belief in her own importance and righteousness brought back memories of the meddling church people I had left the ministry to avoid.

"I'll make inquiries to identify the most appropriate people you should approach," I said, standing to end this unpleasantness quickly.

"Don't you know who they are already?" Mrs. Pitcher asked, implying some deficiency on my part. I confessed I needed more precise information.

"Well," she responded, "I expect to hear from you in a few days, Doctor. We want to register our demands while the public and the newspapers are interested in what goes on in the far north."

She started to leave, then abruptly turned. "In addition to our other good works," she said, "my ladies collect castoff clothing for those natives." I didn't encourage response, but she continued. "You should have several bundles to take with you next spring."

With that, the whirlwind that was Mrs. Pitcher swept away

without so much as a "thank you" for my patience in being lectured. Given the reports I had yet to write and the experience with Mrs. Pitcher, I began to think braving the Bering Sea was not the worst that could happen to a person in my position.

Thankfully, that very afternoon's mail delivered hope I could satisfy Mrs. Pitcher in time to keep from being subjected to another dose of bombast. Deliverance came in the form of a note from Devlin, scrawled in pencil on one sheet of lined paper. It said, "Knowles: I have some encouraging information of interest regarding the reindeer idea. When you have a minute, attend me at my home in Oakland." He included an address I recognized as being in the hilly section adjacent to Berkeley. It was not all that far from my boardinghouse.

The very next day, I borrowed a horse and buggy, asked detailed directions and with little difficulty found the house in a tree-shaded neighborhood. It was a modest two-story structure, newly painted in a shade of tan with pleasant light green, contrasting colors on windows and doorframes.

A rail-thin, dark-haired woman, her blouse sleeves rolled up and her dress covered by a brightly colored floral apron, opened the door.

I introduced myself, apologized for the intrusion and said the Captain had asked me to call.

"I'm Amy Devlin," she said with a welcoming smile. "I've heard the Captain speak well of you, Dr. Knowles, and I know he'll be pleased to see you."

She led me through a darkened hallway past a parlor and dining room to the rear of the house and onto a bright, glass-enclosed sun porch with a fine view of the bay. In the distance I could make out San Francisco partially obscured by fog.

Devlin rose from his wicker chair, greeted me, and offered

coffee, which I declined. Copies of several newspapers lay scattered on the tile floor. Two books were open on a round wicker table near his chair. I recognized one as the volume of Emerson's essays I had seen in his cabin.

"Good of you to come, Knowles," he said as he gathered up some of the newspapers and motioned me to the only other chair. He wore an old sweater over an open-collar white shirt, his feet enclosed in a pair of brown, scuffed leather slippers. The sailor at home from the sea, I thought.

"The timing of your note was fortunate, Captain. I need your guidance on an inquiry from a very persistent woman."

He seemed genuinely pleased I was seeking his guidance until I told him about Mrs. Pitcher and her group.

"Those old busybodies," he snorted. "Sticking their noses into everybody else's business, while some poor Negra or Chinawoman does their chores for 'em."

He said that if they wanted to give "me and the *Walrus* boys a pat on the back, they should contact the Treasury Department in Washington."

On the other matter, he recommended writing to Captain Benson in San Francisco. "Ben's a good Bering Sea man," he said, "and he'll know just where to put their damned letter."

While Devlin left the porch to retrieve the proper titles and addresses for Mrs. Pitcher, I glanced at his books. In addition to Emerson's *Essays*, there was a small-sized, cloth-bound copy of Thoreau's *Walden*. It surprised me he was reading two of the Massachusetts philosophers whose notions scandalized most clergymen, including uncertain ones like me.

He saw me examining the Emerson volume as he handed me a paper with the titles and addresses.

"I bet you think I'm some sort of pagan, reading Emerson,"

he said.

"Not a pagan, exactly, Captain. It's just that Emerson and his friends seem determined to disparage long-established Christian doctrine, something I don't understand."

"I don't see it that way, Knowles," he interjected. "Old Emerson is on the right course, but we can argue about that another time."

Sitting across from him in such an informal setting, I was impressed when he told me what he had accomplished in the short time we had been ashore. He had already spoken with Captain Benson and had wired people in Washington concerning the idea of introducing reindeer into north coastal Alaska.

"Benson, as I expected, likes the concept, but realizes we'll have a helluva time getting any decent money out of the government to pay for the animals."

He stood, moved to a sunny spot near the porch windows, stretched and then turned toward me. "That's where you come in, Knowles. I'm hoping you can get some money from your connections. It shouldn't take more than three or four thousand to start."

"I'll certainly try, Captain," I said, "but it will be hard to get that kind of money. There are so many other charitable demands these days."

"Don't be bashful, Knowles." He moved toward me, blocking the glare from the windows. "Make a strong personal case to school people and the missionaries. You've witnessed how those poor buggers live, haven't you?"

"Yes, of course. But everyone will want to know why the government shouldn't support this kind of experiment."

Devlin, his face grim, began pacing with his hands clasped behind his back as he did on the quarterdeck. "Washington will come around. Eventually." He stopped and pointed at the pile of newspapers on the floor. "We'll shame them into it. Recruit the editors."

"But how, Captain? We don't even know if reindeer will survive in Alaska, do we? Or if the Eskimos can learn to herd them."

"One step at a time, Knowles. We'll start small. Show 'em it can be done, ya know."

Devlin took his seat, leaned my way, and began to outline his thinking in a civil manner, so different from his abrupt belligerence at sea.

"You have to think big, take the initiative, like all pioneers do." He sat back and stared through the windows at the bay. "Emerson has it right. One or two self-reliant men with a mission can make all the difference in this life."

"That may be true, Captain, but we still need lots of support to make this happen."

"Yes, but think of it, man," he exploded, "if we succeed, we could wipe out starvation for hundreds of people for years to come."

He then began a not-to-be-interrupted monologue like those heard in the *Walrus* wardroom. The lifeblood of the Eskimo centered on whale, seal and walrus hunting, he explained. Now most whaling ships had steam engines and harpoon cannons, allowing them to hunt far into the Arctic Ocean for longer periods. They were taking the animals in amazing numbers, he said. The natives, with small boats and hand-held harpoons, were left to hunt whales that were left closer to shore. He shook his head and sighed. The meat and blubber from one whale can feed a village for months, he said.

"The government should be thinking about this," he went on, "but to Washington the Arctic Ocean might as well be on the far side of the bloody moon."

He told me he had taken the first steps in attempting to interest federal departments other than Treasury in what could be done to help the natives provide for themselves.

"I've got the attention of the Smithsonian natural-history people," he said with a broad smile. "They've promised to send north an expert to figure out if reindeer will thrive in Alaska."

"It's a beginning, Captain, I admit."

"Of course it is. I'll put in a few dollars of my own, get some from the whalers I know, and if you can get some more, Benson will agree to let me buy and transport a dozen or so reindeer to St. Michael as a test."

"These are all hopeful signs, I agree. But the difficulties in getting funds—" I said with a shrug.

"For the love of God, Knowles," he said as he stood and began to pace again. "I thought you were beginning to understand what we face up there. You saw the St. Lawrence beggars, didn't you? And then you even volunteered to trek with us in the search on shore—"

"I do understand, and I sympathize—"

"Now you're talking like a Washington politician," he said as he looked over the bay once more. "All sympathy, but won't raise a solitary dollar to help the freed slaves in the South or the Alaskan natives feed themselves."

"I resent that, Captain. I said I would try. It's just that we have to be realistic."

I told him I would get to work immediately petitioning my former colleagues in the church for permission to solicit contributions, but that I couldn't guarantee anything.

"All right. All right. Just tell those preachers and those school people that if something isn't done soon, we'll have a real human disaster on our hands."

"I will, Captain, I promise."

"Tell 'em our diseases and alcohol are killing enough of them as it is. There can be no excuse for letting them starve. They're wards of the government, for God's sake!"

He removed his sweater and tossed it on the table. "You can also tell 'em I know that money-grubbers in San Francisco are getting organized to exploit natives and whites alike even more than they are already."

"What do you mean, 'getting organized'?"

"A bunch of railroad people, I'm told, have created a company to control shipping, mining and trading up there," he said, beads of perspiration forming on his brow.

"Couldn't that prove to be progress?"

"Not with the railroad barons involved," he said raising his voice. "You have to open your eyes, Knowles. There are evil people in the world, and some of them have designs on Alaska."

Devlin's negativity and passion unsettled me. Even on a delightfully warm, sun-filled day, he could see nothing but black and white, good and evil. I wanted to argue that the arctic frontier could use some progressive thinking, but thought the better of it. I shied away from another rebuke.

His arguments made, he collapsed into his chair and changed the subject. "Will you be sailing with us on the *Walrus* next season?"

"That depends on your sailing orders and those of other cutters," I said, explaining I had already booked passage on the first commercial steamer to Dutch Harbor in May. "I've arranged to meet the seal company's early supply ship to St. Paul. I'm concerned about Miss Cartwright."

"That's wise, and overdue," he said. "Convince that young lady to get off the island and to a safer place, will ya?"

"The orphanage at Dutch Harbor needs a teacher. I've written them about Miss Cartwright and her situation. I have no idea how she will react to my intervention into her affairs."

"Maybe after a winter as the only white woman on that rock pile, she'll be more realistic, grasp the chance," Devlin said.

I didn't tell him I had also explored the possibility of her teaching at a mission school in Oakland, and that the prospects there were encouraging. Less said to him about my feelings for Sarah, the better, I thought.

In the days that followed, I drafted a paper outlining the need for the introduction of reindeer, how it could help support natives at both government and missionary schools. I also made a request to the Methodist Mission Board to allow me to present my case at its December meeting. The note to Mrs. Pitcher, with the names and addresses she required, I entrusted to the Post Office. I knew if delivered personally, I would invite additional lectures and unwanted assignments from that determined female.

The pastor of Mission Church and his wife invited me to spend Christmas with them and their extended family. With a delightfully decorated tree, friendly people and a hearty feast, it was a joyful occasion.

But as soon as I began to walk the four streets to my boardinghouse, I was overcome with remorse. All I could think about was Sarah alone in the cold and long months without sunlight in that tiny cabin with wind rattling its siding. Devlin was right. I should have persuaded her to leave with her grandfather, I said to myself.

The only thing I could do after I entered my warm bedroom was to ignore my nagging spiritual confusion, and get down on my knees and pray for her safety; to ask forgiveness for my lapse of judgment, and to help me be reunited with her as early as humanly possible. And then wait impatiently for May to arrive.

PART TWO

Variations of White

Chapter Nine

Mud-stained patches of ice made for a treacherous climb to St. Paul's school in mid-May for my much-anticipated reunion with Sarah. A whirlwind of terrifying questions tortured my mind during the one-mile trek from the seal station loading dock in a chilling wind.

What if she's changed? Doesn't feel for me what I feel for her? Am I taking for granted she'll want as a suitor a man at least a dozen years older than herself?

I had asked myself these questions over and over through the long winter. Memories of her warmth during the short time we were together last year always pushed them aside. Now, within a few hundred yards of seeing her, doubts assailed me again. I put down my heavy seaman's bags, resting a minute to rehearse what I would say, to think over what I would do if she spurned me. I truly believed this woman was my best chance for happiness, to end my loneliness. So I picked the bags out of the mud, and resumed the climb with determination to succeed.

Then I began to fret that she hadn't come to greet me. She must have heard the ship's horn, I thought. Was something wrong? Was she ill? All sorts of horrible possibilities presented themselves until I neared the top of the rise, and was heartened by a wisp of smoke from the schoolroom's metal chimney. She was there, I realized, and, knowing her, I realized that she wouldn't leave her young charges alone for anything.

Sea conditions and heavy fog had conspired to delay the sealing company's supply ship from sailing as early as I wanted, to arrive in early May. Now my naïve plan to convince Sarah to board the steamer with me for its return trip seemed in doubt. The vessel had to unload supplies and sail early the next evening to make up for the late start.

When I entered the chilly schoolroom, Sarah had a gray-checkered shawl wrapped tightly around her as she gave individual attention to one of the four children present. A warm smile radiated her ever-so-pale face when she saw me, burdened as I was with the two large seaman's canvas bags.

"You remember Dr. Knowles, don't you, children?" she said. "Now, let's give him a proper welcome back to St. Paul."

In the singsong manner of schoolchildren everywhere, they bade me welcome even if they had much trouble pronouncing my name.

As I loosened the cord securing one bag, I told the youngsters I had presents for them. Until that moment they had stared at me with something akin to suspicion. Now, squeals of delight echoed off the unpainted wooden walls as I held up a handful of colored pencils, and counted out four copies of *McGuffey's Reader*. Sarah distributed the items to each of them in turn, reminding them to say "thank you." She then told them to draw pictures of the schoolhouse while she spoke with the visitor. With my trimmed beard and brown jacket, I didn't look like St. Nicholas. But I felt like him anyway, accepting their thanks and watching the smiling, gap-toothed children handling new pencils and searching for illustrations in the book.

As I followed Sarah into the adjacent cabin, I was dismayed to see how much thinner she had become since last fall. But as soon as the door closed, the seaman's bags were dropped, and I pulled her toward me, pressing her against me and kissing her brow and her cheeks. She didn't attempt to disengage.

"I've missed you, too, Stanton," she whispered so her students wouldn't hear. "But I'm all right, really I am. You shouldn't have worried."

Embarrassed at my impulsive and unwarranted behavior, I held her at arms' length to get a good look at her. "I apologize, Sarah. But I've been tortured all winter—you out here alone while I was—"

"Now stop that," she said softly. "It was my decision. I'm not a schoolgirl and nothing awful happened, as you can see."

She came back willingly into my arms, rested her head on my shoulder and whispered, "But I was very lonely. I thought of you many times, and of your kindness to my grandfather and me."

I took her face in my hands and kissed her on the lips. First gently. Then passionately. Her cheeks were coloring when she slowly pushed away.

"Well, Doctor Knowles," she said taking a breath. "You certainly have found some boldness since last we met."

She laughed, and touched my cheek, saying she had to get back to the children. I could hear them distinctly. Benches were being knocked about as they yelped, and they seemed to be chasing each other around the room.

"Unpack the rest of your precious packages," she said, her eyes wide with amusement. "I'll give them the rest of the afternoon off, and be back in a few minutes. Then we can talk."

Relieved that Sarah received me with affection I really didn't deserve, I arranged the things I had brought on the kitchen table: small packages of tea, coffee, sugar, flour, bacon, six precious eggs packed securely in cotton and a loaf of bread from the ship. In the place of honor, I placed a box of San Francisco chocolates. At the other end I also spread out several books I had bought her, letters from her grandfather, and copies of newspapers describing last year's rescue of Howell and praise for the Captain.

By the time she returned to the room that seemed bleak by the absence of her grandfather's photos, diplomas and pieces of furniture, I had added coal to the stove and put on the kettle.

"I'm delighted with your thoughtful gifts," Sarah said. "My provisions, especially anything that could be considered a treat, are nearly depleted."

Without ceremony, she busied herself frying bacon and eggs, filling the cabin with one of the most pleasant aromas known to man.

As we ate, I told her about my inquiries at the Dutch Harbor orphanage school and at the mission school in Oakland. She raised many questions about potential duties, salaries and living arrangements, most of which I couldn't answer well enough. Obviously, she had given serious thought to what she might do after leaving St. Paul.

"The supply ship will be here until tomorrow evening," I said, taking a sip of coffee. "I hope that with my help and some assistance from the Aleuts, you'll be willing to pack up and return with me when she sails."

The school would be closed temporarily in any event, I told her. She'd have no reason to even contemplate staying here.

"At Dutch Harbor," I said with rising enthusiasm, "you could meet the people at the orphanage. If that arrangement wasn't of interest, you could return to the States on a commercial steamer."

We sat close to each other, dirty dishes pushed side, and discussed those possibilities as well as what would happen to the pupils left at St. Paul. The school would be reopened in the future when there were more children, was all I could say.

She leaned toward me, took my hand and urged me to tell her all I knew about her grandfather's health, my visits to the other schools, and my life in Oakland. She was eager to hear the story of Howell's rescue, the Siberians who saved him, and Devlin's determination to steam through the ice pack. She was so eager for news of any kind, in fact, that it grew dark before I was able to get her to talk about her winter on the island.

"The provisions grandfather left were adequate until the last month or so," she said. "Oh, Lord, I became so sick of salt pork and navy beans I could have cried. I actually did once or twice."

"Is that all you had?"

Her laugh was a joy for me to hear. "Almost. If it hadn't been for occasional gifts of fresh fish from two of the families, I would have turned into a proper maniac."

She said there had been several severe storms, and one, lasting two days and nights, had really frightened her.

"I thought the old cabin was going to blow away. Some skins on the inside of north windows and some tarpaper blew off the walls. I spent hours trying to nail them back in place."

"Honestly, Sarah," I said taking her hand, "I'm so sorry I wasn't more forceful in convincing you to leave, to avoid facing the winter alone."

"I brought it on myself," she said. "It's one of my many failings, the belief I can do anything. A little like your Captain Devlin, if what you say about him is true."

"You're nothing like Devlin," I said heatedly, shocking her. "He berates everyone around him; you build them up, invigorate them." I rose and circled the table. "That man sees evil everywhere; you see the good."

"Please sit down and calm yourself, Stanton. It was only a little joke."

"I'm sorry, Sarah. It's just that Devlin's manner often infuriates me. He's devoted to Emerson and the Transcendentalists, for Pete's sake."

"Is that so bad?"

"It is when he believes he's destined to be one of Emerson's 'great men,' changing the world."

I sat, and she told me more about her winter on St. Paul. The months of darkness were the worst, but she kept busy keeping the cabin and school warm, and instructing her charges when weather permitted them to come to school.

"And I read every book grandfather left behind, even those that didn't interest me at all, like the one with interminable suggested sermons."

She wrinkled her nose into a sour expression. "I'm not one who likes sermons in any form. Had too many 'Amen's' growing up, thank you."

Hearing that, I was pleased that novels were among the new books I had bought for her on the advice of friends in Oakland.

She sat back, paused and then added, "One unusual thing did happen in December. Even though it was foggy and dark, I saw a ship close offshore over by the sealing station."

"Was it the same one that you saw last summer?"

"I couldn't tell, Stanton. It was too far away and I knew better than to go over there."

I was immediately apprehensive. I knew only government and seal-company vessels were allowed to land here except in emergencies. Certainly, none but the most foolhardy would attempt it in winter seas. I told her I would inform Devlin as soon as I was able.

Freezing rain began to rattle the windows before we had time to discuss her future in any detail. Or, as I hoped, *our* future. I dreaded the thought of walking back to the ship in this weather, but knew it would be scandalous to stay overnight in the cabin, alone with Sarah.

As if reading my thoughts, Sarah filled the cups again and said, "Stanton, don't be a prude and try to get back to the ship tonight. It'll be proper for you to stay here under these circumstances."

She said I would be exiled to her grandfather's old room.

"Yes, but people will talk, and…"

"Who's here to worry about?" she said, laughing and clapping her hands. "You're on the Seal Islands now, Doctor, not on some campus of busybodies."

I had never seen her so amused, so ready to laugh with abandon. It inflamed my desire for her even more.

"Stay, and tomorrow morning we can discuss at leisure what is to become of me. And, of course, dine on the delicious food you brought. Tastiest I've had for months."

About midnight, sequestered in the old parson's spartan room covered by heavy blankets against the chill, I was unable to sleep. With rain pounding the tin-clad roof above me, all I could think of was Sarah in her little nest not more than twenty-five feet across the hall. Remembering her lithe body as it pressed against me that afternoon excited me physically, but tormented me emotionally. I had not experienced this level of arousal since my teens. I never felt this inflamed about the pastor's daughter I was supposed to marry, a prospect that had forced me to flee the pulpit to the safety of a professor's bachelor life. I should have prayed as I did regularly when my faith was strong. I tried then, but I couldn't.

After tossing and turning a while longer, desire and need overcame torment. I had gone to bed wearing warm clothes, but even with them, I shivered when I got up and lit the oil lamp. Shoeless, I opened my door; its squeaky hinges more piercing than the sounds of the rain. The uncarpeted floorboards likewise were awakened as I crept into the narrow hall. Self-consciously I stood in front of her door, listening for any sound to indicate she might be awake. I realized how ridiculous I must have looked, and after a moment, my sense of duty and shame won out. I turned to return to bed when I heard her voice, muffled by bed covers.

"Stanton, please go back to bed, my dear. If it's any consolation, I want to feel your warmth tonight, too. But neither of us would ever forgive ourselves if we went further, would we?"

"I'm sorry I awoke you, Sarah, it's just that—"

"We have to wait, dear one. We'll have time later to enjoy each other in that way."

I was shocked. Excited. I almost dropped the lamp. I wasn't sure I had heard clearly.

"Does that mean you think we'll be married?"

She giggled. "Since you haven't asked me yet, we'll have to talk about that tomorrow. Now please, go to bed before you catch pneumonia. Goodnight."

"Goodnight. Stay warm and well. But excuse me if I shout."

And I did. As ludicrous as it may seem, this middle-aged schoolman, in his freezing stocking feet in a cabin in the middle of a Bering Sea night, shouted "Yippee" at the top of his lungs. I heard more laughter from Sarah's room, and gave another holler. And another.

When I came down the next morning, Sarah had already brewed coffee and was starting to fry the remaining bacon. With a broad smile on my face, I hugged and kissed her and said, "I love you, Sarah." And then, like some college sophomore, I actually knelt on one knee right there in front of the stove and asked her to marry me.

Standing above me, with a dishtowel in one hand and a lock of her hair falling over one eye, she frowned and said, "That's a very serious decision to make so early in the morning." Then, with a mischievous smile, she took my hand.

"I might consider marrying you, Stanton Knowles, but only if you'll get up from that dirty floor and help me make breakfast. The children will be here in half an hour."

We embraced again and kissed each other tenderly before she suddenly jerked away and turned to flip the bacon just starting to smoke and burn. "See what you've made me do?" she said, smiling. "You get a girl excited and the breakfast gets ruined."

At breakfast, she grew serious, and said we both needed time to consider marriage.

"I'm extremely fond of you, Stanton, and attracted to you. But we hardly know each other." She twisted her long braid around her hand and studied it. "I haven't seriously considered marriage at all. Some of the boys back home said I was too opinionated to be a proper wife for anybody."

"I've known since my visit last year that I desire you, Sarah, in more ways than one," I said holding her hand. "I didn't know what love was until I meet you."

She got up, came and sat on my lap.

"Let's decide when we're both in Dutch Harbor in two or three weeks," she said. "You might change your mind, you know."

Reluctantly, I agreed to the postponement, saying, "Be aware, m'dear, I will not change my mind."

With the most important decision deferred, we discussed her immediate future. She said she preferred to take the position at the orphanage school, if that proved possible. We agreed to be married by the pastor there if we still wanted each other. We both knew it was impossible for her to close St. Paul's school and pack all her things in time to leave on the supply ship that evening. I would go on ahead and she would take passage to Dutch Harbor on the next available cutter after saying her farewells to the Aleut children and their parents.

The temperature hovered around freezing, the wind from the north was steady and the clouds were low and gray when I left the cabin. But nothing could dampen my joy. All I remember seeing was the vivid green grasses and the occasional wildflowers beginning to cover the hillside. All I remember thinking was that my lonely bachelor life would soon be a memory if only I could keep my enthusiastic desires from frightening her away.

I boarded the supply ship that afternoon a happy man, not in the least concerned about sailing the angry Bering Sea or facing Devlin's scowls and suspicions. I believed I had found a companion for life, her name was Sarah, and I was determined to do whatever was necessary to make her my wife.

Chapter Ten

The seal-company's supply ship took almost three days to make the two hundred eighty miles in heavy seas. I was anxious to leave my damp, unclean cabin and the monotonous ration of fish and potatoes by the time we lumbered into Dutch Harbor, spotting the white-hulled *Walrus* riding at anchor, its sails flapping in the breeze.

Reverend Potter, the orphanage's director, was pleased when I told him Sarah was enthusiastic about teaching at his school, and would arrive in several weeks. His wife, on the other hand, was excited by the possibility of a wedding in the chapel. So was I.

Upon boarding the Walrus, I realized that Devlin was using a rare light-wind day with high clouds and occasional sunshine to good purpose. Portions of the deck were covered with the crew's hammocks drying after being scrubbed clean. The sails, coated with coal soot from the stack and salt from sea spray while under way, had been hosed down and were drying.

Lieutenant Norris, supervising the work from the pilothouse, introduced me as "Commissioner Knowles" to two new officers. The young men were so much alike in appearance, I could only tell them apart by the number of stripes on their uniform sleeves. One of them, Second Lieutenant Dowie, told me he had several years' experience on a cutter in the Great Lakes. The other was Third Lieutenant Mueller, a recent graduate of the Academy in New London. Both were about six feet tall, clean-shaven and with sandy hair and matching mustaches. I wondered how these two eager fellows would respond to arctic duty and Devlin's unrelenting criticisms.

Carter, Norris said, had been reassigned to another vessel. That was disappointing, for I had grown fond of that young man's sense of humor and friendship toward me during the voyage to Siberia.

Norris added that Lt. Heath was still on board after unsuccessfully attempting to obtain another assignment, now that he was married and his wife was expecting their first child.

I went below and found Devlin in his cabin having a drink of whiskey with Chief Engineer Anderson.

"Here's our reverend school commissioner at last," Devlin said, continuing to taunt me with the "rev-er-end" label. "I trust he's bringing us good news."

Anderson excused himself, and I sat opposite the Captain as he puffed his odorous tiny cigar, relaxed with his jacket off and his stiff collar unbuttoned.

"Eight hundred sixty-two dollars is all I've been able to raise for the reindeer experiment so far," I said. "I have high hopes for about five hundred more."

"Dammit," Devlin said with a glower. "That's not enough to get the Siberians to sell the animals we need. I expected more of you, Knowles."

"You always do, Captain. But I've sent letters to the shipping companies and had a conversation with a board member of one of them. They have the most to gain if our experiment works, don't you think?"

I added that my discussion with the board member convinced me we could expect two hundred dollars or a little more from two of the most active companies, giving us enough to buy trade goods for about a dozen animals.

"I suppose it's a start," he said leaning back in his swivel chair. "But, dammit, I expected more generosity from the church and school people." He leaned forward, and pointed at me. "'Nothing great was ever achieved without enthusiasm,' Knowles. Emerson said that somewhere. Be more enthusiastic, man. Don't you understand the urgency?"

"I do," I said, getting more annoyed by the minute, "and I have been enthusiastic. Hard cash is difficult to come by these days." I rose and ambled toward his shelf of books. "In any event, the people I approached are certain to support a petition for government money if our experiment works."

Nodding acknowledgment, Devlin added that a Dr. Peabody from the Smithsonian was due aboard later this season.

"He's supposed to determine if reindeer herding is feasible in Alaska," he said. "He damn well better."

"That is progress," I said, astounded by the Smithsonian's speed in making the appointment. I went on to tell him I had some additional news of my own.

"Miss Cartwright tells me she saw an unknown ship at the sealing station last December."

That got his attention. "Could she tell if it was the same one that sent boats ashore last summer? Did she see them loading anything?"

I explained that the weather was bad and that she didn't dare go and investigate after her experience last August.

"Just as I thought," Devlin said, leaping to his feet and pacing the cabin. "A bunch of goddamned bandits are smelling around St. Paul, looking to make off with our furs."

He paused for a minute and, as if talking to himself, said, "I'll have to see if we can get permission to trap them. It won't be easy in winter, but it'll have to be done."

Still pacing, he explained that the government only allowed limited harvesting of immature males to maintain the size of the fur-seal herd, and that each pelt taken produced a royalty.

"If what I'm thinking is true," he said, "Uncle Samuel is losing thousands of dollars a year and hundreds of animals are being slaughtered illegally."

Desperate to avoid another Devlin lecture, I walked toward the door, and said, "I have to get my gear, Captain, but before I do, I have another piece of news—splendid news, in fact. Miss Cartwright has agreed to leave St. Paul and is considering marrying me. She'll be here on the next supply ship."

He stopped pacing and looked dumbfounded for a moment. Then a smile began to accentuate the wrinkles around his eyes. "Why, you old fox. I know I told you to get her off that rock, but didn't dream you'd marry her to do it. I suppose congratulations are in order."

He sat again and, leaning toward me with elbows on the desk, went on. "I always thought you were a confirmed bachelor, Knowles, a regular Protestant celibate or some such. But here you are a prospective bridegroom after only meeting the girl a couple of times."

I said nothing, as he continued. "Let's hope you can work with that kind of passionate speed to get the money we need for those reindeer."

Not sure if he was sincerely wishing me well or having a little fun at my expense, I took his congratulations at face value and thanked him. I said I hoped to visit potential school sites in Bristol Bay before Sarah arrived, and asked if the *Walrus* might be heading in that direction.

Devlin said he had to inspect the salmon fleet in that general area and would take me along. "We'll be back here in plenty of time for you to greet, marry and bed Miss Cartwright," he added. And the old rogue actually winked.

As we approached Bristol Bay under scattered clouds with temperatures in the low fifties two days later, the magnificent snow-capped peaks of the Alaska Range were clearly visible to the north. I was trying to make casual conversation with Norris when Lieutenant Dowie, the duty officer, shouted, "Look at that, will ya!"

Puzzled, I looked to where he was pointing, a mile or so ahead of us to the north, and saw nothing but open sea. Then suddenly a huge killer whale flew twenty feet or more out of the water, twisted in midair and splashed down. Then another animal, dazzling in its distinctive white and black markings, took a similar leap closer to the ship. Then another closer to shore mimicked the others.

"They must have just feasted on a big school of something," Norris said. "They'll play for a while longer and then get to serious hunting again."

"Whatever the reason," I said, thrilled by the beauty of the animals, "that was one of the most marvelous displays of sheer power with grace I have ever seen."

Norris agreed. "I grant you it's inspiring, Dr. Knowles, but you should see 'em when they've surrounded a bunch of seals. Relentless, they are. Nothing stops them until they get all they want."

The display went on for more than a half hour as the Orcas slowly swam north, still breaching and splashing, and we continued east entering the wide mouth of Bristol Bay. Separating flat tundra on the mainland shore from the Alaska Peninsula, Bristol Bay, I was told, extended more than eighty miles inland to some of the finest salmon streams anywhere.

As we moved farther into the bay, I noticed a number of fishing vessels sailing apparently in circles near the entrance to a smaller bay on the mainland coast. Norris said a cannery had been established near there last year, but he too was curious why so many fishing boats were sailing aimlessly instead of heading to the cannery. He sent word to ask the Captain if he wanted to investigate and conduct a sanitary inspection at the cannery.

Devlin came on deck, surveyed the situation and set a new course. After consulting a chart, he said it would be too dangerous for the *Walrus* to anchor inside the smaller bay with so many small craft milling around.

We set anchor near the entrance, and Devlin ordered the launch and one other boat lowered.

"Dr. Donaldson, Knowles and I will take the launch to inspect the cannery. Heath, you and Dowie take the other."

We were already in the launch when Devlin shouted, "And Heath, teach that new two-striper the right way to check for fishing violations, will ya. I'll bet he didn't learn anything that useful at that fancy Academy of yours."

The small bay made a turn to the right about a mile in, so we couldn't see the cannery as we wove through the fishing vessels. As we neared one, its skipper yelled: "Do something, will ya Captain! The cannery ain't workin' and my fish are going to go bad."

As we rounded the bend, fishing boats were anchored every which way, their crews sprawled on decks, smoking and chatting. A few men stood up, pointing at us. The cannery was now visible. It was a long wooden structure set on tall pilings at the far end of the waterway, still about a mile away.

A fisherman from one of the boats stood and through cupped hands shouted: "The fuckin' Chinks won't work, ya hear? The whole place is shut down."

From this distance the cannery building looked as if it were alive with crawling insects. As we got closer, I realized what I had seen were arm-waving men leaning out of a series of small windows near the roofline and others clustered on a narrow walkway along the building's length.

Devlin stood as we approached the docking area, pointing to the words "Arctic Circle Corporation" painted in large, white letters on the cannery's otherwise unpainted siding. It was then I noticed that the men shouting and waving were Orientals. Some wore pigtails and traditional skullcaps. Others sported western clothes and hats, but all had oilskin aprons reaching from their chests to the top of their boots. A good many carried what looked like filleting knives. A few clutched and waved the small hatchets used to chop off fish heads and tails.

We were unable to dock at the crowded wharf itself, but rafted to one of the fishing boats already moored. It forced us to clamor over its deck, still slippery and smelling of fish, and up a rickety ladder to the wharf.

Our presence had not been noticed amid the hollering of unhappy fishermen and the constant din in some Chinese dialect from the building. But as Devlin led us with a determined stride down the wharf, the knot of fishermen slowly fell silent and separated to let us through. The Chinese stopped their yapping, and some pointed at the uniformed figure advancing on a group of cannery company men.

Two men were lying on the wharf near a cluster of four white men and two natives holding rifles. One of the injured men was writhing and groaning in pain. The other was a Chinaman, the right side of his face covered with blood.

"What in all hell is going on here?" Devlin barked.

One of the white men introduced himself as Abernathy, the cannery manager. As he spoke, the two natives with rifles, as if on orders, separated from the group and slowly moved toward shore. Among Abernathy's three other companions was a tall, muscular blond with beard to match. He held what appeared to be an axe handle at his side. Hanging from his belt was a length of rope with a large tarred knot on one end: the kind I'd been told was used in the old British Navy to punish seamen.

"The goddamned Chinks won't work," Abernathy said. "They've tied up operations throughout the bay and are costing my company— as well as these fishermen here—good money, I'll tell you."

"Why won't they work?" Devlin demanded. "And what about these two injured men?"

Abernathy, a beefy man in a heavy, checkered shirt, his wide belt cinched below a bulging stomach, said: "All this is really not your concern, Captain. We have a permit to operate this cannery and we'll get 'em back to work, don't you worry."

Devlin advanced to within two feet of the man and said, "Don't give me any of your shit, Mister, or I'll make sure your precious permit ain't worth the paper it's written on. Now answer my questions and be quick about it."

Abernathy stepped back and almost fell off the edge of the wharf, causing laughter from the Chinese and even a few snickers from some of the fishermen. His three companions stared at Devlin in disbelief and took a step or two toward him.

It was only then I came to a dreadful realization. We were unarmed and surrounded by furious Chinamen with knives, angry fishermen and hostile, burly white men backed up by two riflemen. And Devlin was acting like we owned the place.

"They complain about the food. And these two bastards were insubordinate," Abernathy said, regaining his footing and trying to reassert his authority.

Devlin went over the Chinaman and asked if he could speak English.

"Little speak," the small man said, and added that his name was Chou.

"Well, Chou, what's wrong with the food?"

"Chow bad. Rotten. Make sick," the man said. Devlin asked Donaldson to attend to the gash on his face. "All right, Chou, get somebody to show me this bad food."

The man shouted something in singsong, and several Chinese ran toward shore and disappeared behind the cannery building.

Devlin then turned his attention to the other injured man. He was a broad-shouldered Negro with graying hair. His arms were tightly wrapped around his midsection and his legs were pulled up in a fetal position.

"That nigger is my employee," Abernathy bellowed as he walked toward the fallen man. "He's my responsibility, not yours."

Devin ignored him and knelt on one knee near the man and asked his name.

"Caleb, Suh," he said hoarsely. "I'm the cook."

"Leave that nigger alone," Abernathy hissed.

Before Devlin could answer I spotted the two natives with rifles approaching the wharf again with their weapons raised. On impulse, I shouted, "Don't even think of threatening a cutter Captain you two, or you'll spend the rest of your lives rotting in a cage!"

Devlin looked up at me in astonishment, stood, saw the riflemen and said: "Listen to the Commissioner if you know what's good for you, you sons of bitches."

The men, probably more used to seeing and obeying cutter captains than cannery people, lowered the rifles and just stood where they were. My hands were shaking. I was amazed any command of mine had such a result. And not a little pleased that Devlin had called me "commissioner," noting he failed to add that I was only a commissioner of schools, not police.

Donaldson began examining the extent of Caleb's injuries the best he could, while Devlin asked the suffering man, "What happened here, Caleb?"

"I wouldn't dish out rotten stuff to the Chinks and Carlsen over there kept hitting me with that stick of his. I'm all broke up inside."

Donaldson said Caleb had several broken ribs and maybe even a fractured collarbone. "But I'm more concerned the blows may have ruptured a kidney," the ship's surgeon added. "I'll know more if we can get him back to our sick bay."

Rising to his feet, Devlin headed toward the man with the axe handle, when a scrawny little Chinaman came shuffling onto the wharf with a tin pot about the size of a small dish tub. Devlin took it, looked at its contents and gave it to me without a word.

The cold brown rice it contained was infested with maggots and what appeared to be the slick, wire-like tail of a rodent of some kind. Devlin snatched back the bowl, walked to Abernathy and pushed it into his chest.

"You think that's dinner fit for humans, you bastard, then you eat it. Right here and now!"

This caused some high-pitched squeals from the Chinese, who probably didn't understand a word but certainly recognized the intention. A steady drizzle was beginning to fall as Abernathy, his face now red with anger, threw the bowl and its contents into the bay.

"Fuck you, you self-important little revenuer," the cannery manager said, "and get the hell off my wharf before something happens to you."

There was complete silence for a moment. Everyone—fishermen, Chinese, Abernathy's men, Donaldson and me—waited to see what Devlin would do. I admit I was really frightened, my mouth dry even in the rain.

Still staring at the clenched-fisted Abernathy not more than three feet away from him, Devlin shouted over his shoulder,

"Mister Chou, do you have anybody who can cook decent rice?"

The small Chinaman, now standing uncertainly, seemed momentarily confused by the question. Then in a soft voice said, "Plenty cook here."

Devlin defiantly turned his back on Abernathy and pointed at Chou. "Then tell 'em to go find and cook decent chow for these workers now, by authority of the United States government, you savvy?"

"You can't do that!" Abernathy hissed as his three companions began to move menacingly closer to the Captain and me.

When Chou sang out his instructions, the Chinese workers responded with shouts of approval. Some of them, those closest to the main wharf, began to advance with hostile glares toward the cluster of white men. The fishermen, who had been quietly observing the standoff, started to back away from possible danger. The Captain, Donaldson and I were trapped in an ever-smaller open space between the cannery men, the moaning Caleb, Chou and the advancing workers.

Acting as if he were on a routine inspection with a squad of armed sailors to support him, Devlin brushed past Abernathy and went directly to the tall blond man, who was tapping the axe handle against his leg while keeping an eye on the Chinese coming toward him from the other side.

"Where are you from, Carlsen?"

Carlsen, who appeared to be in his late thirties, was momentarily taken aback by such a routine query. "Seattle," he finally answered.

"No, not where you just came from. Where were you born?"

Again a puzzled silence. Everyone within hearing distance stared at the unlikely pair. Carlsen was at least a head taller and twenty pounds heavier than Devlin. "I was born in Norway, so what?" he snapped.

"Well then, Mister, you have to learn that Alaska is a federal United States possession, and you can't go around beating innocent, unarmed men. Now hand me that axe handle!"

Carlsen surveyed the cluster of Chinamen with their knives and hatchets, and looked toward Abernathy for some kind of support. Not receiving any, he finally shrugged and slapped the wooden weapon with force into Devlin's outstretched hand.

"I was only teaching that dumb nigger a lesson like anybody would," he said with a sneer. "Take the goddamn handle and shove it up your arse. I ain't going to stay around to take any shit from you."

Carlsen turned to head toward shore. Devlin told him to stay put. But Carlsen proceeded to brusquely push his way past several Chinese.

"Come back here, you coward," Devlin shouted. "You're under arrest!"

When the Norwegian continued to walk away, Devlin, using both hands, swung the handle and crashed it into Carlsen's left knee. The sound of wood crashing bone sickened me, and made me flinch.

The big man stumbled forward in pain for a second or two. Then with a roar, he turned and tried to get traction on the now-wet wharf to lunge at Devlin. The Captain moved quickly to his right and with another vicious swing of the handle hit Carlsen hard on the left side of his neck, sending him sprawling.

The Chinese workers roared. A few were laughing.

Carlsen attempted to get up again. The Captain brought down the axe handle once more and the Norwegian, moaning, fell over in a heap.

Abernathy and his companions, cowed by the mob of shouting

Asians and Devlin's violence, remained wide-eyed in shock. I was appalled. Ashamed, actually, at the Captain's brutality. My god, I thought, he could have crippled that man. He's acting like a character out of the Old Testament.

Deliberately, Devlin, the axe handle positioned on his right shoulder, turned in a half-circle surveying the entire crowd as if to say, "Who wants to be next?"

I saw that Heath, Dowie and a small number of *Walrus* sailors, having completed their inspections, were on the fringes of the crowd of fishermen. Devlin saw them, too.

"Heath, come over here and arrest this son of a bitch for multiple assaults and resisting arrest," Devlin commanded.

Heath appeared nervous and frightened as he and the others approached the still-menacing Carlsen. But Dowie stepped forward, eager to prove his worth, I guessed. His chest puffed out and his parade-ground stride very much in evidence, he went directly to the stricken man, pulled him to his feet and with the help of two sailors began to drag him limping toward our launch. Carlsen was swearing at the Captain in English and, I presume, Norwegian.

"Chou," Devlin shouted over the noise of the crowd, "tell your people that the overseer's been arrested. They'll get good food soon. Tell 'em it's time to get back to work."

Chou did as he was instructed and the chattering workers began to return to the cannery building. Devlin asked Donaldson to borrow some sailcloth and planks from the fishing captains so Caleb could be carried to the *Walrus*. He grabbed my arm and told me to come with him. "I want a witness," was all he said.

The Captain went to the still-protesting Abernathy. He told the cannery manager we would sail across Bristol Bay to Naknek, but be back the next afternoon for a hearing on charges against

Carlsen, followed by a full-scale sanitary inspection of the cannery.

"When you see my vessel return, get yourself out there and bring Chou with you or I'll send armed men in to get you. Understand."

"I'm going to file a protest to the highest authorities about your conduct," Abernathy said, "and I hope they court martial your ass."

"That's your privilege," Devlin retorted, "but be advised I'm the highest federal authority in these waters as far as you're concerned. And one other thing. If that Negro dies, I'm charging your bullyboy with murder and you as an accomplice."

A heavy rain began to fall as we walked away from Abernathy and his men. The crew of the nearest fishing boat started to shovel their catch onto the now-activated hoist to bring it into the building, which resonated with the sounds of machinery in motion.

What an incongruous sight we must have presented on the march down that smelly wharf in the rain. Devlin, water dripping off the peak of his cap, the axe handle on his shoulder, led our little procession. He nodded to acknowledge respectful comments from some of the fishermen. It was as if he were a conquering emperor, with Donaldson and me his faithful retainers. Even more improbably, we were followed by four white uniformed sailors carrying an improvised stretcher for a Negro cook.

I didn't say anything to the Captain on our return trip to the *Walrus* because the now-subdued Carlsen was in the launch. To my further shame, I didn't say anything when we went aboard, and Jameson was instructed to lash the man to the mizzenmast in cold rain.

Later, as the ship headed toward Naknek, I went to Devlin's cabin to belatedly register my abhorrence of the beating and on-deck confinement of the prisoner.

"Don't second-guess me, Knowles," Devlin shouted. "These are bullies who don't understand anything but violence. I know what I'm doing."

"But you acted like a bully, yourself."

"Nonsense. I didn't beat helpless men. Those bastards had weapons and numbers on their side. I didn't." He took a step toward me. "Truth is, white men up here figure the law only applies to natives and foreigners. I've been proving otherwise for years and I won't stop now for you or anybody."

"If you're so enamored of the law, Captain, why did you bash Carlsen a third time and have him dragged away like that? Why not send armed sailors to shore to arrest him?"

Devlin sighed and gave me his penetrating stare. "Didn't you see how those Chinks looked at the bastard? He's been smacking them with that tar rope of his. Their hatred of the man should have been obvious, even to you. If I didn't punish him right then, there could've been real bloodshed."

Now it was my turn to sigh. "Listen, Captain, I have to work with you to get to our schools. And I want to bring reindeer to Alaska, but I don't approve your methods."

"Fine," Devlin said. "After I lock up Carlsen in Dutch Harbor, you can go your own way. Marry Miss Cartwright and live happily ever after, somewhere there's a steeple on every corner and a courthouse in the square."

"I'm as committed to Alaska as you are, Captain. Our ways of going about it are very different. Yours are brutal, even by frontier standards."

He moved toward me in anger. "What the hell do you know about what it takes to get respect for the Flag up here? We're not dealing with Sunday-school teachers, for Christ's sake! They're hard men who feel they can do anything they want in the north."

He turned, pulled off his jacket and threw it with force on his bunk. "All right, Knowles, all right. From now on, you handle the schools and I'll handle the sons of bitches who want to pillage all they can. Now get outta here!"

As I began to leave, I turned and said I had one last question. "What made you think you could face down that hostile cannery manager and his men when we weren't armed?"

"Intuition, Knowles, intuition. Emerson had a lot to say about that, too. You should get off your high horse and read him sometime."

Chapter Eleven

My thoughts were as bleak as the slate-gray sky on the voyage back from Bristol Bay. With alternating emotions of hot anger and deep shame, I avoided the Captain and other officers as much as possible as our small vessel made her way along the coast of the Alaska Peninsula. My visits with the prisoner and with Caleb only stoked my sense of impotence. What in the world am I doing? I thought. Why did I ever think I could do anything to improve how human beings are treated up here?

I refused to participate in Carlsen's hearing on the naïve assumption my absence would absolve me somehow from Devlin's violence. But I didn't feel absolved at all. Just cowardly.

Donaldson, good friend that he was, kept me informed. He said Carlsen was charged with assault with a weapon and resisting arrest and was to be transported eventually to the marshal at Sitka for trial. Abernathy was fined for allowing unsanitary conditions at the cannery, and was ordered to reimburse the government for Caleb's medical care and to pay the Negro's wages for the season. Abernathy threatened to go to court, Donaldson said, to challenge the fine and payment and to seek judgment against Devlin.

Not even moderate seas, mild temperatures or productive visits to inspect schools relieved my depression until, near the end of the ten-day trip, I caught sight of the snow-draped cone of Shishaldin volcano with its crowning plume of smoke. Its grandeur was undeniable evidence of nature's beauty, power and permanence. Along with the knowledge that I soon would be reunited with Sarah, that sighting lifted my spirits, gave me hope for the future—my own and Alaska's.

As we sailed, the crew went about its business as efficiently as ever, but the men kept their distance from me. They knew of my confrontation with Devlin, noticed my absence at the hearing, and couldn't help but hear Carlsen's angry shouting. Heath and the younger officers gave me wide berth, too. Jameson, the consummate diplomat, was polite when we met but was unusually noncommunicative.

Caleb, on the other hand, showed great resilience and good humor. Donaldson had set his broken left arm, wrapped his chest with tight bandages, and bound his right shoulder in a makeshift leather harness to keep fractured bones in their proper place. The damage to his wounded kidneys was still undetermined, but caused him pain despite regular doses of laudanum and water.

"Capt'n, his self, came to see me," Caleb said on my visit to the tiny sick bay, redolent of the acrid odor of liniment. "Asked very kindly if I needed help gettin' back home and all."

Slowly and painfully the black man shifted his position. "Tole him I wanted to go back to that cannery place once I was better. That boss owes me for the season. Won't get anything unless I get back there, I s'pect."

"You may not be able to go back this season, Caleb," I said. "Your injuries may take months to heal. Best to make other plans. Let the Captain get you the money you have coming."

"Capt'n do that for a darky?" he asked, clearly suspicious.

"I believe he can and will," I said, thinking of Devlin's relentlessness once he put his mind to anything. I gave Caleb some tobacco and helped him light his short pipe, a difficult maneuver for a man with minimal use of his arms. He thanked me and continued to shake his head in disbelief that "the Capt'n" would help him get his pay.

Carlsen, with his left arm in a sling and his knee held in a wooden brace, had only anger to sustain him. "That son of a bitch beat *me* and calls *me* a criminal, and now you want to know how I'm faring?" he shouted as I ducked into his locked cabin. He was sprawled on a bunk too short for his lanky frame with only a wobbly table, a tin cup and plate to keep him company.

"I'm going to see the lot of you pay for what you done me. That's how I'm faring," he said.

I left him to his hollering as soon as I could.

A smiling and waving Amy Devlin was on the pier awaiting our arrival at Dutch Harbor. She had taken a steamer from San Francisco, and was now accompanied by a portly young fellow with frameless glasses. He introduced himself as Dr. Peabody of the Smithsonian Institution, the expert assigned to determine whether reindeer herding could succeed in arctic Alaska.

Amy was fighting to keep her city-style hat, complete with feather and veil, from blowing away in the wind when she approached me. "I've heard there might be a wedding in the offing," she said, smiling. "I do hope and pray it's true, and it will take place before the *Walrus* leaves. The Captain and I would be so honored to attend." She took my hand, and gave it a conspiratorial squeeze.

I didn't know what to say, so I smiled and said nothing. She invited me to have dinner with the Captain, Peabody and herself so she could hear all about the prospective bride and our plans. I politely demurred, saying I had to go ashore to speak with the pastor at the orphanage. I wished Peabody luck, stressed the importance of his work to our experiment, gathered my gear and disembarked.

*
**

The arrival of two additional Revenue Cutters for the traditional Dutch Harbor Fourth of July celebration was the only thing that kept the following week from being unbearable as I waited for Sarah. As far as I knew, this celebration was the only time during the summer patrol that the men had any opportunity for some amusement. It couldn't compare with the liberties their colleagues had in lively port cities, but the competition among crews, the parade of seamen with their rifles, and fireworks did provide some distraction from hard duty. This year there were whaleboat rowing races, two prizefight bouts and a marksmanship match. A *Walrus* man was declared winner of one of the prizefights, but the laurels for most of the other contests went to crewmen of the *Shield*, the Bering Patrol's flagship.

Captain Benson, the Patrol's Senior Captain, invited some officers and a few white civilians to the *Shield* for dinner and to watch the fireworks. As luck would have it, I was seated near the end of the long table between Amy Devlin and Lieutenant Norris. The four captains were clustered at the center, engaged in lively conversation, interspersed with laughter. In all, there were a dozen of us in the well-appointed wardroom, leaving very little space for the Japanese steward to serve.

Amy prodded me for information about Sarah, her family and our uncertain plans. Her tiny hands constantly in motion, she recounted the difficult voyage from San Francisco and her enthusiasm in being able to visit reindeer herding areas with her husband this summer.

"Oh, Stanton," she said lowering her voice, "we went through three nights of a fierce gale last week. Every passenger, I'm sure, was bruised from the battering, and most were constantly seasick."

She rolled up the left sleeve of her dark dress and displayed a deep purple bruise on her forearm. In a conspiratorial voice, she leaned closer and said, "Whenever I weather storms like that, I realize why sailing in the north causes many men to go mad or at least lose years off their lives. Frankly, I don't know how the Captain does it year after year."

During the fireworks display, Captain Benson, Devlin and the other captains went below. I wondered if they would discuss Devlin's determination to return here in December to search for the mysterious ship Sarah had seen at St. Paul. I wondered, too, if Devlin would be honest in relating what he had done at the cannery.

Amy took my arm and guided me away from the others on deck. "Stanton," she said over the noise of fireworks on shore, "the Captain told me about your angry words to each other. I'm so sorry."

"It's a disagreement over methods, Amy, and I—"

"Oh, I don't mean to intrude," she said, gently touching my arm. "It's just I believe he needs a friend like you. Someone who'll talk back to him when he needs it."

"We'll still work together on the reindeer transfers, Amy, and in other ways, too, I promise. But there's a fierceness about him. Seems driven to overcome the ills of the world all by himself."

"I know," she said, pulling her shawl tightly around her in the increasingly chilly air. "I also know he's determined to prove to everyone he's the best officer in this forbidding place."

"Why, for God's sake, Amy? He's already thought of as the best navigator up here. Respected by natives and whalers, and feared by the seal poachers."

"He has his reasons, believe me," she said as we walked to the harbor side of the deck. "He'll confide in you when the time is right, I'm sure of it." She sighed. "For better or for worse, Stanton, he has come to trust you, and trust's not something Edward Devlin bestows easily."

I thanked her for her advice and concern and for her courage in being willing to sail with Devlin for the next several months.

"All I ask is you try to be his honest friend and critic, Stanton. He really doesn't have any real friends, except me. And, God help us, he's always quoting that Emerson fellow. Something about a real friend being a masterpiece of nature."

By this time we had circumnavigated the deck, and saw Captain Benson, his arm over Devlin's shoulder, heading for the gangway trailed by the other commanders.

I thanked Benson for a delightful evening, shook hands with Devlin, and told Amy again how much I enjoyed her company. I went ashore immediately. Walking through gathering fog to my room at the orphanage, I wondered if I'd ever learn what went on in Devlin's mind.

The *Walrus* sailed north on July sixth, leaving Lieutenant Heath behind to catch the next steamer for San Francisco. When I approached him, he appeared agitated, nervously pacing back and forth on the gravel track near the pier. He said his wife was having a difficult pregnancy, and he had been granted liberty by Captain Benson himself to be with her. Devlin, he said with a scowl, had been opposed, claiming he needed every officer assigned to him for the voyage to the Bering Strait.

Thinking to calm him, I suggested a stroll along the vividly green hill facing the harbor, anticipating a pleasant outing to help overcome my own impatience for Sarah's arrival. The temperature was just above 60 degrees and only a light wind was blowing from the north. Wildflowers of every imaginable color were blooming in profusion among soft blankets of moss.

"Devlin could not have been more disagreeable," he said, shattering my hope for congenial conversation. "I know I shouldn't be saying anything to you, Dr. Knowles. But, damn it all, that man is no gentleman."

"He's a tough taskmaster," I gasped as I struggled up a particularly steep incline. "And, as you know, I disagree strongly with many of his methods, but he's your commanding officer, man. And he's well regarded in these waters."

We halted at the top of a rise, and Heath turned toward me. "Maybe so," he said, "but at what price? He bullies junior officers, and goes looking for troubles that endanger ship and crew just so he can pose like a hero."

He turned to face me, making me aware of his seriousness. "The man is a throwback," he said with vehemence. "Wants this place to be *his* precious frontier forever. Resists all progress like the new ships, new ideas and investments of the Arctic Circle Corporation."

I raised my hand to stop him, but he continued.

"You saw how he berated the captain of the *Arctic Rose*; how he treated the people at the Bristol Bay cannery."

Heath quieted down, and bent to pick a brilliant arctic poppy, toying with it for a second or two. "I know I am being indiscreet, Dr. Knowles, and I beg you to keep my anger in confidence. My career would be over if it were known I spoke this way about my Captain."

"Don't worry, Lieutenant. I understand. I'll do as you request."

He thanked me and offered his hand as if to seal the understanding. "Be assured, Doctor, some other officers and I are watching and noting every unseemly move Devlin makes."

Looking down on the harbor, he paused for a moment. "For instance, did you know that last night he pleaded with Captain Benson to permit him to take the *Walrus* up here again in December to search for some ship that might be stealing fur-seal pelts?"

I kept to myself my fears about the dangers involved, telling him only that I had heard a ship had been spotted at the sealing station last winter.

"Imagine. He actually wants to subject us to howling seas in the dark of winter on the microscopic chance of finding a ship in hundreds of square miles of ocean. It's madness!"

He looked directly at me and, in a conspiratorial tone, said "Believe me, when the time is right, we'll make sure the authorities realize what a danger he is to the Service."

On our descent to the harbor, Heath's demeanor changed. He walked briskly and smiled as he spoke lovingly of his wife, his joy at becoming a father. There were no more outbursts against Devlin. He had unburdened himself. And placed an unwanted burden on me.

Sarah arrived three days later, one day after the *Walrus* had sailed with Amy and Peabody on board. I rushed onto the deck as soon as the gangplank was in place, and pulled Sarah into my arms. Oblivious of the stares of seamen securing the vessel and the unloaders on the pier, we hugged and kissed, and said not a word.

And so began several frenetic days of wondrous joy tinged with sadness as events forced us to make abrupt decisions, changing our plans. There would be other times when we had to accommodate the reality of being thousands of miles— and many weeks—away from California. This one was occasioned by a letter to Sarah, dated June fifth, from the director of the Methodist Mission in Oakland.

The director wrote that Reverend Cartwright, her only close living relative, was desperately ill and probably would not last the summer. We both realized he had been in poor health when we urged him to leave St. Paul a year ago. Now, the director's month-old report on his condition devastated Sarah.

"Oh, Stanton," she said, "I never should have allowed him to go to Oakland alone in his condition. I was only thinking of myself in my devilish stubbornness to stay with the children."

I embraced her gently as she dug her head into the rough shoulder of my woolen jacket. Hearing and feeling her muffled sobs, I felt as helpless as any man when his woman cries. But after a few minutes, Sarah wiped her tears away with a dainty handkerchief. Once again, she was a decisive woman of resolve, and to my great relief, her first resolve was to be my wife.

We decided to be married in Dutch Harbor immediately, explaining our situation to the pastor at the orphanage. We would also tell him that given the circumstances, Sarah would be unable to teach there this year. The passenger vessel that had transported Amy here was due back from Nome in three days, and we agreed to book passage south to be with Cartwright.

The pastor and his wife were gracious and understanding. The minister married us that very afternoon with a simple ceremony in his cramped, wooden chapel. The only attendees were orphanage staff members and two old Aleut women who wandered in. I had purchased a wedding ring before coming north on the hope Sarah would say "yes," but it proved to be too large for her tiny finger, causing amusement among the witnesses, but humiliation for me. The pastor's wife came to our rescue, and loaned us her ring for the ceremony.

By some feat of magic, that same wonderful woman prepared a dinner for all attendees, found time to gather a wildflower bouquet and located a bottle of sherry for imbibers to make a proper toast.

As soon as we were alone, I promised Sarah we would have a more joyous celebration in California, even though I didn't have the slightest idea how I would arrange it. Still chagrined, I said I would provide her with a ring that actually fit her finger.

That night, I paced nervously outside the cabin provided to us by the pastor. Waiting for Sarah to get ready in privacy and into bed, I was beset with doubts. Would my inexperience make me appear less a man in her eyes? I had hungered and dreamed about this moment all my bachelor years. Now it had arrived. The girl I loved was waiting just inside the door, but my ardor was deflated by fear of failure.

When I finally entered the drafty, unheated room, Sarah said, "Hurry and get out of your clothes and under these covers, my dear, or else you'll have a disagreeable cold to start our life together."

I got under the covers, and feeling the warmth of her body, apologized for my cold hands and feet. She said nothing, but worked closer to me. Awkwardly, I put my arms around her and we kissed with solemn tenderness. Then my wife of six hours—a girl more than a decade younger than myself—began to instruct me with an instinctive naturalness I found astounding.

She took my right hand and guided it to her soft breast, gently stroking it through her flannel nightgown while we kissed. I felt the nipple harden, and my fear was overcome by the joy of discovering she wanted me as much as I wanted her. I became fully aroused as we kissed urgently, and she pulled my hand slowly down her side and then gently up between her legs, ignoring the fabric barriers between us.

At first tentatively, and then more excitedly, I stroked the damp, yielding flesh she guided me to. Sarah raised her hips. She let out a soft moan. Then another. I wasn't artful. I didn't know how. But the dim light of an arctic summer night leaked into the room as we urgently fumbled with nightclothes and heavy bed covers. Then, with Sarah's helping hand, we consummated our marriage with delirious pleasure. At my rapturous release, I gasped loudly, "I'm inside you, dearest. Now we're one."

Chapter Twelve

Sarah's grandfather was dying.

In his sparsely furnished, whitewashed room at the Mission infirmary, he tried to be cheerful when we arrived the first week of August. He pushed himself up in bed with great difficulty to greet us, but soon fell back onto his pillow, took Sarah's hand and fell asleep. Sarah tried, but failed, to hold back tears when she saw the transparent skin on his face drawn tight, accenting sunken eyes, and heard his shallow breathing.

We didn't have any opportunity on that first visit to tell him of our marriage. At that point, I'm certain he wouldn't have realized who I was or care why I was there. Visiting the sick had been a frequent pastoral duty in my former life, but it did not prepare me to see my new wife's dearest relative in such a condition.

Sarah and I rented rooms in Oakland close to the infirmary so she could tend to her grandfather every day. I often saw tears in her eyes, but she refused to allow sadness to overwhelm her. Her antidote to grief was to relieve the nurses, and give him constant doses of personal, loving care.

It may make me seem coldhearted, but despite Cartwright's condition and its impact on Sarah, that sun-filled autumn in California in 1887 was one of the happiest and most illuminating of my life. I actually found purpose and fulfillment in the demands of domestic life, demands I had been oblivious to in my lonely years. I believed my willingness to take on mundane chores allowed Sarah to spend as much time as possible with her revered grandfather. It also allowed me to be of service to the woman I came to love more each day.

Through it all, Sarah was a marvel. She not only cared for Cartwright but showered me with affection, and, yes, all the marital intimacy I could have asked for. She still found time to organize my haphazard way of work, making me more efficient in discharging my duties than I had ever been.

With her encouragement and common sense, I realized I should spend less effort inspecting remote government schools, and more time convincing religious denominations to open their own schools in the north. Given the government's parsimony, that would be the only way basic education could be provided in reasonable time to a decent number of native children.

As that wonderful girl organized my reports and transcribed letters to the missionary authorities, I almost succeeded in pushing out of mind the disappointments, setbacks and violence I had witnessed in Alaska. I almost forgot my abhorrence of Devlin's stubborn need for reckless confrontation.

But it wasn't to be. In early September, I was unexpectedly exposed to the troubling reality that determined people, more powerful and influential than the likes of Devlin or me, had different—and, to my mind, darker—plans for Alaska and its people.

Sarah and I were invited to a social gathering at the two-story, San Francisco hillside home of Lt. and Mrs. Heath to celebrate the arrival of their first child. When we arrived I wondered how Heath, with a lieutenant's salary, could afford a home in such a neighborhood with its glorious views of the east Bay and Alameda Island.

We were just being introduced to his demure young wife, the sleeping infant in a pink blanket, and a few other well-wishers in the sunny parlor, when Heath pulled me aside. I thought it rude under the circumstances to whisk me away from the guests, leaving Sarah on her own, but he insisted there was someone who wanted to meet me.

He took my elbow and guided me out of the parlor and into the adjacent dinning room with its bright floral wallpaper. The room was dominated by a mahogany table covered with lace and resplendent with colorfully decorated desserts and a large punchbowl. In the corner behind it stood a slim man less than five feet tall wearing an expensively-tailored gray suit and striped silk cravat. He was sipping punch from a crystal cup. It looked to me as if he were holding court.

Heath ignored the four gentlemen listening attentively to the man, and said: "Governor, may I present Dr. Knowles, the Alaskan education commissioner you wanted so much to meet."

Heath then introduced the man as Thurston N. Godfrey, the former governor of Georgia and his wife's uncle. "But everybody calls him governor," Heath added, making sure I was duly impressed.

The grip of Godfrey's small hand was strong, and he held mine firmly as he looked directly up into my eyes. "A great pleasure to meet you, Dr. Knowles. Lieutenant Heath has told me much about you and your work. I think I may be able to be of some little assistance to you."

Godfrey asked the others if he could have a word with me in private and, using his walking stick to hold open the screen door, led me to the back porch. It faced a small but well-tended lawn and garden with several orange and lemon trees arranged to provide privacy from neighbors.

"California weather is magnificent, isn't it, Dr. Knowles?" he said. "Much better than where your travels take you, I suspect."

He spoke rapidly for a Southerner, pausing for a second after each thought. Even in his high-pitched voice, the effect made each sentence seem like a burst of gunfire.

As he leaned his slight frame against the railing, which ran the entire length of the house, I thought one could mistake him for a well-dressed boy of thirteen or so. His high forehead ringed by light brown hair mixed with gray strands, his pince-nez glasses, and his unwavering stare quickly spoiled the illusion.

After confirming his opinion of California weather, I said, "You're a long way from Georgia, aren't you, Governor?"

He chuckled. "I haven't been an elected official since Reconstruction, Dr. Knowles. I'm free to pursue my purposes anywhere. I choose this fine city to be as close as reasonably possible to the outstanding opportunities in Alaska."

Without another word, he stood erect, reached into the inside pocket of his coat, pulled out a plain white envelope and handed it to me. In it was a check from the Arctic Circle Corporation for two hundred and fifty dollars. It was made out to me personally.

"My niece's husband tells me you're trying to raise funds to buy reindeer. To keep the natives happy. Very laudable, indeed. Good for business."

"Thank you, Governor," I said. "But this check is made out to me personally."

"My colleagues and I are certain you'll know how to put it to the best use," he said, patting my arm. "We're enthusiastic about the prospects up north. As I'm sure you are, too. In your own way."

He went on to explain that the Arctic Circle Corporation was formed by investors who "were among the most highly regarded national figures in railroads, finance and other businesses."

"The people in the Cleveland Administration have neglected Alaska," he said, taking off his fragile glasses and polishing the lenses briskly with his breast-pocket handkerchief. "They have no imagination. Can't even conceive of the opportunities up there. We can."

Without losing eye contact, he went on to say the government should be reaping substantially greater royalties from the fur-seal trade. "That's only the beginning," he said in his rapid-fire manner. "There's money to be made by people who know what's what. In mining and fisheries and canneries."

He took a few steps away from me. "And with hundred of miles of unexplored mountains and rivers, there's bound to be deposits of copper and coal. Maybe even gold." He turned abruptly. "The key, Dr. Knowles, is transportation and supply. Arctic Circle will operate the most efficient shipping lines ever seen in those waters."

I told him this was all interesting, but that I was only an educator, a government employee.

"Don't underestimate yourself, Doctor. Schooling's very important. Have to teach the dark-skinned folk how to read, write and do sums." Grabbing my coat sleeve, he added, "Just don't give them any unrealistic ideas. We suffered that kind of nonsense at home after the War."

I'm ashamed I didn't rebut at once his low regard for the natives, but he strode with tiny steps to the porch swing, sat down and motioned me to join him.

"We've already invested millions in Alaska. We're willing to spend millions more," he said, his short legs barely reaching the floor to put the swing in motion. "We just need a few well-placed land grants and respect for the law up there."

With that, he said his ships could do for Alaska what the rail-roads did for California. "Think of it. Tiny fishing villages and mining camps could become thriving towns if they allowed us exclusive transportation rights."

I tried to bring some reality to this discussion.

"Whiskey sellers and violent ruffians preyed on the natives, causing near-starvation in some villages," I said. "There was no effective civil government, and hunters at sea were decimating the seal population."

"We know all that, Doctor," he said. "That's why we'll use our influence to get the Cutter Service more ships and crews. Got to curb lawlessness and keep the natives in line."

He leaned toward me and lowered his voice. He said there'll be a new Administration—"a new day"—in Washington. He had confidence that Harrison would be elected President, and would handle the Populists and their annoying ilk.

"We'll have many friends in the Administration, I assure you," he continued with a sly smile. "We can do much for progress in Alaska with the support of knowledgeable people like you."

I couldn't believe he was so ignorant of the difficulties his company would face getting permits and land grants. Alaska was only a "possession," without the legal status or governmental structure of even a "territory."

"With the right encouragement," he said, "we'll fashion Alaska and the North Pacific into a domain fit for the white man."

Before I could comment, Sarah came out of the house, and Godfrey leapt to his feet. Bowing like a courtier, he surprised her by taking her gloved hand and kissing it lightly.

"A great pleasure, Mrs. Knowles," he said. "I apologize for kidnapping your husband. We were just discussing how my colleagues and I want to support the reindeer project. Teach the natives self-sufficiency and all that, eh?"

"Interesting," Sarah said after acknowledging his greeting, "I thought the natives had been self-sufficient for thousands of years before we came."

She smiled when she said it, but I could see by the set of her jaw what she thought of his attitude. I could have kissed her right then and there.

Godfrey mumbled something about how things have changed, and asked if he could have just five minutes more with me.

"Five more minutes, then," she responded. "Stanton really must go in and pay his proper respects, as we have to leave soon."

After she left, I told Godfrey about Sarah's work at the school on St. Paul and he seemed genuinely interested.

"The sealing operation there is old-fashioned," he said, tapping his walking stick on the floor. "We're determined to take over that contract when Harrison is in office." He began wiping his glasses again. "The government's losing thousands of dollars in royalties each year," he added. "Seal skins are a lucrative business, Doctor. People are getting ten dollars a pelt or more on the open market these days. Would you believe that?"

I wanted to ask how he knew the government contractor was inefficient, that royalties were being lost, but thought the better of it.

He went on to say his corporation already had controlling interests in several coal mines and canneries and had launched the Arctic Circle passenger and freight steamship line.

"We'll follow the railroad example," he said, "like in California. Small, dusty towns like Los Angeles give the Southern Pacific some funding, and get rail services. Then they grow. Helps the railroad as well as the town."

The more I heard from Godfrey the less I liked him. I'd learned from Sarah tales about towns desperately paying railroads' ransom to get service. But I was intrigued that in his litany of schemes, he hadn't even mentioned whaling, with its profits and devastating impacts on the Eskimos. I asked why whaling wasn't a part of his plans.

"We're studying all the possibilities," he said, spreading his arms as if to contain the world. "But believe whale oil will be replaced by kerosene made from cheap crude oil. We'll let the whalers find that out for themselves," he smiled. "But they'll still have to buy our coal."

In a conspiratorial tone, he leaned close and actually whispered. "Dr. Knowles, there's a lucrative future in our company for educated men like you. Instead of searching for school sites in some muddy village, you could prospect for financial opportunities." He pointed at me and winked. "I suggest you think about it. Get in at the beginning of a worthwhile enterprise, eh?"

At first I was flattered. Then I became appalled that anyone would think of me other than an educator. Controlling my growing uneasiness, I said, "I have too much to do building schools as it is, I'm afraid."

He pursed his lips and slowly shook his head. He said he was disappointed, but that he admired my dedication. He insisted we both wanted progress and growth for Alaska. I became certain then that the offer was not genuine, for in the very next breath he sat back and asked for my opinion of Captain Devlin.

Trying to be as nonjudgmental as possible, I said the Captain was widely recognized as a superb navigator, feared by lawbreakers, but respected by Aleuts and Eskimos alike.

"Yes, he should be commended for keeping the damned foreign poachers out of our waters," he said. He sat staring into the garden for a moment. "But I don't think he's the kind of man who supports development and free enterprise."

I stood, setting the porch swing in motion, and said, "Governor, for the life of me I can't figure out what really drives that man." I turned toward him. "But I do know he believes in Alaska's future."

"I hope that's so," Godfrey said, "otherwise he'll suffer the fate of all fanatics who try to stop progress." He wagged his tiny finger at me. "At any rate, Devlin has to stop going around harassing legitimate ships like our *Arctic Rose*, and beating cannery foremen."

He took me by surprise. "Did Lieutenant Heath tell you what happened in Bristol Bay?"

"No need," he said with a satisfied smile. "We own that cannery. Abernathy has dropped charges against Devlin. For now." He got to his feet. "I can't comprehend what all the fuss was about," he said. "That foreman was only trying to teach the Chinks and that nigger cook a lesson or two. Has to be done once and a while."

"I was there, Governor," I said, my voice rising. "It was a sad situation all around, but your foreman did more than teach a lesson. That cook could have died."

"The point is," he said, "government officers should support enterprise, not go out of their way to impede it."

On our way down the hill to the Market Street tramline, Sarah chastised me for "abandoning her in the parlor with the ladies."

"They were all very polite, asking casual questions about Alaska," she said with a sigh, "but all they really wanted to talk about was whose husband would be promoted, what dinners they were invited to attend, and on and on." She gave my hand a hard squeeze. "All I could do was smile sweetly, nod and sip that awful punch."

But when I recounted my conversation with Godfrey, she halted abruptly and turned to face me.

I had to laugh whenever she began by saying, "I'm just a poor farm girl." Even in our short time together, I knew that phrase meant I could expect strongly held opinions well beyond the ken of any farm girl I ever knew. She didn't disappoint.

"For Pete's sake, Stanton, everyone knows how the railroads operate. They demand ransom from towns, then charge anything they want and demand anything they need from politicians."

Trying to keep an open mind, I said maybe things would be different in Alaska. There wouldn't be tracks, just open water that any shipping company could use.

"Just the same," she said, "that kind will try to bludgeon Alaska, too." She took a few steps and turned. "Be realistic with men like this governor, my dear. I wouldn't be surprised if that contribution for the reindeer and his offer of employment weren't subtle bribes for your support."

I had already thought of that possibility, and told her so.

"You really are too gentle—too gullible—sometimes, dear," she said in her most enticing voice as she took my arm and cuddled closer. "Don't let Godfrey, Devlin or anybody else keep you from standing up for your ideals."

I took her comments in good grace. I knew she was right. Years of seminary teaching had dulled my ability to deal with ruthlessness or the manipulation of politicians like Godfrey.

I'm a good student, I thought as we continued down the steep sidewalk. I'll have to learn from the likes of Devlin and Godfrey how to succeed for once in my life.

I only know that at that moment, I was determined to try.

Chapter Thirteen

Cartwright's funeral was as stark and lonely as the last years of his life.

Sarah handled all the arrangements. She wrote letters to whatever relatives might still be alive in Ohio and to the pastors of churches he had served decades ago. She even provided the presiding minister with sermon notes extolling her grandfather's nineteen years of devotion to scattered missions in Alaska.

In the process, I shared the traumas and joys of her early life. The people who cared for and shaped her became more than unfamiliar names. I already knew that her father, like thousands of others, was lost at Gettysburg, and that her mother died of diphtheria when Sarah was six. Now I heard stories of how she spent several years being dragged along as her grandparents shuttled from one revival meeting to another, from one small town boarding house to the next in Kansas and Missouri.

It seems a cousin on her mother's side is the one person to whom I owe gratitude for trying to make sure Sarah would be more than a hardscrabble farmer's wife on the plains. A school-teacher with four children of her own, and a husband who led unsuccessful crusades against railroad freight rates, Cousin Betty taught Sarah to value learning, to be self-assured. She saw promise in Sarah, and somehow arranged for her to enroll at a normal college in Ohio for a year. Sarah cried when she told me how her cousin depleted meager savings, and badgered college administrators to give her that opportunity.

Like many who serve either their God or their country in the far north, only a dozen strangers attended Cartwright's funeral. None of the Aleuts or Eskimos he had tried to help were there. Neither were his fellow missionaries, far away at their stations, preparing for the long winter.

"At least he wasn't buried in some forgotten hill on St. Paul," I said as Sarah and I ordered a marker for his grave in the Methodist cemetery. We scraped together enough money for a simple memorial that didn't do justice to his life of sacrifice in cold, wet places:

Rev. Thomas L. Cartwright
Servant of the Lord in Alaska
b. 1820   d. 1888

I was sad that my wife had lost her only close relative, even though we had anticipated it for months. Death had vanquished his suffering, we told ourselves. More important to me, it relieved the anguish his suffering had caused Sarah. But I didn't grieve. The kind of grief that shrouds and strangles the spirit would overtake me at a later time.

In the months that followed, Sarah banished her sadness with planning and activity, mostly on my behalf. She arranged for me to meet religious authorities willing to support schools in villages I helped to choose. Pleas were made to Washington for additional school supplies and teachers. And through it all, she became more amorous and loving even while complaining about my lack of organization.

On New Year's Eve we had a delightful evening with Lieutenant Norris and his family. His wife was as gregarious as he was taciturn, as plump as he was rawboned, and their three children, all in their early teens, were energetic and amusing. We played parlor games before a blazing fire while we awaited the arrival of 1889. I even tasted a little Champagne at the appointed hour, discovering I didn't like it. This convivial celebration with a fine family was a rare treat for Sarah and me. Living on one government salary, we had been embarrassed to accept invitations from the Norrises or others since we were in no position to reciprocate.

Arriving home a little before one o'clock, we celebrated the New Year in our own way, entwined in delicious and exhausting satisfaction. After that tender moment, she turned and asked if I would listen as she outlined an idea she had been considering for some time.

"Please, dearest, hear me out before you say anything, all right?" she whispered as we cuddled under the covers. "I want to go back to Dutch Harbor next spring to teach at the orphanage."

I sat up protesting. "Sarah, I want you here," I said with enough volume to fill the dark, chilly room and perhaps disturb the upstairs neighbors as well. "You're the most important..."

She covered my mouth with her hand. "I know, darling, I know. And I value your love and respect above all else. But you'd be away visiting schools all summer, while I'd be sitting here alone with little to do. I can't abide being useless, you know that."

I argued she would be safer and more comfortable here; that she could find a teaching position in Oakland. Eventually I relented. I could never deny her anything, especially when she had a practical as well as a moral argument. The savings on rent and other expenses for six months, she said, just might possibly give us a modicum of financial stability in the fall.

Throughout June and early July, with Sarah happily engaged at the orphanage, I toured possible schools sites in Bristol Bay with a Catholic priest. He said his bishop in Oregon would agree to build and staff a school at a village we jointly selected. The best choice turned out to be near the cannery where that violent incident occurred the year before.

With that good news in hand, I returned to Dutch Harbor, and spent a few days with Sarah and her charges while awaiting the arrival of the *Walrus.* As it steamed past brooding "Missionary Rock" and into the harbor, I was more determined than ever to stand up to Devlin if he continued his ruthless ways. But I was also anxious to get the reindeer experiment under way, now that I had raised a little more money to buy trade goods.

The *Walrus* sailed north on July 14 with a stiff wind at her back and dreary, dirty gray clouds low above. We hailed and inspected three vessels en route, looking for illegal liquor or fur-seal pelts. Finding no irregularities, we arrived without further incident eight days later at the spot in Anadyr Bay, Siberia, where we had found Howell four years earlier. This time, we were greeted by sunny skies, thin sea ice offshore and muddy terrain. Lieutenant Carter and Jameson, joshing each other about becoming arctic cowboys, were sent ashore to determine if any reindeer were available at the village where Howell had lived. They returned that night accompanied by one of the headman's sons, a lad about sixteen who was quickly renamed "Chukchi Bill" since no one could pronounce his real name. Chukchi's shiny black hair was held back from his smiling, pockmarked face by a knot of deer hide. He said the herders had taken the animals south for better grazing.

Chukchi, who had some knowledge of pidgin English, gleefully accepted several ounces of tobacco, and agreed to come aboard as interpreter and guide, as we headed south to search for the herd. On the two-day trip, now accompanied by constant rain squalls, Jameson's men fashioned hobbles to restrain the reindeer when they were loaded onboard, and used odd pieces of wood and line to construct a pen for the animals on the afterdeck. All we needed then was to find the herd, bargain for as many pair of young reindeer as possible, catch them and devise a method to bring them from shore to the vessel. It would prove to be a job easier described than accomplished.

When we arrived at a location Chukchi believed would be closest to the herd, he was rowed ashore with Carter, Jameson and two other men. Devlin had equipped them with a modern rifle, two hundred cartridges and two pounds of tobacco to begin the trading.

Later that day, as the rain ceased, we watched as our men returned to the shore with three pairs of reindeer herded by several Siberians. I wanted to cheer.

Then, much to our amusement and to the guffaws of the watching herders, Jameson and his men slogged through the mud trying to lasso the frightened animals. The Siberians were pointing and waving their arms and even rolling on the muddy ground with riotous laughter.

Although we were about two hundred yards offshore, I could hear shouted obscenities referring to parentage and profane uses of the Lord's name as the men tried to catch the elusive deer. There was much slipping, sliding and wide-of-the-mark roping on shore, and hoots of derision and catcalls from the entire crew, cooks, coal handlers, mess boys and officers included.

"Hey, 'Boats'," some sailor with a booming voice shouted from his perch in the rigging, "make believe you're ropin' a Barbary Coast whore. Ya have more experience doin' that, don't ya?"

"They may be only deer, laddies," shouted another, "but they're makin' asses outta you." This was greeted with wild cheers from the crew.

A smiling Devlin had been enjoying the spectacle from the pilothouse up to that point. Now apparently he had enough. "All right, you good-for-nothing loafers," he bellowed, "let those men get about their work and you get about yours."

The men began to disperse, but the smiles didn't. The title "sea asses" would follow Jameson and his detachment for years to come.

It took two hours, but the job was accomplished after the herders took pity on the frustrated seamen. They gently quieted and captured the reindeer, helped hobble their legs and carried them to our whaleboat. Two by two the beautiful young animals with luminous, frightened eyes were rowed to the ship, fitted with slings and hoisted aboard. The hobbles were removed and they were led into the improvised pen. As if in retribution, the poor disoriented beasts left droppings all over the whaleboat and the deck. Devlin ordered the whaleboat washed out and coal ash spread in the pen, making clean-up a little easier. "And get that deer shit off my deck," he shouted to no one in particular.

The Captain, with a grin softening his dark face, then marched forward to greet the mud-caked shore party. "Well, men," he said for all on deck to hear, "I do believe the Revenue Cutter Service should establish a new specialty: 'Reindeer Roper Third Class.'" This caused an explosion of laughter loud enough to frighten the deer even more.

As we headed east the next morning toward the herding experiment site near my school at St. Michael, Devlin sent word he wanted to see me. He was in high spirits, which might have had something to do with the half-filled glass of whiskey in his hand. He said we both were to be congratulated for getting the experiment under way with as little money as we had been able to raise.

"We proved the Siberians would sell live animals if the trade's fair enough," he added. "Wasn't sure they would. Some of 'em believe it's a sacrilege to let outsiders have animals they can use to build new herds." Devlin was particularly pleased that Chukchi Bill had been allowed to come with us and teach the Eskimos how to herd.

I wasn't ready for congratulations, but I was convinced the Siberians would not have been so obliging for any captain other than Devlin. His reputation for straight dealing with natives along Bering Sea coasts was well known. Certainly the headman wouldn't have allowed his son to be taken aboard any ship other than the *Walrus*. Eskimos knew their people, men and women both, could be shanghaied and treated badly on other vessels.

"The real test will come," I said, "when we try to entice Alaskan Eskimos to become herders as well as hunters, when we deliver larger numbers of animals to places with no school staff to oversee the operation."

"Knowles, you're too much of a pessimist for your own damned good, you know that?" Devlin took a book from a shelf and threw it on the desk. "You ought to read Emerson. He says a man has to take the bull by the horns, act on his best instincts if he wants to achieve anything worthwhile."

I nodded, left the book where it lay, and changed the subject, asking him about the prospects of government funding.

"With the way Washington works, nobody knows," he said taking a sip of the whiskey. "We have to get the newspapers riled up about this, shame the politicians into doing something positive for the poor beggars they've ignored for twenty years."

He drained his glass, took a bottle of Old Smuggler out of his desk drawer and poured himself another inch or so. "But anything's better than depending on the charity of the likes of Godfrey." He leaned across his disorganized desk with a fierce look. "He's one of those Southerners who promised the darkies a mule and an acre after the War, and then made it tough for them to survive. To be self-reliant."

Trying to avoid being on the receiving end of one of his lectures, I said nothing.

"He's the kind of bastard who'd try the same stuff here. Give you a few dollars for reindeer, will he? Hah! Tell you to teach the wretches their ABC's, and then he'd push 'em off their hunting lands. Best you stay away from him and his pals, Knowles."

"I don't like Godfrey's attitude either, Captain," I said. "But you have to admit he and his friends can bring needed resources to develop the north."

"Bull! Wake up, Knowles. Those kind of potbellied pirates won't develop anything or help anybody they can't control. They're the same as the goddamned railroad barons in California."

He went to his bunk, propped himself against the pillows and said he had dealt with all kinds of "low-lifers, whether wearing frock coats or patched pants" years ago in his rise from cabin boy to deck officer in the Merchant Marine.

"I've been in these godforsaken waters for more than twenty years now, Knowles. It's where I can kick ass to get things done without 'Fancy Dans' looking over my shoulder. Where I can prove myself, and do something to help these poor bastards."

He paused, pointed a finger at me and said, "Now it's up to people like you and me to beat down the carpetbaggers and the scallywags. All they do is take, never give anything back."

He calmed down, and looked at me with a quizzical look on his face.

"Knowles, can I trust you to keep something in confidence? It'll prove I know what's what."

I said I'd respect his wishes. He got up and lit one of his small, smelly cigars.

"I got permission from Benson to search for that ship Sarah saw hovering around St. Paul in the dead of winter, remember?" he began. "Late last December, I assembled a crew of volunteers, and sailed the *Walrus* around the most likely pass through the Aleutians a smart captain would use heading south during the scant hours of good light that time of year."

After fighting heavy seas for six days, he continued, a lookout spotted a steamer heading southeast, and the *Walrus* gave chase.

"It was getting dark when they finally became aware of us. We were about five miles behind, but closing in spite of heavy swells. The bastard turned off all lights. Thought he'd lose us in the dark."

Devlin grew excited in the telling, waving his arms. He said he figured the "mystery ship" would head for the Inside Passage to avoid the raging North Pacific, and plotted a course to intercept her.

"We surprised the bejesus out of 'em the next morning when we were east of 'em, cutting them off. I had the lads run out one of the guns. Damned dangerous to do in those seas. But I wanted to show 'em we meant business."

When they were close enough, Devlin said he signaled the vessel to heave to, and used the megaphone to order its captain to steam to Sitka.

"I told the son of a bitch I'd fire as many shells as I needed to sink him if he refused. He knew I couldn't get off a straight single shot in those swells."

He said the *Walrus* followed the other ship to Sitka in the dark, fully aware its crew would be throwing illegal seal pelts over the side. He, Norris, Carter, and five armed Cuttermen boarded the steamer, the *Claire* C out of San Francisco, the next day. No store of pelts was found in her hold.

"But those sons of bitches weren't as smart as they thought

they were, Knowles," he said with a sneer. "Several crewmen had traded for pelts for their own use, and hid them in their bunks. Each pelt had been scrapped, washed and salted. They could only have come from the St. Paul operation."

The *Claire C's* papers proved she was owned by Arctic Circle, he said, and one of the men caught with an illegal pelt admitted they had been trading illegally with some St. Paul natives for several years.

"I thought I had 'em," Devlin said, frowning. "But when we got home, I was ordered to report nothing about the incident or the arrest. The directive came straight from Washington."

He said he learned later that President Harrison had already awarded the lucrative twenty-year sealing contract to Arctic Circle, and Treasury didn't want the company's illegal activities to embarrass the Administration.

"Think of it, Knowles. The politicians had fired a company doing a credible job of protecting the seal herd, and gave it to a bunch of Godfrey's bandits."

Devlin said he wrote personal letters to acquaintances in Treasury, outlining Arctic Circle's landings at St. Paul. He even went further: alleging that he knew Godfrey had financed sealers hunting at sea for years.

"Remember when we boarded that British-flagged ship? Well, Norris discovered Godfrey's name in her papers, listing him among her backers."

"Didn't you disobey orders in writing those letters?" I asked, astonished at his recklessness.

"Nah, they were personal letters, not formal reports. I obeyed the letter of the order, don't ya see?"

"But what good did it do?"

"Don't know. We'll have to wait and see if the silk hats want word out they gave seal plunderers the keys to Alaska's most valuable resource."

Devlin's effrontery—his self-confidence—continued to amaze me. I was a government appointee, and wasn't comfortable being apprised of his unorthodox political maneuvers, even though his story helped explain his hatred for Godfrey, his suspicions about Heath's loyalties. I quickly changed the subject to our plans for the experiment with reindeer at St. Michael.

We agreed that Chukchi Bill would be in charge of teaching the locals how to make herding pay off with food and useful skins: that is, if we could convince Alaskan Eskimos to trust their Siberian cousins, and overcome their instinct to kill the animals immediately for the meat. My schoolteachers would oversee the effort, and provide progress reports so we could urge the government to become involved.

Any doubt about how our gift would be received was banished two days later. Arrival of the reindeer delighted the villagers at St. Michael. The schoolchildren couldn't seem to get close enough to the animals, much smaller and more docile than the wild caribou they had seen.

Our delivery was the occasion for a driftwood bonfire, complete with native drumming and dancing. It wasn't as elaborate as the feasts and festivities held by Eskimo whaling captains at the end of the hunt. My teachers told me the natives call it "nalukatag," and it's a very important ritual to honor the spirit of the whale, so central to their beliefs.

But all that didn't interest Jameson, who leaped uninvited into the circle of dancers. With his uniform jacket off and his pipe in his mouth, he did an Irish jig with such enthusiasm and abandonment that perspiration rolled down his cheeks.

The Eskimos were wide-eyed, pointing in wonder at the

gyrating white man. Along with several of the officers, I was laughing so hard my spectacles fell off when several natives tried to mimic Jameson. Tracing jig steps in bulky mukluks proved too difficult, and soon they reverted to their own, more sedate, shuffling dance.

"Lieutenant Carter," I said, wiping the tears of laughter from my face, "you are witnessing the clash of artistic expressions. One born in the isolated Arctic, the other on a crowded, green island a half world away."

Even as I enjoyed Jameson's spectacle, I wondered if these Eskimo dancers, so imbued with the sanctity of the whale hunt, would be willing to become herders.

I wondered, too, if Devlin's efforts to subvert Godfrey would anger his Washington supporters. Opposition from the Harrison Administration would kill all hope of government funding, I thought. Then the Eskimos wouldn't have to worry about learning to herd.

Chapter Fourteen

S t. Michael was a lively, even frightening, settlement that mid-August.

Located within striking distance of the Yukon River, the village of some thirty small, unpainted wooden structures and a few barabaras attracted colorful, even bizarre, strangers that time of year. Eskimo families from isolated upriver camps, mud-spattered prospectors toting pistols and trappers with their furs, rifles and native "wives." Not to mention the dense swarms of large tundra mosquitoes determined to make the most of their short lives by making humans miserable. Without letup, they attacked eyes, ears, nose and any other patch of exposed skin. They almost drove me mad.

With temperatures in the high 60s, the moldy tents and transient lean-tos were everywhere. The stench of unwashed bodies and clothing, rancid grease and decaying skins was nauseating. The up-river Eskimos came to trade or to find work as harpooners or as workers in the shore whaling stations. The white men were waiting impatiently to ensure that they wouldn't miss the last August steamer. They knew if they weren't aboard, they might have to spend the winter in the wild. St. Michael had neither provision— nor any willingness—to house more than a few outsiders.

About noon on the second day of my extended school inspection, a volley of shots pierced the air. The two teachers and I hastily herded the children into the most secure schoolroom. As it turned out, we had little reason to be concerned. The shots came from a drunken trapper shooting gravel at the feet of an

Eskimo boy. He apparently believed the youngster was trying to steal his otter furs.

The ruckus was loud enough to cause Devlin to row ashore with four men to investigate. I watched from the schoolhouse's wooden walkway as he marched up the beach toward laughing white men surrounding the trapper. They became quiet and fell back as if Devlin were leading a company of Marines, leaving the muttering trapper alone and staggering in the open space.

"Hand me that weapon, you stupid son of a bitch," Devlin demanded as he approached the stoop-shouldered, heavily bearded fellow.

"Go to hell!" the trapper slurred, as he waved the revolver in the air. "It's mine. I'll shoot your fuckin' head off if you try to take it. I'll shoot that slant-eyed kid, too, if he comes near my stuff again."

Devlin continued his measured stride until he was about six feet from the trapper. He then lunged at the wobbling man, knocking him to the gravel, and sending his heavy weapon clattering out of reach. It looked to me like the kind cavalrymen used in the War. Jameson followed a second later. He straddled the trapper, pinning his right arm. The man howled, "You're breaking my arm, you goddamned swabbie."

Devlin ignored the screams. In a voice loud enough for all the onlookers to hear, he said, "There's to be no shooting in this village. And no sale of hooch to the Eskimos either, ya understand?"

"Old Seth was only trying to keep the thieving savages away from his furs, for chrissake," came a shout from the crowd.

"I don't give a good goddamn what he was trying to do," Devlin said. "Anyone caught firing a weapon in St. Michael, especially at a native, will spend the next two months in the bowels of my ship. I promise you won't like it."

While this was going on, a group of locals gathered around the Eskimo boy the trapper had accused. They stood expressionless watching as the Captain punished a white man for shooting at one of their own. I have no doubt they were astonished.

Apparently believing he had made his point, Devlin jammed a tiny cigar in his mouth and walked slowly toward the twenty or so white onlookers. A few had affected scowls and clenched fists. Several had thumbs hooked on their belts near their low-slung holsters, making me very anxious.

Devlin stood directly in front of a snarling, shirtless young fellow with muscles like an ox. He was at least six feet tall, broad-shouldered, and had a mop of unruly brown hair falling unbound down his back. The Captain held the trapper's revolver by its long barrel. Without a word he made a big display of removing the unexpended cartridges and pocketing them. In a conversational tone he said, "In the interest of peace, I expect all of you men to do the same."

"Who the hell do you think you are, old man?" brown hair shouted as he moved within inches of the Captain.

One of Jameson's men began to approach, but Devlin waved him off. Without moving away from his challenger, he told the crowd, "This feller thinks he's still out in the wilderness somewhere, not on territory of the United States government." He surveyed the group, stuck the revolver in his belt and added, "which as far as you men are concerned, means me. Now get about it."

I couldn't see his face, but he must have used one of his hellacious stares on brown hair. The man moved back a pace, spat some tobacco juice on the gravel and hesitantly emptied his weapon.

"Now, men, we can all have a more congenial time in lovely St. Michael," Devlin said with a smile. He ordered Jameson to release the trapper, and to remain onshore. He cupped his hands around a match to light the cigar, turned his back to the crowd, and strolled to the knot of Eskimos for an animated conversation I couldn't hear. After a few minutes, he turned and ambled to the beach through the milling white men without a word, and boarded his whaleboat. I was relieved to see him go.

Sailors being sailors, the Cuttermen left ashore took the opportunity to do a little trading of their own. It was quite a sight to see the clean-shaven seamen in their work uniforms dickering with jostling men in soiled leather hats and a wild assortment of tattered clothes. Jameson, who considered himself an astute bargain hunter, was prominent among them.

"Look here, Dr. Knowles," he said as he sauntered over to me with his rifle slung over his shoulder. He showed me two almost intact walrus tusks, each about nine inches long. "With a little carving, these fellers will make my winter in 'Frisco really, really adventurous altogether," he added with a broad wink and a sly smile.

Ten days later, the *Walrus* was abreast Nome, heading to the northernmost American village of Barrow, when a whaling vessel signaled us. On board was a shipwrecked passenger, Captain Collins of the whaling ship *Orca*, who asked for our immediate assistance. He explained that the *Orca* had been caught in the ice pack south of Point Barrow a week earlier, was crushed and sank within minutes, he and his men were barely able to escape with the clothes they were wearing.

"I can't explain it," he told Devlin. "The *Orca* was built specifically for arctic whaling only three years ago." The man looked defeated. Embarrassed. His broad shoulders were sagging, and he continually pulled at his shaggy, white-flecked beard. He said he and some of his crew had slogged over the ice for two days before reaching ships anchored in protected waters north of Icy Cape. The fate of his other men was unknown, he said.

Devlin ordered a course change to get us to the Cape as quickly as weather conditions allowed, and took Collins below so he could get some rest. I'm sure a glass or two of Scotch was also on the agenda.

The solid mass of the icepack was still far to the north when the *Walrus* cleared the Bering Strait and entered Chukchi Sea. Heath told me we were at least five hundred miles from Icy Cape. It meant we couldn't reach the *Orca* crew and the whaling fleet for three days even under the best of conditions.

The next day as we neared the latitude of the Arctic Circle, it became obvious we would not have such luck. An imposing, brilliant white barricade extended from horizon to horizon some miles directly ahead. It looked to me as if a newly whitewashed wall, almost perfectly flat on top, had sprung from the sea to bear the burden of the clouds above.

"That's some fog bank," said Norris, who happened to be in the pilothouse. "No way around it. That monster'll slow us down some."

Until that day, I never appreciated what visual marvels nature could produce using only variations of white and black. Above the snow-white brilliance of the fog bank, strands of clouds were slowly transformed into a granite shade, then to tints of mouse gray, slate gray, lilac, purple, darkening further into ebony. And the entire panorama contrasted with a restless sea reminiscent of old unpolished pewter.

My awe at the display was replaced with foreboding a few hours later when we sailed into a strange, ghostly world. I couldn't see anything for more than thirty yards on any side of the ship. Even the tops of our masts were obscured. The fog above, faintly illuminated by the sun's waning light, became a translucent ceiling for the gray-tinted cavern of white wetness we traveled. The fog dampened and distorted sound; the eerie silence was disturbed only by the soft thump of engines and the low, intermittent growl of the foghorn. It felt as if our ship carried the only mote of humanity left on earth; that we were groping blindly from the reality we knew into the unknown.

The engines were slowed. Lookouts were posted on deck since the crow's nest itself was enveloped in the watery ceiling. But it was not fear of collision that unsettled me. It was that haunting feeling of utter solitude as we sailed through tiny droplets in immeasurable number that smothered our world.

The *Walrus* steamed for more than six hours to get through that bank. When it became possible to use the sextant, Devlin ordered both Carter and Heath to make separate sightings to be as certain as possible of our position. He said we would most likely hit more fog and might have to approach Icy Cape in the dark, requiring the most precise use of dead reckoning.

Wardroom arguments became quite heated as we neared the Cape. Heath, backed by Dowie and two other junior officers, argued vehemently for delay in proceeding until the fog lifted. Anderson, Donaldson and even young Carter countered that Devlin was the best ship handler there was and knew what he was doing.

"Dammit, Norris," Heath said, his face flushed with anger. "It's suicide to approach shore in these conditions. You're the First Officer. You have to convince the Captain to lay offshore."

Norris studied Heath for a time, removed the pipe from his mouth, and said simply, "There's only one captain on this vessel, Lieutenant. And you ain't him." He rose from his chair. "It's best if you and your pals stop second-guessing the man and find out how to help." He then left the wardroom and headed to the deck.

I couldn't hear what they were saying, but Heath and his supporters huddled in the opposite corner in intense conversation.

Despite the fog and the dark, Devlin sent Captain Collins and several men in a lifeboat to locate the whaling ships. He had heard their bells, he said, and knew they were nearby. Within hours, our boat returned with the news that all the survivors of the *Orca* were accounted for among four vessels in a partially sheltered bay. Collins was sent back the next morning to let the other captains know we would return from Barrow in a few days to pick up the *Orca* survivors.

As the *Walrus* headed north through leads in the ice pack, most of them close to shore, Devlin told me to organize the cargo of school supplies. "It's only about one hundred and thirty miles to Barrow," he said. "I don't want to spend more than a day there unloading at this time of year." He pulled up his collar, swept his arms to indicate the white expanse of sheet ice reaching to the far horizons. "That is, unless you want to be away from that pretty wife of yours all winter."

When we arrived off Barrow, all hands were assigned to help muscle crates of school supplies and provisions for the refuge station into small boats. The approach to the isolated village was so shallow, and the ice near shore so fragile, this time-consuming procedure was the only way to bring material ashore.

I barely had opportunity to spend two hours with the teacher in his one-room schoolhouse before the *Walrus'* shrill whistle summoned landing parties back onboard. A somber Jameson pointed out the dark, angry clouds building to the northwest. They signaled the coming of "one hell of a storm," he said. "We don't need no September blow this far north," he added. "It could shove the icepack closer to shore and get in our way making it outta here."

The frigid gale hit us when we were within fifty miles of Icy Cape by Carter's reckoning. It did push the ice shoreward, forcing the *Walrus* to pick its way at quarter speed through the floes. When the Cape came into sight, I was relieved to see that a concave barrier of rocks of varying heights protected the whaling vessels from the winds.

But just as the *Walrus* started its turn to enter the bay, the wind shifted direction radically, gathering force. It now whistled from the northeast over open tundra with not even a hillock to slow its fury. Responding to the new situation, Devlin set our anchor toward the northeast, close to the shore. The four whaling ships, all of them positioned to fight wind from the opposite direction, were suddenly in a precarious situation. They had set anchor near the barrier, letting out extended anchor lines sailors call rodes.

I had learned during my time on the *Walrus* that vessels had to feed out lines at the very least seven times as long as the distance from their deck to the sea bottom to get an anchor to hold securely. Now, as the ships swung around to face the new wind direction in such a confined space, their anchor lines were far too long to keep them off the jagged rocks of the barrier that had protected them moments before.

"They'll have a damned tough time surviving the night in one piece," Devlin shouted over the howl of the wind as he observed men scrambling on the nearest vessel, about a mile away. "They'll burn up their windlass and their energy trying to shorten those lines." He kept the long glass on the ships, shaking his head slowly. "Even if they make it, with such a short rode the anchor won't hold worth a damn in this wind."

In the growing darkness, holding on as best I could, I resisted the temptation to shut out what was happening to a second whaler about two miles farther into the bay. The vessel was being blown slowly but inexorably toward disaster. Her anchor could not hold.

"She's gonna wreck, Captain," Carter yelled as the vessel spun broadside to the wind.

In minutes, she was thrown violently against the rocks. I couldn't hear the crash of splintering timber or the shouts of her crew. But to my horror, I somehow sensed these sounds in my mind.

"Jesus, those lads are being thrown into the ice water," Carter said. "If they don't get smashed on the rocks, they'll spend a miserable time freezing tonight." The young lieutenant, desperately holding onto the rail, looked as if he was about to sob. "And we can't do a goddamned thing," he said.

Darkness now made it impossible to see how the other vessels were faring in the wind and heavy, steep swells. The *Walrus*, being larger and properly anchored, was not in imminent danger. But she was climbing and diving and listing radically all the same, forcing me to envision the frantic fear that must have overwhelmed the men on those ships.

At first light, the carcasses of all four whaling ships became visible, strewn grotesquely along the barrier. I was sickened by the thought of the men thrown into the sea, now trying to survive in piercing cold among rocks pounded by surf and winds still above forty-five miles an hour.

The stern of the ship closest to us was wedged high on the rocks, her forward deck awash in the surf. The two ships farther away had spun broadside and wrecked, their sails blown loose, whipping like torn laundry on a clothesline. The ship farthest from us had sunk in the shallows about five miles distant. Only lopsided masts and torn canvas marked her location.

With Devlin and most of our officers, I watched in dread and apprehension as men on the nearest vessel struggled to launch their two seaworthy lifeboats. One almost capsized as soon as it hit the water. It was quickly righted as its crew struggled to gain headway to reach the *Walrus*. The other had nine aboard. It was pushed sideways in the swells halfway to us, almost foundering as seawater poured over its low gunwales. In panic, some of the men bailed frantically, using anything at hand, including their caps. The others strained to the oars, their arms and backs bent to the almost impossible task of moving a boat heavy with water. I prayed that somehow they would be spared.

Nobody on the heaving deck of the *Walrus* said a word. All were focused on the struggling seamen in the boats. It was as if we were collectively willing them to safety. I knew men would die if tossed into the waves. There was little chance for rescue before their blood froze.

After a heart-wrenching half-hour, both boats were within thirty yards of our stern. Lines were thrown toward them repeatedly. The wind blew them tantalizingly out of reach. A man in one boat leapt from his seat and caught a line. He lost balance for a moment. His shipmates grabbed him and pulled him down, barely keeping him from going overboard.

The other boat's coxswain caught a second line a few minutes later. The *Walrus'* crew used winches and sheer manpower to pull the boats through the rain and swells close to our plunging sides. The boat half filled with seawater was cut loose and sank.

Devlin, bracing himself against the wind, was at the rail, supervising the treacherous task of bringing the soaked and exhausted men aboard. He ordered a boom extended and a sling lowered to bring up injured sailors. The others carefully climbed rope ladders with wooden footholds as our ship rose and fell like a bucking horse. One poor fellow, who days before had survived the sinking of the *Orca*, had the fingers of his left hand crushed between the ladder and the hull.

After the fifteen survivors were at last aboard and sent below, Devlin assembled his officers. He said we would never be able to reach the men from the remaining ships in this weather from our present position. "It'll take some doing," he said, "but we'll up anchor, steam closer to those other fellers and re-anchor. Look smart, now."

Heath, cautious as usual, said something about the shallowness of the bay and the close quarters for maneuvering. "So what would you have me do, Heath?" the Captain said with a dismissive wave of his hand. "Leave those poor bastards to freeze until the weather is pleasant enough to suit you?"

I went to assist Donaldson as best I could while the *Walrus* changed position. Besides the man with smashed fingers, the doctor had to deal with two broken or fractured arms and one man with a dislocated shoulder. All were in a great deal of pain. It seemed to me that every survivor of the *Orca* was either sneezing and coughing or suffering from frostbite.

It unsettled me at first to invade the privacy, to be in such intimate contact, with other men. But following Donaldson's lead, I was surprised at what I was able to do, how quickly I adapted. I helped men, their hands disabled by the cold or by being curled desperately around oars, to get out of wet clothes, and to swathe them in blankets against their clammy nakedness. I removed boots and massaged feet with greasy, smelly liniment. I spooned dark cough syrup into their mouths, and handled basins of vomited seawater. I accepted their expressions of thanks, but had no idea how we could assist them further.

Devlin's initial attempt to anchor near the remaining ships failed. The anchor dragged, putting the *Walrus* herself in danger of crashing stern-first into the rocks. It was difficult and dangerous to handle heavy anchor and chain in such weather. But the *Walrus* men, working on a water-sluiced forward deck rising ten feet and falling a like distance, succeeded on the second try.

Devlin ordered Carter and Dowie to assemble and to take charge of one boat each. As far as I could see, Heath, who was nowhere to be seen, wasn't even considered. Both boats were to go to the wreck almost astern of our position. Her crew had been stranded among the surf-pounded rocks since the night before.

There was no safe landing spot on the barrier. I saw our boat crews struggling mightily, using oars as poles to avoid submerged rocks. They came as close as possible to solid ground. The survivors fought through surf to reach them. The exhausted, soaked men, lacking strength to board on their own, had to be pulled over the gunwales into the boats.

Even with the wind abating somewhat, it was a backbreaking job for the two *Walrus* parties to row the half-mile or so back to the ship. But they did. We then had a bit of unexpected luck. The third whaling ship had salvaged two of its boats, and her crew used them to fight the swells without need of our assistance. As before, in my mind I was pulling hard on their oars, willing them to succeed. They reached the tenuous safety of the *Walrus* in about an hour. It must have been the most harrowing hour of their lives.

The vessel that had been anchored in the shallowest part of the bay was completely underwater. I saw that a few of its crew had somehow made it to shore, while the remainder were signaling from the barrier itself.

Devlin devised a new tactic that caused more grumbling among Heath and his supporters. The Captain upped anchor once again, detailed fresh boat crews for Carter and Dowie, and steamed slowly toward the wreck. Being broadside to the wind, the *Walrus* was listing heavily to port. Our lee rail was no more than two or three feet above the roiling water.

When Devlin maneuvered the *Walrus* into the wind, we all heard the frightening sound of keel scraping gravel. Without seeming to share our fear, he reversed engines, and somehow found deeper water. He ordered the boats lowered while our engines struggled to hold us steady. He sent one boat to each survivor location.

We then steamed slowly the five miles or so to the entrance of the bay, and carefully reversed direction. Devlin repeated this racetrack movement three times until Carter and Dowie, with survivors aboard, were in position to come alongside. There was at least a foot of seawater, as well as cold and sick men, in each boat.

Devlin's dangerous but expert ship handling, and the courage of his disciplined crew had saved fifty-nine men from the four whalers and the *Orca*. I shuttered to think how many would have perished if they had not been picked up in time. With our regular complement of forty-four, there were more than one hundred men aboard the *Walrus* when she steamed into the ice pack the next morning.

The storm blew itself out as we headed southwest toward the Bering Strait, and a good thing it was. The *Walrus* could hold no more than sixty with any degree of comfort. There being no room to house everyone below decks at all times, the healthiest survivors had to take turns huddled topside with only spare sail canvas to protect them. I shared my little cabin, hardly large enough for one man, with two whaler officers. The wardroom, the officer's cabins, the crew's mess and every companionway were packed with coughing men sprawled in wet wool or oilskins.

The physical condition of many survivors caused the most concern. Beside broken limbs and one serious concussion, it seemed that half suffered from deep chest colds. Three or four had very high temperatures and were isolated on Donaldson's orders. Cough remedies were depleted before we even reached the Strait. Laudanum was in dangerously short supply.

Devlin called the whaler captains, his officers and me to the pilothouse as the *Walrus* slowed to quarter speed to find leads through the ice.

"Gentlemen," he said, "we could be facing one hell of an epidemic of pneumonia or la grippe. Too many sick men at close quarters can bring us all down." Lines of exhaustion and dark pouches under his eyes were evident. Leaning on the bulkhead for support, he told us that food, medicine and coal were running low. "And we'll probably hit heavy ice goin' through the Straits given this damned early winter we're having."

He pushed himself erect. "None of the villages, including Unalaska at Dutch Harbor, will have medicine or food enough to help, so I intend to steam directly to 'Frisco. Gotta get these men proper medical attention."

He asked the whaler captains to select their most able-bodied men to work with the *Walrus* crew. He specifically asked for help in taking on coal quickly at the Port Clarence coaling station, our only stop.

With the help of the whalers, the *Walrus* made the fastest passage possible through late September seas to San Francisco, bypassing every port.

Personally, the swift passage might mean I would be deprived of the person dearest to me for the winter. Sarah had planned to wait for us at Dutch Harbor. I hoped she had the good sense to take the last steamer south when we didn't enter that port by mid-month. If not, I wouldn't see her or hold her for six long months.

It took us 27 days of steaming, first through ice floes and then two storms, to reach home. All hands cheered when we passed through the Golden Gate on October 11, the pennant declaring "injured on board" flying from our mast.

I prayed that Sarah would be there to meet me.

Chapter Fifteen

D evlin looked out of place, nervous. The focal point of a semicircle of loud, back-slapping well-wishers with whiskey-throated laughs, he seemed reserved and managed only a tight smile as he slowly found his place of honor at the head table.

I had delayed entering the ballroom of the Occidental Hotel, wanting to escape as much of this exuberant good fellowship and nautical chitchat as possible. It was the Captain's night, the whalers' night. Not mine, especially given my distaste for liquor-induced hilarity on any occasion.

How can this man who never loses an opportunity to boast about his exploits, be so ill at ease being honored by fellow ship-masters? Especially with news reporters in the room, I wondered.

"It's about time you got yourself here, Dr. Knowles," Chief Engineer Anderson said as I arrived at the table reserved for *Walrus* officers. "You almost missed the she-crab soup. It's first-rate, even if you won't let them put in a little Sherry for kick."

"Sorry for my tardiness," I said as I took my seat. "Sarah needed medicine. Been fighting a persistent chest cold developed on her voyage back from Dutch Harbor. I'm just glad she took the steamer by herself when the *Walrus* didn't return as planned."

A waiter in white gloves appeared, and with some ceremony poured the steaming, thick liquid into my china bowl, unleashing pleasing aromas of paprika. While he performed, I surveyed through the fog of tobacco smoke the resplendent head table, its crystal sparkling in the candlelight. A small carafe of amber liquid, which to my dismay I surmised was whiskey, was set at each of eight places. I hoped "Roaring Ed" would have the sense to abstain on this of all nights. Above hung a banner spanning almost the entire length of the table with rosettes in red, white and blue at each corner. In deep blue lettering against a white background, it declared:

The North Pacific Whaling Association
Honors
Capt. Edward M. Devlin, USRCS

I felt a tap on my shoulder, and turned in surprise to see a smiling Governor Godfrey. He nodded to the officers, telling them not to stand, and whispered to me. "I need your help, Doctor. I've been urgently trying to talk privately with the Captain for days."

I told him I had not spoken with Devlin for weeks and didn't know his plans for this evening.

"Please try to arrange something," he insisted. "I want to introduce him to some very prominent men. And discuss another matter important to his career."

Promising I'd speak to Devlin after the banquet, I watched as he threaded his way around tables with those tiny, quick steps of his. He took his seat among sullen-faced men in dark suits at a table near the rear of the room.

A plate with a huge slice of bleeding roast beef was set before me. I liked my meat well done and arranged to trade mine for Donaldson's charred piece, much to his satisfaction. Only then did I notice the absence of several of our officers.

"Where are Heath and Dowie?"

"Our constant malcontents found convenient excuses," Anderson said with a smirk. "The Captain's refusal to promote

Heath because of his constant bitching and all probably has something to do with it. Don't miss either of them, to tell the truth."

Before I could begin to attack the beef, Donaldson poked me, and pointed to the head table. Devlin, leaning forward over the white tablecloth, was motioning me to approach.

"What did that bastard Godfrey want?" he said softly so his nearby dinner companions couldn't hear.

"And a 'good evening' to you, too, Captain," I said indignantly.

"Yes, yes, Knowles, I'm glad you could be here for this. Really I am. But tell me what that slippery bandit said."

"He asked me to set up a meeting. Something about introducing you to important people."

"Introductions, my ass. He probably got his hands on that letter I sent to Washington."

"Don't tell me you had a few too many drinks and wrote something you now regret."

He fixed me with that icy stare of his and said, "I never regret anything I do, Knowles." Then with a shrug and a wave of one hand, "But I guess I'll have to meet him. Don't want him making a scene with Captain Benson and others around here."

The president of the Whalers Association was calling for silence as I returned to my seat.

Captain Joshua Foster cut an imposing figure. More than six feet tall with girth to match, he had a head of graying, wavy hair and mutton-chop whiskers. Together they framed his fleshy, florid face, making him look like a prophet of old. He introduced the head table. Its occupants included Captain Benson, the Bering Patrol Senior Captain, the San Francisco mayor, the U.S. Collector of Customs, and two vice presidents of the Whalers' Association.

Foster elaborated on Devlin's long career in the north in excruciating detail. When he finally arrived at descriptions of the Icy

Cape rescues, he repeated "heroic," and "unselfish," and "brilliant seamanship" in virtually every sentence. This went on for almost a half hour. I saw many around the room nodding off, while others began to talk among themselves. Foster then read congratulatory telegrams from the Secretary of the Treasury, Senators George Hearst and Leland Stanford, one a Democrat and the other a Republican, among many other notables. He said the Association had produced a petition to Congress and Treasury, signed by thirty whaling executives and shipmasters extolling "the heroism and the value of keeping men like Devlin in the Arctic."

When he called Devlin to the podium, one hundred fifty or more attendees stood and cheered, the sounds echoing in the high-ceilinged chamber with its oak paneled walls. Some whalers stood unsteadily on plush-cushioned chairs; others clinked crystal glasses with forks or knives. The enthusiasm, I suspected, was engendered not only by respect for Devlin, but for cessation of Foster's monologue.

Foster presented the Captain with a solid-gold watch, and intoned the inscription: "To Captain Edward M. Devlin, USRCS. In grateful appreciation. North Pacific Whaling Association, March 1890."

When the cheers abated, Devlin thanked the Association for the gift and the support it had provided him over his twenty-plus years of service in the Bering Sea.

"Most of us here tonight," he said, "know first hand the dangers and the discomforts of sailing in that fog and cold. We also know a captain can do very little without the support of his officers."

He then asked the *Walrus* officers to stand and be recognized. "When you see them ashore, gentlemen," Devlin added, "stop and buy them a drink or two." This was greeted with forced laughter.

"There's a civilian member of the *Walrus* family at that table, too. He's our esteemed Alaskan School Commissioner, who rides along with us quite a bit. But, fellers, don't try to buy this man a drink. Please give a hand to Dr. Stanton Knowles, who left the ministry for the classroom. But we're the ones who taught him to tell the difference between a capstan and a bowsprit."

I was secretly very pleased to be singled out. I'm not embarrassed to report I blushed like a schoolboy as I acknowledged the applause of these sea-hardened men.

Devlin seemed to have regained his bravado. He told the audience that as much as he appreciated the honors he had received, he had two requests to make.

"You gentlemen have been so successful in harvesting whales," he said, waving his arm to embrace them all, "many Eskimo villages are in a bad way. Some suffer starvation for lack of whale meat before spring hunting season arrives."

Amid murmurs of agreement, he told them of our experiment with transporting reindeer to Alaska, providing food and skins in areas with the greatest need.

"I ask you all to contribute funds so we can buy goods to trade the Siberians for the animals. Captain Foster has agreed to collect whatever you can give."

Devlin then requested that the Association provide, "a fine steak dinner for my outstanding enlisted crew when the *Walrus* is being outfitted for the season next month." Foster agreed to that also, and the ceremonies ended, unleashing the chatter and laughter of men anxious to find their way to the bar.

By the time Devlin extracted himself from the clusters of well-wishers, Godfrey was standing alone near some potted palms at the back of the room. Waiters and Chinese busboys scurried amid sounds of rattling dishes and utensils. They were turning the festive hall into a sad, bare room.

"Congratulations, Captain." Godfrey extended his hand accompanied by his usual hint of a smile. "Well deserved. A spectacular rescue, indeed."

Devlin motioned him to sit at a bare, splintery wooden table, its cloth already on its way to the laundry.

"Apologize that my guests had to leave," Godfrey said. "Important members of my board. Two from the Southern Pacific, and all wanted to meet you."

"I suspect you and I have more important business to discuss than that, don't we?" Devlin said.

"We surely do, Captain. Are you certain you want Dr. Knowles to be present?"

"Yes, I want a witness to what you have to say."

Godfrey's smile vanished. He ceased playing with his watch chain, leaned toward Devlin and tapped a manicured finger on the table. "I'm told on good authority you wrote letters to Washington opposing Arctic Circle's bid for the seal-harvesting contract. Could that be true?"

Devlin admitted he did write to oppose the contract. "It was my duty to do so."

"Your duty?" Godfrey raised his thin voice above the clatter around us. "Sir, you are a cutter captain. You have no duty to get involved in high-level government decisions." He looked toward me, then continued in his staccato manner of speech, keeping time with his tapping finger. "Are you aware, sir, that President Harrison had already agreed to award us that contract? That your impertinence has delayed a final decision, embarrassing the Administration?"

Devlin leaned forward in his chair, put both hands on the table and stared directly into the slender man's eyes. "Listen here, Godfrey, and listen well," he said. "I've been odd man out my entire life. It has never kept me from doing what I believe to be right. And I'm right now. You know I am."

Godfrey appeared taken aback by the Captain's intensity. I certainly was, regretting that I was the one who arranged this contentious meeting.

"All right, Captain," Godfrey said sitting up straight and fingering his watch chain, "tell me why you oppose us. You've probably been misinformed. I can set you straight."

Devlin took his time to respond. "Letting Arctic Circle have that contract would be like sending killer whales to protect seals, to my way of thinking."

"That's preposterous. Unfair. Slanderous." Godfrey was on his feet, looking down on the seated Captain. "We are a responsible company, with investors respected on Wall Street and Washington. You'll have to answer for such defamation if you let it stand."

Devlin rose to confront him. "It's not defamation to tell the truth, Godfrey."

I became apprehensive, and tried to insert myself between them, but the Captain held me off with one hand.

"You apparently have allies at Treasury," Devlin said. "I have mine among seamen all over the Pacific, some on your own vessels."

Godfrey turned and moved away, pulling down the cuffs of his expensive, well-fitted jacket, clearly trying to compose himself.

"Shall I tell you what I've learned, what I told Washington?" Devlin continued, following him at a distance. "That for years you and your investors have financed ships to poach seals in the open sea. That you sent at least one vessel to land illegally on St. Paul Island, allowing its crew to sell hooch to the natives."

Godfrey swung around, pointing his finger. "You, sir, retard progress. You discourage new investments. New ideas. And to think my company declined to charge you for unwarranted violence at our cannery."

172 | WILLIAM E. DUKE

"Unwarranted, hell!" Devlin boomed, causing the noisy waiters to stop and stare. "Your bullyboys had beaten a defenseless old darky and a Chink, and thought they could get away with it."

"We'll protect our own workers, and the natives, too, if you'll only mind your own business. It's the white man's role and duty to civilize Alaska."

Devlin seemed ready to charge the man. I stepped between the two, and placed a restraining hand on the Captain's chest. "Gentlemen, please," I said, "can't you discuss these things in a more civil tone?"

Devlin started to walk toward the rear door, then turned. "I don't trust your Arctic Circle crowd to protect anybody but itself," he said in a level voice. "I know how you treated the darkies when you were governor of Georgia."

"You know nothing about Georgia and its problems during Reconstruction," Godfrey said, his face turning crimson with rage.

"I know a helluva lot more than you'd like to believe. How you and your crowd scared the hell out of 'em, kept them out of school and on the land."

Devlin stood in the darkened alcove near the door, put on his cap and stared at Godfrey. "I'll do every goddamned thing I can to protect Eskimos and Aleuts from you and your ideas of civilizin'."

Devlin went through the swinging doors, and Godfrey slumped into a chair, shook his head and toyed again with his watch chain.

"That man is an uneducated, foul-mouthed ruffian, Doctor. I'd advise you to disassociate yourself from him while there's still time."

I said nothing. Godfrey stood for a moment watching two waiters tear down the banner over the head table. "We're the future of Alaska, not Devlin, and that contract is crucial to our plans." He turned and pointed at me. "If the President is forced to void that contract because of Devlin's allegations, there'll be grave consequences for that man and anybody associated with him."

Controlling my anger, I walked through the hotel lobby as boisterous laughter and tinny concertina music spilled from the barroom. Is "Roaring Ed Devlin" holding forth in there? I wondered. Is he bragging about his confrontation with Godfrey? I debated whether to go through the swinging doors, and force him to see the damage his warning to Godfrey—his outright dare—could do to the reindeer project. I realized the man savored arguments with anybody at any time, especially before an audience, that my pleas for reason would mean nothing to him this night.

All I thought to do was to trudge sadly home, vowing never to forgive him if Godfrey's friends in Washington jeopardized funding for the reindeer or my schools.

Chapter Sixteen

An unrelenting barrage of vicious Pacific storms forced our passenger steamer to retreat into the Inside Passage as we headed north that June. With the vessel shielded by verdant barrier islands from high wind and twenty-foot waves, it became possible to stand without being battered against the peeling gray bulkheads, to do something useful. The cook indulged me with a tray of plain wheat crackers and a pot of weak tea that I set on the table beside Sarah's narrow bunk, and then rearranged her pillows.

"I'm too sick to appreciate your fussing, dear," she said. Soft light from the one cloudy, leaking porthole illuminated her ashen face, wreathed by an unusual disarray of hair. "But don't fret. The baby isn't due until December at the earliest."

The baby! I had quivered with joy and disbelief when Sarah informed me of that marvel the day before we left San Francisco. I continued to be surprised—and a little frightened—when her morning retching confirmed it.

She held the cup close to her lips and sipped the tea as I bent forward, elbows on knees, and watched from the hardwood chair.

"I insist you stop frowning so, Stanton. I'll be all right, and so will the child. As to the other things bothering you…"

"It seems as if all I've tried to do up here is coming apart," I moaned.

"Bosh. You sound like a child yourself," came the instant reply from behind the cup. "You're letting Devlin's stupid challenge to that Godfrey creature get you down. The reindeer project is still intact, isn't it?"

It was true the government had finally authorized token amounts to begin buying and transporting the animals. I told her I feared Godfrey would induce Washington to cut off additional funds as long as Devlin was involved; that we certainly couldn't expect more donations from Arctic Circle. My own superiors, I lamented, declined to authorize teachers and construction money for two of the three schools I had promised native elders last year.

"What are you doing way over there?" Sarah said, putting the cup on the tray and making room for me on the bunk. "Bring your litany of woes over here where we can both suffer through them."

Sarah pouted mischievously and took my hand. The sour odor of her most recent retching clung to her nightgown. "Now, let's see. You're already beginning to make the Captain at least listen to reason." She smiled wanly, pulled me to her and kissed me tenderly. "And, my dear, you're going to be a father. Isn't that enough to make you happy?"

"Oh, don't mind me, m'love," I said returning her kiss. "Of course I'm happy and excited. Overjoyed, actually."

But not completely, I thought. I still harbor fears of failure, of not being a good provider, a model for my child. Why in God's name, I asked myself, do I always favor the darkest prospects? Why can't I be an optimist like Devlin?

The remainder of the trip was a time of intimacy, of oneness. Despite my darling's bouts of nausea, our intimate conversations, the plans we made for our child's future, enlivened my spirits. I didn't realize the hopes raised during those few carefree days would have to last me a lifetime.

*
**

We landed at Dutch Harbor two weeks later than expected, disappointed that the *Walrus* wasn't in port. I was eager to get under way before any barriers could be erected against the delivery of the reindeer. Success in that endeavor, at least, might make the 1890 season worthwhile after all.

Devlin's ship soon returned and crates of school supplies were quickly hoisted aboard. Then came enough trade goods to fill a country store: pound sacks of tobacco, kegs of powder and shot, thirty steel traps and a like number of large case knives, six bales of calico, an assortment of tin plates and cups, iron spoons and even a tea chest with portions wrapped in tiny paper packages.

The *Walrus* steamed into the Bering Sea in early morning two days later, heading west of north toward Anadyr Bay and its herders. About midday we emerged from heavy fog to discover a sealing schooner not more than three miles distant. I could imagine the horror her captain must have felt when he saw a Revenue Cutter plowing toward him. His hunters, in their small boats, were spread out for miles among the migrating herd of fur seals. He couldn't abandon them even if he thought by some miracle he could outrace the *Walrus* to the safety of another fog bank.

Devlin ordered assembly of a boarding crew. Told Lieutenant Dowie to run out the cannon, and the duty officer to reduce speed and put us alongside the schooner.

"I've caught you in the act, no doubt about that, captain," Devlin shouted into the megaphone. "Call in your hunters, and prepare for boarding and inspection." He started to leave the rail, but quickly returned. "Once my men are aboard that scow of yours, come on over here for coffee. And bring your papers."

Having witnessed the boarding of the *Adele* four years earlier, I feared another armed confrontation. But Devlin was smiling and relaxed as he went below.

I watched the sullen hunters, their weapons cradled in their arms, as they were rowed back to the schooner.

"Those fellers are good and mad," Norris said as he joined me. "We interrupted 'em having a very profitable day." Gesturing to encompass the scene around us, he added, "That's one of the largest herds I've ever seen in open water."

It was a thrill to see the swells aboil as thousands of mammals splashed and breached, instinctively hurrying to reach mating grounds on the Seal Islands.

I was puzzled when Devlin put Lieutenant Carter, his most junior officer, in charge of the boarding party. He said he wanted Norris to supervise on deck, while Heath, Dowie and I were to join him in the wardroom when the schooner captain arrived. I couldn't understand why on earth he wanted me involved.

In the wardroom, Devlin positioned the sealer, whose name was Dixon, across the table from him, offered coffee and introduced the rest of us. Dixon sat in silence. His eyes, under full black brows, flitted from face to face as he wrung his dirty hands as if he were trying to keep them warm.

"Mr. Dixon," Devlin said, sipping his coffee, "if you truthfully give me information I need, I'll consider going easy on you. Maybe even help salvage something of your season."

Now I was really flummoxed. I couldn't believe I had just heard Devlin offering leniency to a poacher.

Dixon looked surprised as well. He removed his cap and scratched his graying hair. "I'm just a simple sailor with one old ship," he said. "Owe people money, I do. Can't afford to lose a season of work."

"Then tell me where you got the money to make this voyage," Devlin said, slapping the table hard enough to make us all jump.

"Who's backing you?"

Dixon looked puzzled. Like most sealers and whalers, he said he had investors. He and his crew commanded definite shares of any profit, but the remainder was owed to people in San Francisco.

"Who are they? I want names, goddammit."

The sealer shrugged, shuffled through his papers and slowly read a list of his backers. That didn't satisfy Devlin. He leaned forward, riveting the man with a stern look.

"Are any of them agents doing the bidding of some company? Or for one of those new corporations we've been hearing about?"

Dixon shrugged, ran his hand over his bristled chin, and said they were just wealthy individuals, most of whom had backed him in earlier ventures.

Devlin sat back, and in a conversational tone asked, "Mr. Dixon, have you ever heard of some outfit called the Arctic Circle Corporation?"

I knew then what Devlin was up to as Heath came bolt upright at mention of Godfrey's firm. His eyes widened and his face went rigid as he stared at Devlin, who returned his gaze. It was an uncomfortable moment.

It was obvious to me that Devlin was intentionally provoking Heath, daring him to object, to be insubordinate. Heath, his arms folded across his chest, just glowered, saying not a word.

"Yeah, I've heard scuttlebutt about that crowd," Dixon said, relaxing somewhat. "Some say they price their coal to put other shippers out of business." He sat back, shrugged and sipped his coffee. "Others bitch and moan they're taking over the Bristol Bay fishery. But it's only gin-mill gossip, as far as I know."

Devlin nodded. He told Dixon the pelts he had harvested would be inventoried and seized, and he'd be assessed the minimum fine.

"You'll have to turn them into the warehouse at Dutch Harbor yourself," Devlin said, "but I'll check, you can be sure." He stretched his arms behind his head. "Then you can go hunting off northern Japan for all I care. Just stay the hell out of my territory."

The Captain showed the sealer to the door. "If I catch you here again, Dixon, I'll confiscate that wreck of yours. It'll take you years in court to get it back."

Heath, his face still contorted in anger, remained seated with his friend Dowie as I followed Devlin to the deck.

"Why must you always stir up trouble?" I said, making him turn to look at me. "You're provoking another fight with Godfrey. It could jeopardize everything."

Devlin looked me up and down with what bordered on disdain. "This place offers nothing but trouble, Knowles. I thought you'd be smart enough to understand that by now."

My face reddening, I shadowed him as he strode away. "You know Heath is related to Godfrey by marriage. You must realize that young man resents you, that he'll tell Godfrey about this."

Hands on his hips, Devlin turned and said, "I also know prevention is a helluva lot easier than cure. I'm warning that fancy-pants bandit to stay out of my way." Devlin took a step closer, and whispered, "He's not the first carpetbagger to come sniffing around here. Won't be the last, either."

"Things are changing, Captain. Here and in the whole country," I said, keeping my anger under a semblance of control. "Somehow, you'll have to learn to get along, to be more accommodating."

"What I've learned—and you apparently haven't, Knowles—is up here a man has to face down every challenge as it comes, and keep at it for as long as it takes." He put both hands on the rail, watching the sealer captain reboard his ship. "Do you think I don't know that feller we caught today is only one of dozens we didn't? That he'll be out here killing seals again next year?" He looked resigned as he took out a small cigar and lit it.

"Life here's like a Bering Sea storm, ya know? You have to climb that mountain of angry water ahead, take a steep plunge down, and rise up again, knowing you'll have to climb all the watery monsters coming at you for hours on end."

My bravado expended, I said nothing.

"The difference," he said as he walked toward the pilothouse, "is in a storm you eventually reach safe harbor. For me, there's no such thing. There ain't any for you either, Knowles, if you have the guts to stay and do something useful."

The sun was toying with the horizon the night we approached Siberia a week later. A sparkling necklace of sea ice, futilely resisting the coming of summer, was the only obstruction as we anchored. The ground at the landing location remained frozen. All hands, especially Jameson and his "sea ass" wranglers, felt that solid earth would make capture of the reindeer easier than last time.

Trading with the village headman went smoothly, the old man smiling when he saw the quantity and variety of trade goods. He and his two acolytes were dressed for summer in western shirts and trousers instead of reindeer skins. Especially taken by the large steel knives, the headman played with a red-handled one and tested its blade with his thumb throughout the talks.

I was surprised that Devlin asked me to join him in the trading circle of herders and crewmen on the forward deck. I couldn't understand much of what the elder said, but it became apparent Devlin insisted the Siberians corral, help put on hobbles and load the deer into our small boats. There was little argument when the Captain offered an additional half-pound of tobacco.

The entire operation was complete in four days, and we headed east with twenty frightened animals aboard. The doe-eyed, docile creatures found it difficult to keep footing in their slippery pens as the ship pitched and rolled. I laughed when I saw several sympathetic seamen trying in vain to calm the animals with offers of oats and soothing words, only to get a deluge of droppings—liquid and solid—as their reward.

I found Devlin in his cabin smoking his cigar and sipping a glass of whiskey when I went to see him.

"You and I should be pleased as all get out," he said, taking off his uniform jacket and motioning me to sit. "We may have started a whole new arctic industry this afternoon. Could feed thousands of people one day."

"It's a good beginning," I said. "But we still have to convince the Eskimos to become herders, have to keep government money coming."

He waved me off. "I know you don't approve of me, Knowles. Think I'm a stubborn old troublemaker." He put some pillows behind his back and flopped on his bunk.

I didn't disagree.

"I can't unlearn what years working with all kinds of rascals have taught me. You can't shake off your world of books and classrooms and religion. Just let's leave it at that."

I was wary of where this conversation was heading. "Captain, I want the reindeer experiment to succeed, but I don't want to be drawn into one of your schemes against Godfrey and his powerful friends."

"Godfrey's a symptom," he said taking another sip. "He's just the first boomer with real money to set his sights on Alaska. He'll bleed the place dry, and take all he can lay his hands on back to his potbellied banker friends in the East."

"How can you possibly know that?"

"Because I've seen it all before. In the South, in the Merchant

Marine and in California, too," he said sitting up and staring at me. "I couldn't do anything about it then, ya understand? But I can now, and I will." He poured several ounces from the Old Smuggler bottle into his glass. "Up here I can prove what I'm made of. Can do something to keep the thieving bastards halfway honest."

"Whatever made you so bitter, so suspicious of everybody?"

"My history is none of your concern, Knowles, or anybody else's. What's important is who I am now, and what I'm willing to do."

I sighed, and stared at the gently swinging ceiling oil lamp. I told him I also had suffered disappointments and betrayals. My unceremonious dismissal as pastor, the professional backbiting at the seminary that led me to resign, my lonely, undirected life that ended only when I came to Alaska and found Sarah.

"This region gives me the opportunity to show what I can do, too," I said, turning only to find him snoring quietly. He hadn't heard a word of what I said.

There were no Independence Day festivities to greet me as I came ashore in Nome along with the deer, school supplies and a consignment of lumber, tarpaper and tin roofing sheet. The full magnitude of the task ahead overwhelmed me as I watched Cuttermen unload the cargo on the gravel beach. In a matter of weeks I had to convince a trader at the Arctic Circle Corporation store to manage the herd, build a school and teacher's quarters, and entice parents to allow their children to take lessons.

To my great relief, Devlin granted use of the carpenter's mate and some men for a few days to get construction of the one-room schoolhouse started. Without them, I could not have coped with the incessant problems.

The site I had selected for the buildings was near a gently rising hill some distance from the shore. It proved to be too soggy to sustain a foundation. Even when we found a better location, swarms of mosquitoes and July heat made work difficult and slow.

For the next month, while the Captain was buying and transporting reindeer to other locations, I became desperately lonely for Sarah. I yearned for her gentle, loving embrace, for the way she kept my spirits from sinking. Her natural bonding with natives, especially with their children, would have been invaluable as I struggled to complete the building and enroll students.

Without her, I couldn't shake a feeling that I wasn't living up to my self-proclaimed pledge to construct and staff decent schools where they were needed.

I was constantly distracted. The local Eskimos resisted herding. The prevailing attitude held that it was unmanly to kill animals that weren't tracked and hunted. They reviled their herding Siberian cousins as "old women." In the end, the trader, who reluctantly agreed to help me, had to bribe some men with knives and axes to get them to even try to learn.

The lumber we brought was inadequate for the construction. One wall of the teacher's cabin had to be fabricated with odds and ends and driftwood, a highly valued commodity in country without trees.

Most depressing of all was the attitude of the new teacher recruited by my superiors in San Francisco.

The tall, slender, middle-aged fellow wearing a tweed suit arrived with three steamer trunks, a second-hand parka and a decidedly haughty manner. It was all I could do to get him to accompany me on visits with village leaders, who sensed his disdain at once. He didn't seem to care when they squatted staring at him without saying a word. He spoke in a soft voice, looking over their heads, and used multisyllabic words a college

184 | WILLIAM E. DUKE

student would find laughable. His demeanor didn't change even with my repeated urging, throwing into doubt any hopes I had for the school's immediate success. With all his credentials, I thought he belonged in some private city school, not in the isolation of frontier mud and ice. I shuddered to think how he would behave in the dark and cold of the Arctic winter.

When the *Walrus* returned in early August, I was anxious to part company with that obnoxious fellow. I couldn't have known that within weeks I would be forced to deal with really despicable men.

Chapter Seventeen

I t was at the northernmost American village of Barrow, with its chorus of howling sled dogs and lingering odors of thawing whale blubber, that Devlin's informants put him on the chase. The resident teacher and I were discussing plans for the school when Jameson barged through the two separated doors used for protection from winter cold, saying the *Walrus* had to leave within the hour.

"Sorry to interrupt, but you'd better get aboard, Doctor," he said. "The Captain's on a tear, and I don't know if we'll get back here at all this season."

I was annoyed, but reluctantly gathered my papers and reports and complied, being used to Devlin's "tears" by that time.

Without any explanation, Devlin headed north, rounded Point Barrow, and steamed out into the Beaufort Sea, north of Alaska. Even in mid-August, the ice sheet was only a mile or two offshore, and he had us crunching through its thin crust at three-quarter speed.

"You're always bitching about my methods, Knowles. That I don't treat people gently enough for your taste," Devlin said, when I asked where we were going in such a rush. He scanned the horizon with the long glass. "Well, if what I heard in Barrow is true, you're about to see why my way's the right way up here."

When darkness came, a lookout saw lights northeast of our position. Devlin reduced speed, and ordered our own running lights turned off.

"I wanna sneak up on that bastard before he can throw all his hooch overboard," he said with a wide grin. "You're about to get an education, Knowles. Just wait."

As the overcast sky brightened the next day, we were closing at the highest safe speed on a freighter, the sole identifiable object in the expanse of white. I noticed men scrambling on its deck. The ship had a mast configuration similar to the *Walrus*, with the addition of three large cargo booms. Norris was told to bring us directly alongside, since the ice-tamed sea was calm and there was an unusually gentle breeze.

Devlin had assembled an eight-man armed boarding party, and as we neared the vessel he ordered the skipper of the steamer—the *Narwhal* out of Seattle—to prepare for boarding. Lines were attached and, led by Carter, the Cuttermen climbed over the rails and onto its deck in minutes. Devlin went with them, motioning me to follow.

The freighter captain, his face flushed with anger, an artery in his neck throbbing, strode toward the invaders shouting, "You have no fucking right—"

"Stow your indignation," Devlin shouted back, glaring at him, "and have your men uncover the cargo hatch for inspection."

The tall civilian with his well-trimmed gray beard and brass-buttoned navy jacket looked like someone used to giving, not taking, orders. But he withered under Devlin's stare. Our Captain then ignored him and casually walked toward the knot of seamen surrounding their distinguished-looking skipper.

To me, the ragtag white members of the freighter's crew seemed to embody the menace and scowls of the Barbary Coast and Seattle's Skid Row.

"Do any of you bastards think I would've boarded this wreck with armed men if I didn't already know what I'd find?" Devlin asked. He took one of his small cigars out of his uniform pocket and lit it. "No? Well then, open that goddamn hatch, and we'll get down to business."

The freighter captain, who said his name was Gibbs, nodded grimly. Three of his men activated one of the booms, cleated a heavy line to a metal ring on the cover and hoisted it easily, unleashing an overwhelming sour smell of raw alcohol and soggy wood. It stung my nostrils and brought tears to my eyes. Devlin peered into the hold, and grinned.

"Looks like you tried to empty your hooch into the bilges, Mr. Gibbs. Pity we got here before you got the job done."

He sauntered toward the captain. "Looks to me like there are thirty or forty kegs down there. That'll cost you plenty in fines."

"It's not illegal to carry alcohol," Gibbs said, with what seemed little conviction.

"It is when it's unlicensed rotgut intended for the Eskimo trade," Devlin sneered.

Gibbs continued to protest, saying he intended to sell it to wintering whalers. Devlin ignored him and put Jameson in charge of getting the liquor barrels up on deck.

"Make sure you get an exact count, Boats," he said, "then smash 'em up real good and pour that poison into the scuppers."

I was astounded when the Captain addressed the two dozen or so *Narwhal* crewmen directly. About half were whites wearing a variety of ill-matched jackets and caps. Eskimos in woolen clothing and a smattering of Orientals made up the rest.

"You men are to stay on deck, understand?" Devlin told them with a grin. "Mister Gibbs and I are going to continue the sanitary inspection below."

His last statement elicited howls of protest from the *Narwhal* crew, especially the white men. "Stay the hell outta there!" "That's private, you goddamned copper!"

Gibbs joined in. "You found the liquor you wanted, dammit. Now fine us if you have to, and get the hell off my ship."

"My, my, my," Devlin said pursing his lips, "could it be there's something down there you don't want us to see?"

As we headed toward the companionway, one broad-shouldered *Narwhal* crewman moved to block us. The Captain pushed him aside, hissing, "If you want to impede a federal officer in his duty, you son of a bitch, I have a prison cage waiting for you in the States."

The man swore but moved aside, and we descended into the dim light, heading forward toward the crew's quarters.

There was a galley in one corner, partially partitioned off from a crew's mess room dominated by a stout oaken table at least eight feet long. In the far corner, two short, fat, giggling Eskimo women sat sprawled on the floor next to each other. Each wore head scarves tied under their chins, accenting their round facial features. One had on a faded western ladies' dress with a floral pattern more suited to the tropics than the Arctic. The other wore torn sealskins. They were obviously drunk, and had difficulty standing. They kept looking at Gibbs while the Captain tried to determine where they were from and what brought them here.

"It's not what you think," Gibbs said. "These women—"

Devlin, unable to get the women to say anything intelligible, had already walked away, heading for an opening at the far end of the room shielded only by a canvas sheet. Inside was a dark, dank corridor with bunks along the inner bulkhead. Three Eskimo women were huddled on one disheveled bunk, diligently chewing on sealskins.

"You see?" Gibbs said, joining us. "The women are just softening skins for clothing and will sew parkas and such." He gripped the back of Devlin's jacket to make him turn. "They'll be helpful to the whalers wintering up here, don't you know that?"

"You think I'm stupid, Gibbs?" Devlin bellowed, the sound ricocheting down the narrow corridor. "You don't have a haberdashery here, you have a floating brothel."

Gibbs tried to argue, but Devlin turned to the Cuttermen with us. "I want every female on this vessel taken topside with their belongings, right now."

As we retraced our steps, the two drunken women were swearing and spitting in protest as our men tried to force them to go on deck.

"Some won't want to leave," Devlin said to me in a low voice. "After centuries of wife-sharing up here, they think fornication with strangers is a routine housekeeping chore."

Devlin went on deck, and Harry, one of Jameson's men, joined me as I headed aft checking other cabins. In one dimly lit room reeking of alcohol, we found two women sleeping soundly. In the relative warmth of the cabin, one was naked from the waist up, her brown arm draped over her companion, who wore only a threadbare nightgown, her legs exposed.

Embarrassed and disgusted, I averted my eyes. But Harry had no such compunction. I asked him to get help, and bring these two to join the others topside.

Moving farther toward the stern, I entered a cabin twice as large and more elaborately decorated than the others. I lit a lamp on the desk, and as weak light crept into the crannies of the oak-paneled interior, a motionless figure materialized through the gloom. Moving closer, I saw a small young woman or girl sitting on a bed arranged against the rear bulkhead.

"What's your name?" No answer.

"I'm Doctor Knowles from the Revenue Cutter," I said softly.

"I mean you no harm." Still no response.

Unlike the other women on board, she was thin, and wore a fur hood that accented an angular face with delicate features. Even in the dull light, her skin looked a shade too pale and her nose a bit too narrow for an Eskimo. Her almond-shaped eyes betrayed one part of her ancestry, but their pale blue color signaled another.

I squatted to be level with her, and speaking slowly, asked how old she was. She shook her head slightly, but said nothing. I showed her all ten of my fingers. "This old?" I said, pointing at her. "Nah." I raised the ten again and then five. She reached out, and took two of my fingers and bent them down.

"Leave her alone, and get out of my cabin," Gibbs shouted as he strode toward us. "She's my, my... daughter."

He pushed me away from the bed as I was trying to rise, causing my right shoulder to careen into the bulkhead.

"If you have anything to do with selling this child, I hope Devlin throws you in jail for the rest of your squalid life," I sputtered, sickened by the thought of this girl being despoiled by some brutal whaler.

"Keep your mitts off her," he said, as I regained balance and took her hand to lead her out. "I told you, we're related."

He blocked the way toward the door. I lowered my aching shoulder and rammed into him, throwing him onto the bed. He was up and after us when Harry and one other Cutterman appeared and cut him off. Gibbs wrestled away from Harry, and was about to grab the girl when the other sailor knocked him to the floor with the butt of his rifle. I kept going, holding her hand, until we arrived at the base of the main companionway.

I looked into her eyes, pointing at her, then back toward Gibbs, and moved my arms as if I were rocking a baby. "Is that man your father, your daddy?" I asked. She shook her head from side to side. "Good," I said. She lowered her head and a tentative smile appeared.

The freighter's afterdeck was slick with stinking spilled raw whiskey and littered with broken barrel staves when I went to find Devlin. Carter, who had become adept at pidgin, was interviewing the noisily protesting women near the bow, with two Cuttermen helping him keep control.

"This youngster was hidden away in the captain's cabin," I said. "She indicated she's thirteen, but I think she's younger."

Devlin had been joking with Jameson while compiling a report on the uncovered whiskey. He turned to appraise her, and his smile morphed into a stern glare.

"Was she molested by that bastard?"

"Don't know, Captain. Gibbs says she's his daughter, but she denies it."

"Daughter, my arse," he said. "He traded hooch for her, and planned to pawn her off to a whaling ship for winter sport."

He squatted down, and asked her in pidgin where she came from, what happened to her mother. The Captain's disgust at Gibbs was evident in his manner, so I wasn't surprised she was frightened, and hesitant in answering. As I watched, I wanted desperately to let her know she was safe, that we would take care of her.

"From what I can gather," he said, "her mother is dead and the woman's husband didn't want her around because of her mixed blood. Gave her to Gibbs in Nome."

Gibbs rushed up, telling us to leave her alone, that he planned to adopt her as his own.

"If I find out this girl was molested on this ship, you'll go to jail for sure, Gibbs," Devlin said. "The fact she's aboard this whorehouse at all will cost you a pretty penny in fines, so forget about your adoption crap."

Devlin braced Gibbs, and told him what he had to do to keep from being locked in the *Walrus'* brig. "You'll turn your ship around and follow us," he said, jabbing his finger at the man. "We'll stop to put those women ashore where they came from, and then on to Nome."

"We can't do that," Gibbs said waving his arms. "Whalers wintering up here depend on us for supplies, for chrissakes. They'll starve to satisfy your high and mighty interference."

Devlin rubbed his chin and walked to the rail.

"All right, Gibbs, you'll get your first mate to supply the whalers, and pick you up at Nome later." He turned to face him. "You broke so many goddamned laws, I want to see if the new civil authorities there can sort 'em out and level punishment."

The Captain was in his element. "If they don't have the guts to make you pay dearly for this, you'll shiver in my brig until we get home. It'll take months."

"You don't have that authority," Gibbs shouted.

"Do you want to gamble on that?" Devlin shot back, as he turned to Jameson. "'Boats,' gather this man's belongings, escort him on board, and keep him in the wardroom until I get there."

"And by the way, Gibbs," Devlin added, "tell your men if the *Narwhal* doesn't appear at Nome within a month, I'll get the court to impound it and charge every man aboard with fornication."

Gibbs and the Eskimo women were ushered aboard the *Walrus*, but I kept the girl with me as I clambered over the rails. Devlin had given permission to settle her in the sick bay, adjacent to Donaldson's cabin, to provide some privacy and protection. Later that day, I arrived with a tray of hot tea, toasted bread and pudding of some sort, and noticed she wore long strands of colorful beads attached to braids of her hair on each side of her face. When I mentioned them, Donaldson said they were the kind that inland natives gave young girls before they reached puberty.

"I've just finished examining her," he said, "and she's in good general health." He began putting his instruments into the cabinet. "But I regret to tell you she's been penetrated, probably several times recently."

"God forgive me," I said trying to keep my voice under control, "I want to grab a scalpel, and cut out the groin of that child-molesting devil."

"Hold on there, my outraged professor," Donaldson said, packing his pipe. "It might not have been Gibbs. She's been shuttled around for some time, can't tell who done the deeds."

Things like this happen, I told myself, but my fury was unabated, realizing if I had married when the old pastor I had worked for wanted me to, this defenseless girl could have been my own daughter.

Ignoring my obvious fury, she was smiling as she nibbled the toast. Then she quickly snatched the stethoscope from the doctor's desk, put the hearing buds in her ears, and came with a laugh to listen to my heartbeat. Donaldson and I laughed as she mimicked his examination method, and I tapped my chest in rhythm with the beat, saying, "heart."

"Hoooart," she responded, and I roared in appreciation. Then I pointed to my eyes, ears, nose and mouth, identifying each as distinctly as possible. She made a valiant effort to repeat each word, giving me an idea.

I went to my now-depleted cache of school supplies, found three books that might be helpful, and presented them to her with a flourish. The words meant nothing to her, but every time she came across an illustration of children, she pointed and raised her eyebrows questioningly.

For the next three weeks, this doctor of theology spent every spare minute in the surgeon's office sounding out words of people and things depicted in a third-grade reader. I knew Sarah would have been better at it, more patient, and I longed for my wife, thinking constantly of the child we would soon have.

Neither Donaldson nor I could pronounce the girl's name, which sounded something like "Obeuka." The reader gave me the solution. One of the young women portrayed was called Mary, so I suggested we name our foundling "Mary." And since we rescued her on the Beaufort Sea, she became "Mary Beaufort" in the closed, little world of our ship.

The *Walrus* stopped at Barrow, and two of the Eskimo women were taken ashore. Three more were sent back to their villages in Kotzebue Bay, followed by two others when we arrived at Nome. Devlin spent his days there filing charges and providing testimony against Gibbs, while Carter and I tried to find information about Mary's family, or at least her village. Not one person knew anything about her, suggesting to us that she must have come from a village far into the interior.

I asked for permission to take Mary to the Dutch Harbor orphanage. It was granted the very day we received word an epidemic had swept through that community earlier that summer. Filled with anxiety for Sarah and the baby, I was thankful when Devlin agreed to leave immediately.

Two Revenue Cutters were in the inner harbor when we steamed past Missionary Rock at the entrance, and, much to my relief, epidemic signal flags were not flying. Before our anchor was down and set, Captain Benson and his surgeon came alongside, and I rushed to help the senior captain aboard, asking about Sarah. He patted my back, and looked grim.

"Your wife had a bad time of it," Benson said, "but I hear she's recovering."

MANY COLORS OF WHITE | 195

I was stunned. I always pictured the energetic, vibrant woman I found on St. Paul smiling confidently, defeating any obstacle.

Before I could respond, Lieutenant Gilbert, the surgeon assigned to Benson's ship, took me aside.

"That's not all, I'm afraid," he said. "She lost the baby. It was a girl."

I put my hands over my face to cover the tears, and leaned against the rail for support. I knew how devastated Sarah must have felt, how much she wanted the child.

"We don't know what caused this epidemic," Gilbert said, "but whatever it was, it attacked nerves and muscles." He put his arm on my shoulder. "Mrs. Knowles has not regained the use of her legs. I'm so sorry."

Guilt and grief overwhelmed me as I stumbled to get away from him, to banish his news. Almost immediately I felt small arms encircle my waist, and a powerful arm hug my shoulder. I tousled Mary's hair and took Donaldson's hand, only half hearing Benson say that the epidemic had lasted two months, and that eleven had died, four of them children at the orphanage.

The *Walrus'* launch headed directly toward the orphanage on a knoll above the gravel beach more than a mile from the pier. The clapboard building seemed to grow larger as we approached. So did my fears, my uncertainty. How would Sarah greet me? Would she hate me for leaving her to face the greatest traumas of her young life alone? Would I be man enough to cope with her grief, with her condition?

"She's still weak, poor dear," Martha Potter, the parson's wife, said as I stepped ashore. "We've made her comfortable, but she hasn't gotten over the loss of the child."

I bent down and hugged the thin, gray-haired woman, thanking her for all she had done to help Sarah even while she mourned the loss of her own charges. I introduced Donaldson, and presented

Mary, asking if the girl could live at the orphanage until her situation was clarified. Mrs. Potter agreed without hesitation.

As the four of us walked toward Sarah's room, I pleaded to be allowed a few minutes alone with my wife. I hesitated outside Sarah's door trying to compose myself, as I had that night on St. Paul. This time, it wasn't passion that detained me, but foreboding. Was this God's punishment for my lack of faith, I wondered? Certainly, this would not be an occasion for cheers of joy.

The rays of the setting sun filtering into the room through a glass vase on the windowsill splintered into multiple colors, and undulated over the figure sitting up in bed. When she saw me, she wailed through tears, "Oh Stanton, I lost our little girl. Forgive me!"

I ran to her, and cautiously took her into my arms, not sure if she would feel pain.

"Forgive me for not being here," I said, kissing her repeatedly. "Don't say you lost the child, my love. It was the sickness."

"But now, I can't walk or even stand," she said, as she started to sob. "What will we do? Where can we go?"

I brushed back the hair falling over her face and the rivulets of tears from her cheek. "We're together now, and like always, we'll find our way, don't you worry."

"But I'm a cripple, don't you see? I'll be a terrible burden to you. Don't even know if I'll be able to do my wifely duties."

"Sarah Knowles, I love you, and as long as you love me, we'll be fine."

There was a knock on the door, and Donaldson poked his head in, asking if it was all right to visit. He entered with Mrs. Potter, and said he'd like to examine Sarah, to be sure earlier assessments of her condition were accurate.

As I waited in the hall, my fears returned. I had just told my devastated, grieving wife that everything would be fine. I had no idea how, or if, I could make that claim come true.

Donaldson agreed with Gilbert's diagnosis, and visited daily. He made height adjustments on the crutches and leg brace she had been given, and showed me the correct way to help Sarah into a chair. Many other *Walrus* officers came to pay respects, but nothing seemed to cheer her. Not even Jameson, who arrived all smiles and pleasantly teased about her husband's peculiarities, could raise her spirits. That wonderful little man presented her with a gift of scrimshaw on a walrus tusk. It depicted an Eskimo ready to strike with a harpoon with a silhouette of our ship in the background. I knew what such a piece would be worth to him in San Francisco trade, and was overwhelmed by his generosity, his friendship.

Devlin arrived alone on the day the passenger steamer we were to take home entered the harbor. He handed me a letter he had written to Amy, asking her to house us and help us in any way possible when we got back to San Francisco. I was even more taken aback and surprised when he offered me a loan of several thousand dollars. "Just to help you both get settled," he said. Given our situation, I had to accept.

Donaldson, the good friend that he was, provided the most help. He had heard of specialists in the kind of paralysis Sarah seemed to have, and wrote to ask them, as a personal favor, to make arrangements for her treatments.

When the time came for us to leave the island, Cuttermen helped carry Sarah to the launch on a litter fabricated by Jameson and his men. As the procession passed in front of the orphanage, all the attendants and children were lined up to say goodbye to their teacher.

"Get well soon, Missus Knowles," they intoned. Sarah waved to them with tears in her eyes. Just then, to my astonishment, Mary Beaufort barged through the ranks, ran to me and hugged me fiercely. I kissed the top of the child's head. Seeing this, Sarah opened her arms and motioned Mary to come to her. She embraced the youngster, then held her at arms' length.

Without a word, Sarah removed the shell-and-bead necklace the Aleut children had made for her, and draped it around Mary's neck.

"Use this to remember us," she said, placing her hand on Mary's cheek. "And keep it until we return some day, all right?"

My heart gladdened as Sarah's transcendent smile returned for the first time since I returned.

That ended my last voyage with Devlin, Jake. In the nearly five years since, I've come to believe that despite the drinking, the violence, and his stubborn refusal to compromise, he's a man with the flaming drive needed to help Alaska and its people. I hope my recollections help you see why his trial is more than "a squabble among officers," as you put it.

Unfortunately, I can't give you a personal perspective on the specific charges against Devlin. Except for the cannery riot, I wasn't a witness. You'll just have to see for yourself what develops when the Board of Inquiry resumes Monday. Maybe, we'll both learn what drives that complicated man.

PART THREE

Sykes Takes A Stand

Chapter Eighteen

The throbbing at my temples and lingering nausea were almost gone when I neared the top of Nob Hill. As I rested to get breath and bearings, sweat rolled down my back and wilted my collar.

What in the hell are you doing up here, Jake Sykes? I thought. Why not just cover the dreary trial and ignore Knowles' interminable stories and suspicions? I like my villains black and my heroes pure, but this Devlin is too much of a puzzle. Are a front-page piece and a pitiful bonus good enough to forego the convivial joys of the gin mills for this blather?

I trudged on and found the house, a two-story, brick structure surrounded by a fieldstone wall at least three city lots wide. It seemed a socially suitable nest for a banker's wife, for the president and loudest howler of the Women's Temperance Crusade.

A plump Mexican maid in black uniform and white apron told me curtly to wait outside among the flowering bougainvilleas. She would see if Mrs. Arthur A. (Lucy) Pitcher was "at home" to me. Shortly, I was escorted into a parlor with lace doilies on every conceivable surface. Closed drapes gave the room a funereal look.

My card in her hand, Mrs. Pitcher waddled in. "It's highly unusual for people I don't know to call on Sunday afternoons," she said, frowning.

I apologized, explaining that I needed accurate information about her organization before the trial resumed the next day.

She might have been deemed pretty if she didn't present herself with such damned arrogance. As it was, her oval face and pug nose were eclipsed in layers of flesh and satisfaction.

She didn't offer me a seat. "I have heard horrible things about your newspaper, Mr. Sykes," she said, looking at my wilted collar and scuffed shoes. "I agreed to meet you only because the Devlin trial is so important to our cause."

Trying hard to remain polite, I swallowed the urge to tell her to go straight to Biddy hell. I'd get even with her soon enough in the pages of the *World*.

I told her I'd observed her associates picketing at the Customs House, and wanted to know their interest in this particular case.

"We don't picket! We inform!" she said as she took a seat on the last forward inches of a velvet-cushioned chair. "Drunkenness is the curse of our nation."

"I truly understand," I responded with all the conviction of a hell-fire preacher. "But why get involved in such an obscure military squabble?"

"It's not obscure." She stood to face me. "You're here interviewing me, aren't you? You witnessed our outrage over that devil's drunken barbarity." She paced and flailed her arms, unleashing a cloying scent of lilac. "We're getting national attention to the evils of liquor."

With the hangover roiling my insides, I almost agreed with her, but just nodded knowingly, and told her the cause certainly was deserving. With my most sincere smile, I asked how she had come to learn about Devlin and the charges against him.

"We have friends in high places and low. Good Christian men."

"When did Governor Godfrey speak to you about it?" I said softly, taking a gamble since I had never spoken with the man. "He told me he had a particular interest in the charges."

She stopped pacing and came toward me. "We are fortunate to have Governor Godfrey and his nephew among our supporters. Being the fine gentlemen they are, they told us the entire disgusting history of that inebriate Devlin, and what he does to hapless workers."

I tried to be convincingly sympathetic. "That must have been very disturbing for you and your ladies to hear."

"We didn't know what to do about those tawdry stories," she said, her hand on her ample bosom. "Then Lieutenant Heath gallantly told us some of his fellow officers were preparing charges against that man, and offered to help us make our case." She favored me with a pleasant smile. "They even convinced that new sailors' union to join the cause."

"That's a strange alliance, isn't it?" I said. "I've heard sailors are known to like their grog."

"We need all the allies we can get to make an example of Devlin. His actions prove what depths of depravity liquor can cause."

"The arrangements you've made are very impressive," I said, trying to look supportive. "Will you be testifying at the trial?"

"Certainly not! It's not proper for ladies to be on public display in places like that." She lifted her nose as if smelling a vile odor. "Besides, I made our position very clear in letters to Washington last November."

I commended her on her timely reaction to events she only heard about in September, and asked for the names of officials she had contacted. Before she could respond, a chubby boy of four or five wearing a white sailor suit with blue piping came shuffling into the room.

"Aren't you going to read to me, grandmother?" he said pleadingly.

Her face was transformed by a wide smile as she placed her hands on the young feller's shoulders, saying, "Where are your manners, Toby? Say hello to the gentleman." He mumbled something. I bent to shake his tiny hand, and Mrs. Pitcher said, "Now run along to the sun porch and get your book. I'll be there in a minute or two."

She went to the door saying, "As you can see, Mr. Sykes, I have a very important task to perform. As to your question, let's just say they were prominent government figures recommended by Governor Godfrey and by my husband. Mr. Pitcher's very well connected, you know."

I said I was aware of Mr. Pitcher's position in financial circles, but pressed for the names. She just shook her head.

"We're extremely pleased that some people in government have finally agreed to make that uncouth Devlin pay for his drunkenness."

"One last question, Mrs. Pitcher, if I may?" I said as she directed me into the tiled entrance hall. "Did Governor Godfrey provide funds for your placards and printed materials?"

She held open the oaken front door, and said in a teasing voice, "That's something you'll have to ask him."

Out on the sunny street, I admired the view of the bay and Alcatraz Island for a moment before heading downhill in search of that "fine Christian gentleman."

Godfrey was not at his lodgings on Sutter Street or at his office. Since I was awake and relatively sober, and the day was still young, I decided to ferret out Charlie Lumsden, head of the seamen's union.

He didn't fit my notion of what a tough organizer should look like when I found him holding forth with three of his big, beefy cronies in the ground-floor saloon under Sailor's Hall. His foot on the brass rail of a copper-covered bar, he was shorter and thinner than his colleagues, and wore a gray Sunday-go-to-meeting suit.

"I wondered when ya'd get around to see me and my boys," he said eyeing me as I approached. "Already jawed with those *Examiner* and the *Sun* fellas. Now, what can I do for the Noooyork *World?*"

"The question is what the *New York World* can do for you," I said picking up a handful of unshelled peanuts from the bar.

Claiming I desperately needed a quick one, I bought a round of drinks for the four of them. Sailors being sailors, they ordered whiskey. I stuck with dark ale to settle my stomach. Raising my mug to them, I casually mentioned I had covered the Pullman Strike. I had their complete attention for almost an hour recounting the riots and beatings. Two of the men, arms around each other's shoulders, began an out-of-tune chorus of a weepy union ballad.

To squash the singing as much as anything else, I said, "One of the greatest afternoons of my life was when I interviewed Eugene Debs himself, and some of the other strike leaders after the bastards dragged them off to jail." I embellished a bit, but I made those blokes my friends for life.

Lumsden agreed to speak with me privately, and we walked through the sawdust smelling of stale beer to a wobbly table that hadn't been wiped in days. I noticed he walked with a limp.

"Charlie," I said in a conspiratorial tone, "I've heard all the usual palaver about this case, but I need your god-honest appraisal of what's really going on. One working man to another, all right?"

He laughed, but didn't say no. I shouted to the bartender for drinks for the two of us.

"Why is this set-to among the brass buttons important enough to put you in league with battleaxes who'd padlock all the bars in North Beach, for chrissakes?"

"It has nothing to do with those hi-falutin' busybodies," he said straightening out his lame left leg. "It's about building this fucking union. We're fightin' the big boys to give working salts decent money, and a little respect."

I nodded my best union solidarity nod. "I know how rotten sailors are treated, Charlie," I said, patting his arm, "but why put your effort on this case? Do you have it in for this Captain Devlin?"

"Nah. Some of my lads think he walks on water, came up through the ranks, and all that shit," he said blowing through his lips in disbelief. "He's going to get us attention, is all." He turned to look hard at me. "You can, too, Jake, in that scandal sheet of yours."

I promised to write a piece on the union's grievances just as the drinks arrived in the shaky hands of an old waiter, wearing an apron emblazoned with all the brown and charcoal stains of a bar rag.

"So why get involved, Charlie?" I asked. "Was it that punishment crap they call 'tricing up'?"

"Hell no," he said, "captains do a lot worse things to ya than that. I got plenty of stories to tell ya on that score." He sat back and took a sip of his Scotch. "Besides, everybody around here knows that bastard Swenson who's supposed to testify against Devlin tomorrow is one vicious son of a bitch."

I pressed him to tell me how he heard of the torture charges against Devlin.

He stared into the corner of he room for a long time, then smirked and said, "Guess it's all right to tell ya, since you're such a union lover, and all. It was one of his own officers that done it. Some fancy-dancy lieutenant told us the whole thing. Gave us a few dollars for signs and shit and asked us to hold a protest meeting upstairs."

"Was his name, Heath, by any chance?"

"That's the feller. And a smooth-talking gent, he was. Said we had to keep it all quiet."

"Did he say where the money would come from?"

"He didn't." Lumsden smiled and drained his glass.

"But you know, don't you, Charlie?"

He shrugged, waved a goodbye to the idle bartender. I didn't want him to leave yet.

"Come on," I said. "You can tell me."

He chuckled. "Sure, I suppose you're the most closemouthed fella in San Francisco right now, eh?" He studied his empty glass, and said. "I'll tell ya what everybody on the waterfront knows and no more."

Checking to see that his mates were still hanging on the bar, he whispered, "The Arctic Circle bunch, that's where the money comes from. But ya didn't hear that from me, right?"

"Jesus, Charlie, what in hell did they have to offer you?" I said, amazed at his willingness to go even that far. "Did they tell you they'd recognize your union or something?"

His laugh echoed in the nearly empty room. He shook his head and said, "Whatta ya drunk, Jake? They're as crooked as all the other high-hat bastards." He put his face close to mine. "Arctic Circle didn't promise us shit. But they're putting a lot of money into the Alaska trade, and everybody knows Devlin did somethin' to deep-six their fur-seal contract."

He sat back and chuckled. "They're just gettin' even with the sawed-off Irishman, is all. But we'll get the bastards eventually. They'll owe us after this Devlin business."

He stood, favoring his bum leg. "I wanna see that story on my union in print, Jake. Don't forget." He winked and slapped my back hard. "I better get home now or maybe that old lady of mine will trice *me* up, whaddaya think?

So, all the sign-waving and shouting gets back to Godfrey and his errand boy, Heath, I thought as Lumsden left by the back door. One way or t'other, I'm going to have to corner one of 'em.

Chapter Nineteen

WESTERN UNION NIGHT WIRE:
TO EDITOR, NY WORLD

TORTURE SKETCHES IN MAIL STOP SAVE SPACE
FOR SUNDAY PROFILE STOP HERE'S TODAY'S PIECE
STOP MORE TO COME STOP SYKES

San Francisco, January 23—A nautical Board of Inquiry witnessed a shocking demonstration of cruelty to sailors today, the first day of testimony in the trial of Captain Edward Devlin of the US Revenue Cutter Walrus on charges of inflicting cruel punishment, dereliction of duty and drunkenness.

Seaman George Swenson graphically illustrated how Devlin four years ago caused extreme pain and injury to two other sailors and himself with a punishment called "tricing up." Gasps of horror were heard in the chamber when, with the prosecutor's help, Swenson had his hands manacled behind his back. He showed what happened to his arms and shoulders as a rope was passed through the manacles and he was hoisted aloft until his toes barely touched the deck. He testified he had been a crewman on the whaling bark Hannah, anchored off Port Clarence, Alaska, when Devlin put him through this procedure twice for minor offenses. He claimed he was left hanging for about ten minutes each time.

Testimony by the first mate of the Hannah and Revenue Cutter officers indicated Devlin was called to the whaler after Swenson and his companions threatened to "cut the throat" of their captain. They

208

also stole and hid a rifle from their captain's cabin, the witnesses
said. Swenson denied the allegations, claiming Devlin was under
the influence of alcohol during the episode. The other two victims of
the punishment did not testify.

Lieutenant Jeffrey Wilson, the prosecutor, presented affidavits
stating that the U.S. Navy considers tricing up as cruel and has
outlawed its use. Devlin's attorney submitted documents from some
twenty seamen who witnessed the punishment asserting that Devlin
was sober on the day in question.

The Board dismissed a second cruelty charge against Devlin based
on an incident at a Bristol Bay cannery in 1888, ruling the statute
of limitations had run out. In that case, the Revenue Cutter captain
allegedly used an axe handle to savagely batter an Arctic Circle
Corporation foreman who was resisting arrest for beating a Negro
cook and a Chinese laborer.

The trial has sparked fierce animosity between factions in this port
city as hundreds of demonstrators block entrance to the Customs
House daily. Members of the Women's Temperance Crusade and
seamen's union protest Devlin's actions, while whalers and ordi-
nary seamen hail him as the life-saving hero of sailors stranded in
the arctic ice. San Francisco policemen were called in to keep the
unruly mob from entering the chamber being used as a courtroom.

Called to the stand, Devlin defended his actions.

MORE TO COME

My editor insisted I file short articles, so my readers were deprived
of my incisive accounts of the more colorful antics in an otherwise tedious day of testimony. For instance, I was flabbergasted
by Devlin's relaxed, even meek, demeanor when he first took the
stand. Sitting comfortably in his full dress uniform, complete with

comic-opera sword, he wasn't the "Roarin' Ed Devlin" of Knowles' tales. You'd never believe the old bastard was being accused of cruelty, so matter-of-factly did he relate his story in a soft, even voice. He readily admitted he had ordered Swenson and his mates triced up, saying they'd been mutinous for days before he had been called to intervene. He claimed it was his duty as a lawman. "It's not a customary punishment," he said, "except in frontier areas."

Lulled, as I was, by Devlin's tameness, the inexperienced prosecutor misjudged him.

"If you're so keen on law and order, Captain," he said striding toward the witness, "why did you torture these men?"

"I torture no man, sir!" Devlin shouted, jumping to his feet, sending the witness chair crashing noisily behind him.

The clattering chair and the shout shocked every one in the room, including me. Wilson staggered back as if punched. Devlin remained standing, and pointed at the prosecutor.

"I taught a lesson to three mutinous bastards who refused to work. Threatened to kill their skipper, they did."

Cheers and stomping of feet arising from the cluster of whalers sitting behind the press section, echoed in the chamber. Most of the Temperance brigade covered their mouths, horrified, I suppose, by the language. Personally, I was happy to have some dramatic tidbit to add interest to these drab proceedings.

Captain Johanson, his eyes wide and his face reddening, repeatedly pounded the gavel for silence. He ordered Devlin to pick up his chair and sit down.

Wilson, his face still flushed, regained a modicum of composure. He approached Devlin warily. "Why didn't you arrest those men, turn them over to civil authorities?"

Devlin smirked. "If such a crime happened in San Francisco, Lieutenant, you'd arrest 'em and turn 'em over," he said leaning forward and speaking as if to a child. "The nearest marshal to Port Clarence was at least two thousand sea miles away on the south side of the Aleutians."

Johanson couldn't contain himself. He took off his glasses, leaned across the judge's table, and interjected. "You could have put them in irons and transported them on your vessel, couldn't you?"

Devlin turned to face the presiding officer. "Yes, sir. But the *Walrus was* the only cutter assigned to far north patrol. We would've been off station for months. Who knows what skullduggery would have happened while we were gone."

He faced front, crossed his legs and looked toward the group of whaler captains. "Almost as important, the *Hannah* was shorthanded. Couldn't continue its cruise without those men. Wouldn't have been able to make a living for her officers and crew."

"What you're saying, Captain," Wilson said, "is that you take it on yourself to act as judge and jury in such cases. Is that right?"

"What I believe, sir," Devlin said, shifting in the chair to lecture the younger man, "is that Congress empowered us to suppress mutinies. I triced up those ruffians as a last resort. It was justified by conditions at the time."

Wilson went to confer with his civilian advisor at the prosecutor's table. "Captain Devlin," he said, turning toward the witness, "please explain to the Board how you can claim your use of this gruesome punishment was a 'last resort,' that it was 'justified'."

Devlin pulled over his knees the sword and scabbard that had been distracting him. He said he told his men to "frighten those three toughs, but not injure them," and had given them opportunities to foreswear violence, return the stolen rifle and go back to work. His efforts were rewarded with foul-mouthed refusals, and curses directed at him personally and at all officers and men of the Cutter Service.

"Swenson was smirking, and swore at the top of his voice," Devlin said, pointing to the sailor. "He said something like 'I won't take orders from any half-pint Irish revenuer.'"

"Only then did I order punishment," he said, showing the palms of his hands. "Two of those mutineers agreed to behave at once. It took two hoists to make Swenson see the light." Devlin allowed himself the trace of a smile on his swarthy face.

"As to justification, that's easy to explain. It worked. The master and mate of the *Hannah* didn't have their throats cut, and the ship sailed north with a manageable crew. Had a very good season, I'm told."

Devlin seemed anxious to step down, but his attorney stopped him, saying he had questions of his own.

"Tell us, Captain," McGowan said, in a voice like slowly rolling thunder, "did you drink any alcoholic beverages the day of this incident?"

"I do not drink on duty," Devlin replied.

"I assumed as much, Captain," he said as he put his foot on the witness riser as if he were having a friendly chat. "But please think back and tell the Board whether or not you imbibed any whiskey whatsoever on this specific day."

Devlin, sighing as if exasperated, said he had not.

McGowan nodded, causing a portion of his long gray hair to fall over one eye. "Now, sir, are you aware of any Revenue Cutter Service regulation that forbids tricing up as a punishment for serious offenses?"

"There is no such regulation," Devlin said, looking directly at Johanson, then at members of the panel one by one. He smiled at his small victory, and returned to the defense table.

Johanson huddled with his panel, then called it a day. He added that verdicts on all charges against Devlin would be announced separately at completion of the full hearing. What a disappointment! I had hoped for an immediate decision on this nonsense to give me something solid for an overnight story.

I struggled to elbow my way through the dispersing crowd amid screeching of chair legs and the kind of loud, nervous chatter kids used when released from school.

My target was Godfrey, who had been observing from the aisle farthest from me. He certainly had a right to be angry over dismissal of charges involving the Arctic Circle cannery incident: charges he and Heath helped raise. I wanted his reaction, but before I could get to him he dodged me, his small frame lost among the retreating ranks of the anti-liquor ladies. I was getting really annoyed by that prissy son of a bitch.

Knowles stood in the very last row under a dusty portrait of Lincoln. I guessed he was waiting until exits cleared so he could maneuver his wife's wheelchair into the hall. I was anxious to meet that woman, wanting to see if reality could possibly match Knowles' obnoxious recounting of her virtues during our long night of talk.

I introduced myself to the lady so politely it would have made my stuffy Aunt Minnie proud. Then I asked Knowles his opinion of the day's proceedings.

"It went all right, I guess," he said, removing his spectacles and rubbing his eyes. "I wish Devlin would learn to be a little less combative."

Sarah agreed with her husband. She gave me a wide, warm smile that transfigured her lean face. "I could see by their expressions the Board members despised that Swenson fellow," she said. "But they seemed disturbed when the Captain made every effort to get the whalers on his side."

"Sarah's right," Knowles said, "and remember, the same Board members have to render judgment on the more serious charges against Devlin in the days to come." He came forward into my row, pointing at my note pad. "You got your sensational fodder today, Sykes, but dereliction of duty and drunkenness can end the Captain's career."

I pulled up a chair to be at the same level as Sarah, taken by the liveliness, the humorous glint in her large dark eyes. Her legs hung lifeless on the chair ledge, but her smile, expressive use of hands and vibrant manner made me forget her condition. Her plain, light gray dress contrasted with her dark-brown hair, pulled back into an intricate braid. A large pad of sketching paper and a packet of pencils lay on her lap. She said she had been scribbling during the proceedings.

"This ain't scribbling," I said when I examined her detailed pencil drawings of Devlin, Johanson and Swenson's demonstration. "These are very good, good enough to send to my editor. Would you mind? Might be worth a dollar or two."

She laughed. "It would be fun to see these in print, wouldn't it, dear?" she said taking Knowles' hand.

I marveled at how accurately she had captured Swenson's distinctive mug. One corner of his upper lip had been cut away, exposing a cluster of brownish teeth. It seemed to freeze his countenance into a perpetual sneer.

She dismissed my praise for the Swenson rendering. "I've been haunted by that look for years, Mr. Sykes," she said with a frown. She struggled to put her lifeless legs on the floor so she could lean forward. "I'm certain he was one of the liquor traders who accosted me when I was teaching on St. Paul's."

Chapter Twenty

WESTERN UNION 8 PM, SEPT. 24—
TO EDITOR NY WORLD

DAMAGING TESTIMONY OF NEAR SHIPWRECK STOP NOT FRONT PAGE WORTHY STOP BETTER STUFF COMING STOP SYKES

San Francisco, Jan. 24—Damaging testimony alleging a drunken captain endangered his ship in Aleutian Islands fog and mist was chillingly related today by one of his officers. Appearing at the trial of Captain Edward Devlin, US Revenue Cutter Service, Second Lieutenant Richard Dowie claimed that had not the vessel's first officer assumed command in time, the ship would have wrecked and its crew thrown into icy waters.

Captain Devlin denied the allegations, and claimed they were made by several junior officers conspiring against him.

Lieutenant Dowie said the USRC Walrus was sailing in heavy fog the night of June 6 last when he spotted the treacherous rocks of one of the Shumagin Islands emerging from the gloom ahead. Captain Devlin, who appeared to be inebriated, ignored warnings of potential disaster, and retired to his cabin, Dowie added.

First Lieutenant Luther Norris, the first officer, testified he was unable to rouse the captain to obtain orders, and took it upon himself to change course to avoid the rocks. Under heavy prodding by the prosecutor, he refused to say Devlin was intoxicated, claiming the Captain had been on deck constantly for several days and needed sleep. Lt. Norris admitted, however, that with the help of the ship's surgeon he found and removed from the Captain's cabin an unopened case of Scotch whisky.

Several junior officers also told the tribunal that Devlin was under the influence of alcohol last September while making courtesy calls on a visiting British warship and other vessels in Dutch Harbor. They said on that occasion Devlin insulted several younger officers, was disoriented and abusive while at a reception on the warship, and fell off a pier into the harbor the following day.

Devlin, hailed for decades by many in this city as an arctic hero, faces dismissal from the Service if convicted on charges of endangering his ship. He is also charged with counts of inflicting unusual punishment on three whaling ship crewmembers, and conduct unbecoming an officer.

Following today's session, Mrs. Arthur Pitcher, president of the Women's Temperance Crusade, said testimony supported her group's demand for legislation outlawing liquor aboard all government ships. A Devlin supporter, who declined to be publicly identified, stated the captain's future seemed bleak, judging by today's testimony.

I'd have preferred to find more pleasant diversions among the Barbary Coast's whorehouses than listening to daylong spinning of conflicting, tawdry tales to sink an old salt's reputation. But something about this case intrigued me even if it lacked the allure of an axe-murder trial. So I suffered through dreary recitations in that stuffy hearing room, and paid close attention. I'm damned glad I did.

The four spit-and-shine junior officers gave the same precise accounts of Devlin's drunken behavior. Difficult to believe, I thought, when the events occurred at different times and places.

Then a parade of enlisted men and warrant officers, some who had sailed with Devlin for a decade or more, swore they had never seen him drunk on duty. Ever. Their unlikely stories varied, but Wilson couldn't get even one to change his testimony. He subjected them to hours of hostile, repetitive questions, accompanied by theatrical eye-rolling, shrugs and sighs of disbelief.

Dowie, ramrod straight, and with a commanding voice to match, described the business at the Shumagins as if he were reciting from the Bible. There was no rustling in the room as he spoke. The officers on the Board stopped squirming in their hard wooden chairs. Not one of those whiskered worthies asked a single question.

Defense attorney McGowan, who often seemed to be nodding off, surprised me and everybody else. He rose for a bit of cross-examination. In his unhurried, avuncular manner, he asked Dowie, "You had guidance from other officers in preparing your very precise testimony, did you?"

Dowie blushed, ran his hand through his blond, well-trimmed hair. "I resent your insinuation, sir," he said, "and I object to your question."

Devlin, his arms folded, glowered at the witness.

"It's not for you to object," McGowan said, picking up a yellow pad from the defense table. "Is it not true that you, and several of the officers we heard from today, agreed more than two years ago to monitor and record in a book your Captain's every decision, his every action?"

The spectators whispered as McGowan, pulling the wattle under his chin, cautioned the lieutenant to remember that he was under oath. I saw Godfrey and Heath lean toward each other in conversation. Sarah, in the back of the room, appeared to be sketching. I hoped she was getting a good likeness of pretty-boy Dowie.

"We only agreed to watch the Captain, that's all," Dowie said, looking toward his colleagues in the front rows for support.

"Only agreed to watch, is that it?" McGowan seemed to be conjugating the statement is his mind. "Well then, Lieutenant, what, precisely, was your collective objective in doing all that watching and writing, eh?"

Dowie's voice grew louder as his face reddened. "It was for the good of the Service and our ship."

Wilson objected, but McGowan, saying he was almost done, was granted permission to continue.

He removed his spectacles and shuffled toward the witness. "For the good of the Service; do I have that right?" Without waiting for a response, McGowan asked, "Please tell us, Lieutenant, who organized this little group of Service protectors? Was it Lieutenant Heath? It didn't spring spontaneously out of the Bering Sea foam, did it?"

Wilson was on his feet. "The witness is being badgered," he said. "These questions are irrelevant."

I noticed that Heath had his hand shielding his mouth, and had turned in his chair to whisper to Godfrey, who stared ahead, showing no emotion.

Johanson hesitated, smoothed his mustache, and then agreed with Wilson. McGowan took exception to the ruling, bowed his leonine head, smiled benignly and sat down.

Devlin grinned and nodded at his attorney, who within seconds had his palms clasped under his double chins as if he were communing with the Deity.

That smile won't last long, I thought, as the old sailor was called to answer the prosecutor's questions.

"Do you deny your ship was in danger, given conditions on the night in question?"

"I certainly do, sir." Devlin stared hard at Wilson. "I know those waters like I know San Francisco Bay. We were in heavy fog, steaming slow ahead under bare poles, and there's not a rock or shoal around."

"How do you know there wasn't danger? You weren't on deck, were you?"

"I surveyed the situation before I went below. Remember, I've sailed that patch of water hundreds of times over the past twenty-five years."

"Why, then, wouldn't you rouse yourself to give orders when your officers expected trouble?"

"I'd been on deck continually for days after we left Sitka, and I was exhausted." Devlin turned to address the Board members. "Unfortunately, I didn't hear the call. Probably it was the whiskey and quinine the doctor gave me when I came down with a bad case of la grippe."

Wilson pounced. "So you were drinking whiskey, were you?"

"A dram or two for medicinal purposes, is all," Devlin said.

"A dram or two, eh? Then how do you account for the fact that several of your officers swore here today that the ship was in danger of going aground and you did not respond?"

"I've learned some officers have been in cahoots for a long time, trying to paint my actions in the worst possible light. They're the ones making these accusations."

"Is it your testimony, then, that you were not under the influence of alcohol, that you were fully cognizant that night?"

"It is. I was simply exhausted and ailing."

As Senior Captain of the Bering Sea Patrol, E.M. Benson should have been the most compelling witness for the prosecution. The officers of the Board certainly knew well his reputation for decades of service in that godawful assignment. A tall, trim man with a weathered face and graying walrus mustache, he carried the aura of hard experience in the north as he walked with a sailor's swaying stride to the witness chair.

"If what the junior officers said today is true," he said matter-of-factly, "it would constitute a serious breach of conduct on Captain Devlin's part."

"Are you qualifying your assertion, Captain?" Wilson asked, clearly taken aback. "Don't you believe the younger officers' testimony?"

"In general, yes," he said without changing expression. "But the explanations of Captain Devlin and Lieutenant Norris—that the Captain was exhausted and needed rest—must be taken into consideration."

That wasn't something Wilson wanted to hear, and as he went to consult with his advisor, Benson just kept speaking. "I, too, have been made aware recently of an unusual degree of antagonism against Captain Devlin by some of his officers."

Wilson whirled around. "Why is that so?"

"Devlin is demanding on junior officers," Benson said, looking toward the Captain. "He expects them to work as hard as he does, which is very hard indeed. Refuses to promote people who don't measure up to his standards."

The prosecutor shook his head. "Be that as it may, sir, is it your testimony that the young officers lied to this Board?"

"No, that's not what I'm saying." Benson leaned forward and stared at the prosecutor. "I'm trying to make it clear that commanding a vessel in those devilish fogs day in and day out without navigation aids can exhaust any man. That such duty could explain the Captain's conduct."

"We've heard testimony Captain Devlin was inebriated on the occasion in question," Wilson said, reacting like a bulldog on a scent. "Would you agree the Captain has a reputation as a heavy drinker?"

Muffled clucking of tongues and whispers could be heard. His elbows on his knees, Devlin looked at the prosecutor. Nothing like a little smell of Barleycorn to titillate the crowd, I thought.

"He has a drink, of course. We all do." Benson took time to reposition his sword. "As to how heavy a drinker he is, I don't know." He sighed, sat up, and added, "As to his abilities as a seaman and navigator in the north, there are none better."

Devlin smiled. I cheered silently on behalf of all imbibers everywhere.

Johanson held up his hand to halt Wilson's questioning. "Would you agree, sir," he said pointing his gavel toward Devlin, "that whether or not the Captain was inebriated, his inability to be awakened to give proper orders for the safety of the ship was a most serious infraction?"

Benson looked toward the President and then at Devlin. "I have to agree, yes," he said, his voice barely audible.

I almost missed spotting Godfrey among the crowd in the blinding sunshine outside the Customs House. He was with Heath and two well-dressed civilians, and all four were laughing. This time, he didn't try to avoid me, so I politely asked his opinion of the day's proceedings.

"I believe," he said with a broad smile, "Captain Benson's testimony said it all. We can't have untrustworthy men commanding government vessels, can we?"

"Is it true, Governor," I persisted, as he started to walk away, "that you have a particular interest in seeing Captain Devlin removed from the Cutter Service?"

"My interest isn't personal, young man." He turned to face me. "I'm a businessman. It's just good business to have men of temperance and judgment in command positions."

Like a foppish character in a political cartoon, he put both hands on the knob of his walking stick and leaned toward me. "From what I'm told, Devlin spends time and government money transporting reindeer for the Eskimos," he said pursing his thin lips. "Time he should spend making Alaska safe for productive ventures, don't you think?"

"Were you disappointed the Board dismissed charges against Devlin for his actions at your Bristol Bay cannery?"

"The man escaped punishment for his outrageous violence on a mere technicality," Godfrey said. "The fact he was charged at all got the attention of my investors. Made them understand what a man like Devlin, who lives in the past, can do to hinder our plans for the future."

"I'm a little confused, Governor," I said, putting on my most helpless expression. "You say there's nothing personal between you and Devlin, but isn't your nephew here one of the officers who brought charges against him?"

Heath started to answer, but Godfrey silenced him with the wave of a hand.

"Lieutenant Heath is a fine officer just doing his duty." Godfrey glanced at his gold pocket watch and said he had to leave, but added, "Like all good Americans, the lieutenant just wants to see progress and civility come to Alaska. It's not the wild frontier anymore."

What claptrap, I thought, as he took Heath's arm, and walked away using short, mincing steps, his cane clicking on the cobblestones.

"Whaddaya think of that slippery bastard?" someone said from behind me. It was Boatswain Jameson, in uniform and wearing a look of disgust.

"Well, Jameson, what's your opinion of the trial?"

"It looks bad for the Captain, that's a fact," he said, walking toward Pacific Avenue.

I caught up and said we should have a drink or two and discuss it.

Jameson's somber mood vanished as he led me through the swinging doors of Scotty's, and shouted, "Listen up, laddies, 'Boats' is back."

Scotty's was a pleasant sort of place for a side-street gin mill, and Jameson's greeting was met with laughter and friendly catcalls of derision.

We were "Jake" and "Boats" by the time the second drink arrived at our corner table. I stayed with dark ale, he insisted on Scotch.

"That shit about the Old Man not rousing to give orders," Jameson said, shaking his head. "It's happened countless times to plenty of skippers on long voyages, and nobody gives a hoot 'n a holler."

I liked this bantam rooster of a man, and clinked his glass. Blind loyalty wasn't a trait I encountered often in my business.

"The Old Man drinks a little, so what?" Jameson said, shrugging as he took a sip. "You don't hear any of those snobby young officers like that back-stabbing Lieutenant Heath tellin' what Devlin does to keep hooch from killing natives, do you?"

He leaned forward, put his arms on the table, adding, "And that half-pint Godfrey and his politician friends don't give a damn about such things. There's no money in it for 'em."

He said he could tell me things about Devlin I wouldn't believe. I ordered another round and some baked clams, and urged him on.

"About a dozen years ago," he began, "Devlin was skipper of a cutter smaller than the *Walrus*. It was early in the patrol—June, I think—and we were going to stop at some village on one of the Bering Strait islands."

When the drinks and the clams arrived, he sat back, and closed his eyes.

"When we got close, no locals came out in a rush to trade. Smoke came from only a half-dozen of the thirty barabaras and shacks scattered willy-nilly over a flat, uninteresting patch of tundra.

"After we anchored, I saw some Eskimos slowly gathering along the nearest shore, about a mile away. Only a few raised arms in any kind of greeting, and I had a bad feeling. Then an oomiako, the skin-covered boat they use for hunting, came along side with four men in ragged, loose-fitting parkas. There was none of the usual shouts about trading."

Jameson sat up straight, and looked directly at me. "That's when I knew there was real trouble, Jake. Eskimo whalers always dress in clean, new clothes, and put new skins on their oomiaks to go huntin' in the early spring. Has to do with their respect for the whales, or some such thing."

"But these people were actually in rags, you say?"

"Yeah, and they was so weak, Jake, we had to help 'em aboard. They pleaded for grub. It was pathetic. One of them, not more than five feet tall, he was, had a face like a skeleton with sunken eyes. He spoke that pidgin shit and made gestures like a wild man."

I tried to interrupt, wondering if this were true or just whiskey talking, but Jameson rushed on.

"Between gulps of canned salmon, this Eskimo said a whaler came the fall before lookin' for whalebone, ivory, baleen and furs. The whites stayed for a couple of weeks, taking anything of value in trade for rotgut hooch.

"That tiny feller babbled something like 'No peoples hunt. Much wild drunk.' He scooped the last bit of fish from the can, licked his fingers, and held out his hand for more.

"The Captain ignored him, and asked Cookie to get what food could be spared from our stores, and load it into one of the boats. He told me to muster some men with rifles ready to go ashore. He said, 'Jameson, those hooch-selling bastards know any Eskimo would barter his very soul for that poison. We oughta hang the sons of bitches.'"

"He actually said that?" I interjected.

"Sure did, and I have nightmares about what I saw in that godforsaken place, Jake. The liquor disabled 'em, made 'em crazy. Couldn't hunt to stock up for winter, ya see? Hundreds had starved after the whale meat and muktuk in their ice cellars was gone.

"In some shanties, bodies were every which way. They'd been frozen, but were getting ripe in the spring warmth when we got there. Some were partly eaten by dogs that'd escaped. The smell was awful, Jake. I still remember the mixture of rottin' bodies and wet decay. Worse than a 'Frisco' slaughterhouse, it was. Had to go outside at least twice and throw up. Others did too."

"Jesus, Jameson," I said, sickened by the image of half-eaten corpses, "how could you and your pals stand that duty?"

"It was damned tough, I'll tell ya. But Devlin went into all those stinkin' shacks the same as us. He ordered us to shoot any dogs not in harness, saying they'd most likely tasted human flesh. Then he organized our lads and Eskimos who were able, and ordered them to remove bodies and bury 'em under gravel."

He took a large gulp of the Scotch, ignoring the clams.

"Christ, I remember some of those bodies fell apart when we moved 'em. I swear the Captain looked frozen in hatred one minute, and close to tears the next. Me, I was just sick."

I had a hard time envisioning Devlin with tears in his eyes, but ordered another round and asked, "What did you do then?" This was my kind of yarn, and I didn't want him to stop.

"We stayed for more than a week. Several of my lads went hunting on land, while four others came with me and two Eskimos to hunt along the coast in a small boat. With a steady southeast wind, I was cold as hell altogether since I was steerin', not rowin', ya know? We got nothing the first day dodging ice to the west. On the second, Harry, who's a good shot, killed a monstrous seal that we towed to the village for people to divvy up."

His words were beginning to slur. "'Boats,'" I said, "then what?"

He said they left as much food and spare clothing as they could, and steamed east to pass the word of the disaster, asking every whaler to give assistance as best they could.

"I'll never forget what the Old Man told me when we left that village," Jameson said. "'Boats,'" he said, 'we have to catch every bloody bastard what sells that swill to these people. It's murder, as far as I'm concerned.'

"So, Devlin drinks," Jameson said, his eyes half closed. "I bet we've smashed hundreds of barrels of hooch and fined dozens of hooch sellers since then, but nobody cares about that."

"Why not tell all this at the trial?" I asked.

"Can't. Not part of the charges," he mumbled, "that's why I told you, for chrissake. See if you have the balls to write about it. Might even shake up Godfrey's hi-falutin' investors a little."

I left him sleeping, his head on his arms on the corner table at Scotty's, and wondered if even stories like this one could save Devlin now.

Chapter Twenty-One

Only a handful of protesters remained on Plymouth Square the next morning. Under low-hanging clouds hurrying east, two small groups of Lumsden's men silently waved their "No Torture for Sailors" placards. Five Temperance women stood like skirted railroad guards near the Customs House steps, thrusting "Demon Rum" handbills at spectators.

For the first time since this nonsense began there were empty seats in the makeshift courtroom with its lingering coal-fire smell. "I'm not the only one bored with this long-winded blather," I said, as I found a place toward the rear next to Sarah and Knowles.

"It's not boredom," Knowles said. "Everyone believes Benson's testimony sealed Devlin's fate—that it's all over."

In my weariness, I agreed, and spent the opening hour of the session watching Sarah's fluid pencil strokes outline McGowan's multiple chins. I was so fascinated, in fact, I only heard snippets of the prosecutor's drivel as he questioned the sanctimonious Heath on every tiny aspect of Devlin's drunkenness at some party aboard a British warship in Dutch Harbor. I still couldn't fathom how supposedly reasonable people could spend so much time on such pettiness.

Thankfully, in his cross-examination, McGowan probed Heath's motives rather than who said what to whom at some drinking bout.

"You have been at work for some time recruiting witnesses and preparing evidence for the prosecution, have you?"

"Yes, I have," Heath said, raising his chin like a preacher denouncing sin, "from the very moment these events occurred."

McGowan put on his spectacles and consulted his large pad. "From the very moment they occurred, is that what you said?" Heath nodded.

"Now I'll ask you about things that happened much earlier, say two or three years ago. What, in that period, drove you and others to secretly record every action and statement of your commanding officer?"

Wilson objected, saying the question was irrelevant to the specific charges. He was overruled after McGowan argued the existence of a group of disgruntled officers had been established earlier, and the Board should hear why it existed.

"Captain Devlin consistently treated us in a unofficer-like, rough and insulting manner, and was often inebriated," Heath said. "I believed something had to be done."

McGowan, hands clasped behind his back, sauntered toward the Board's elevated perch, then turned back to Heath and casually asked, "Was that before or after Captain Devlin disciplined you for your performance, assigned you to guard duty on St. Paul Island...?"

Wilson interrupted in a loud voice, saying Heath was not on trial. McGowan shrugged his shoulders, affecting a pose of innocence, but the President wasn't fooled. He sustained the prosecutor. Heath stepped down. Devlin smiled broadly. I did, too, being a fan of any charade to sneak damaging statements into the record.

In a surprise move, Wilson then recalled Norris as a witness.

"I advise you to choose your words carefully, lieutenant," the prosecutor said. "I ask you again, was Captain Devlin drunk the night you were forced to change course near the Shumagin Islands last June?"

Norris stared hard at him, leaned forward and said through clenched teeth, "You impugn my integrity, sir. I resent it, and damn your effrontery in making me out a liar to my superiors in Washington."

Wilson looked dumbfounded. He turned up his palms and shrugged. "Lieutenant Norris, I haven't the faintest idea what you're talking about."

"Then how come I got an official telegram warning me to be truthful in my testimony?" Norris said, his usually placid face contorted by anger.

Johanson resorted to the gavel to silence whispering. "The Board would like to hear the contents of such a telegram," he said.

Norris reached into his breast pocket, retrieved a crumpled paper, and in a loud voice, read, "Informed your Devlin case testimony less than forthcoming. Crucial you tell full story."

Norris looked toward the dais, and blurting out, "This was delivered to me while I was at home with my family, sir." Turning to the prosecutor, he said, "It was signed Chester L. Macy, Assistant Secretary of the Treasury."

Johanson turned to confer with his panel when McGowan roused himself. "Mr. President, I object to the prosecution's treatment of this witness. He has already testified on this matter, and is a respected officer and gentleman."

Devlin was leaning forward. He looked first at Norris, then to the dais, apparently trying to hear the discussion. For me, it was amusing as hell to see sparks fly when the brass buttons got wind someone was going over their heads. These worthies could handle charges of cruelty without flinching, but, heaven forbid, not chinks in the chain of command.

His powwow with the panel over, Johanson waved his gavel at the prosecutor. "Lieutenant Wilson, what do you know about this blatant attempt to interfere with our deliberations?"

"I would never even consider contacting Washington about any aspect of the case," Wilson said.

"Do you know who did?" Johanson thundered. "Did you speak to any party to this case casting doubts on Lieutenant Norris' earlier testimony?"

The prosecutor said he might have voiced his opinion of Norris' story to Heath and a few other officers.

"Consider yourself reprimanded," Johanson said, pointing at Wilson. "I'm asserting my prerogatives. I excuse this witness, and recall Lt. Heath to the stand."

I enjoyed the delicious sight of the self-important Heath and his conspirators in disarray. They all seemed to be whispering to each other at once until Johanson stormed, "Now, sir! Not next week."

As Heath walked slowly toward the witness chair, Knowles, with a broad smile, whispered, "I'll bet he's behind this. Thinks the Arctic Circle vendetta against the Captain will turn against him."

Wilson, his head bowed, retreated to the prosecution table. I couldn't see Devlin's face, but noted he leaned over the defense table to stare at his accuser. McGowan, as usual, looked relaxed and oblivious.

Johanson coughed into his fist, then took charge.

"Did you appeal for Washington's involvement, Lieutenant?"

"I did not, sir."

"Do you know who did? Remember, you're still under oath."

The clicking of the clock above the dais was the only sound to fill the void as Heath hesitated. He seemed to sink into the chair. He cleared his throat, and in a husky whisper said, "I may have mentioned my concerns to some people at Arctic Circle Corporation."

I scanned the room looking for Godfrey. He was nowhere to be seen.

"Why, for God's sake?" Johanson made no effort to hide his fury. "Do you think this Board is unable to judge the charges you are a party to?"

Heath remained silent. His face reddened. He gripped the arms of the chair. Then with a burst of fury, he pointed to Devlin and declaimed, "Because, sir, that man is no gentleman. He's a disgrace to the Service, and his supporters will say anything to save him."

Johanson gaveled. Gasps and excited conversation came from all sections of the room. Devlin tried to stand, but was gently restrained by his attorney, now fully awake.

I wanted to cheer. At last I had some decent fodder for old Pulitzer to chew on.

In his anger, Heath leapt to his feet and shouted above the tumult. "He's a Negro! The son of a Georgia slave woman. He's not fit to command."

There were a few seconds of stunned silence. Then, like other spectators, I stood wondering aloud if I had heard correctly. Voices in varying pitches and volumes melded into a discordant, ever-rising volume of sound. "Did you hear that?" "No-good slanderer." "Always knew there was something odd about that Devlin." "Throw that disloyal bastard out."

Everyone, it seemed, turned to look toward Devlin, as if Negroid features might appear mysteriously on his wind-tanned Caucasian mug. He remained seated, staring at the floor and sadly shaking his head. Amy, located directly behind him, appeared to be sobbing, her hands over her eyes. Norris and a few whalers gravitated toward the defense table. Heath's supporters congealed around him, as he left the witness chair without Johanson's permission. Wilson, looking forlorn and dismayed, remained with his advisor, his thoroughly prepared case thrown into confusion.

Well, well, I thought as I hurriedly stuffed my pad into my coat, Pulitzer will love this crap. A subaltern calling his commander a nigger in open court! Unheard-of, outrageous stuff. But it'll sell some papers, and get me on page one. Doesn't matter if it's true or not, it's one helluva story.

It was impossible for me to hear Johanson when everyone in the room was talking loudly at the same time. He motioned to the Master at Arms to restore order. In desperation, that confused, lonely sentinel repeatedly pounded the butt of his baton on the coal stove, releasing wisps of black smoke. The action gave Johanson enough silence to be heard shouting, "This room will be cleared. Proceedings are adjourned until tomorrow morning."

"I expected something like this," Knowles said with a frown.

I didn't have time for an explanation. I scrambled around Sarah's chair, went into the foyer and ran to intercept Heath and his gang as they left by the far door.

"Mr. Heath," I said, jumping to get his attention over the uniformed shoulders of his colleagues, "what do you know about Devlin's mother?"

He and his defenders kept moving. "I have evidence," his over-the-shoulder shout echoed off the marble walls. "He fooled us all. I'll say no more until tomorrow."

His group swiftly descended the stairs. I scrambled after them until I heard a booming voice behind me. "What in hell did you think you were doing in there?" It was Wilson, trying to get Heath's attention. "You've fouled the prosecution's case with that slander, and probably wrecked your own career, for Chrissake."

On the chance I might corner Devlin, I ran through the Square and around to the side entrance. A dozen spectators, including the *Examiner* and *Chronicle* neophytes, were shouting to get Devlin's attention as he, Amy and Norris got into a hansom cab.

Three beefy whalers and an agitated Jameson blocked their way. I circled around the guardians, and almost had my hand on the cab's door handle when one of the whalers shoved me away. "Give the man some privacy, won't ya," he hissed.

As the horse gained traction on the cobblestones and trotted away, I noticed Charlie Lumsden and two of his hangers-on edging into the crowd.

"I'm almost ready to feel sorry for that old bastard," he said, motioning toward the retreating cab. "Imagine being called a secret nigger for all the world to hear."

"Whaddya think this brouhaha will do to the case, Charlie?" I said, catching my breath.

"The brass buttons will deep-six that prissy lieutenant, that's for goddamn sure," he said. "But, if it's true, they'll get Devlin's hide now, one way or the other." He clucked his tongue. "There's no black faces at Treasury, but they'll be a lot of red ones today."

"Why d'ya think the Arctic Circle bunch was stupid enough to lobby Treasury, Charlie? It showed they were out to get rid of Devlin, didn't it?"

"It's gonna be a tough election year, Jake," he said, shrugging. "Politicians will do anything for anybody who'll give 'em campaign money."

At that moment, Johanson and some Board members exited the side door. The ever-increasing crowd of the curious gravitated toward them.

"What are you going to do now, Captain?" the young *Chronicle* reporter asked.

Johanson stopped, and waited for the rest of us to cluster around him. "We will not let an improvident, slanderous outburst derail these proceedings," he said, his face stern. "We'll deal with it tomorrow, and that's all I'm willing to say."

WESTERN UNION 11:30 AM Jan.25—
TO EDITOR NY WORLD. DEVLIN CALLED A SECRET
NEGRO STOP TRIAL IN DISARRAY STOP STORY
TO COME STOP SYKES

Their boardinghouse was wedged between a cut-rate dry-goods emporium and a grocer, and looked as if it hadn't been painted since Lincoln split rails. Sarah shouldn't have to stay in a place like this, I thought. I'd like to kick Knowles' miserly ass.

Sarah put down her book, and smiled when I entered the drab room with peeling wallpaper that served as the parlor. The odor of grease and sizzling sounds of chicken frying in the back announced that the dinner hour was near. I told her I came to take them both out for a decent meal.

"It'll do us all good to forget the trial for a while," I said. "And I suspect a little reprieve from boardinghouse fare might be welcome."

"I'd like that very much, but Stanton hasn't returned yet." With her strong arms she wheeled her chair nearer to me. "He went to make sure the Captain and Amy were comfortable. They had to leave the hotel, you know, to escape those pestering newspaper friends of yours."

Knowles bustled in almost immediately, no doubt unwilling to miss the delicacies of a paid-for boardinghouse meal. It took little persuading, and before long the two of us took turns pushing Sarah's chair to a Market Street restaurant I'd been told was noted for its seafood.

With its red-and-white-checkered tablecloths and paneled walls, Stewart's was a quiet, pleasant place with the faint odor of baking bread in the air. Knowles lifted Sarah from her wheeled contraption and into a regular chair with stoic efficiency just as a wicker basket of warm rolls and oyster crackers arrived. I ordered ale. Sarah surprised and delighted me by asking for a glass of Sherry. Maybe she hasn't been completely tainted by her time with Holy Rollers, I thought. Knowles stayed with coffee.

"This reminds me of the fine times we have had with our colleagues at Louise's Chop House in Los Angeles," Sarah said.

Knowles beamed with pleasure. "We're considered exotic down there," he said. "None of our new friends have ever been anywhere near Alaska, you see."

Sarah laughed. "And never had to learn how to deal with a chair-bound female teacher, either."

Knowles seemed pleased with himself as he related how Sarah and he found employment and made friends at some hifalutin' school. I ordered scallops. They went for the halibut, Sarah remarking she missed the seafood she enjoyed at Dutch Harbor.

"I'm curious, Knowles," I said as the food arrived. "What did you mean when you said this afternoon you expected that idiot Heath's outburst?"

"This was supposed to be an outing to forget the trial, remember, Jake?" Sarah said, frowning.

Knowles put down his fork, sat silent for a moment. "I've known for quite a while Heath and his friends would do anything—say anything—to sink the Captain." He sighed deeply. "God knows they have cause to dislike him. He terrifies officers who haven't come up the hard way, who don't fit the frontier mold."

The ale was tasty, dark and cold, so I ordered another. "That's understandable, but are they doing Arctic Circle's bidding?"

"Heath certainly is," Knowles shook his head sadly. "I'm not sure about the others. It's not clear if it's an organized conspiracy, or just a group of disgruntled officers who feel they've been abused."

A party of four well-dressed men and two women was being seated near our table, and I couldn't help but overhear their chatter.

"Have you heard that one of those cutter captains is a nigger?" one of the men asked. "Claimed to be Irish. Couldn't tell him from a white man, I'm told."

One of the women said, "It's shocking. Everybody in the city's talking about it."

"Isn't he the fellow who keeps rescuing sailors stranded in that Alaskan icebox?" one of the other men asked.

"That can't be, can it?" said the second woman. "I don't believe darkies like the cold at all. It must be some other seaman."

I lowered my voice to a whisper. "Do you really think it possible Devlin's the son of a slave?"

"Whatever the truth," Sarah said, her voice rising, "it was outrageous to blurt out such a thing with such venom."

Knowles stopped eating and stared vacantly into a corner of the room. "In all our conversations, Devlin never once alluded to his childhood. To where he was born and raised," he said. "With his Irish name and tiresome quoting from Emerson's essays, I presumed he came from the Northeast."

He had a forkful of coleslaw halfway to his mouth when he paused again. "If he does have Negro blood," he said, looking at Sarah and me in turn, "it might explain why he savored the freedom to act as his own boss in Alaska."

Sarah reached for Knowles' hand. "You were just with him, dear. What did the Captain say about that shocking accusation?"

"He said he'd set the record straight at trial tomorrow, that's all."

"If Heath and Godfrey wanted to get Devlin that bad," I said, between bites of scallop, "wasn't it foolish to bring up the black-blood business?" Not getting an immediate response, I added,

"I think being ambushed that way could generate the Board's sympathy for the man just when the evidence was going against him."

"Maybe," Knowles said. "It's obvious someone went to a lot of trouble investigating the Captain's past." He stared into his coffee mug for a time. "I don't think Godfrey planned to make that accusation in public. He's too smart."

"You mean, errand-boy Heath just lost control and blurted it out?"

"I think so," he said. "Out of his frustration getting caught doing Arctic Circle's dirty work. One way or the other, if it's true it could be Heath's trump card—and Godfrey's, too."

He leaned across the table and looked directly into my eyes. "To my knowledge, Sykes, no Negro has ever knowingly been permitted to command an American ship, much less an armed government cutter."

Chapter Twenty-Two

WESTERN UNION NY JAN.26 7AM—TO JAKE SYKES,
OCCIDENTAL HOTEL, SAN FRANCISCO—KEEN
INTEREST IN NEGRO CAPTAIN STOP FILE SUNDAY
PIECE STOP PULITZER NY WORLD

A cacophony of excited conversation filled the packed courtroom when I arrived late and hung-over the next morning.
Ladies, gents, sailors in uniform and ordinary seamen leaned
against the smoke stained-walls and stood in the aisles. I was
squeezed between two whalers against the wall closest to the
press section, directly under a smelly, hissing kerosene lamp.
I shouldn't have been surprised. I knew that even a whiff of a
nigger scandal brings out the worst in American bumpkins, and
the newspapers that pander to them. Mine included. I told some
itinerant scribes for New York and Washington sheets to get the
hell outta seats usually reserved for me and the three 'Frisco
rags. They told me to go play with myself.

Godfrey wasn't present, but Mrs. Pitcher and her sour-faced
ladies were back in full force, as were Lumsden and his union
bunch. Devlin, sitting on the edge of the defense table, was in
animated discussion with his attorney, who repeatedly shook his
head from side to side. Three sailors with holstered batons were
chatting with a diminutive San Francisco copper as they awaited
arrival of the Board members.

Johanson followed the panel to the dais and, wearing his
almost comic schoolmaster scowl, declared that no repetition

of yesterday's disruption would be allowed. Gesturing toward the policeman, he said he would order him to clear the room of spectators at the first sign of trouble.

Wilson and McGowan simultaneously tried to get Johanson's attention, McGowan raising his hand like a schoolboy wanting to go to the outhouse.

"The prosecution planned to recall Lieutenant Heath to the stand," Wilson said after receiving Johnson's go-ahead. "Unfortunately, he has not arrived. We have been unable to locate him so far."

"Then send a Master at Arms to find him, lieutenant," Johanson commanded. "I want that officer to explain his inflammatory statements under oath."

His hands raised palms up in supplication, McGowan approached the panel. "Against advice of counsel, Mr. President," he said with a shrug, "Captain Devlin respectfully requests to testify at this time."

Murmurs of hushed excitement spread through the room. Johanson noted that the prosecution's case was still being presented. Did the Captain realize that he would be subject to cross-examination, he asked. Devlin nodded his head, indicating approval.

"He does, sir," McGowan said, "but he also desires to make a personal statement, if you will permit."

"Very unusual," Johanson replied, staring at Devlin, who held a sheaf of papers in his hand. "I strongly advise you against it." He turned to the panel for support. Whatever the brass buttons advised, he said with apparent reluctance, "If Lieutenant Wilson does not object, I will allow it in view of the scandalous accusations made against Captain Devlin yesterday."

Wilson, a broad smile on his face, said he had no objection, that he was prepared to question this witness at any time.

Devlin strode to the witness chair, sat as if at attention, and settled the ridiculous sword across his knees. He thanked the

Board for allowing him to speak out of order, and began a recitation of his service in the north.

"We appreciate all that," Johanson interrupted, fingering his gavel. "Confine yourself to the facts of this case."

"The Cutter Service and the Bering Sea Patrol have been my life and my passion for decades," Devlin began. "The accusation that I'd consciously endanger my ship—that I was drunk on duty—that night last June is outrageous. I deny it."

Wilson couldn't wait to get at him. "Then please explain why you were unable to take command of your vessel in a precarious situation. We've heard sworn testimony to that effect."

"Disloyal officers misconstrued the facts for their own purposes." Devlin said, his voice rising. "As I've said before, we had been in heavy fog for three days. I rarely left the pilothouse in all that time. I was exhausted, and they knew it."

Pacing back and forth in front of the witness, Wilson asked, "You feel that's an adequate excuse, do you?"

"It's the reason, sir," the Captain said, playing with the yellow tassel hanging from the sword's hilt. "It's not an excuse. I should have risen regardless of exhaustion, but I didn't hear the call."

Young Wilson was no dullard. With his lip curled, he said, "We've also heard testimony of your drinking and ungentlemanly conduct in Dutch Harbor last September. Were those episodes caused by exhaustion, too?"

"No," Devlin said softly, rolling the tassel between his fingers, "On reflection, I admit I'd been drinking, probably too heavily, the three days we were moored there."

Before Wilson could interject, Devlin looked directly at the panel, stressing that the *Walrus* had been safely moored, was not on patrol duty. He had apologized to the other captains present on that occasion, he said, and recently received a letter from the

British Navy skipper stating that his conduct the night in question had not been considered disrespectful.

Wilson pounced. "Am I correct in understanding you now admit being under the influence of liquor during that period?"

"Your understanding is correct," Devlin said, his voice barely audible. "I apologize if I caused the Service any embarrassment."

Lucy Pitcher was beaming, her ladies tittering, when Wilson favored them with a broad smile of victory in this skirmish against the forces of devil alcohol. If my head hadn't been throbbing, I would have laughed. Only military martinets and busybody women would make so much fuss about so little.

But, still I was enthralled to see Devlin squirming after hearing Knowles' stories of the man's strutting antics. His drinking habits were of little interest to me, or to the bumpkins around me. Most of them, I'll bet, didn't care about this drunk-on-duty blather.

Like the sadists who go to the circus hoping to see the high-wire bloke take a fatal fall, they were leaning forward, cupping their ears, paying close attention to everything Devlin said. They smelled blood. Wanted to witness the downfall of a celebrated hero. If he proved to be the son of an octoroon, the thrill would be so much sweeter.

Wilson, prancing before the dais, seemed mighty pleased with himself. Despite yesterday's reprimand, he had gotten Devlin to compromise himself on two of the charges against him. But the prosecutor wasn't ready to quit.

"On the charges of dereliction of duty and conduct unbecoming, sir, you allege you're the victim of disloyal officers," he said. "Why do you inspire such disloyalty? Other commanders work officers hard. Why are you singled out?"

"I've been sent to command in the most hostile waters we have," Devlin said. "I do not—I will not—accept slipshod work from pantywaists who would like an 'if you please' with every order." He rearranged the sword on his lap. "Where we sail, there's no margin for error. Not in seamanship, not in enforcing the law against scoundrels of every sort."

"And you do this by insulting treatment and harsh punishment of officers?" Wilson asked.

"I never punish an officer unless I'm forced to speak to him several times," Devlin said. "I teach 'em to be self-reliant. Tell 'em what they must know to survive in frontier waters."

He turned abruptly to face the panel. "But my gruff manner is not the reason for their constant carping and spying."

Devlin sat forward and looked directly at Johanson. "I believe, sir," he said, "well-known railroad barons and Wall Street people who would control Alaska incited these men to conspire against me."

Johanson frowned, and gaveled to contain the rising noise level. "No matter who incited whom, Captain," he said, "restrict your answers to your own actions and to charges this panel has to deal with."

"I will, sir," Devlin said, "but the members need to know why these charges were leveled against me in the first place." He shifted his weight in the chair, let the sword droop to his side, and asked if he could make a personal statement.

Johanson asked the prosecutor if he were done with the witness for the time being, and nodded at Devlin, telling him to be brief.

Devlin began solemnly with the usual palaver about his loyalty to a Service that gave him a chance to prove himself. He apologized once again if anything he had done had injured the Service's reputation. Sly devil that he was, he casually slipped into the record his theory that junior officers were organized against him by Heath on behalf of the Arctic Circle Corporation. He even added that Arctic Circle was headed by Godfrey, a former governor of Georgia.

Johanson rolled his eyes and looked toward the ceiling, but didn't warn Devlin again. Coughing and foot-shuffling were heard throughout the room. These people aren't hearing what they came to hear, I thought. They didn't have to wait long, for what Devlin said next caused gasps and audible cries of "Oh, no," then silent attention.

WESTERN UNION SEPT. 26 11:30AM TO EDITOR NY WORLD HERE COPY OF DEVLIN'S STATEMENT STOP SUGGEST RUN FULL AS SIDE PIECE STOP STORY TO COME STOP SYKES

"Full confession of his secret racial identity made by Captain Edward M. Devlin, USRCS to a Board of Inquiry. Official court document obtained by our San Francisco correspondent.

"In his hysterical accusation yesterday about my parentage, Lieutenant Heath told the truth for the first time in these proceedings.

"The wonderful, light-skinned woman who was my mother was, in fact, a slave on my father's plantation in Georgia. It was a felony in that state for whites to marry anyone with even a drop of Negro blood, so my mother and my father lived together as man and wife for more than 20 years without the blessings of matrimony. What mattered to them was that as the son of a slave, I was legally a slave myself by the laws of that time and place.

"I have not revealed my true heritage until today, not out of shame, but in the belief that prevailing prejudices would make it impossible for me to serve my country and accomplish my life's mission. I'd like to explain.

"I last saw my mother the day my father took me north and arranged for me to be educated at a school near Boston. I was eight years old.

Before the Union victory in the War, the fact that my father was an Irishman who once served in the British army, and was a successful plantation owner couldn't protect me. So as a sad and frightened lad, forced to leave home and cope with New England winters among strangers, I learned self-reliance. For those who believe that common-law marriages like my parents' union can not be loving, I'd like to record that they died within a month of each other, and were buried side by side in red Georgia dirt. Not a week goes by, even to this day, that I don't remember fondly the warm, loving woman who bore me. She urged me to stand tall and fight for what I knew to be right.

"*I was fifteen when I learned my parents had died. I ran away to sea, and advanced through the ranks to become first officer on merchant ships before joining the Service. That's of no importance here. What is important for this Board to know is that all my life I have pushed myself to excel at every task assigned to me. I've tried to help anybody down on his luck, whether he be a stranded whaler or an Eskimo. My mission was to prove that a son of a slave could be as good or better at his profession than any man.*

"*My greatest regret—my greatest fear—is that accusations made in these proceedings will destroy the reputation I have earned as a seaman, a protector of Alaskan natives and a lawman. And in doing so, will undermine my struggle to prove the worth of citizens with Negro blood.*

"*I read recently that a Mr. Homer Plessy, a successful businessman in Louisiana with the same birthright as mine, has gone to court to ensure that people like us have the same rights as any American. His case is supposed to be heard by the United States Supreme Court this very year. I hope and pray that distinguished body will have the wisdom to outlaw once and for all the injustices suffered by children of slaves. I hope my testimony today will be helpful in that endeavor.*"

*
**

It was astonishing to hear this rough-edged man, called "Roaring Ed" by his whaler pals, slowly read his credo in an unfaltering voice into the silence of the chamber. After a lifetime of deception, he had just hoisted a flag of identity, an identity that could sink him. "I'm the son of a slave," he told them. "Now, what are you going to do about it?"

I admit, I was moved, as I wondered if this could be the key to understanding that complicated, contrary man, someone I had come to regard as capable of being a bully one day and a zealot the next in protecting natives. A man who couldn't handle his liquor, but loved to pose as some sort of hero.

When Devlin asked permission to be excused, Johanson sat dazed for a moment. He then gave his consent, and most of my fellow scribes climbed over chairs, and ran to the Western Union office. Amid the clamor as the crowd hurriedly exited to spread the news, Johanson recessed proceedings until after lunch.

There would be more testimony then and tomorrow, but I wasn't interested. I already had the circulation-building stuff old Pulitzer wanted. He'd tell the boys in the composing room to set the largest headline type to titillate the trolley riders jostling to dreary jobs in New York.

ACCUSED CAPTAIN IS SLAVE'S SON
CHARGED WITH CRUELTY, DRUNKENNESS
IN ICE BOUND SEAS OF ALASKA

That'll help the newsboys hawk papers on Broadway and probably in front of the White House, too. Every bartender and lunchroom philosopher in the bloody country will shake his head in repeating the tale of a nigger who fooled everybody to become a captain commanding white men. And, of course, he was a drunk to boot. "It's true," they'd say, "it's in all the papers."

But Jake Sykes didn't come three thousand miles cross-country to be fooled. I knew this was all a sensational sideshow. There was a better story here somewhere. I filed my daily piece like the other scribes, had a mug of dark ale, and went off to find and corner the old devil himself.

Chapter Twenty-Three

K nowles was surprised and flustered when I appeared on Norris' doorstep in the Mission District that evening. Since he was the only one who could have told me where Devlin was hiding, he tried to quietly shoo me away.

"Might as well let him in, Knowles," came a voice from the darkened hallway behind him. Devlin, smoking a small cigar, his uniform jacket unbuttoned, was motioning me forward. "This son of a bitch can't do any more damage than I didn't do to myself today."

The parlor they led me to was not much larger than my hotel room, and was wreathed in swirls of tobacco smoke. Sarah had secured a place between the only window and the fireplace. Norris was not in the room, and neither was Amy, who, I was told, was ill. Before taking a seat on a worn leather sofa, Knowles apologized for my being there.

"Whaddaya want to know, Mr. *New York World*?" Devlin said as he stood before me, his hands in his hip pockets. "I'd have thought you had all the stinking bilge you needed from my sorry performance."

I remained standing. "There's more involved here than your bloodline, Captain." I turned to look at Sarah. "I think that 'son-of-a-slave' crap was a cheap, low-down trick to get you the hell outta Alaska. I'd like to know why." He raised his eyebrows, pursed his lips, and gave me a penetrating stare. "All right," he said, "what do you know? Let's have your theory."

"Listen, Captain, I've covered Tammany Hall, Wall Street and a half-dozen bloody strikes." I flopped down next to Knowles. "I know how the cow eats the cabbage in this country, and this trial smells of pure, moneybags politics to me."

The old buzzard threw his cigar butt in the fire, pulled up a chair in front of me and straddled it as if he were riding a horse.

"I know something about cheating bastards, Sykes," he said, looking apologetically toward Sarah.

"Don't mind your language on my account, Captain," she said. "I grew up the only girl in a family of boys. Besides, I really want to hear what Jake has to say."

Devlin leaned back and looked at the low plastered ceiling. "Whatever your theories or mine, Sykes, they got me, don't ya see? They've won."

"Maybe not," I said. "Don't underestimate the New York World. If Pulitzer feels like it, he can scare the drawers off the people who want you gone. He'll sell a lot of papers doin' it, too."

Both Sarah and Knowles nodded, supporting me.

Devlin closed his eyes, and rubbed his hands on his trousers as if he were kneading his thighs. "Why would Pulitzer or anyone else back East give a damn about me now?"

"They won't," I said, "unless you tell 'em exactly why the big shots want to bury you." I leaned closer to him, adding. "Every dirt farmer with a grudge against the railroads, every sweatshop seamstress, every working bloke would love to hear how you fought those stuffed shirts."

I stood and went to open the window to get some air circulating. "And they'd want you to win, beat Godfrey and his pals. You know, David versus Goliath stuff."

"After today's testimony, I'm just another drunken darky bastard," Devlin said. His voice was sad, but his dark eyes were smoldering.

"Stop thinking that way, will ya," I said from across the room.

"That statement of yours today was powerful, courageous."

I walked to his chair and looked down at him.

"The country is ripe for change," I said as if I were a genuine political commentator. "The Panic of '93 and the bloody strikes must have taught the bumpkins something. Maybe we could get that gasbag congressman from Nebraska, William something or other..."

"Jennings Bryan," Knowles offered.

"That's him," I said. "He's been bellyaching about the dangers when a money bags like J.P. Morgan had to bail out the country's Treasury last year. Maybe I'll send him a copy of whatever I write. See what kind of hell he can raise."

Sarah said she'd heard Bryan was trying to unite the Populist and Democrat parties in a reform movement for the Presidential election.

"He'll need stories of how financiers beat down the little man, won't he?" she added. "Your fight with Arctic Circle would be a good one."

Thinking of my own story needs, I interjected. "Planting Heath as a spy on your own ship would only make Godfrey look worse."

"All that may be so," Knowles said, "but Democrats still need Southern white votes to win. The Captain's story won't help that cause one bit."

Devlin stood, rubbing his hands together. "Now that I'm admittedly a man with Negro blood, the Democrats can't help, and the Populists won't give a damn one way or the other." He shook his head, and chuckled softly. "Strange, isn't it? I was so relieved this morning to let everyone know my mother was a slave. Lifted a burden that haunted me all my life, only to find it now keeps me from doing what needs to be done."

He went to the fireplace, and leaned on the mantelpiece, speaking to the fire.

"It's too bad, because I know what the Arctic Circle sons of bitches with all their political friends will do up north, given the chance," he said. "I've seen their kind of skullduggery in Georgia."

He said that just before he was assigned to the west coast in '67, he took a dangerous gamble, and returned to his birthplace. "The Union Army was supposed to be in charge even then. Wearing my blue Cutter Service uniform, and buying a potload of drinks for some Army officers, I learned what the bastards were doing."

Southern-born and -bred men like Godfrey were called "scalawags," and got rich manipulating the Reconstruction Acts, he said. "They allied themselves with slimy carpetbaggers from places like your New York, Sykes. Formed phony companies, foreclosed on distressed plantations and businesses, and sold them to each other for a pittance."

He began pacing the tiny room. "Remember, Sykes," his voice louder, "they did these things right under the noses of the Army brass."

He told us he hired a driver to take him from the still-charred chimneys of Atlanta to see what remained of his father's plantation. The house where he was born still stood, but the prosperous farm he dimly remembered had vanished. Most of it had been divided into two- or three-acre sharecropper plots where Negro families had to scratch out a living as best they could. The white family living in the old Devlin home had converted the barn into a crossroads general store, he said. "Those poor, ignorant sharecroppers had to buy everything they needed to survive from that damned store, and the landowner set the prices and terms."

Sarah angrily slapped the arm of her chair. "That's just a different kind of the slavery," she said, her voice harsh. "Couldn't you—couldn't somebody—do something about it?"

"It's all legal, Sarah," Devlin said as he went to stand near her. "Remember, Godfrey was governor. That snake knows all the tricks. How to bend the law if he has to, bribe lawmakers and sheriffs, even judges."

"The railroads are using the same kinds of tricks in California," Sarah said, her fists clenched. "They control the politicians, and dirt farmers and townspeople have to take whatever the railroads give them."

"Sarah's right," Knowles said, rising from the sofa. "But if Sykes gets some of this in his newspaper, maybe the Populists will side with the Captain yet."

"Hold on," I said. "These Reconstruction horrors are old news. So is the story of the railroad bullies. You'd need facts to tie Godfrey to the Captain's situation."

That dampened the atmosphere. "You'd have to show that the moneygrubbers were actually afraid of him. That they used the Captain's parentage to disgrace him, to get him out of their way," I added.

Everybody sat down. I was getting depressed myself. I desperately wanted dark ale, or anything wet with alcoholic content.

"I torpedoed the Arctic Circle's fur-seal contract," Devlin said softly. "Know that gang has been backing seal killing at sea. That made them as mad as hell."

"You never made a formal report on all that, did you? It's just your word against theirs," I said, "unless you can get people to back you up under oath." I went to the window again, adding, "And frankly, Captain, the reports about your drinking won't help one damned bit."

"Sykes is right," Devlin said. "All my suspicions won't get my ship back. Even if Johanson and the others ignore the one-drop-of-Negro-blood thing, they'll have to beach me for a while, at least." His shoulders sank and his face looked glum. "As Emerson said somewhere, 'It's time to be old, to take in sail'."

"Oh, blather!" Sarah said as she struggled to push on the wheels of her chair to approach him. "Whatever Johanson decides, there's much you can do—that we all can do—to protect the Aleuts and Eskimos from the kind of men you describe."

She blushed, and pointed toward the Captain. "And besides, my good sir, your Emerson also said something like 'God won't allow his works to be manifest by cowards.' And from what I hear from my husband, you're no coward."

I was amazed by her fierceness, and, not incidentally, by her knowledge of that Emerson's drivel.

The ticking of the mantel clock made the only sound until she sheepishly explained that Knowles had directed her to some of Emerson's works in the school library.

"What I mean," Sarah said, "is that Stanton and I need your fighting spirit and your guidance to go back to Alaska. To be useful as the frontier era ends." She leaned forward in her chair to look directly at Devlin. "We'll try to moderate, at least, the evils you fear will happen."

"Alaska still *is* the frontier," Devlin said forcefully.

"Not really," Knowles said, taking his wife's hand. "Captain, you have to admit things are changing. Big business runs the country, and Alaska won't be spared, no matter what any of us do." He spoke of the influx of mineral prospectors on the coast and far into the Yukon, of the steady increase in the number of steamships, barges and fishing vessels.

"Right," Sarah said. "And we want to be there to bear witness, and so should you, Captain, whatever the outcome of the trial." She said she had been invited to teach at the orphanage at Dutch Harbor. "Those marvelous people told me they'd accommodate my disabilities, would build a wooden walkway for my chair."

Her eyes were wide, and her face aglow as she spoke of the Aleut children she would teach. Knowles looked at her with pride and affection, which I believed was genuine. Devlin sat transfixed. I was in awe of this woman whose useless limbs could not retard a soaring spirit. I was ashamed that my only purpose in all this was to get some wretched paragraphs to please a crotchety editor and help him sell a few thousand more newspapers.

"I wouldn't be much help," Devlin said, shaking his head. "If I'm not captain of the *Walrus*, I'd be just another out-of-work sourdough with a blot on his record and Negro blood in his veins."

Sarah attempted to argue, but Devlin held up his hand. "The five men on that Board will determine my immediate fate," he said, "but that shouldn't deter you and Knowles from doing what you plan."

He seemed to regain his swagger as he came and looked down on me. "And what are you going to do, Mr. Sykes of the *New York World?*"

"I'm going to scratch out an article in soaring Sykes prose, find some congenial company until the verdicts come down, and go home."

"When you're composing that prose of yours, remember that Roarin' Ed Devlin's not dead yet. Heath and all his Arctic Circle string pullers haven't heard the last of me. I'll find a way, goddammit."

Images of Sarah's enthusiasm and Devlin's glum determination for vengeance remained in my mind as I struggled to write the profile for Sunday's supplement. With a bottle of Scotch within easy reach, I spent most of Friday trying to weave the "Captain as hero" yarns Knowles told with the revelations at the trial. All the other rags, I knew, would feign horror at the Negro who fooled everybody to become a U.S. Cutter captain, and a drunken one at that. Pulitzer would love that garbage. I don't know if it was Sarah's bravery, Devlin's bluster or the Scotch, but old Sykes took the risky path for once.

WESTERN UNION NIGHT WIRE—
TO EDITOR, NY WORLD

LEAD FOR DEVLIN PROFILE STOP RUN WITH HIS STATEMENT STOP MORE TO COME STOP SYKES

San Francisco, January 27, 1896—Captain Edward M. Devlin has been called many things, but a coward isn't one of them. The U.S. Revenue Cutter captain was described during a Board of Inquiry in this city as the most knowledgeable and heroic commander in the Western Arctic, a protector of natives and fur seals, a drunkard who cruelly punishes lawbreakers, and the son of a slave woman.

Investigations by the New York World show he should also be called a crusader. This rough-talking seaman, who rose through the ranks, demanded an official hearing to expose his longstanding fight to keep the Alaskan frontier free from the corruption of absentee financiers. In doing so, he risked his reputation, his livelihood, revelation of the lifelong secret of the circumstances of his birth, and his self-appointed mission to prove the worth of people with Negro blood.

MORE TO COME

Chapter Twenty-Four

A different, sinister cacophony enveloped misty Plymouth Square six days later on February 1. The usual "Demon Rum" and "Stop the Torture" chants were hard to hear over the bilious ravings of bumpkins come to witness a "scheming black man getting what he deserved."

One skeleton of a man, wearing a parson's round hat and a black suit too small for his gangly arms, waved a Bible as he shouted repeatedly, "The Almighty will smite evil ones who mix the races." A gray-haired gent sporting a top hat rode a tricycle with a huge front wheel, and displayed a placard stating "My Country, The Whiteman's Country."

They and other howlers like them mingled with union men, some whalers, a few Cuttermen, and the feathered-hat teetotalers. Someone just passing by might well believe they were witnessing the opening hysteria of a Bible-thumping revival meeting. All that was missing was the tent and white-hooded vigilantes.

There was less confusion in the chilly courtroom. The usual cast of characters predominated. It appeared the four city coppers with polished shields on their gray helmets had helped the Master at Arms keep the most obvious race-baiters from entering. I found a seat in the rear with Sarah and Knowles who squirmed nervously in his chair.

"I'm so glad Amy isn't here to see all the viciousness against the Captain," Sarah said. "Her health hasn't been good, and the trial just devastated her, even before the Negro-blood revelation."

255

"How do you think the fine ladies of San Francisco will treat her after all this?" I asked.

"I hate to say it, but I believe they'll both be shunned, no matter what verdicts come down," she said trying to get comfortable in her chair.

"No doubt about it," Knowles added. "Amy will be affected the most. Devlin is a proud man with the stubborn willpower to overcome almost anything, but she'll pay a heavy price."

As the Board members filed in, the chamber became silent before the Master at Arms even called for it. Sourpuss Johanson elected to forsake his usual perch on the platform, and spoke from a rostrum in front of the witness chair.

"I want the record to be absolutely clear," he said, hands clutching each side of the polished wooden stand. "In its deliberations, the Board of Inquiry gave no consideration whatsoever to statements regarding the parentage of the accused. They are not relevant to the issues before us."

I turned to Knowles. "Yeah, and I'll be the next Pope." He smiled wanly, but was focused too attentively on Johanson to be amused.

When he had silence, Johanson asked Devlin and his attorney to rise. Devlin arranged his sword in its proper position, tucked his gold-braided hat under his left arm and stood at attention. You had to admire the old warhorse's composure, but I admired Johanson even more. He knew all hell would ensue no matter what the verdict on the first charge, but he read it as calmly as if it were a list of ship's stores.

"By a vote of four to one," he intoned, "the Board declares the charge of cruel and unusual punishment is dismissed, there being no Cutter Service regulation forbidding the use of tricing up." He raised his voice to be heard over the buzz of spectator groans. "We declare Captain Devlin had authority to order this punishment for mutinous conduct in the absence of civil law at the time and place in question."

His final words were drowned out by catcalls from the union men and squeals from the anti-liquor ladies. I couldn't see Devlin's expression as his attorney clapped him on his back, but the old sailor remained at parade-ground attention. Sarah threw back her head and emitted a distinctly unladylike laugh. The coppers formed a line in front of the rostrum as several chairs in the front rows were toppled, and everyone stood and began babbling. Except Lumsden.

"What now, Charlie?" I asked, as I pushed my way toward him.

He just shrugged. "We live to fight another day, or some such bull." He took hold of my jacket and pulled me close. "Tell you the truth, I'm as happy as hell to say goodbye to those busybodies," he said, nodding toward Mrs. Pitcher and her posse.

I asked him if he had seen Godfrey or Heath today.

"Haven't you heard about that stalwart lieutenant?" he smiled, flashing a startling collection of gold teeth. "Scuttlebutt has it he submitted his resignation last Friday, when you were nowhere to be found." He stretched out his bum leg, pursed his lips. "Too bad, really," he said. "I would have liked to see 'em fry his shiny arse. Never liked that prissy gent."

I laughed and repeated my inquiry about Godfrey, raising my voice so I could be heard over the growing volume of heated remarks.

"He's probably sunning himself in Santa Barbara or somewhere," he said. "Why not? The bastard's made his point: Mess with Arctic Circle, and they'll get you one way or t'other."

Mrs. Pitcher was surrounded by her supporters and some newspapermen. Tears had sculpted rivulets on her powdered cheeks.

"This is an outrage!" she sputtered in indignation, dabbing her eyes with her lace handkerchief. "These captains protect each other, even when it was clear Devlin is a drunk with power to torture people." She put one hand to her throat, and shouted, "We'll send protests to Washington this very day. You have not heard the last of this."

"Will you allege misconduct by the Board members?" the *Chronicle* scribe shouted.

"We certainly will," she responded, looking directly at Johanson, who ignored her by concentrating on his notes.

"The Revenue Cutter Service is to be condemned for allowing a violent, foul-mouthed man to command a government vessel; a man who for all intents and purposes is a Negro." She gasped, her eyes wide in disbelief at the very thought. "It's a disgrace to our Flag."

Her friends were leading her toward the rear door just as Johanson commented, "Furthermore, the Board unanimously agreed to request the Secretary of Treasury to authorize new regulations forbidding the use of tricing up as a punishment by the U.S. Revenue Cutter Service under all circumstances."

Devlin remained at attention as the hubbub swirled around him. I would have loved to know what was going through his hard head at that moment.

Johanson waited for the spectators to resume their seats, and read the verdict on the second charge.

"On the charges of conduct unbecoming an officer and inebriation to the scandal of the Service, the Board by a three-to-two vote finds the accused guilty."

The young officers who had supported Heath were talking excitedly and gesturing in the front row. The few whalers present were shaking their heads. I heard one of them say, "What a load of shit." It was a sentiment I shared. Devlin, still partially hidden from my view, leaned slightly toward McGowan to whisper something. What can he possibly be saying about that ruling, I wondered.

"So far this is better than I expected," Knowles said. "'Conduct unbecoming' might warrant only a reprimand or short suspension of duty."

Johanson waited for silence, shuffling his papers.

"It should be noted," he said, "that our deliberations were contentious, due to the conflicting statements made by many witnesses. We believe there was rampant perjury on both sides. We urge the Department to investigate further."

"Now we'll see if your profile on Devlin did any good, Jake," Knowles said when the verdict on the most serious charge was about to be read. I told him I received a telegram from Pulitzer saying the article was well received: that the *Washington Star* had reprinted it. I'd been pleased as hell yesterday when Hearst's scandal mongering 'Frisco rag ran a clumsy rewritten version. Those slackers had a helluva nerve stealing from the master, I thought.

Not a cough, a voice or a rustle of skirt were heard in the room as Johanson removed his spectacles, and cleared his throat.

"The Board unanimously finds Captain Devlin guilty of dereliction of duty last June while his vessel was underway in fog near the Shumagin Islands."

Howls of approval issued from a covey of younger officers allied with Heath. Devlin remained at full attention facing Johanson. McGowan's shoulders slumped, as he ran his fingers through his hair. Wilson, sitting primly at the prosecutor's table, just smiled. Sarah sighed deeply, and grasped her husband's arm. The sketch she had been making of the scene remained unfinished, the faces of the Board members blank.

"Based on our findings," Johanson bellowed over the rising noise, "the Board recommends to the Secretary of Treasury that Captain Edward M. Devlin be dismissed from the Service."

Groans and curses arose among the whaling captains. They probably were among those who petitioned Congress just five years earlier to grant Devlin a gold medal for his diligence in rescuing shipwrecked sailors.

"Until the Secretary makes his decision known," Johanson said, "Captain Devlin will be on leave without pay, under orders not to board any U.S. Revenue Cutter Service vessel." He surveyed the room for a moment. "Having completed its assignment, the Board of Inquiry is disbanded," he declared with a trace of a smile.

Is that all there is to it? I thought. No epaulets torn from his shoulders, no ceremonial surrender of that comic sword. No shouts or wails. Just a few words, and everybody but Devlin can go about their business.

True, spectators talked excitedly as they walked to the exits. Wilson, who had just won a big case, looked almost sad as he shook hands with his advisor. Officers of the panel gathered their papers and chatted quietly with each other. Other than a few young officers wearing smiles, there was no jubilation in the cavernous room. It was reminiscent of that first day when the makeshift courtroom had felt like a funeral parlor.

Devlin took three steps toward Johanson and stopped. He slowly raised his hand to his forehead in a silent salute. Johanson stared at him, finally nodding acknowledgment. Devlin lowered his hand, turned and marched out the side door, alone.

Outside on the Square, clusters of former protesters were chatting amiably among themselves, with only an occasional outburst of jubilant laughter. Discarded signs and placards were scattered indiscriminately, their messages no longer relevant.

The bumpkins got what they wanted, I thought. The old hero was brought low, and it didn't matter to them how or why it was done.

Only the skeletal preacher was animated. He bellowed from his perch atop a low wall, proclaiming that the Almighty had punished a man who was the "fruit of fornication between the races."

I hastened to the Western Union office, hoping I never had to visit this place again.

WESTERN UNION 11AM FEB 1—
TO EDITOR NY WORLD

FIRST PART DEVLIN VERDICT STOP MORE
TO COME STOP SYKES

San Francisco, February 1, 1896—Captain Edward M. Devlin, considered by many a hero of the Alaskan Arctic, was found guilty today of dereliction of duty and conduct unbecoming an officer. A US Revenue Cutter Service Board of Inquiry issued the verdicts following a weeklong trial, and recommended that the Treasury Secretary remove Devlin from the Service. He has served for more than thirty-one years, most of it in arctic waters.

The courtroom was in an uproar earlier in the day when the Board dismissed charges of cruel and inhuman punishment against Devlin, declaring he acted within existing regulations. The President of the panel claimed many contradictory statements on both sides indicated possible perjury, and urged further investigation.

The trial was a sensation in this city, the major port for the Pacific whaling industry, and for the Revenue Cutter Service's Bering Sea Patrol. Public interest intensified when it was revealed that Devlin was the son of a slave woman, a fact he had not disclosed to authorities.

Devlin's fate now rests with Treasury officials in Washington. A final determination is not expected before March.

MORE TO COME

"There's still some hope, I suppose," Knowles said when I caught up with the two of them at their boardinghouse. "The Secretary could opt for a more lenient sentence."

"Not much chance of that," I said. "All he has to do is certify the Board's decision, dodging what could become a political problem in an election year."

"You're too cynical, Jake," Sarah said, frowning. "The Captain is proud, believes he personifies Emerson's self-reliant man. He won't give up. He'll appeal to the Secretary."

"Probably," I said with a chuckle, "but he might just find comfort in a bottle or two of Old Smuggler, then go strangle Heath and Godfrey."

"There you go again." Sarah's face reddened in anger. "Always thinking the worst of people."

I apologized, saying such thinking was an occupational attribute, and asked if either of them had seen Devlin after the verdict.

"We're going over there this evening," Sarah said. "He's promised to help us make arrangements to return to Alaska. We'll keep him busy for a while."

Knowles asked why I couldn't write another article, pointing out the severity of the sentence in view of Devlin's years of service. I told them my assignment was over, that I'd been called back east.

"Old Pulitzer's sending me to Cuba," I said, pumping my arms with enthusiasm. "Revolution, sinister Spaniards, soft nights and charming señoritas. What could be better?"

"Why so soon?" Sarah said looking up at me. "Don't you ever get—I don't know—captivated by the stories you write and the people you meet?"

I looked into her dark eyes for a long moment. "Sometimes I do, Sarah," I said softly. "But can't afford to. Gotta go where the news is happening." I turned to avoid her gaze. "I just hope the war doesn't start before I get to Cuba."

When I finally got back to New York in March, none of my friends wanted to talk about anything but Cuba and the national elections. My brilliant dispatches from San Francisco were all but forgotten. Pulitzer, getting crankier by the day as his eyesight failed, had other things on his mind. He was determined to beat Hearst in a circulation war that was driving the scribes and the newsboys of both the *World* and the *Journal* to exhaustion.

I was assigned to cover Tammany Hall trivia while anxiously awaiting passage to southern climes, when I spotted a short piece on the Associated Press wire.

Washington, March 10—AP—The Treasury Secretary today reduced the sentence of Captain Edward M. Devlin, US Revenue Cutter Service, convicted by a Board of Inquiry of dereliction of duty in the Alaskan Arctic last year.

Devlin will be relegated to the lowest level of the captains' seniority list, and removed from command for four years. Following a week-long trial in San Francisco, the Board had recommended Devlin's outright dismissal from the Service.

The Secretary's statement said the reduction in sentence was based on Devlin's valuable service in the far north over more than twenty-five years.

There was absolutely no interest among my colleagues. I had to badger a copy editor just to get this tidbit into the back pages of an early edition that no one outside Manhattan would ever see. I sent a note and the tiny cutting to Sarah and Knowles in care of the orphanage at Dutch Harbor, because I didn't know where else to send it.

I didn't send a copy to Devlin, a man who continued to confuse and confound me. Sometimes he seemed to embody a myth of his own making. Not all white, not quite black; not quite selfless hero, but not really a regenerate bully, either. It pissed me off no end that I couldn't grasp the real shape of the man, couldn't bring myself to swallow whole his story of being motivated to prove the worth of people with black blood.

I wondered, for example, how he was able to get the Secretary to soften up with Godfrey, his cohorts and the Negro haters allied against him. I convinced myself my widely reprinted profile of Devlin as "hero of the common man" surely had something to do with it. But despite my soaring prose, he really might be just a self-promoting blue-jacket whiskey swiller with vengeance in his heart. I really didn't know.

Of one thing I was certain. The old seadog, who seemed to relish crisis, would be able somehow to work his way back to Alaska, to keep the myth alive.

But that was as far as my musings about the past would go. With thoughts of the Cuban señoritas foremost in mind, I went in search of some dark ale to bolster me for the going-away party my pals were throwing me at McSorley's saloon.

PART FOUR

Northern Lights

Chapter Twenty-Five

1898

Devlin confounded Sarah and me during our frequent dinners with him following Amy's funeral last November. The man had lost his wife, his reputation, and his ship, but acted as if nothing had changed.

He claimed he had given up his beloved Scotch whisky, but his defiant bravado remained intact.

We had hoped these friendly occasions would help him to adjust to his new situation. Personally, I found them unsettling, even disagreeable. We had our own pleasant news to share about progress in adopting Mary Beaufort, about plans to return to service in Alaska, but he wasn't really interested.

He complained incessantly about the Klondike Gold Rush. "It has infected Alaska with ruffians and scoundrels of every description, and the government's not doing a damn thing to contain them," he said. He obviously believed he was the man who could.

He refused to talk about the status of Negroes.

"Separate but equal, my arse," was all he would say when I asked his opinion of the Supreme Court's momentous Plessy v. Ferguson decision.

It amazed me that a man who had such a personal stake would have nothing more to add. After all, the Court had made it legal for states to restrict the rights of people like Devlin with a drop of Negro blood in their veins.

When we dined with him at Stewart's one evening in July, he quenched his thirst for anger and fury by playing the role of Devlin, the man with a mission. His performance became less convincing when the names of his enemies were raised.

"Heath is a scurrilous viper," he said, downing his third cup of coffee, "doing the bidding of poisonous swamp life sworn to destroy me."

Sarah motioned him to lower his voice, as arriving patrons were seated in the hushed dining room. Devlin wore a dark, ill-fitting civilian suit, but several newcomers recognized him, pointed and whispered among themselves.

Would they object that a man of Negro parentage was dinning in a white establishment, I wondered? Did Devlin face that kind of thing in his daily life? Or would he ignore it, as he always did when I gave him an opportunity to discuss it?

"Heath certainly was treacherous," I said, keeping my voice down, "but Godfrey's group isn't as destructive or as evil as you seem to believe." I passed him the dish of oyster crackers. "You have to admit Arctic Circle is bringing benefits to Alaska. Like those modern passenger ships they've built."

He waved his hands, brushing my comment aside. "Knowles, they're all money-grubbers, as bad as the Wall Street gang that elected McKinley, painting Bryan as nothing more than a hayseed." He looked fondly at Sarah. "Don't you agree, m'dear?"

"I really thought reform had a chance in '96," she said, sadly shaking her head. "Now with the war all but over and Manila in American hands, we'll be bombarded with more 'white man's burden' nonsense."

"Exactly so," he said, leaning over the table to take her hand. "With the Manifest Destiny crowd running things, God knows what that Heath bunch will be able to get away with up north."

He sat back, swirled the halibut on his plate into the mashed potatoes. "I haven't stopped making inquiries about Arctic Circle and its operations," he said, his mouth full. "I want them to know I'm watching every move they make."

"What good will that do?" I asked.

"It'll make them think twice before they skin natives and gold miners at the trading posts they're taking over all along the coast."

With such single-minded ferocity, I couldn't understand how he had managed to get the Treasury Secretary to reduce his sentence. When I prodded him, he smiled and said, "I have friends in useful places, too."

Scores of letters had been written on his behalf by whaler captains and seamen he had rescued, he explained.

"Even the missionaries I fought when they demeaned Eskimo whaling ceremonies wrote to say my reindeer had averted hunger," he added.

But the most telling support, as far as he was concerned, came from Captain Benson.

"Ol' Benson told those high hats I should be punished, but they'd be foolish to deprive the Service of my experience and knowledge of northern waters." For the first time that evening, he was gleeful.

The Northern Pacific Whalers Association had given him a small office, he added, and were paying him to update Bering Sea charts.

"Gives me a chance to see who's doin' what up north," he said.

I continued to be flabbergasted by his ability to ignore reality and play the role of the law-and-order commander.

But he wasn't putting on an act when he arrived at my cluttered closet of a home office in August, a little more than two and a half years after the Treasury Secretary reduced his sentence.

"They've recalled me, Knowles," he said with a loud, cynical laugh. "Forget four years in useless purgatory. Forget the black-blood nonsense. They need this skipper right now."

Waving the yellow pages of a telegram, he explained that the new Treasury Secretary had ordered him back to active service.

"He says right here I'm the best choice to find and save some steamer with engine trouble missing above the Bering Strait. He might be a McKinley appointee and all that, but he's goddamn right I am!"

I was startled. Was this a victory, or another Devlin illusion?

"You can't seriously consider accepting," I sputtered, "not at this time of year." I pushed aside the papers on my desk and faced him. "It'll be October before you could get there, and everybody expects an early winter in Alaska this year. You'll face an ice pack and shortened daylight, for God's sake."

"So much the better. It'll prove I'm still the best there is, ya understand." He was pacing in circles in the tiny room when Sarah wheeled herself through the inner doorway, smiling broadly to see him so excited.

Once she heard his news, her smile vanished. "That's insane, Captain," she said. "They may be making you a scapegoat, knowing nobody can succeed."

"There's little chance of that, m'dear," he said sitting down on a pile of reports littering my only extra chair. "If this were a political trick, they wouldn't give me the *Walrus*, the best ice ship they have, and allow me to choose a volunteer crew."

I leaned over my desk and urged him to reconsider, outlining all the objections I could muster.

"I'd take this assignment if they asked me to sail to the gates of hell," he said, favoring me with one of his defiant stares. "It's a miracle that the good old *Walrus* is at Mare Island undergoing repairs right now, and available."

Then his voice grew soft. "My one concern is how the men will react to taking commands from the son of a Negra."

"That could be the least of your problems, Captain. This wouldn't be the first time a rescue mission was lost above the Strait in an early winter, and…."

"Stop being a Cassandra, Knowles," he interrupted. "I'm the feller who can find that crippled steamer with its load of gold fever crazies."

He rose and took Sarah's hand. "I know you two mean well, but I have to do this for my own sanity." He turned and glowered at me. "I can't fail, Knowles. Have a chance to prove Godfrey, his sniveling nephew, and all the other bigots wrong, ya know? Even if I can't find that ship, the very idea that I'd be willing to try will prove my point."

He said Jameson, now a warrant officer, was recruiting trustworthy crewmen, while he would contact the officers he wanted.

"If we can get 'em to volunteer, we'll have a solid, loyal lot, not a bunch of those Academy brats we had last time," he added with a broad smile.

"And there's one delicious irony here, Knowles," he grinned mischievously. "The missing ship is one of the new ones Godfrey claims will tame the Arctic. What a laugh, eh?"

Sarah looked into Devlin's eyes. "If you're determined to go, Captain," she said. "I think Stanton should be aboard."

"Nonsense," he said. "I don't need Knowles as a nursemaid, and you need him here."

"I always need Stanton," she said, putting her hands on her lifeless knees, "but before we return to our Alaskan duty next spring, I want him to have time away from the endless chores of taking care of me."

"It's never been a chore, sweetheart," I said, tears gathering in the corners of my eyes. "Someone else can try to curb the excesses of this old renegade."

Even as I said it, I knew she didn't believe me.

As I had hundreds of times, I lifted her from her chair, and with her arms around me, her soft kiss on my neck, carried her behind the screen so she could relieve herself.

"Bring the crutches when you come to get me," she said.

"It's no bother for me to carry you."

But she insisted. When I pulled her upright, she put a crutch under her left arm, and with an effort tucked the other into place. She swung her body to the bed using the one leg that could bear her weight for a few minutes. She had practiced the seemingly impossible maneuver for years, getting more expert with each passing month.

"See, dearest," she said, "I'm quite capable of managing." She patted the covers and motioned me to join her. "Now, don't give another thought about not going, do you hear?"

"I want to be with you, Sarah. Despite your progress and amazing determination, you still need help. I want to be the one who gives it."

"Stop that, Stanton," she said frowning. "Mrs. McCreary's a strong, capable woman. She'll do just fine until you return."

I lifted her legs onto the bed, and put my arms around her. "You're not ready to be left alone yet. And besides, there's always the possibility I won't return."

"You will, I know it," she sighed. She turned her upper body, removed my spectacles, and kissed me fervently. "I've realized for years you've struggled to make yourself a match for Devlin. Now's your chance to prove you've done it." She gently smoothed my beard that needed trimming. "He needs your kind of strength and common sense, whether he acknowledges it or not."

She pulled me closer. "Let's not argue, dear. Hold me, and let's make love right now in the light of this sunny afternoon."

The day before the *Walrus* was to leave, I was busy in San Francisco making arrangements for Mary Beaufort to join our family at long last. With Devlin's help, we recently had received court approval to make the darling child our ward. Now, at the last minute I scrambled to telegraph funds to the orphanage for her steamer ticket, and to make sure one of my colleagues would meet her at the pier, and deliver her safely to our home in Oakland.

Sarah was in her chair in front of the kitchen window when I arrived home well past six, the rays of the setting sun painting a pastel glow around her. I ignored the cold supper Mrs. McCreary had left me, and went to hug my wife. When I came near, I was immediately concerned. Her eyes were red. She appeared to have been crying, something her stoic nature rarely allowed her to do.

"What's wrong, darling?"

"Oh, it's silliness, I suppose. It's just that the Captain has been here all afternoon, and he seemed, I don't know, agitated and depressed."

"Devlin?" I said. "I've seen him in all kinds of moods, but never depressed. He's too damned self-confident."

Sarah said he had come by to leave a large envelope, saying papers inside would be important if he didn't return from the rescue mission.

"He kept saying there was nothing to worry about, but his manner disturbed me. He went on at great length quoting Emerson's ideas about intuition, and that one great man can make all the difference." She took a handkerchief from the sleeve of her gown, and dabbed her eyes.

"Darling, I haven't seen you this upset for years. Please tell me what else about his ranting made you so sad."

She said he told her to put the papers somewhere safe, but not to open them unless he failed to come back. In that event, she was to send some of the addressed contents to Norris and Jameson, and to Sykes, as well.

"Maybe Sykes would like to have the real story of 'Roaring Ed Devlin,' he said forcing a laugh."

Her thin face was drawn, and she appeared to be on the verge of tears again when she took my hand. "He doesn't fool me. His last will and testament are in that envelope, and I shivered as I thought of you—"

"Please, darling, don't make a hasty judgment. He's still the best seaman in the Arctic. We'll be all right, and I'll get home to you and Mary soon."

"How can you be sure, Stanton? I think Devlin believes he'll be lost." She sobbed into her handkerchief. "And I'm the one who urged you to go with him."

"My God, why did he trouble you with all his superstitions? Why not just leave his damned papers with his lawyer, or me?"

"He said he trusted me more than anybody because I had the 'strength and resolve' of Margaret Fuller, you know, the famous abolitionist writer and one of Emerson's cronies."

Devlin had told Sarah that Fuller, a woman old enough to be his mother, had befriended him when he was a cabin boy on a voyage from Italy to New York in the 1850s. That she enchanted him, taught him Emerson's philosophy, and urged him to be a witness for the anti-slavery cause.

"He sat in that kitchen chair there," she said pointing. "He had his head down near his knees, grieving for something that happened almost fifty years ago. It was eerie to see him that way."

Devlin's story was that the ship, heavily laden with marble for ornate buildings, smashed into a sandbar in a violent storm off

New York Harbor. It broke up in a short time, sweeping Fuller and most others to their death.

"He had tears in his eyes when he told me Fuller had strapped her two-year-old son on his back in an effort to save the lad. Devlin survived the swim to shore, but the boy drowned."

"No wonder you're unsettled. What a tragic tale to tell on the eve of a voyage."

"That wasn't all. The Captain swore he regretted to this day his failure to fulfill a promise to Fuller to use his own racial predicament to prove the stupidity of slave laws."

Sarah motioned for me to come to her, and she hugged me tight with her strong arms.

"I regret ever urging you to go, dearest," she whispered. "I don't want you to sail up there with Devlin harboring such black thoughts."

"I'm committed, now, Sarah, and you said yourself I'm more forceful in facing Devlin down when he tries his crazy antics."

"I'll never forgive myself if anything happens to you on this voyage," she said, her face buried in my shoulder. "I love you, and need you."

"I love you, too, dearest," I said, "and everything will turn out fine, you'll see."

She wasn't convinced, and neither was I, but I ate the cold chicken in silence, packed my bag for the morning, and took my precious wife to bed.

Chapter Twenty-Six

The *Walrus*, outfitted with extra provisions, two sledges and a volunteer crew of thirty-nine, steamed through the Golden Gate on August 20. Jameson had done a first-rate job. If there was reluctance among the men to take orders from Devlin, I couldn't detect it as we plunged through heavy North Pacific swells.

My reluctance to be aboard was another matter. Sarah's recounting of her conversation with the Captain unsettled me greatly, although I tried desperately not to let it show. Devlin seemed his old, brusque, commanding self as we got underway. But I couldn't overcome the feeling that the dark foreboding he displayed to Sarah might lead him to make some disastrous, heroic gesture. I decided to monitor his moods closely, and to act as best I could if his melancholy returned. Neither my shipmates nor I should be made to suffer for Devlin's fanatical schemes.

We steamed through Akutan Pass the first week in September, the shallow Bering Sea greeting us daily with regiments of waves twenty-five feet or higher. They made difficult, and sometimes frightening, the eight-hundred-and-fifty-mile journey from Dutch Harbor to Port Clarence, the last known location of the missing steamer.

I'll never forget one monster of a wave that enveloped us while I was in the pilothouse with Norris. The crest was so high above, it blocked all light from the sky. In seconds, tons of seawater exploded along the entire length of the deck, sending vibrations through every timber and chills through every nerve and sinew in my body.

A few days later, as we neared our initial destination, sleet driven horizontal by a strong southeast wind tormented us. Devlin was forced to order the crew to chip ice from the rails, blocks and rigging, while the ship reared and plunged. Being more surefooted, or more reckless, than years before, I lashed myself to a lifeline, determined to prove my worth. The men in their fur parkas hung on with one hand while wielding tools with the other. I made myself useful by holding two of the men in turn, bracing them as they hammered three inches of ice from the pilothouse bulkhead. I was cold and exhausted, but satisfied I was now a working member of our short-handed crew of volunteers.

"Are you still trying to be a hero?" Donaldson asked with a smile. We were in his cabin adjacent to sick bay, where the nearby boiler room provided delicious warmth. I shrugged, and lit my tobacco, now barely dry enough to burn.

"Still don't know why you came on this joy ride," he said. "You're a civilian and older than my forty-seven years, so you didn't have to come. And Devlin won't listen to you any more than he does the rest of us."

"He might." I removed my parka and made myself comfortable on his bunk. "Why, my good doctor, did *you* volunteer?"

"Mostly to show the brass what I thought of that trumped-up Board of Inquiry," he said, packing his own pipe. "But to be completely honest, my wife's nagging made the decision easy." He laughed, and leaned back in his chair, putting his feet up on the bunk. "She's after me to resign and go into practice with her father in San Luis Obispo."

"I have a completely different problem," I said. "I wanted to be here and at home with Sarah at the same time."

"We all admire you, Knowles, for how you take care of her; did you know that? It has to be tough on you."

"I don't think of it that way," I said, shamefully masking the resentment I often felt for the never-ending caregiver demands. "Her bravery is what keeps me going."

"You have my admiration, my friend. As for me, I'd rather deal with Devlin's demons than face the dreary combination of my wife and her sanctimonious father in some dusty ranch town."

I was more than pleased when we spotted Port Clarence Bay ahead. It was clogged with chunks of floating ice in all shapes and sizes, holding the angry swells captive by their weight. From a distance the ice floes looked like an undisciplined flotilla of tiny sailboats, although I knew what a menace they really could be.

We soon spotted two whaling ships hunkered down for the winter near the Eskimo village where we had delivered reindeer seven years ago. Devlin got as close as he dared to the vessels, now firmly secured in ice, and spoke with their captains. But the only information of any possible use to us was provided by two prospectors wintering aboard the larger ship.

"Them passengers was gold-crazed fools," said one, a scrawny fellow with full white facial hair surrounding a toothless mouth. "When me and ole Jerry saw the ice forming early, we elected to stay put here and let 'em go north in that cracker box."

The man called Jerry spat tobacco juice over the side. "They wanted to winter near the Noatak Delta," he said. "Heard there'd be gold up there. Were bound and determined to be the first to lay claims next spring."

Devlin asked how many people were aboard the missing steamer, named *Arctic Cross*. They looked at each other, shrugged, and said about twenty-five, including the crew, and "that fool captain."

"Them idiots'll freeze, as Christ is my judge," Jerry said. "I knowed none of us should've come even this far north, gold or no gold."

They asked if we were heading home. When Devlin said he was going to search around Kotzebue Sound near the Noatak Delta, they declared us crazy, too. I didn't say anything, but I was beginning to agree with them.

It took us the better part of four days to round Cape Prince of Wales and enter Bering Strait. As I peered through the haze, Little Diomede Island on the American side looked like nothing more than the back of a giant white whale. With reduced hours of gray light daily, Devlin was too focused on the search for open leads to engage in conversation. He didn't find any heading in our direction, so we broke through two-foot ice sheets four more days before entering the Sound. It was October 4. As unlikely as it was this time of year, the thermometer read two degrees below zero, while the unrelenting wind made it feel much colder.

The *Walrus* steamed no further than four or five miles into the expansive Sound, it being too dangerous to navigate closely packed ice floes in darkness. Carter shot flares to signal any vessel that might be seeking shelter there. He received no response, but an hour later, a lookout rushed into the wardroom saying he saw what could have been a small signal fire in the general direction of Kotzebue Village. I hoped it came from survivors of the *Arctic Cross* so we could head home.

When I went to his cabin with the news, Devlin used both hands to push himself out of the chair. "Finally have a chance to rest," he explained, failing to hide a glass of whiskey behind an uneven pile of books.

"Oh, don't be an old woman, Knowles," he said when he saw my sour expression. "This cold is crucifying my aging, aching bones, and the ship is safely anchored in the ice."

He stretched out on his bunk, and emptied the glass. "Tomorrow we'll see what's up in the village. Maybe that wayward vessel is safe in one of the bays farther east." He yawned, and turned on his side, saying, "I sure as hell hope so."

"Given the thick ice and the temperatures we're encountering," I said, remembering my promise to Sarah, "isn't it best to head south regardless of what we find here? The men tell me it'll be difficult enough as it is."

Sleepily he ignored me. "We gotta find them no matter what." He turned toward the bulkhead and went to sleep, snoring softly.

In stingy light the next day, Devlin moved the *Walrus* as close to the village as the shallow bay allowed, and sent a boat ashore. Our parka-clad men used oars and boat hooks to break ice and then pole and push their way through floating pieces. I marveled how the ice wore many colors of white. Some pieces were pure and brilliant as newly fallen snow. Others had picked up grains of gravel or sand and had subtle grayish and reddish tones. A few had been pushed to shore, and now featured irregular, faintly blackish blemishes. They reminded me of the cloud shapes that so intrigued me as a child, when I would lie in a field and search with delight for dragons or mustangs among the fleecy white.

About an hour later, I watched with admiration as our men labored to return with four passengers bundled in woolen coats, scarves or pieces of odd cloth in many faded colors tied around their heads.

In the wardroom, steam rose from the ice-encrusted clothes and boots of the new arrivals as they were given coffee. Two were prospectors, each loudly proclaiming thanks for the warmth of the ship.

"I haven't been warm, or had a decent hot meal in a month," one said.

The other two were crewmen from the *Arctic Cross*. They had jumped ship in late September, they said sheepishly. One was a short, stocky young man with an unkempt black beard, and he was noticeably nervous.

"I swear to God, Captain," he said, gulping down coffee. "Me and Henry here had to get off that fucking ship. Captain Heath is a crazy bastard, insisting on going to Barrow in this weather with an engine acting up."

"Did you say 'Heath'?" Devlin demanded. "The same man who left the Cutter Service?"

"That's him," the seaman said. "Kept saying he had his schedule to keep. Schedule, hell. He's like to get the whole bunch of them killed."

"Did you hear that, Knowles?" Devlin bellowed, startling the visitors. "They pulled me off the beach to save the same slimy, incompetent son of a bitch who tried to get me cashiered."

He circumnavigated the table, waving his arms. "I just knew there was something otherworldly about this," he said, puffing on his cigar butt. "Something pulling me to keep going forward."

He seemed to be muttering to himself. After what he had told Sarah, his talk of unnatural forces frightened me.

"Don't hold it against us, Captain," the seaman named Henry said. "We wouldn't have jumped ship, I swear, if the *Arctic Cross* was working right."

He verified it was one of the new vessels the Arctic Circle Line had recently rushed into service with much fanfare in San Francisco.

"Those money-grubbers will do anything for a quick dollar," Devlin told them. "I don't blame you men for bailing out, what with that treacherous Heath acting as if he knows what he's doing."

He turned to the sailor and asked how many *Arctic Cross* passengers and crew were ashore at Kotzebue and how many wanted to come with us.

"There's fifteen of us," he said, "and all but these two miners want to stay right where they are until spring, thank you. You should, too, Captain. There's reindeer at that village, so we won't starve."

Devlin continued to pace. "I know there's reindeer. Who in hell do you think brought them?" he said. "But I'm compelled to search for your crippled ship."

"Wish you wouldn't," Henry said, "I was one of 'em you saved up at Icy Cape years ago. Wouldn't want you and your lads to get marooned for this stupid business."

The Captain shook hands with both sailors, and wished them luck. He then told Jameson to feed them and take them ashore.

"I'll get you some trade goods," he told Jameson. "Buy three reindeer, and have the villagers butcher 'em." He took two silver dollars from his pocket, and gave them to Jameson to use if necessary. "We'll need all the strength we can muster before this is over."

The meat was frozen solid by the time it was hoisted aboard. Devlin told cookie to secure the choicest cuts for an all-hands dinner to be served before we left the Sound. The remaining pieces were wrapped in canvas, divided equally and stored for "the people we rescue," he said.

His certainty of success was unwarranted, I thought, so I decided to try to reason with him.

"The men are reluctant to tell you," I said forcefully when we were alone on deck, "but we all believe it's past time we turned south. The *Arctic Cross* could be snug at Barrow for all we know, and at least a dozen passengers are safe wintering here."

His head down staring at the deck, he ignored me. "We have to go north," he finally muttered. "Tell that good-for-nothing Dowie I want to see him." He turned directly into the wind, and with a strangled voice said, "That bastard Heath is out there. I want to throw him at Johanson's feet."

Startled, I stammered that the trial had ended years ago. That Captain Johanson was probably patrolling some eastern harbor, and Dowie was no longer one of his officers.

"Don't tell me what I should do, sir!" he said, his eyes wide with fury. I was sure he didn't know who I was at that moment. He pointed to the northern sky, where a barely visible display of northern lights could be seen through the heavy clouds. "That's an omen, I tell ya," he said. "They're out there, all of them, and I'll get 'em."

He stomped to the companionway and went below before I could say another word. It was obviously not a time for reason, so I went immediately to consult with Donaldson.

"He's confused, not thinking straight," I said. "Maybe he's drinking heavily again."

"He's been acting stranger than usual the last week," Donaldson said, relighting his pipe. "I assumed it was nerves. God knows the nerves of everybody aboard are getting frazzled."

Donaldson agreed to search Devlin's cabin for whiskey when the Captain would be in the pilothouse, frantically searching for Heath, now the personification of everything evil to his fevered mind.

The savory odor of broiling reindeer wafted through the ship just before noon our last day in Kotzebue Sound. Anticipation of fresh meat lifted spirits of all from engine room to wardroom. For several hours, as sounds of laughter emanated from the crew's mess, we all tried to forget the cold and impending darkness.

Jameson, impish as usual, pulled me aside. "Don't worry, my dear Doctor," he said with a wink and a grin, "I won't be tellin' the lads any of my Last Supper jokes."

I laughed, even while silently appealing to the Lord for safe return to California.

In the wardroom, Devlin, seemingly his old self again, was embellishing tales of his past exploits and ribbing his officers, and me.

"Gentlemen, I give you the Reverend Doctor Stanton Knowles," he said, raising his coffee mug in mock salute. "The seasick, bookish gent who poached a free ride with us to the Seal Islands a dozen years ago. He's now a genuine Arctic Ocean sailor."

I was embarrassed—and delighted—as cries of "Here, here," arose among the laughter.

"And, he's not a bad surgeon's assistant, to boot," Donaldson said, clapping me on my back.

Thankfully, the steward entered at that moment, keeping me from saying anything to dampen the spirits of my colleagues. The young Japanese served reindeer steaks with stewed tomatoes and stewed corn, with canned peaches for dessert. If the meat was gamey and stringy, I certainly didn't mind.

It was only when we relaxed over pipes and cigars that the dark cloud of reality intruded. I liked and respected these hardy fellows, but I ached to be with Sarah. Vivid memories of her warmth, her good sense and her warnings had haunted my dreams since we left San Francisco. I'm sure the others were thinking of home and loved ones as well, but all were reluctant to show it.

"Just a thought, Captain," Carter said with a cheerful smile, "if we start today, and the good Lord willing, we might be home for Christmas."

Devlin frowned. "No more talk like that, Carter," he hissed. "We're here to do a job, and we'll continue at light tomorrow." He looked from face to face. "Emerson said it, gentlemen. 'The only reward for a job done well is just to do it.' We'll head home when we do, understand?"

I shuddered, but kept my dark thoughts to myself, for now.

Chapter Twenty -Seven

In the days that followed, Devlin walked with a noticeable limp. He rarely left the pilothouse, even for meals, as the *Walrus* slowly crunched its way toward Point Hope. I never saw him use his usual maneuver of climbing into the rigging to search for leads, but with his uncanny senses he somehow found ice thin enough to break. As it was, we had at most four hours of twilight each day, and the farther northwest we steamed, the more the ice thickened. Low-hanging clouds were present day and night, making accurate sextant sightings impossible.

"How in the world can we steam by dead reckoning without sightings?" I asked Norris over the rush of the wind.

"He's feeling his way," came the answer. "We can't keep this up much longer." It was a startling admission from that stoic seaman, and I agreed with him.

On deck the fifth day out, I braved cold that pierced through my parka like needles. The ice pack looked like the white coverlet on a rumbled bed, surrounding us as far as the eye could see. In places it was as flat as the plains of Kansas. In others, upcrops of rafted ice reminded me of irregular, gray and white boulders in snow-drenched Sierra mountain valleys. I shivered knowing we were alone in the unrelenting grip of a gigantic force of nature with little immediate hope of release. I saw a few leads of open water, but none were in the direction Devlin wanted to head.

Nerve-wracking noise assaulted me whenever we were able to lurch forward. Often, the *Walrus'* bow would ride up on a block too thick to ram through. It would hang there for a time until our weight shattered it, producing a sound like cannon fire. Ragged ice screeched and scratched along the metal-plating and wooden hull whatever our ship's direction. The noise, like chalk on a blackboard, made me cringe.

The ice pack itself delivered a discordant chorus all its own. Currents and wind splintered resisting blocks that groaned angrily at being disturbed. On occasion, one large piece would be lifted protesting over its neighbor, creating a low monolith of ice. It was if the pack were a living thing.

We came to an abrupt halt the eighth day out of Kotzebue. The *Walrus'* bow hung over a block that refused to crack. Devlin put the vessel in reverse to provide running room for a counterattack. Within seconds, the helmsman was thrown violently over the wheel that revolved with such speed its spokes were a blur. I cringed as the seaman smashed into the bulkhead with a scream of pain.

The Captain stopped engines. Three crewmen and I carried the moaning fellow as gently as possible, passing him feet first down the steep, narrow companionway. In the sick bay, Donaldson had to use a serrated hunting knife to cut away his heavy parka and shirt, as the seaman looked away, his jaw clenching a rag someone had given him.

"Taylor has a dislocated shoulder and a broken arm," Donaldson said after administering morphine. "We'll use a tight sling and splints. That's all we can do for him right now."

Jameson later explained the cause of the accident. An underwater ice keel had pushed the rudder sharply in the opposite direction while the ship was in reverse. Whatever the cause, the incident unnerved us all. It made the *Walrus* captive to the ice. It was October 16, and I knew that in a matter of weeks we would be unable to steam our way out in the dark arctic winter.

I realized then it was no longer a case of finding a lost ship and its crew. It was a matter of survival. Mine and those of my shipmates.

"These things happen," Devlin told the glum-faced lot of us during the evening meal. "Nobody could have foreseen that underwater ice was in exactly that position."

Everyone silently listened, eating their canned corned beef, until Norris spoke up.

"Can't go farther north, Captain," he stated without emotion. "We'll be in almost total darkness soon, and then we'd have a helluva time getting out."

Such an assessment by the man we all considered his most loyal, seasoned officer stopped Devlin, who stared at him with disbelief, his coffee mug half way to his lips.

"And with all the ramming, Captain," the chief engineer added, "we're taking on water faster than we should. Have the extra bilge pump running already."

"I'm in command here!" Devlin thundered. "I say we have to find that goddamned ship." He then surprised me, and everyone present, by actually explaining himself. He said his calculations of the ice pack's movement showed that the *Arctic Cross* should be directly northwest of our position if she'd been frozen in near Point Hope.

"It'll do no good to find her if we get trapped ourselves," Norris, the man of few words, said softly. "You and I've been in situations like this before, Captain. You've always put the safety of this ship first."

"Don't lecture me, Norris! I know my goddamn duty. I've never lost a ship."

The tension intensified in silence.

It took Carter, the Gloucester fisherman's son, to have courage to break it. "With your permission, sir, I have a suggestion that might help."

"I don't believe you or your daddy ever faced this kind of thing off the Grand Banks of Newfoundland, Carter," Devlin said with a wave of his hand. "But let's hear it anyway."

Carter beamed with enthusiasm as he proposed we use the two sledges stowed below to continue the search on foot during hours of light.

"If we plot two courses about forty-five degrees apart," he said, illustrating the angle with his hands, "and the teams make five or six miles, they'll be able to scan miles ahead and on each side of their position."

Norris immediately supported the idea. I had the impression he and Carter had rehearsed it. "If nothing's found the first try, fresh teams could follow a different course the next day," Norris said. "We'd cover more territory than we ever could by ramming ahead."

Norris walked to the Captain's side and placed a hand on his old friend's shoulder. "That's more than anybody could expect you to do in these conditions."

Devlin, his chin on his chest, said nothing for what seemed like minutes. "All right," he said looking morose, "we'll try it your way tomorrow. Carter will command one team. I'll get Jameson to take the other."

Loaded with flares and provisions in case survivors were found, the sledges were lowered to the ice before light. To my astonishment, Devlin did not appear on deck to supervise. Even bundled in my parka, the dry, zero-degree cold assaulted me as ten crewmen were assigned to each team. Three were to break trail looking for open leads and crevasses, three would act as rearguard. Four men would pull and push the sledge, spelled regularly by their mates. Rifles were bundled in the sledges to keep them warm enough to fire in the unlikely event a polar bear had wandered this far offshore.

Within ten minutes of their leaving, I could barely make them out through the blowing snow and ice crystals. They just disappeared into the haze of the icescape.

"If you still have any influence with the Almighty, my friend, this is the time to use it." Donaldson had silently joined me at the rail.

"As unworthy as I have become, I've been saying silent prayers for their safe return," I told him. "Also made a vow to do my part tomorrow."

"All us old fogies will have to take turns," he said. "With Taylor out of service, half of our short-handed crew is trudging over the ice right now."

As we went below, Donaldson whispered that he was concerned over Devlin's physical condition.

"For one thing, the cold is wreaking havoc with his rheumatism," he said. "I've prescribed quinine and whiskey to help a little."

"Is that wise?"

"I think it best," he said. "The steward and I searched every inch of his cabin, and didn't find any hidden whiskey. A toddy a day will help him rest."

His usual sunny disposition turned grave, and he grabbed my sleeve. "You gotta remember, professor, that Devlin's bones have been battered by this goddamned cold and fog for thirty years, half his lifetime. He's got all kinds of problems I don't even know about."

When time neared for the teams to return, I went to the pilot-house. A brilliant white flare was launched and the foghorn blown repeatedly to help them find us. Jameson's team to the northwest answered with a flare, as instructed. No responding signal came from the northeast. The exhausted first team arrived in murky darkness about an hour later. It had found no trace of the missing ship. Devlin appeared briefly, and ordered a second flare fired toward the northeast. Still no response.

Driven by anxiety, I went to the rail staring into the darkness. Several times I was certain I detected movement. But each turned out to be a mirage, a common phenomenon in the Arctic, especially at night. Or maybe those visions were conjured up by my visceral desire to see the men safe.

Two hours later, as Devlin was organizing a search party, the unsteady, flickering light of a hand-held flare was seen to the east. Men were sent to guide the freezing, disoriented team members and help them aboard. To my great relief, all were accounted for.

The crew's mess was the rallying point for the returnees, and the low-ceilinged room soon was filled with the wet-dog odor of soaked animal skins, fur and wool. The men were plied with buckets of hot cocoa and coffee. Most just wanted to get out of their clothes and flop on bunks, but Donaldson rausted them out. Several had exhibited signs of frostbite on toes and fingers. Two had severe wind and cold burns on their faces. I volunteered to help, and following the doctor's instructions spent several hours rubbing limbs and applying greasy salve that smelled like used engine oil. Not unexpectedly, it made me remember the many times I had provided somewhat similar services on the shriveled limbs of my darling Sarah.

"I'm done in, Knowles," Devlin mumbled as I entered his cabin. He was sprawled on the bunk, running fingers through his graying hair. "It's not just my aching leg, but my failure."

Trying to cheer him, I said I had just left the returning team, and all were weary and hurting, but would be able to work given some rest.

"But they found nothing," he said through clenched teeth. "I know you all think I'm crazy, but I feel Heath is just beyond my grasp." He grimaced, kneading his left leg and knee. "Sometimes you have to reach beyond bare facts to find the truth. Emerson wrote about it often. I believe it."

"Don't be so downhearted, Captain," I said. "We're not done searching yet."

He swung his legs off the bunk and pointed at me. "This is all Heath's fault, goddamn him. That stupid bastard with his superior airs refused to learn anything from an old deckhand like me." He pulled himself up with an effort, and flopped into his swivel chair.

"He should've learned the Arctic won't tolerate fools or folly. Now that devil probably has a crushed ship and a dozen dying men to answer for."

His look was sorrowful—almost painful—as he asked me to sit down and be patient. "I've something I have to get off my chest, something you should hear."

"If it's the story that frightened Sarah," I said, perching myself on the edge of his bunk, "she told me all about it, and I must say you were insensitive in raising her fears."

He said he was sorry if he disturbed her, but what he wanted me to know transcended his infatuation with Margaret Fuller.

"The truth, Knowles, is that my life's mission hasn't been to prove the worth of people with black blood. I had convinced myself that it was. But now I realize it's been guilt and vengeance that bedeviled me."

"Good God, you never cease to amaze me," I said, throwing up my hands. "You're an enigma, you know that?"

He waved me off, and leaned forward in his chair.

"I've been wracked with shame I didn't follow Margaret's urging to enlist in the abolition cause; that I refused to join the navy in the War, and turned my back on poor, struggling darkies in Georgia."

He scraped his scalp roughly, as if to expunge the memories. "I could've made a real difference in those days, could've become one of Emerson's 'great men'. But I didn't, ya see?"

The springs of his swivel chair squeaked as he leaned back, and told me the truth about his trip to Georgia in '67.

"Before the War," he said, "I regularly received small remittances from a lawyer in Atlanta. I never questioned them. They came from a past—from a place—I wanted to forget. When I finally met the old attorney in Atlanta, he told me that after my parents died their slaves were "hired out" to other plantations. He sent a portion of the money earned north to pay for my education and upkeep. I knew then, Knowles, I'd been carousing and drinking for years on the sweat of human beings with darker skin than mine."

He closed his eyes, and absent-mindedly kneaded his leg again, saying he asked the lawyer for copies of Chattahoochee Corporation documents foreclosing on the Devlin plantation, and for an introduction to the current owner, a former sergeant in the First Georgia Volunteer Regiment, named Spencer.

"I asked Spencer if any of the former Devlin slaves were still on the property, and he directed me to one of the tin-roofed tar paper shacks scattered in the fields."

It was there he encountered a toothless, nearly blind old Negro named Neb Devlin. The man was startled by questions about the days before the War, especially about any Negro mistress of the place. The old man said he had been a field hand, but he dimly remembered a "light-skinned woman from the southern islands who wore fancy clothes, and bossed the house niggers."

"I didn't tell that old feller I was probably her son," the Captain said. "His pitiful condition repelled me. Depressed me. All I thought to do was give him the leavings in my tobacco pouch and the few dollars I had with me, before fleeing that hot, smelly shack."

He sat bolt upright in his chair and pointed at me. "Here was an old black man with the same name as mine," he said in a loud voice, "but I couldn't wait to get away from him. He might have been one of the slaves who toiled among the cotton rows to fill my pockets with coin and my glass with liquor."

His vehemence made me recoil. I didn't know what to say.

"But what did I do?" he shouted. "I fled back to the white man's world I had claimed for myself, feeling nothing but revulsion for the lot of Negroes. Do you understand now why I feel guilt?"

Devlin said it was only in a devastating Bering Sea storm that he vowed to atone.

"If I hadn't done anything to help the Negro, I would be a tireless white man protecting the dark-skinned natives of Alaska, and the animals that sustained them. It was easier, you see? I'd be a hero without facing the daily indignities and cruelties inflicted on black men. Would be the personification of Emerson's notion that one man with resolve could change the world, even as I refused to alter my own."

It was about a decade ago, he said, when he learned from me that a former governor of Georgia had created the Arctic Circle Corporation. My comments led him to search through old documents on the Devlin farm, discovering that Godfrey had been a principal of the corporation that had taken over the property shortly after the War.

"From then on, guilt was transformed into vengeance against Godfrey and his like. I now realize my hatred of his racial beliefs actually reflected the loathing I felt for my own lack of honesty."

He said he had convinced himself that if he could defeat Godfrey's designs for Alaska, could find his sniveling nephew's ship, his conscience would be clear.

Shoulders sagging, his body seemed to melt into the contours of his chair. "But my conscience isn't clear," he said in a whisper. "That's why I can't fail now, no matter what."

He swung his chair around, put his elbows on the desk, and his head in his hands. He seemed to forget I was there, and began mumbling to himself. "I'll have to find them, keep him from destroying what's left of me."

Deeply concerned, I put my hand on his shoulder. It startled him, and he looked up at me with wide eyes. "Oh, it's you, Knowles," he said. "Be a friend. Have Donaldson send me a mug of that medicine. Must be ready to go onto the ice myself."

I urged him to rest. Give his leg time to get better. My hand was still on his stooped shoulder when he retreated into silence, staring at the desktop.

The officers avoided eye contact when I entered the wardroom and described Devlin's condition. "He's not talking sense," I told them. "Seems to blame Heath for all that's wrong in the world."

I was puzzled when no one responded. After an embarrassing few minutes, Jameson came and took my arm. "It's rotten to hear that, Doctor," he said with a shake of his head, "but there's something else bothering the lot of us."

He looked to his colleagues for permission before continuing. "You're so close to the Captain these days, we've kept you in the dark. Nothing personal, ya understand. The reason Lieutenant Carter's team was delayed was they found a human body."

"Do you know who it is?" I asked as I leapt out of my chair in shock. "Is it an Eskimo or white man?"

Carter was sprawled on the floor, his back to the bulkhead. "He's covered in ice, and weighs a ton," he said. "He's tall enough to be a white man, but can't be sure until he thaws a little. We have him down in the boiler room."

"And you haven't informed the Captain?"

"We figured if he knew, he'd keep us searching for days. We'd get trapped," Carter's exhaustion was evident in his response.

Norris, the by-the-book first officer, defended him. "We have to work our way south right now, Doctor, whatever the Captain's condition," he said. "The new wind direction is opening leads. They won't stay open for long."

I knew the fierce wind from the northwest now came from the northeast, forcing the pack to subtly change direction, splintering parts of the surface.

They all looked at me to gauge my reaction. "But if you found one body, there may be more out there," I said, still discomforted by the news. "At least, we have to search the area where you found that man."

They knew I was right, despite the urgency we all felt to head south. Their internal turmoil was obvious in the way they avoided my gaze. I argued for sending out at least one team to retrace Carter's route, while Norris and the rest attempted to turn the *Walrus* southward. Their attention to me only returned when I said, "In his present frame of mind, I don't see why we have to notify the Captain immediately."

"All right," Norris declared, "I'll make the decision. One team will go. With the Captain out of sorts, I'll put the remaining able-bodied men on the ice to set gunpowder charges. We'll blast our way out of here."

I volunteered to go with the team, but Carter objected. He said I was needed on board with the Captain, that he would lead the team since he knew the area to be searched.

Chapter Twenty-Eight

It was still dark, the low-hanging clouds scattered by the wind, when Carter's team was lowered. Donaldson had given Devlin a concoction of whiskey with a little laudanum to help him sleep. I decided not to disturb the man for a while, dreading the time when he would awake and discover what we had done without his consent. So I stayed in the comparative warmth of the pilothouse to observe the frantic activity throughout the hours of light.

Under clear skies it felt much colder than the two degrees below zero registered on the thermometer. The sharp crack of gunpowder charges could be heard over the moaning wind as Norris carefully put the vessel in reverse and then forward, lifting the bow over a five-foot thick shelf. This time, weakened by the blasts, it gave way. He repeated the procedure again and again. As darkness intruded, I was overjoyed to realize that the *Walrus* was pointing southwest. We had turned more than ninety degrees.

I went below to inform the Captain. He wasn't in his cabin. I looked in the wardroom and the galley, and with deepening panic asked the steward and a mess boy to aid me.

"I can't find the Captain anywhere," I sheepishly told Norris. He was receiving Carter's report of an unsuccessful search, but it was my announcement that sent him wearily slumping against the pilothouse bulkhead, dumbfounded, dejected.

"You mean, he's nowhere on board? Are you sure?"

"Sadly, yes," I said. "We looked all over the ship. And the steward says Devlin's parka and mukluks are missing."

"Dammit all, Knowles, how did this happen?" Norris sighed, shook his head sadly, and ordered flares fired at regular intervals, and posted extra lookouts. He then called for immediate assembly of all officers in the wardroom.

"He must have gone over the side with the search team when it was still dark this morning," Jameson said, his usually cheerful face glum. "He'll freeze or fall into open water. For chrissake, gentlemen, we have to go find him."

"I'm completely to blame," I said. "I should have watched him more closely." Guilt overcame my natural fear, as I said. "I'm prepared to go right now."

"Like hell you will," Norris said. "You'd just freeze, too. We can't do anything in the dark." He stroked the stubble on his chin. "One team will look for him tomorrow. You'll have three, maybe four hours of twilight. You go with the team, Doctor. The rest of you will be needed to help break us outta here."

For the first time on this voyage, I knelt on the hard wood next to my bunk and prayed with a fervor I hadn't felt in years. It was probably useless, I knew. Nobody could survive alone more than a few hours in the subhuman cold and dark.

But even with his muddled mind and bum leg, Devlin's stubbornness and determination might produce a miracle, I thought.

Through tears of anguish, I asked forgiveness for my wavering faith, for denigrating Devlin's belief in Emerson's intuition nonsense. I implored the Lord to help us find him. I knew we had to escape now whether we found him alive or dead. If we didn't, I might never see Sarah again.

In the chill of my cabin, I realized a truth about myself. Despite my silent grumbling and posturing as the heroic husband of an invalid, I needed the strength and the wisdom of that extraordinary woman much more than she needed me.

Next morning, I was determined to be a useful member of the search party, despite the fear that overwhelmed me as I stepped off the ladder and onto the ice. The dry cold assaulted my senses. It flowed into my nose, freezing my nasal hair and sinuses, forcing its way into my lungs. The ship's gauge read minus five degrees, but that was just a number. To my aging body, the cold was like a frigid, aching stone inside my temples and joints. It penetrated my parka skins, wool, and fur to seize my limbs in its painful grip.

Initially, Jameson and I took the lead, weaving around rafted upcrops and crevasses, heading northwest where Devlin believed the *Arctic Cross* would be found. Even under clear skies, it was difficult to see very far with the steady wind blowing ice granules off the surface. I began to tire within an hour, paying the price for a lifetime favoring libraries over playing fields.

While plodding forward against the wind, I almost fell into an open lead of congealing water. Jameson pulled me back just in time, and I landed hard on the ice. Frightened by my carelessness, I retreated to join the sledge crew, electing to be a pusher. It was more to give me something to hold on to than to help its progress.

I was losing track of time and everything but the cold, when the sledge halted near an upcrop of rafted ice about ten feet high. With a boost from one of the men, I struggled to climb it, slipping and sliding awkwardly. Near the top, I saw that Jameson was about a half mile ahead. As it was getting dark, we pushed the sledge toward him at a measured pace. Even then, the exertion caused me to breathe in frigid air too rapidly.

Jameson shouted into my hood. "Three of us have searched all around. No sign of him." Over his ice-encrusted muffler, I could see the weariness, the sadness, in his eyes. "Have to start back now, or we'll all be lost," was what he shouted next.

My spirits sank, realizing that we had to give up the search for Devlin to save ourselves. The thought that the Devlin of Old Testament certainty and impulsive action was to be abandoned in this white wilderness was too much for my mind to grasp. I was ashamed of my cowardly readiness to retreat, but offered no resistance.

Jameson and I were helping to turn the sledge around when a flare lit the sky, calling us back. No one even tried to speak. As if on command, we started the trek. In my shame at abandoning him, my mind fumbled to remember the words of the Prayer for the Dead, visualizing Devlin entombed in ice.

We had been instructed to fire two flares when we began our return, but the gun, hampered by the cold, wouldn't operate. Jameson tucked it under his parka to give it some warmth. Then, in deepening darkness, the dangerous march around open leads began, carrying with it only the bitterness—the sadness—of our failure.

There was a faint glow from the ship's lights, but it was too diffuse to provide a reliable course. New cracks from the shifting ice made it dangerous to move ahead except by measured steps, the lead men searching for crevasses with poles. Jameson tried the flare gun once more. It still wouldn't fire, but a flare from the *Walrus* arched high to our left. It gave me new hope, but not enough illumination to identify the dangers ahead.

Jameson tried again, and the flare ignited this time. Its brilliance blinded me for a second, but unveiled a mostly flat expanse of ice without visible open leads between our position and where we felt the ship lay. Invigorated, the weary team made reasonable time for the next mile or so.

It was then I became terrified. I felt subtle movement: a slight listing to right and then left.

My God, I thought, we're on a floating ice sheet.

Jameson signaled that he felt it also. He shot off our last flare to search for safe passage. Harry, Jameson's old compatriot, used the few minutes of brightness to find a spot where our floating sheet was about three feet from more stable ice.

Six men jumped to the other side. The last landed short. One of his legs dragged in the freezing water up to his thigh. He was pulled to safety by a teammate. Ice was already forming on his sealskin trousers. His misstep broke a piece from the stable sheet, opening another foot of so of water we had to cross.

The injured man could be put under the canvas on the sledge, I thought, as his colleagues began pulling on its ropes. The rest of us pushed, attempting to force its five-foot-long runners over the opening.

The floating piece sank a few inches as the heavy sledge approached the edge. One runner snagged, dipping into the water. The sledge turned on its left side, with one runner and a few feet of wooden frame resting on the place we had to reach.

Jameson, using motions alone, instructed us to strip the sledge of its cover and roll the precious rifle and provisions onto it. We pulled and pushed the heavy, unwieldy burden over the sledge's side. I dimly realized that the floating sheet could move at any minute, sending the sledge and the provisions into the water, taking away the best hope for my escape down with them.

"You go next," Jameson shouted as he pushed me toward the sledge that was bobbing slightly up and down. "The rest of us can jump it."

Weary almost to incapacity, I followed his instructions, slowly scaling the sledge's upturned wooden framework. I backed down once when the frame sank a few inches under my weight. Starting again, my bulky, ice-encased mukluks slipped. I almost fell into the water, but hung on long enough for Harry to pull me across to safety.

Jameson and his three teammates made the leap. One of them landed hard on one knee, and rolled on the ice in pain. The sledge was abandoned. The able-bodied took turns carrying—and sometimes dragging—the provisions, and helping the injured two to move ahead. I stumbled after them, not knowing if we could make it to the ship with the injured men slowing us down.

We halted behind an upcrop of rafted ice that provided some protection from the wind but blocked the lights from the ship.

"We'll deep-six the provisions," Jameson said, "but give me the rifle." He fired three shots in rapid succession, waited a while and tried to fire again. The gun jammed.

Moving once more, the man with the knee injury was seated on the rifle held up by two of his mates, his arms around their shoulders.

By then, flares were rising skyward regularly from the *Walrus*. They gave us enough light to proceed as their rays reflected off the ice-encased masts and rigging in the distance, making the ship look like a ghostly apparition.

What seemed hours later, we saw the lights of wavering handheld flares coming toward us.

"Norris heard the shots, by God," Jameson shouted. "He's sending some help."

The relief team took charge of the injured and led us around open water to the ship, where we faced another obstacle. Norris and the crew had been able to free the vessel from the grip of ice, creating about six feet of open water we had yet to cross.

I was exhausted and fell sprawling on the ice. The next thing I knew, I was harnessed to a sling and hoisted aloft. Gripping the harness as best I could with bulky gloves, I swung above the water, and crashed into the hull before pulling myself over the rail. I fell onto the deck, feeling I might never rise again.

"We found no sign of him," I gasped at Norris, as he squatted close to me. "Lost the sledge and provisions."

"All of us are devastated, God knows. But it was to be expected, and we did all we could," Norris said. He helped me to my feet, adding, "There's some good news for all the rest of us, at least. We've found nearby leads heading southerly."

A seaman helped me into the pilothouse so I could remain close until the last of our team was safely aboard. With my hood pushed back for the first time in hours, I was overcome with delight and awe to see a most magnificent display of northern lights. Vivid crimsons, light greens and yellows undulated, swirled and flowed across the clear northern sky. Faint rose-colored pillars seemed to greet the swiftly moving colors at the horizon.

"Really somethin' grand to see, ain't it?" Jameson said as he joined me.

"Right at this moment," I said, "I want to believe with all my heart they're offering a fitting arctic welcome to an extraordinary man."

Donaldson and Anderson had to help me out of my parka and mukluks in the wardroom. I collapsed on the floor, still trying to shake the memory of the cold, while leaning my back against the bulkhead. The steward gave me a steaming mug of cocoa and helped me take the first sip. My hands were still shaking. Jameson sat beside me. "I never thought the Captain'd just disappear like that," he said. "Always thought he'd get his self killed in a brawl, or shot by a poacher."

He took a long gulp of cocoa. "I almost expect him to come busting in here right now, calling us 'lazy bastards, resting on your backs like 'Frisco whores.'"

I turned to the wizened, small man. "You saved my life out there, my friend. I'll never forget it."

He shrugged and said with a forced grin, "You ain't too bad a feller, either. For a schoolteacher, that is."

Norris pulled up a chair next to us. "What do you think, Knowles, was it suicide?"

"I don't know," I said. "He was so sure the *Arctic Cross* was nearby, his unshakeable belief in intuition could have caused him to take a chance and investigate on his own."

I gulped the hot liquid. "It's unlikely, I know, but given his muddled mind and the laudanum, it's possible." I struggled to sit up straight. "I never could figure out how that man's mind worked, Norris. But no matter what the truth is, can't we all agree to report simply that Captain Devlin died in the search for the *Arctic Cross*. The man deserves that much, doesn't he?"

He was just about to answer when an out-of-breath Carter poked his head into the wardroom, shouting, "Come on, you all have to see this to believe it."

Rising with great difficulty, I joined the others and, we followed Carter to the boiler-room ladder. I had forgotten all about the body found two days before.

I descended slowly into the heat of the boiler room. Pain surged as I stepped on each rung, making cold-impacted joints grate in my knees and elbows.

The body was lying face down in a pool of water, its parka cut away from an outstretched arm. Carter nodded to an engineman, who slowly turned the man over.

The blue-shaded, distorted, but unmistakable, face of Addison Heath stared up at me.

I gasped and slumped against the rail protecting the boiler.

"Good Christ," Jameson said in disbelief, "the Old Man's intuition was right altogether. This traitorous bastard was only a few miles away."

"Yes," I said, "and the Arctic has no favorites. It claimed them both."

Chapter Twenty-Nine

EPILOGUE

San Francisco, 1899

It was just as well his memorial service was scheduled for March 30, more than two months after we limped into San Francisco Bay. It gave us all precious time to adjust to the sounds and rhythms of civilized life; to try to blunt the ragged edges of our ordeal, the horror of abandoning Devlin in frozen wilderness.

It was especially important for me, the only one privy to his last confession, his admission that guilt and vengeance were the burning emotions that tortured his soul. I told Sarah about the condition of his mind in those final days, and pledged her to secrecy. We would tell all that Edward M. Devlin sought reckless—often heroic—adventures on the northern frontier to prove the worth of all descendants of slaves.

Still, the man remained an enigma to me. How could someone who thrived on violence and confrontation one minute be a sympathetic protector of natives the next? How could a student of Emerson, Thoreau and Margaret Fuller, with their ideals of personal freedom, become a fierce enforcer of manmade laws?

Sarah, with her inbred reservoir of common sense, tried to shake me out of useless introspection.

"You may think he was obsessed and self-centered," she said, "but in the papers he left behind he included personal letters to Jameson, Captain Benson and Sykes, and willed his Oakland house to you and me." She positioned her chair so I couldn't avoid her gaze. "Don't be his judge," she said. "Just see the Captain as a tortured, self-educated man who tried to do good whatever his motives. He really believed in Emerson's theory that a 'great man' could change the world."

I wasn't convinced, but savored the months of peace I had before having to participate in his memorial service. The delay also allowed time for the *Walrus* to be refitted and given a new coat of brilliant white paint to hide scars inflicted by the ice. No one would suggest honoring Devlin any place other than on the deck of his beloved ship.

By waiting, we avoided unwanted questions of newspapermen. As a result, their articles focused on the heroism of all involved, especially Devlin, who was officially reported as "tragically lost in the performance of his duty." All the stories made note of the outcome of his trial in '96. One or two even mentioned that the Captain was a man of Negro ancestry. Very small victories for the Captain, to be sure.

I was taken aback by one article in the *Chronicle*. It quoted Godfrey himself as calling Devlin "a captain of the old school, who bravely tried to save the *Arctic Cross* and the people aboard it." He added Heath's body had been recovered, and would be buried following a funeral at the cathedral. The same article noted that a dozen or more *Arctic Cross* passengers and crew were found safe at Kotzebue, but the fate of the others could not be determined until ships reached the region in late spring.

Another newspaper quoted Lumsden, who at long last had complimentary things to say about the Captain. Lucy Pitcher, speaking for the Temperance Crusade, provided the only sour note. She claimed that while never doubting Devlin's courage, his "abuse of alcohol remains a disgrace."

Anxiety gripped me as Sarah and I approached the *Walrus* on the day of the service. Despite warm, sunny weather, the very sight of the vessel resurrected all the uncertainty and confusion I felt about Devlin. Did I really ever know the man we would be honoring?

A telegram from Sykes, who was covering American occupation forces in Manila, made me think. After expressing sympathy, Sykes asked, "Was he hero or fanatic to take you north with him?" It would take more than a memorial service for me to answer his questions, or mine.

The service was simple and crisp, as Devlin would have wanted it. Present were the crew, a sprinkling of officers from other cutters and some whaling captains, several of whom I recognized. No newspapermen or photographers saw fit to attend. The story was old news by then.

A Navy chaplain said some prayers. Captain Benson extolled Devlin's seamanship and record of service, and Jameson told a few humorous anecdotes of the Captain's exploits among the Eskimos.

I had prepared remarks quoting Thoreau's, "If a man does not keep pace with his companions, perhaps it is because he hears a different drummer."

But I discarded them as too ponderous, too pious. How could I claim that Devlin marched to a drummer of his own when, like all humans, he marched to so many, hearing only the beats that suited his purposes at one time or the other.

When my turn came, I told the assembly how much I admired the Captain as an energetic protector of the people of Alaska, despite my disagreement with some of his methods. Ignoring the secret only Sarah and I knew, I said, "Above all, I applaud his dedication to prove by his actions that anyone with Negro blood is as worthy as any other person."

The breeze sent an unpleasant chill through my body as I said it, goading me to move to conclusion.

"The Captain always said he was a religious man, but not one to loiter in church pews." A smattering of polite chuckles came from the ranks. I reminded them that Devlin was a serious student of Ralph Waldo Emerson, and said, "I believe a quote from Emerson's essay, *Self-Reliance*, written more than fifty years ago, is appropriate today: '...*God will not have his works manifest by cowards.*'"

"My friends, Edward M. Devlin was certainly no coward. Alaska will miss him, and so will we all."

As I ended, a modern, well-appointed passenger vessel of the Arctic Circle Line, its whistle sounding, steamed past Alcatraz Island heading toward the Golden Gate and destinations north.

In three months or so, I thought, Sarah, Mary Beaufort and I will take passage on one just like it, returning to take up our new duties in Alaska. Devlin would be horrified to know we had to use one of Godfrey's new, gray-hulled ships to do it.

About the Author

William Edward Duke lived an extraordinary life and one that made it possible for him to vividly portray his fictional accounts of the political side of events in the Pacific Northwest. Initially a journalist, he was a long-time member of the National Press Club in Washington, D.C. He was also a "political insider" serving on the staff of U.S. Senator Jacob K. Javits and the Corporation for Public Broadcasting. As a result, he didn't merely observe life in the nation's capital, he was part of it.

After his public service, Bill served as a director of government affairs and later manager of public relations for the Atlantic Rich-field Company (ARCO), then went on to form his own public affairs firm W.E. Duke & Co. He ultimately retired in Los Angeles.

Bill's passion for the Aleut people was kindled by a story his father told him about an experience he had while in the US Navy.

15548188R00173

Made in the USA
Charleston, SC
09 November 2012